ALSO BY

GIANCARLO DE CATALDO

*The Father and the Foreigner*
*Romanzo Criminale*

# SUBURRA

Carlo Bonini & Giancarlo De Cataldo

# SUBURRA

*Translated from the Italian
by Antony Shugaar*

Europa
*editions*

Europa Editions
214 West 29th Street
New York, N.Y. 10001
www.europaeditions.com
info@europaeditions.com

Copyright © 2013 Giulio Einaudi editore s.p.a., Torino
First Publication 2017 by Europa Editions

Translation by Antony Shugaar
Original title: *Suburra*
Translation copyright © 2017 by Europa Editions

Library of Congress Cataloging in Publication Data is available
ISBN 978-1-60945-407-4

Bonini, Carlo & De Cataldo, Giancarlo
Suburra

Book design by Emanuele Ragnisco
www.mekkanografici.com

Cover photo © THEPALMER/iStock

Prepress by Grafica Punto Print – Rome

Printed in the USA

# CONTENTS

For Severino.
And he knows why.

# INDEX OF CHARACTERS

**The Carabinieri:**
*Lieutenant Colonel Marco Malatesta*
*Captain Alba Bruni*
*General Thierry de Roche*
*Marshal Carmine Terenzi*
*Private Giordano Brandolin*
*General Rapisarda*

**The Prosecutors:**
*Michelangelo de Candia*, prosecuting magistrate
*Manlio Setola*, prosecuting magistrate

*Samurai*, former fascist terrorist and gang leader

**The Anacleti family:**
*Rocco Anacleti*, head of the Anacleti gang
*Silvio Anacleti*, nephew of Rocco
*Marco Summa* AKA *Spadino*, one of Rocco's men
*Max* AKA *Nicce*, one of Rocco's men
*Paja* and *Fieno*, Rocco's men

**The Adami family:**
*Cesare Adami*, AKA Number Eight, head of Ostia's Adami gang
*Antonio Adama* AKA *Uncle Nino*, former head of the Adami's,
    now in prison
*Denis Sales*, adopted son of Uncle Nino
*Morgana*, Number Eight's girlfriend
*Robertino*, one of Number Eight's men

**The Three Little Pigs:**
*Scipione Scacchia*, loan shark
*Dante Pietranera*, loan shark
*Amedeo Cerruti*, loan shark
*Manfredi Scacchia*, Scipione's son

**The Laurenti family:**
*Luigi Laurenti*, head of a development company
*Sebastiano Laurenti*, his son

**The Malgradi family:**
*Pericle Malgradi*, member of the Italian parliament
*Temistocle Malgradi*, Pericle's brother, director of the Villa
    Marianna clinic

**The Church:**
*Bishop Mariano Tempesta*
*Benedetto Umiltà*, his assistant

*Alice Savelli*, creator of the blog www.thetruthaboutrome.it

*Abbas*, a carpenter
*Farideh*, his daughter

*Spartaco Liberati*, "The Voice of Rome," radio personality

*Sabrina*, an escort also known as Lara or Justine

*Eugenio Brown*, film producer

*Tito Maggio*, owner of La Paranza restaurant

*Kerion Kemani*, concierge at the Hotel La Chiocciola

*Shalva*, a Georgian smuggler

*Ciro Viglione*, head of the Neapolitan crime syndicate in
    Rome, under arrest at the Villa Marianna clinic

*Rocco Perri*, representative of the 'ndrangeta syndicate in Rome

# SUBURRA

I n the muggy darkness of a summer night, three men were waiting aboard a Fiat Ducato belonging to the Carabinieri, parked on the riverfront road by the Tiber. They were wearing Carabinieri uniforms, but they were criminals. On the wrong side of Rome, they were known by their monikers, Botola, Lothar, and Mandrake. Botola got out of the van and looked out over the river. He pulled a Gentilini breakfast cookie out of his pocket, crumbled it up, and dropped it on the parapet. He took a few steps back and stood there, watching a seagull as it pecked away at the cookie crumbs.

"I love seagulls."

He got back into the van. The guy they called Lothar lit yet another cigarette and heaved a sigh.

"I'm fucking bored. What are we waiting for?"

"I'm with you!" said Mandrake firmly.

Botola shook his head, inflexible.

"Samurai said two o'clock, exactly. Not a minute before, not a minute after. It's not time yet."

The other two started complaining. What are we talking about here? Just ten minutes early? What difference could that make? And after all, going by the evidence, they were the ones out on the street, not Samurai. And what, did Samurai have eyes everywhere? Who did he think he was, God Almighty, able to check on everything they did every second of the day?

"Well, maybe not God Almighty," Botola conceded with a sigh. "But if you talk to me about the devil, you're not far off."

"Oh, sure, the devil!" Mandrake said sarcastically. "He's just a human being like us! And anyway, I'm sick of it: Samurai this, Samurai that . . . To tell you the truth, I've never seen him get his hands dirty, this Samurai . . . He's good at talking, no two ways about it . . . but it's easy, when other people are running the risks for you."

Botola looked them up and down, with a half-smile of commiseration.

They really didn't have the slightest idea, poor jerks!

"Do any of you remember Pigna?"

That name meant nothing to either Lothar or Mandrake.

Botola told a story.

So there's this boxer from Mandrione, his name is Sauro but he goes by the nickname of Pigna—Pinecone—on account of his murderous left straight. Big as a refrigerator, with arms as strong as his brains are scanty, poor old Pigna. If he'd been just a tiny bit smarter, he wouldn't have gone head-to-head with Samurai over a disagreement about a drug deal. That's right, because at a certain point, after a couple of thrown bouts, the Federation revokes his boxing license, and Pigna starts pushing drugs on Samurai's behalf. The thing, though, is that Pigna thinks he's a smart boy. First he starts skimming off the top, then, when he's feeling more confident, he grabs a major shipment, sells it, pockets the proceeds, and disappears. He stays in hiding for three or four months, and then one fine day he resurfaces. He's used the money he stole off Samurai to buy a gym, he's recruited a few big bruisers from the outskirts of town, and he's started dealing on his own. Samurai tries to bring him back into the fold with kindness and goes down to the gym to pay him a visit. He offers him a reasonable deal: fifty-percent ownership of the gym and his dealing operation in exchange for peace. Pigna doesn't want to be reasonable. He calls his bruisers and charges in, head down. Five against one, so Samurai puts up the defense he can muster; still, when it's all said and done, he gets beat up pretty bad. They dump him, half-dead, in an alley, and it takes a good long while for Samurai to get back on his feet. One evening a guy no one's ever seen before comes in to the gym. He starts a membership, he lifts some weights, he starts shooting the breeze with the boss's four bruisers. When closing time rolls around, and Pigna is all alone with his inner crew, the guy no one's seen before whips out a Škorpion machine pistol, the kind the terrorists used to use, and he lines them up against the wall. Five minutes go by. Pigna and his men do everything they can to get a word out of the guy, but he says nothing. At last, the door swings open and in he comes. Samurai. Under his duster, he's wearing a kimono and he's carrying a katana, the curved, razor-sharp Japanese sword. He heads straight for Pigna and delivers a little sermon: he could have overlooked the money, but not the humiliation. And so, my dear Pigna, he tells him, now you're going to take this sword and slice open your belly, and I'm going to watch you die. In exchange I won't touch a hair on the heads of your hitters here. Pigna starts whining. He begs Samurai's forgiveness. He acknowledges that he was wrong. He'll hand over the gym, all the drugs he has left, his list of customers and suppliers. Samurai heaves a sigh, lifts his sword, and with a single blow, lops the head off of one of his boys. Pigna bursts into tears. The bruisers burst into tears. One of them steps forward and offers his services to Samurai as Pigna's executioner. Samurai gives him a level look and decapitates him. You see, Pigna, you don't know how to choose your men, he sighs, they aren't loyal to you . . . At this point, all three of them, Pigna and the two survivors, made a desperate, last-ditch attack.

"Why am I even bothering telling you about it?" Botola concluded. "Samurai ripped them to shreds. His friend never even fired a shot. Then they shoveled the remains into trash bags and dropped them into the Tiber."

Lothar and Mandrake stared at the narrator, disconcerted.

"That sounds like pure bullshit to me," Mandrake ventured.

"It's time," Botola cut him off. "Let's get busy."

They drove to Piazzale Clodio. The Fiat Ducato flashed its brights three times in the direction of the front gate of the Hall of Justice, which after a few seconds slowly started to swing open. The soldier in the guard booth walked unhurriedly over to the driver's side. He recognized Botola and with a wave of his hand invited the van to move on through. At walking speed, the van proceeded up the reinforced concrete ramp that led to the parking area of Building C, where a system of armor-plated doors protected the vault of Branch Office 91 of the Bank of Rome.

The inner doorway of the courthouse.

The coffer that contained the wealth and the secrets of magistrates, lawyers, notaries, and cops.

The false bottom of what they call Justice, but what is really just Power.

Botola pulled the list of the nine hundred safe deposit boxes in the bank out of the van's door pocket. Samurai had circled one hundred ninety-seven of them. They, and they alone, were to be opened. Lothar grabbed two big burlap sacks. Mandrake checked the tool bags and the ring of fifty keys that made him the only serious safecracker in Rome. All three of them put on tight-fitting black leather gloves.

The Carabinieri that were waiting for them had done their job right. The armor-plated doors that led into the vault stood open, the alarms and the closed-circuit video system were turned off. Botola met the gazes of the soldiers with a sneer of contempt. The two of them reeked of fear and dishonor. The smell that cops give off when they're crooked. And then he dismissed the younger of the two with a pat on the cheek.

They'd memorized the vault. In the last two months,

Botola, Lothar, and Mandrake had been down there at least a dozen or so times, accompanied by one of the tellers from the branch office. A guy in his early fifties with a weakness for cocaine and women. He'd rolled over like a puppy dog. He'd given them the names of the owners of each safe deposit box, allowing Samurai to cherrypick the plumpest targets. He'd provided them with floor plans and updated lists of customer visits. He'd allowed them to make molds of the keys that opened the inner doors to the heart of the bank. All told, what remained was the easy part. Laying their hands on all that cake.

"I'm going to take this uniform off," Mandrake ventured. "It's just that I never could see myself as a cop."

"You're telling me, brother!" Lothar chimed in.

Botola authorized the change in attire. As long as they got busy: good luck wouldn't be on their side forever, and even the best laid plans can run aground on the odd twist of fate.

They decided to work in the dark. With nothing but the light of two large marine flashlights. Mandrake moved fast. As he could and as he should. And the first one hundred seventy-four safe deposit boxes opened up like chocolate boxes.

There was a burlap bag they threw all the cash into, ten billion lire, along with a mountain of jewelry and watches.

Lothar grabbed them with a vulgar explosion of greed. His tongue darted in and out of his mouth, as if in the throes of some uncontainable sexual excitement.

Botola devoted himself to the rest. Because in those safe deposit boxes there was something far more valuable than those tidy strapped bundles of fifty thousand and hundred thousand lire banknotes. He discovered with some surprise that a prosecuting magistrate with powdery nostrils was keeping several spare ounces of coke between his grandfather's pocketwatch and his wife's string of pearls. A flashlight beam lit up the account statements from the Swiss banks where lawyers, judges, Carabinieri officers, cops, and treasury police had deposited the money with which the gang had bought them off over the years.

Samurai had been right. There was no Epiphany in there. More like some new Roman Christmas.

In the last safe deposit box they found a handgun.

Botola had never seen anything like it. And he knew a thing or two about guns, after all his years out on the street. But that pistol . . . a throwback to days gone by: long barrel, with something incomprehensible engraved on it, in German by the look of it. He checked the list, supposing there had been some mistake. There was no mistake. Samurai had actually circled that safe deposit box twice. But what was someone like him going to do with that old piece of junk? Anyway, he grabbed the gun and a couple of boxes of ammunition and stuck them in the bag.

Four in the morning. Mandrake was cursing over a couple of locks that were putting up unexpected resistance.

"That's it, boys, it's getting late."

They went back to the van, while the Carabinieri closed the gates and armor-plated doors behind them. The Fiat Ducato made a three-point turn and descended the entrance ramp at walking speed, returning the way it had come. The gate swung open once again. Botola leaned out his window toward the Carabiniere in the guard booth.

"It's been a pleasure, asshole."

The vulgar laughter of Lothar and Mandrake drowned out the clashing of the gears as the van shifted into first.

They took the Fiat Ducato to the woods on Monte Antenne, where they'd previously stashed Botola's clean Saab. They unloaded the bags and buried them, along with the uniforms. Lothar and Mandrake doused the van with gasoline.

"Give me a light, Botola!" Lothar joked.

The bullet caught him right between the eyes. He fell without a whimper.

Mandrake whirled around at the sound of the shot. In horror, he stared at Botola, who held the 7.65 mm Parabellum in his left fist, the barrel still smoking.

"What the—"

"You know that guy in the gym, the one who was there with Samurai? That was me, Mandrake," said Botola. Then he pulled the trigger.

The sun was already high in the sky when Botola returned to his large apartment near the Pantheon. Lothar and Mandrake were just scraps of charred flesh among the sheet metal. He was sorry about them, a little, but you didn't argue with Samurai's orders. The swag was safe and sound, where it would remain until the hurricane, which was sure to come, blew over. Botola put a couple of bottles of millésimé champagne on ice and looked out over the sleepy piazza. Time was, that apartment had belonged to Dandi. The last leader of the gang had been killed a few years ago at the hands of a crew of old colleagues: lead from the hands of his own men, according to some. An act of rough justice that had freed the territory of the worst glutton around, according to most. Botola had no opinion on the subject. He considered the untimely departure of Dandi, to whom he had also been quite close, as something of a mixture of unlucky chance and sheer necessity. If Dandi hadn't gotten a big head, he would have remained number one for a good long while. But if Dandi hadn't gotten a big head, he wouldn't have been Dandi, either. And so . . .

For a while, that 3,200-square-foot apartment with a spacious terrace overlooking the center of the capital had been occupied by Patrizia, Dandi's widow. Then Patrizia had hooked up with a cop, and things had ended badly for her.

Botola, after serving an acceptable sentence, had bought the place, lock, stock, and barrel, furniture included, for a laughable price. And it was from there, from that place that had once reminded them all of who they were, where they had come from and how high they had climbed, it was from there that they were going to have to start out again.

Like things used to be. Better than things used to be.

Samurai deigned to put in an appearance around noon. He was very tall, and he wore a Korean shirt without the faintest halo of sweat, a pair of dark glasses, and close-fitting jeans. He announced himself with a sort of weary sneer, dismissed the champagne, and barely nodded when Botola started to sing the praises of their exploit in the vault.

"I know that everything went according to plan. They were talking about it on the radio."

Botola's feelings were hurt. Sure, he knew that Samurai wasn't a guy who talked much, you could even say he seemed practically mute, and he didn't necessarily expect glee, but a minimum of demonstrable satisfaction, for fuck's sake!

"Did you bring what I asked?"

Resentfully, Botola handed him the handgun and the bullets.

Samurai took it all with the devotion proper to a holy relic, removed his Ray-Ban sunglasses, caressed the weapon with a gaze of tenderness, and smiled at last.

"What's so damn special about this rod?" Botola muttered. They'd laid their hands on a treasure, and this guy was fixating on a pistol that must have been a hundred years old.

"You wouldn't understand," Samurai replied flatly.

Botola didn't insist. He'd been out on the street for twenty years now, and if there was one thing he'd figured out, it was never to get between a man and his obsessions. If that's what got Samurai excited, it was none of his business.

Samurai pocketed the gun and the bullets, then he focused on the small canvas hanging above a long white sofa.

"That belonged to Dandi," Botola hastened to explain. "He paid a hundred million lire for it at an auction."

"It's a copy," Samurai whispered.

"What the fuck are you talking about? There's even a signature! Look, it says De Chierico."

"De *Chirico*."

"So? I don't know if you remember, but Dandi wasn't the kind of guy to take it up the ass from the first forger to come along."

"I didn't say it was a fake. I said copy. That's quite a different matter. The artist paints an original, then he circulates other copies of the same painting, or else he authorizes another painter to do the same thing . . . In any case, it's not worth that much."

"Okay, you're probably right. And anyway, these two mopes hugging never really convinced me anyway."

"Hector and Andromache," Samurai corrected him.

Botola had had enough. Okay, Samurai was losing his mind, but what was he thinking? Hard to say. Maybe it was just the adrenaline that was having its effects on him. Botola went into the kitchen, popped the cork on the champagne that he'd carefully iced, and poured a little for himself alone, seeing that the other guy was in such a strange mood. Then he went back to the living room, determined to avoid wasting any more time.

Samurai had gotten comfortable in the middle of the sofa and was fooling around with the pistol and the cartridges.

"Samurai, if it's not a bother, I think we ought to talk about our projects."

Samurai waved his hand in a vague gesture for Botola to go on.

Botola grabbed a chair with an unappealing shape (another one of Dandi's investments, God rest his soul, and unbelievably uncomfortable) and sat down across from him.

"Well, I'd say that with what we've got, there's only one path for us to follow."

"Which would be?"

"We take back Rome."

"Oh, really? Go on."

"We've got money, clean fresh cash, and lots of it. That is, clean for us because it's dirty for them, I don't know if you follow me."

"Perfectly."

"Okay. We've got the papers. Which tell us what becomes of all the money that these distinguished public servants have stolen over the last few years. Practically speaking, we've got them by the balls. Which makes us untouchable, and so . . . "

"And so?"

"And so, if you're in on it, the two of us, you and me, from this moment on, we're Julius Caesar and Octavian Augustus."

Botola laughed at his own joke. It took him back to the days of Libano, the founder of the gang. A guy who, speaking of obsessions, had a veritable mania for ancient Rome. And maybe he hadn't been all wrong, after all.

"Well? What do you say, eh, Samurai? Is it something we can do?"

Samurai nodded and started loading the pistol. While he was inserting the stripper clip into the aperture in the barrel, he explained the salient steps in the process to the awestruck Botola.

"This is a Mannlicher, manufactured in 1901 in Austria. Unlike your usual semiautomatic pistol, the way it works isn't powered by the recoil of the bolt, but by the barrel sliding forward. The bolt is, as they say, an integral part of the framework: as you can see, the clip with the ammunition is inserted from the top, not from the bottom. This weapon was adopted by the Austrian army, which used it during the First World War. Later, after falling out of use in Europe, it enjoyed renewed popularity in Argentina. And in fact, the cartridges that you see here are made by Borghi, and were manufactured in Buenos Aires in 1947. When you fire the gun, the barrel, partly contained in this cylindrical guiderail, shoves forward, dragged by the friction of the bullet, and by pushing a specially designed recovery spring, it ejects the shell."

Samurai heaved a deep sigh, aimed the Mannlicher directly at Botola's forehead, and pulled the trigger.

Samurai hibernated for the rest of the summer.

Infuriated by the publicity engendered by such a masterly knockover, the men in uniform sent their very best investigators to Rome. The inside guy was nailed almost immediately and he sang like a canary, giving up the Carabinieri, who in their turn handed over Lothar, Mandrake, and Botola: traitors once, traitors every time. That's what Samurai had expected. And so he had been forced to rub out three very good wiseguys, however reluctantly, three guys who knew how life was lived on the street. To snap the thread that would lead to him. Which is why, around mid-September, while the cops were knocking themselves silly to try to put a name to the mastermind behind the robbery, he went and dug up the loot and showed up punctual as ever for the monthly meeting at Il Bagatto.

Officially registered as a "recreational club," Il Bagatto was the closest thing there was to a left-wing *centro sociale* that the right-wing extremists of Rome had been able to put together. But if the organizational model was copied from the left, the stage setting and the interior decoration, from the pennants with the Fascist lictor's staff to the murals featuring Gandalf and Frodo, from the swastika-emblazoned ashtrays to the iron-core billy clubs that were sold under the counter at improvised booths—all this was unequivocally Fascist in style and intent. Equally Fascist were the young hearts of the kids who, at first in dribs and drabs but then increasingly numerous, were gathering on the creaking benches of the cellar room in the Monte Sacro quarter, eager to listen—in religious silence—to the oracular words of their spiritual leader.

That evening there were at least forty of them, nearly all of them young. Sons of *le curve* at Stadio Olimpico, divided by the teams they rooted for but united—at least, that's what Samurai made them believe—by a shared faith.

*Le curve.* The North and South ends of the stadium united. The future of Rome.

Samurai placed great hopes in his boys. Uneasy people, people with nothing to lose, people who were champing at the bit, eager to take everything they could get their hands on.

He'd baited the hook with ideology, but the project went well beyond any long-obsolete utopia. He was determined to create a finely woven net. They needed to be strong, determined, and ruthless as ancient warriors, but also clever as foxes and, when necessary, as malleable and venomous as jellyfish. Each of them needed to be used according to his particular gifts: stray dogs and double-breasted professionals. And all of them, every last one, would be loyal.

Samurai started to speak. His voice was low and pleasant, but it lit up with sudden surges of energy that electrified the mind and warmed the heart. He spoke of the close, indissoluble bond that linked the Revolution, which they all dreamed of, with life on the street. He explained that what constituted a crime for the bourgeois, can be, under certain conditions, a perfect act for the warrior who can tolerate neither the grimy whining of the weakling nor the acrid censure of an inept justice system. Because the act contains within itself its own ethical, esthetic, and religious justification, and more you need not ask.

He talked and talked, enriching his oration with exemplary parables, until he was absolutely certain that he had them in the palm of his hand, as always. And then, suddenly, just when they expected the definitive revelation, he fell silent and, with a half smile, dismissed them all.

"You can go now. And I want each of you to meditate on the things you've heard. We'll see you again next month."

The young men swarmed off, exchanging enthusiastic comments in low voices, careful not to disturb Samurai's concentration; in fact, he sat with his eyes closed, massaging his temples, as if prostrate from his oratorical efforts.

"Maestro? May I have a word?"

Samurai opened his eyes with a sigh.

And found himself inches from the barrel of a semiautomatic.

He focused on a frank, open face, a pair of deep, glowering eyes, a grimace of tension, and a light tremor that the other man was struggling to control.

Marco Malatesta. Eighteen years old. A hoodlum from Talenti with plenty of heart, plenty of guts, and, most of all, plenty of brains. One of his favorites. A potential designated heir.

"If you were hoping to astonish me, Marco, you did it. Now, if you'd be so good as to explain . . . "

"You're no maestro. You're nothing but a bastard!"

"Watch it, Marco. You're thinking like a petty bourgeois."

"Fuck you and your bullshit, Samurai. This is what you are!"

The young man rummaged in the pockets of his jacket and threw a handful of multicolored pills at him.

"Those are worth a lot of money," Samurai commented, by no means perturbed. "You'd better pick them up."

"Ah, you recognize them, don't you? Of course you do! You're the one who's peddling ecstasy on the *curva*, you're the one who's poisoning us all. You're a pusher, Samurai. No, not just a pusher, the boss of all the pushers. You sent us around to crack the skulls of all the pushers. And you called that a 'revolutionary act.' But what was it really, eh? Free-market competition?"

"My boy, if you're planning to shoot someone, first you should make sure the safety's off."

Marco looked down instinctively.

Samurai smiled, then acted with lightning speed. In an instant, he had the pistol in his hands.

Marco lunged at him, eyes bloodshot with fury. Samurai deftly stepped aside, feinting Marco's assault, and then, with the butt of the gun, landed a sharp blow to the back of his skull. The young man dropped, moaning. Samurai swung around and bent over Marco, rolled him over, climbed over him and squatted down, aiming the gun at the middle of his forehead.

"I ought to pay you back in the same coin, Marco Malatesta. And it wouldn't do you any good to beg for pity."

"I'm not asking for pity from some piece of shit! I believed in you, Samurai, I believed in the things you said. Change this city, change this filthy rotten world, a new morality. You're fine with this filthy rotten world, you wallow in it like a pig, *you're* the traitor!"

"I'm not a traitor. If anything, I might be a bad teacher. I haven't been able to teach you a thing. In that way, I'm far guiltier than you'll ever be. And my punishment is to leave you alive."

Samurai pocketed the gun. Then he got to his feet and gestured for Marco to do the same thing. The young man struggled to stand upright; his vision was blurred, his head was pulsating, each heartbeat intolerably painful. Samurai supported him, his right hand brushed Marco's face, as if in a caress of peace. Marco felt a sharp sting of pain, raised his hand to his forehead and pulled it away, smeared with blood.

"It's just a small mark," Samurai explained, folding up a short blade. "You'll have it with you for the rest of your life. It will remind you of who you are, where you come from, and what you've done."

Two weeks later, after the wound had scarred over, Marco Malatesta went to the Carabinieri's Pisacane Barracks and asked to speak to the officer on duty.

# Rome, the Present Day

# I

Looking out the French windows of the Anna Magnani Suite, on the fifth floor of La Chiocciola—a hotel described in handsomely printed brochures as a "charming and secluded little hideaway just minutes from Campo de' Fiori," but popularly known as an expensive sex pad for the capital's elite—the Honorable Pericle Malgradi, MP, a paladin of Roman Catholic values, opened his black silk dressing gown emblazoned with a picture of the snow-covered peaks of Mt. Fujiyama (*it's a kimono, they call it a kimono*, Samurai had explained patiently, but that guy was obsessed, and everybody knew it), extracted a substantial apparatus whose legendary erections were the pride and joy of the Eternal City, and readied himself to bless, with his stream of murky yellow water, the roofs and pedestrians of the immortal eternal city.

"Sabrina!" he barked, without even bothering to turn to look at his favorite, who had just keeled over in exhaustion and was now lying sprawled on the king-size bed next to the other girl, this one a Lithuanian. "Sabrina, you were born here in Rome, you know that poem, it's by Belli, your great Roman poet . . . how's it go? I'm the king of the world . . . I'm me and the rest of you aren't shit . . . "

Ah, urination, the sublime postcoital urination, what a delight, what pure pleasure! You could direct your spray, weaving and lashing it like a garden hose, a fountain, with recurrent, multiple jets, or straight down like a plumb line, or else you could restrict it drip-drip-drip, or unleash a sudden, foaming waterfall onto the heads of those poor suckers working the night shift.

"Look at that, Sabrina! I got one guy right on his bald dome! That's right, handsome, look up, look up at the sky, and blame the seagulls and the crows . . . I'm up here and you're down there . . . you get it, the way life works? Sabri'? Sabrina-a-a . . . Get out of bed and come watch, why don't you, Jesus Christ on a goddamned crooked crutch, with the money I pay you and that Slavic whore, can't you give me this little bit of satisfaction?"

No response. This shift of hookers seemed to be out like a light. As was understandable. He'd ridden them hard, the two of them. Serious business: we're talking about Pericle Malgradi! He'd see to giving them a wake-up call, the two "professionals."

The Honorable Malgradi stuck his hand into the capacious pocket of his kimono and pulled out his Patek Philippe Annual Calendar 4937G, tenderly planted a kiss of justifiable fatherly pride on the tiny picture of his daughters he'd had inlaid on the dial, clicked the mechanism—you go find someone else like me, who can afford a fifty-thousand-euro timepiece to use as a pillbox—and grabbed a couple of Listra tablets.

"Listra, Sabri', you understand, not that crap that the working poor take, Cialis, Viagra . . . stuff that sets your brain on fire and twists your guts in a knot. This stuff is special, baby girl, top quality stuff, made by the loving hands of my brother Temistocle. One of these days I'll have to introduce you girls to him, you know, because he's hung like a racehorse too, just like me . . . It's in the DNA, girls . . . the Malgradi brothers, good blood don't lie . . . Oh, Sabri', you and that other girl, the Slav, what's her name . . . you want to get your asses up off that bed, bitches?"

Nothing. Not a peep. Goddamn it! Now Sabrina was taking things too far. What, did she think she had the only pussy in Rome? In Rome, a city that was literally swimming in peach-fuzz! Next time, a couple of black women. No, better yet: a couple of black women and a transsexual. Just for fun, and a little company. Minimum wage, really, after a whole lifetime spent in the service of his community. But let it be clear with the transsexual, though: you can catch, bwana, but you can't pitch. He wasn't some faggot, after all!

The Honorable Malgradi put the watch back in his kimono pocket, extracted a hefty line of coke from an aluminum foil packet, and crushed the tablets into the cocaine; then he laid it all out on the counter and took a powerful snort.

"Sabrina! Slavic girl! Look, there's plenty left for the two of you."

More silence. Enough is enough! A violent sense of vertigo made him stagger. He grabbed the railing. The shit was going to his head. And from his head, before long, it would descend to his junk. Meanwhile, the erectile cocktail was starting to have its effect, a giddy sense of invincibility swept through him. Everyone kept telling him to take it easy, everyone said that they were dancing on the rim of a volcano, everyone was afraid that things could change any second. Everyone kept yammering on about yield spreads, spending reviews, morality . . . what the fuck! Italy will never change. We'll always be on top, and the pathetic losers will always be down below.

"Help!"

Oh, at last, signs of life.

"Put in your *brillantino*, here comes Uncle Pericle."

Ah, the *brillantino*. This was the novelty that had finally convinced him that Sabrina stood head and shoulders above the rest of Roman hookerdom. A small piece of diamond-encrusted jewelry plugging up her hole, the hole in her rear. That way, said hole was always distended and, how to put it, ready for use. Malgradi liked to extract the *brillantino* with his tongue. That kind of foreplay was worthy of a sultan! Just one downside: the risk of swallowing the dingus by accident. But there was no way that such a piece of dumb bad luck would befall Pericle Malgradi, *Il Numero Uno* himself.

Malgradi turned around.

Sabrina was staring at him, looking anxious and pale.

"Now what the fuck's the matter?"

"Vicky's definitely not well."

It started to dawn on Malgradi that he might have a problem on his hands.

"*E ora cchi vòli chista*? Now what's she want?"

"She's dying, you idiot."

What the hell had come over Sabrina? And why was she screaming like this?

"*Muta, sangu 'i cristu, staju pinsannu*. Fucking Christ, just shut up and let me think."

Sabrina snorted with fury. Malgradi sized up the situation. *Madonna santa*! The Slavic girl had turned green, bright green like a late-season artichoke. She was gasping like a fish out of water, flat on her back on the black satin sheets, and an unhealthy background noise kept emerging from deep in her lungs every time her chest heaved and sank as she labored to breathe.

"*Madonna mia*! She's dying on me! She's dying on me! This bitch is dying on me!"

Incapable of moving. Incapable of making a decision. Incapable of speaking. Sabrina rummaged through her handbag and pulled out her cell phone.

"We need to call an ambulance!" said Sabrina.

A hint of understanding finally ignited in the Honorable Malgradi's mind: I'm fucked! He collapsed onto the bed, next to the foreigner, who was growing increasingly ashen and breathless. As the languid enchantment of the cocaine subsided and the hysterical lucidity of the amphetamine began to gallop, the inevitable consequences flicked before his eyes in rapid sequence.

Donna Fabiana, wife and mother, devout member of the Oblate Daughters of the Virgin Mary. *Gone.*

His own position as national secretary of the party, fanatically committed to the defense of the Italian family against the twin blights of gay marriage and abortion. *Gone.*

His angry disappointed voters from the district of the Ionian coast of Calabria.

*All gone.* Epic scandal. Poverty. Prison.

The Lithuanian girl was gasping and panting, her mouth filling with a yellowish foam, her fists clenching and unclenching as she labored to suck in one last desperate puff of air.

Malgradi snatched the cell phone out of Sabrina's hands.

"You're not calling shit, you get me? Get out of here! *Jativínni! Vui cca nun siti mai vinuti!* Neither of you were ever here! I never met you!"

"Jesus Christ, she's dying! We have to call for help!"

"That's her problem! Fuck it, I'm getting out of here, now!" shouted Malgradi, as he started desperately flailing around in search of clothing.

Sabrina, suddenly chilly, eyeing him like a vulture, said: "Of course you are; after all, no one saw you come up here with us."

Hotel La Chiocciola, a charming little hideaway. They should have burned it down years ago, damn them and the families that had them! And damn you, he thought. Damn the dick he used for brains, he should have put it on a chain, tied it up in a triple knot: *il triplo nodo t'avía 'a fari!* Damn fucking Vicky, and the rest of her ilk, Italy's been too soft on these immigrants for far too long now, give them an inch and they'll take the whole damned mile and then some. He was fucked, he knew it. Fucked!

Finally, with one last rattle, the poor miserable girl threw up a chunk of puke, and then fell silent.

"She's dead!" Sabrina whispered softly.

She closed her friend's eyes and shot Malgradi a glare blazing with disgust, nausea, and contempt.

The Honorable Malgradi, however, was miles away. From deep in his heart a memory from his earliest childhood back in Calabria had begun to sprout. What was it his grandfather, Nonno Alcide, used to say when they went fishing off the coast of Le Castella? That's right: *prega, prega, c'arriva 'u pisci, picchí è proprio quando non sai che pesci pigliare che devi pregare.* "Pray, pray for fish, because it's precisely when you're at loose ends that you need to pray." And so Malgradi fell to his knees, put both hands together, and called upon the Almighty, that His blessed hand might be laid upon His humble servant, "I'll retire to a monastery, o Lord, I'll take religious vows, just save me from this scandal, You who can work Your will as You please, I beg you, I . . . "

"That's right, on your knees and pray. Look, here comes your guardian angel now, on a flying carpet."

Ah, now the whore was having her say. And she even dared to insult him. On what grounds? You bring me this encephalitic hooker who probably carries all kinds of diseases, and still you lecture me?

An uncontrollable fury took hold of the Honorable Malgradi. He stood up, lunged at Sabrina, and knocked her to the floor with one vicious straight-armed smack.

"Sure, sure, *bravo*," she replied, unruffled, rubbing her cheek with one hand. "Now what are you going to do? Kill me too? So then you'd have two corpses to get rid of, not just one?"

"Oh, what the fuck do you want from me now? Do you have any good ideas, you two-bit whore?"

Sabrina picked up her cell phone and dialed a number.

"Spadino? I could use some help here."

Thirty minutes later, a young man, about twenty-two, knocked at the door. He was wearing a pair of faded jeans and a black T-shirt. He was short, pockmarked, and ugly as unsecured debt.

Sabrina let him in and pointed to the bed.

It only took the young man a quick glance around the hotel room to understand he'd just hit the jackpot. The corpse, Sabrina looking depressed and utterly disgusted, the guy dripping sweat and wringing his hands . . . Yes, this was his shot at the big time. Better than anything he'd dared to dream of when the call came in from Sabrina.

"If you could help us resolve this rather . . . unseemly . . . situation . . . "

The high muckety-muck came over, with the smile he wore for election-day victory speeches and his hands shaking as if he was on the verge of a panic attack. Let's just hope he doesn't start wailing like a two-year-old.

"Well?"

"I . . . you see . . . Sabrina, here, has told me so many good things about you, sir . . . "

"She's told me the same about you, as far as that goes," Spadino replied with a snicker.

The Honorable Malgradi shoved his hand into his pocket and pulled out a fat wallet.

"If you would be so good as to give me a little assistance . . . "

By that point, he just didn't know what to say. More importantly, how to put it. The young man amused himself by leaving the man to dangle for a while, then he nodded and lit a cigarette.

"Okay, let me get this straight. You want me to get rid of one dead whore . . . And that's something I can take care of."

A broad smile of relief spread across the Honorable Malgradi's features.

"Naturally!" he said, opening the wallet. "I was thinking that for your trouble . . . "

"Exactly how much you were thinking, just out of curiosity?"

The Honorable Malgradi handed him a wad of bills.

"That must be . . . "

"We can count it later," the young man reassured him, pocketing the wad of bills with rapacious haste.

Malgradi fell back on the smile he reserved for his most prestigious counterparts when a negotiation had culminated in a mutually satisfactory deal.

"I'll never forget what you've done for me today, Signor . . . "

"Call me Spadino. And as for saying thank you . . . you'll have all the time in the world, later! Right now, get the hell out of here."

Malgradi backed away toward the door, muttering a stream of boilerplate terms of gratitude.

"It seems to me that your boyfriend is quite the asshole," Spadino commented, once the coast was clear.

"You can't begin to imagine how much of one."

"Give me a hand getting this poor girl dressed, Sabri'."

With a sigh, the two of them got to work.

The plan was to dump her in a place Spadino knew well. A safe place. So the important thing now was to get her out of the hotel without letting La Chiocciola's desk clerk, maids, or any chance passing strangers suspect that the girl was dead. But even fully dressed and liberally doused with perfume—the night was hot, and she was already starting to emit a faintly unpleasant odor—there was something unmistakably corpse-like about the Lithuanian girl. So Spadino ordered Sabrina to put some makeup on her, and she contributed the idea of putting on the mirrored Tom Ford sunglasses she wore whenever, after a long night out, she had to pull an unexpected quickie. Even if the effect was less than spectacular, it would work. All they had to do was move the girl fifty, maybe sixty feet, and if they were lucky, everything would work out fine.

They got her to her feet, each supporting her from the side. Jesus, she was heavy, God rest her soul! Moving her was an unwieldy process, and it was obvious she wasn't walking, that the two of them were dragging her.

"This is all we can do," said Spadino. "We'll tell the desk clerk that she's drunk. We can give him a hundred euros, make it clear to him that it's in his interest to look the other way."

His thinking was impeccable.

They headed out the door.

The fifth floor corridor was deserted. The elevator came promptly. Smooth as silk, they strode briskly out into the lobby. Spadino asked the desk clerk to hold the heavy revolving door open for him, which the man happily did with a meek smile. Sabrina slipped him a couple of hundred-euro bills.

Once the odd little trio had trundled off down the street, the desk clerk went back to his chair behind the counter, set aside the *Corriere dello Sport* that he read religiously every day to make himself feel a little more Roman and, when necessary—depending on the guest's loyalties—more of an A. S. Roma fan or an S. S. Lazio fan, and did some thinking. His name was Kerion Kemani, he was thirty-five years old, he came from Albania, and a nagging doubt was bothering him. He owed everything he had to the Honorable Malgradi: his job, for one thing, and his Italian citizenship, which he was expecting to receive any day now. But just how far should he take it with the gratitude? Before he'd decided to stick to the straight and narrow, Kerion had had his own short time on the street. Come to think of it, it wasn't as if the Italians had given him much of an option. He'd landed in Bari with the first wave of immigrants, back in 1991. He was little more than a child when he'd found himself jammed with a small army of illegal immigrants in a soccer stadium that soon turned into a cage full of savage beasts. To pay for their passage across the Adriatic, his father had sold everything they owned: the house, the fields, the few heads of livestock that he'd managed to save from the greed of the Communist regime. In the Bari stadium, the Vlorë Mafia had taken care of the rest: his sister had become a streetwalker and he'd gotten busy working as a debt collector. What that meant was spending his days terrorizing husbands and fathers, breaking a leg or an arm every once in a while, beating down unruly whores. That kind of thing. After that, things had changed of course, but there are some memories that never fade. And if his street smarts meant anything, well, then the girl with the oversized sunglasses on hadn't really been drunk at all.

She'd been dead.

That said, what to do next?

All right, let's think this through.

Whatever it was that happened in the Anna Magnani Suite, Malgradi was in it up to his neck. Which meant what for him, Kerion?

After all, the generosity that the Honorable Malgradi had shown him had hardly been offered free and clear. Malgradi was helping him get ahead in Italy, but in exchange Kerion guaranteed absolute discretion concerning the man's turbulent sex life. Malgradi was never registered at the hotel, no inconvenient documentation was ever sent to police headquarters, no requests for IDs, and moreover, all Kerion's compatriots who managed to obtain their long-sought Italian citizenship—at least a thousand to date—were obliged to vote for him.

So really, more than generosity, this was a pact. And everyone knows that pacts don't last forever. Or if they do, their terms can always be renegotiated.

"Now it's my turn, Honorable Malgradi."

And so it was that Kerion Kemani, Albanian night porter and would-be Italian citizen, went upstairs to the Anna Magnani Suite, took possession of a pillowcase stained with a foul-smelling substance that he thought better of investigating in any detail, and a piece of aluminum foil with residues of a white powder. Then he pulled out his cell phone and took a series of photographs of the scene of the crime. Later, in the two-room apartment he'd been sharing recently with his sister in Pigneto, who had recently been promoted from a street-walker to the caregiver of an elderly lady in a wheelchair, he wrote down a short account of what had happened, and finally turned in for the night.

When the time was right, all these things would come in handy.

Spadino and Sabrina dumped the corpse in the nature reserve of Marcigliana, just a few miles short of Monterotondo Scalo. Spadino identified a small ravine, together they hauled the Lithuanian girl out of the car and laid her to rest on a comfy bed of leaves and dry sticks.

"Rest in peace, amen," Spadino commented, and rolled himself a cigarette.

"Now, would you please take me back to Rome?"

"Oh, relax, Sabri', look at what a beautiful starry night it is. We're just getting started here. It strikes me that this little prank is going to cost your friend the Honorable M.P. a nice tidy stack of euros."

"I don't want anything to do with it."

"Who even invited you in? In fact: you've never even met me, got it?"

"You be careful: Malgradi is a dangerous character."

"Who? Him?"

"He's got powerful friends, Spadi', don't underestimate him."

"Don't talk bullshit! Of the two of us, I'm the one you should be scared of, beautiful! Now, quit your sobbing, eh? What's done is done."

"Spadino, I want to change my life."

"Too bad for you," he snickered bitterly flicking away his cigarette butt. "You want to know something? All this activity has got me horny as hell."

"Please, let's just go back to Rome, all right?"

"You want a ride, you pay your fare, sweetheart," he replied brusquely, unzipping his fly.

Sabrina got busy paying her fare.

Meanwhile, all around them, silent invisible shadows began to circle, attracted by the rank odor. Feral dogs.

## II

S padino phoned the chamber of deputies and asked to speak to Malgradi. They put him through to a courteous secretary.

"The Honorable is at the foundation."

"And just where would I find this foundation?"

"Excuse me?"

"Could you give me the foundation's address?"

"It's on Largo dei Lombardi. Do you know where the old headquarters of the Italian Socialist Party were?"

Spadino, who'd never heard of whatever it was she'd just said, but assumed it had something to do with socializing, took a few moments to realize that the place must be next to the shop where, when business was good, he went to buy sharp new shoes.

He rode over on his scooter, and parked it haphazardly next to a no parking sign.

Six large smoked plate-glass windows overlooking the street formed an L that embraced the piazza and one side of Via del Corso, giving no hint to the kind of humanity and life that might be moving around inside save for the occasional fleeting passage of shadows. The front door, made of impact-resistant glass, opened automatically when electric eyes detected movement, and was surmounted by a tricolor cockade in painted aluminum. A plaque proclaimed: "Back On Your Feet, Rome." Why, when exactly did Rome fall? And who is supposed to get Rome back on her feet, Malgradi? Oh, please!

The two bouncers who were guarding the entrance were well-known faces: bodybuilders from Ostia who'd started out working in nightclubs, when Spadino was selling hash around schools. They let him through with a nod of greeting.

A smiling, fluffy brunette walked to greet him.

"*Buongiorno*. Can I help you?"

"I'm looking for the Honorable."

"Do you have an appointment?"

"We're old friends."

"Could I have your name, then?"

"I brought him back something that he forgot at La Chiocciola the other night," said Spadino, touching his backpack.

"You're going to have to wait, I'm afraid. The Honorable, this morning, is going from one meeting to the next."

"I don't have anything better to do. I'll wait."

"Then if you'd care to follow me, I'll see you to our Italia lounge . . . "

"Gladly."

Spadino allowed himself to be led down a short blind hallway with an epoxy resin-and-cement floor, and from there into a large rectangular space, very spacious but windowless. Down the wood- and slate-lined walls trickled rivulets of water that were gathered in steel drain runnels illuminated by chilly spotlights sunken into the floor. Well, you tell me, Spadino said to himself, my grandfather, god rest his soul, was right: the best way to make money in this world is politics.

In the center of the room, surrounded by a hemicycle of black-leather Chesterfield sofas, to one side of a crystal-topped table with cylindrical legs that were replicas of Trajan's Column, sat a haggard-faced puny guy in a navy-blue pinstriped suit, talking to another man who kept interrupting him and addressing him as "counselor." The two men seemed to be in the midst of a discussion that was as vigorous as it was sensitive.

"This is our Roman political coordinator," explained the fluffy brunette, "Counselor Mauro Lotorchio. If you'd like to speak with him in the meantime . . . "

"Why don't I just get myself an espresso instead."

The brunette pointed him to the short end of the lounge. A steel and glass counter where a highly buffed chrome-plated vintage espresso machine enjoyed pride of place. Leaning against the counter were two cute blondes, around twenty, in black tops, white stretch pants, and stiletto heels.

"Our volunteers are at your service," she said brusquely, with a note of resentment in her voice, then turned and disappeared.

Spadino headed over to the coffee machine and didn't even have to ask. The hand of one of the two volunteers, with a handful of light-blue enameled nails, pushed an espresso in his direction.

"So do you seriously work here for free?"

"The Honorable says that politics is a form of service. A passion. Not a job."

"Oh, really? Is that what the Honorable says? And what do you eat for dinner?"

"The Honorable always takes me out to dinner, or else one of his coworkers does."

"Sounds about right."

Spadino turned his gaze toward Lotorchio and the man with whom he'd gone back to arguing. Even though the two of them were doing their best to keep their voices low, he was able to overhear the conversation. The guy was querously demanding an apartment. Lotorchio was offering, but nothing was good enough for the other guy. There was a problem with all of them. How the fuck many apartments did this guy have to offer? And who did they belong to? Were they all Malgradi's?

The first espresso was followed by a second, then a third.

Time passed and there wasn't the slightest sign of Malgradi. Spadino was starting to see red. Lotorchio and his interlocutor had finally come to an understanding, and shook hands. The other guy left. A uniformed general of city constables made his entrance. He spotted Lotorchio and strode toward him, waving a stack of papers in the air.

"My dear counselor! I've brought you the handicapped stickers that the Honorable asked for."

Well, what do you know about that! Disgusted, Spadino was about to light a cigarette, in open defiance of the NO SMOKING signs that wallpapered the room, when Malgradi's voice broke into the conversation between Lotorchio and the general of city constables. The Honorable was strolling arm in arm with a short, corpulent fellow dressed in a shamrock-green three-piece suit with a pink shirt and a dark brown tie. They seemed to be engaged in the tail-end of the discussion that had made him cool his heels in this waiting room for the past hour.

"So you have a clear idea of what the problem is, Your Honor? This whole problem with hiring for shops is turning into a nightmare. Are you telling me that I can't kick a shop clerk out into the street if there aren't any customers? Where are we, in North Korea? I need employees if I'm making money. If not, out you go, scat. Home with you. Forget about a severance package, reimbursement for unused vacation time."

"You don't have to persuade me. I presented an amendment that we'll debate with the upcoming budget bill. We need to free our country from the dictatorship of the trade unions. Rights, entitlements . . . All the left ever wants to do is blare out those two words. What about duties? What about responsibilities? What ever became of them?"

"Then can I reassure the association? I have your word?"

"Malgradi is only one vote."

"And the association has many votes."

Everyone laughed heartily.

Until Malgradi saw him. Spadino. The guy from La Chiocciola. He went over to him and greeted him with a quaver in his voice, and it was impossible to say whether it was a quaver of rage or terror.

"What are you doing here?"

"Your Honor!" Spadino smiled.

"What on earth do you think you're doing?" he whispered into Spadino's ear, trying to steer him toward the foundation's front entrance with one hand on his shoulder.

Spadino planted his legs wide and braced against the side of the hallway. He grabbed his backpack with both hands and turned menacing.

"Rule number one: from now on, we lose the formality and are on a first-name basis. Like all good friends. Rule number two: favors get repaid. And that means that from today forward, you buy the shit from me. And not from those assholes from Ostia out front who are guarding your ass."

"What shit?"

"So, you really don't want to understand! Here, take this backpack, it's got your colognes and perfumes. Let's just say that you and your girlfriends can snort lines with this for a week. And let's say that that makes five thousand. You can give it to me next time, if you don't have the cash right now."

"And what if I called the police?"

"Why don't you just call the constable over there? He's handier."

Spadino pushed Malgradi away with a light shove of his right hand against the Honorable's sternum. And as he headed off toward the door he stopped one last time.

"I'll call you. You get the money ready. Let's start with five thousand a week. Then, if you decide to throw a party, I can get plenty of shit. It'll cost a little extra, but it's the best. Ah, love and kisses from our mutual friend. You remember Sabrina, don't you?"

Malgradi watched Spadino go until he saw him exit the building and walk out onto Largo dei Lombardi. In the throes of a flush of body heat, he got on his cell phone.

The man they called Number Eight answered on the third ring. Malgradi skipped the conventional greetings. His voice was shaking, on the verge of full hysteria.

"Do you . . . Do you know a certain Spadino?"

"Of course I know him. He's from Cinecittà. Why?"

"Look, it's simply intolerable. The man showed up here at the foundation. He started blathering on in front of everyone that you and I . . . ahem, yes, that is . . . that certain things from now on will go through him and him alone."

"And just how did he wind up there, this Spadino? What does he have to do with a person like you?"

"In fact, as I was telling you . . . It's inconceivable. He says that he got my name from a friend of his, some girl . . . But I tell you, are we playing games here? In fact, you see, I was hoping you might give me some advice. Because, you see, I'd rather not be bothered again. This is pure rabble, the kind of scum that might talk out of turn."

"Don't worry. I'll take care of it, Your Honor. As far as you're concerned, it's already taken care of."

"You're simply exquisite. Really. Exquisite as always."

# III

Number Eight climbed into his black V8 Hummer and checked the time. One thirty. He was in time for his appointment with Spadino. At the usual place. He ran his left hand over his bald head until he located the only strip of hair, an inch tall, that was left on his head, designing on the nape of his neck a perfect Number Eight in high relief.

Number Eight. Fuck, what a fantastic name.

It had started out as a joke when he was just a kid in Ostia, poolsharking in halls from Levante to Ponente. Back when they still called him Cesare, the name his father had given him. There had never been any need for the surname—Adami. Everyone knew his surname and everyone carefully avoided uttering it. The nickname sprang out of the fact that before every game of pool, before the break, he'd developed the habit of lifting one ball off the green felt table—the eight ball, only and always that one—and rolling it around on his prematurely bald noggin.

Then it had become a serious matter. Deadly serious. He had become a serious person. More serious than anyone else around.

"Number Eight," period. The boss of Ponente at the age of just thirty-five.

There were a few pieces of shit who still claimed that he deserved none of the credit. Thirty years ago, Libano had made him an orphan. He still remembered the day that, on the beach of Lega Navale, they'd hauled his father up in a net, half-eaten by grey mullets and swollen to the size of a whale. People said that it if hadn't been for Uncle Nino, there'd be nothing left in Ostia of him and his family, not even the stench. Sure, Nino and Libano had come to an understanding and the Adamis had even outlived the gang. Libano was dead. Dandi was dead. Meanwhile, Uncle Nino's hair had turned white, and in the absence of rivals, he'd remained the sole boss on the coastline. Coke, hashish, heroin. "Everyone needs to come under uncle's umbrella." Neapolitans, Sicilians, Calabrians. Then—since things have to be done the right way—the family had expanded. Uncle Nino had raised another orphan a few years younger than him: Denis. He was the eldest son of the Sale clan, an ancient family in Ponente, one of the first families to be deported to Nuova Ostia from the borgatas of Rome, a deranged psychotic. At age sixteen he'd used a Bic ballpoint pen to carve open the face of his high school teacher who had dared to remind him in class that his family had Gypsy origins.

Denis had married a descendant of the Anacletis, the family that controlled Eastern Rome. A marriage that hadn't lasted long, given that the poor young thing had died when her Mercedes SLK slammed into a pine tree on Via Cristoforo Colombo.

May her soul rest in peace!

In any case, Adamis, Sales, Anacletis—that ain't chicken feed. Uncle Nino's masterpiece. Three families with half of Rome in their pocket. From east to west. Appio, Tuscolano, Cinecittà, Quadraro, Mandrione, and Casilino to the east. EUR, Axa, Infernetto, Casalpalocco, and Ostia to the west. Seventeen miles of high-speed beltway that looked like the crown of a queen. Of course, Uncle hadn't been able to fully relish his triumph. He'd been in the clink five years now. Criminal conspiracy and narcotics trafficking. But he had nothing to worry about. He could take care of things: *he*, Number Eight.

He was the boss, at this point. Which meant Spadino was out of business.

Their rendezvous was fifteen minutes away, at most. The Hummer zipped along, old Ostia and the huge parking lots of the Extreme multiplex, one of Uncle Nino's first undertakings, streaming past on the right. He passed the turnoff for the port of Fiumicino where you caught the ferry for Sardinia. At the roundabout for Leonardo da Vinci airport, after the Shell station, he made a right turn and continued along the secondary road that ran along the R1 runway.

The pine trees of Coccia di Morto rose up before him like the backdrop of a theater. Darkness behind him. Darkness ahead of him. Only the little red lights of the airstrip, beyond the hurricane fences surrounding the airport, gave him any indication of where he was. His father had first introduced him to this place when he was a boy. All things considered, the only innocent memory that he still cherished. They'd go down there together at sundown with a modified transistor radio and tune into the frequencies of the control tower. They'd eavesdrop on the conversations between the tower and the airplanes as they took off and landed. They could find out who was arriving and from where and who was leaving and where they were headed. The good old days. Then Libano had whacked Papa, and the only use for low frequencies he'd had after that was to eavesdrop on the cops.

He slammed on the brakes. Spadino's Smart Car was parked with the headlights off in the little clearing a couple of hundred yards into the pine grove, right where the road curved down toward the sea. He pulled over. He got out of the Hummer and went over on foot. Spadino had remained behind the wheel, with the window rolled down. Number Eight leaned over, his big hands braced against the roof of the Smart Car.

"Hey Spadino, they tell me your business is going great, but I see that you're still driving the same piece of shit car."

"I don't have any time to waste. Especially not with you. What do you want?"

"You don't know what I want? But you're a smart boy, Spadi'. How does that commandment go? Thou shalt not covet . . . "

"Thy neighbor's wife. But you're not here to talk about wives. I know that the Honorable came running to you with his sob story. I've already talked with your people. And now I'm going to tell you what I told them: you and me have nothing to talk about. Malgradi belongs to me, now. And if you want to know why, just ask that chickenshit yourself, 'cause I bet he was afraid to tell you."

"Then why don't you explain it all to me?"

"A whore died on him, in his bed. So I took care of the cleanup. Does that sound like enough, in terms of justification? I earned him, got it? And now he belongs to me."

It was a matter of seconds. Number Eight lifted his right hand off the roof of the Smart Car and darted it in through the car window, grabbing Spadino by the hair on the back of his head. He didn't even sense a great deal of resistance. Up and down. Up and down. He smashed Spadino's face against the steering wheel until he'd shattered it. Then he hauled the body out of the car.

"Well look at what a nice big watermelon we've just cut open."

He dragged him over to a pine tree. And then started in on him again. Up and down. Up and down. Pounding that head, which was basically porridge now, against the tree trunk.

It had been five minutes, at most. He stared at runway R1. He took a deep breath of the night air that smacked of salt water and aviation fuel. He went back to the Hummer and enjoyed a nice big snort of coke. The blast hit his brain. Only then did he pop the trunk. He went around and pulled out a two-gallon gas can.

"Be prepared. Never go anywhere without some spare gas."

Then he put Spadino back behind the wheel, doused the whole car with gas, and set it ablaze. He threw his car quickly into reverse as the Smart Car and its driver went up in a ball of flame.

"Have a good trip, Spadi'. And you were right. You and me have nothing to talk about."

# IV

S tanding motionless on the platform of track 1 at the Tiburtina station, Lieutenant Colonel Marco Malatesta of the Carabinieri's Special Operations Group crushed the butt of his umpteenth cigarette under the sole of his green sneakers. He'd taken command of the anticrime section barely two weeks ago, and two weeks ago he'd also started smoking his Camel Lights again, tossing into the wind three full years of hard-won abstinence from tobacco. He slowly massaged his right temple with small, circular movements. The age-old scar was pulsing furiously. It always happened, whenever action was imminent.

Marco plunged his hands into the deep pockets of his heavy motorcycle jacket, which were useful for concealing his Beretta 92 FS. He grabbed his smartphone. He fooled around on the display until he found what he was looking for. The picture lit up, full screen.

Gennaro Sapone.

A nondescript face. He looked like an ordinary bank clerk. He was one of the most dangerous professional killers in Scampia. The last poor wretch he'd sent to meet his maker had been dispatched with a single shot to the back of the head, but it had been a case of mistaken identity: a laborer coming home, instead of a local mob boss. From that day forward, Sapone had vanished. The neighborhood locals were looking for Sapone. The government was looking for Sapone. Which meant he, Marco, was looking for Sapone. And now, if the tip turned out to be right, Sapone's run from the law was about to end. On that platform.

This was the first real operation since Emanuele Thierry de Roche, the commanding general of the Special Ops, had summoned him back to headquarters, returning him to his beloved Rome after eleven vagabond years in the various diplomatic missions of the MSU, the Multinational Specialized Unit. They'd known each other for a lifetime, he and Thierry. And Marco, who owed so very much—perhaps everything—to Emanuele, still hadn't been able to figure out why they'd become friends, the two of them, so very different. Thierry was tall, slender, and formal, the last living descendant of Lucien Bonaparte, Prince of Canino, many times great-grandnephew of Napoleon the Great, just think. And Marco. Who would remain for the rest of his life nothing more than a hoodlum from Talenti. Perhaps it was because they both felt the same way about it: Rome needed to be saved. Especially from itself.

Malatesta looked at his watch and the arrivals board. Eleven o'clock at night. Another five minutes and the interregional from Naples would be delivering that butcher on the run to him. Out of the corner of his eye he checked the track. A fake conductor at the head of the platform. A janitor at the foot of it. And in the middle, a cop disguised as a vendor, rummaging in the beverage baskets. Thank God, there were no other human beings to complicate matters.

The headlights of the arriving locomotive pierced the darkness without warning, while the loudspeaker warned the passengers to stay behind the yellow line. Malatesta once again slipped his right hand into his jacket pocket, slipped the safety off, and got a firm grip on the butt of his handgun.

The train came screeching to a halt. The doors swung open the length of the cars, and an overheated, variegated humanity burst out of those doors. Too many people.

Where's Sapone?

Malatesta knew that sensation very well. The adrenaline was starting to pump. But there was no sign of the killer.

To hell with him, he thought with a surge of anger, turning his back on the cars and running his gaze over the entrance to the escalators.

And that was when Sapone got off the train.

The two shots fired into the air from the .38 that the Neapolitan was clutching in his right hand, coming just seconds before the screams of a young mother, left no room for doubt. The animal had grabbed her little girl out of the woman's arms. Sapone had spotted them.

Malatesta's men took shelter. Aiming their regulation weapons they demanded a surrender that was never going to happen.

"Carabinieri! Carabinieri! Drop your weapon!"

Sapone aimed his pistol at the head of his little hostage.

"Come on, then, you chickenshit cop. Come on, if you've got the balls!"

The little girl was crying. The mother was screaming. The other passengers were hastening to get away. A stalemate.

"I want a car!" the Camorrista shouted. "Otherwise I'll carve this kid's eyes out of her head!"

Orders, in this situation, were clear and binding. De-escalate the situation. Avoid harm to civilians at all costs.

The Carabinieri lowered their weapons.

Marco shook his head.

There are things that have to be done, and that's that.

He started moving slowly toward Sapone; he was no more than fifty steps away from him. He was perfectly balanced, his right arm was extended the length of his body, clutching his Beretta. His eyes were drilling into the murderer's face, because he'd long since learned that if you want to understand when a man's about to kill, it's deep in his eyes that you need to delve.

"Don't you move! Don't you move, fucker! I'll kill you. I'll kill you and the girl . . . I'll kill yo-o-ou!"

The closer Malatesta got, the stronger the whiff of sweat and fear that came off of Sapone.

"I'll kill you, you piece of shit Carabiniere . . . I'll kill yo-o-ou! I'll kill this girl!"

"Colonel, be careful!" one of his men shouted from behind him. He didn't answer.

He stopped at a distance of no more than five yards, forcing himself not to lock eyes with the little girl. He knew that he wasn't going to waste a lot of breath on this. The words were going to be good for just one thing: to gain a few fractions of a second.

"Sapone, it's over!"

"There are two possibilities, you piece of shit Carabiniere. Either I kill you or I kill the little girl!" he said, with the wide eyes of a cokehead.

And those were the last words the Neapolitan uttered.

Malatesta's right arm shot up perpendicular to his body as if it was spring-loaded. He fired without taking aim. The bullet shattered Sapone's hand. The pistol flew away and Sapone collapsed to the ground. Marco rushed over to the little girl. He threw his arms around her and dried her eyes. He whispered gently to her to calm the tremors that were shaking her body.

"It's all over now. It's all over . . . "

The mother yanked her little girl out of his hands. She shouted: "You're a madman!"

She stared at him with blank eyes, while Marco lowered his gaze. There was nothing to explain. Sapone would have killed the little girl. That was the simple truth.

There was bound to be no end of controversy, certainly. And there would almost certainly be disciplinary measures. And, as always, Marco would continue straight on his way.

He turned his back on the woman to focus on the Camorrista whose wound his men were treating.

"Three possibilities. There were three possibilities, you piece of shit. And you got the third."

He was still explaining how things had gone to the men from RIS, the forensics division, when, a couple of hours later, the call came in from Thierry on his cell phone.

"Pine forest in flames. Smart Car burnt. Corpse charred. Go and report."

Marco went to get his motorcycle, a white Triumph Bonneville 800, in the square outside the Tiburtina train station. He angled gently through the last few curves on the crosstown highway, roared through a deserted Porta Maggiore lit by the neon suns of the porchetta vendor's food truck, and in a rosary of blinking yellow traffic lights, he went past St. John Lateran, took Via dell'Amba Aradam, Piazzale Numa Pompilio, and rode past the arches of the Baths of Caracalla. He savored the shiver that the five or six degree drop in temperature of a summer dawn could bring as he headed west, along Via Cristoforo Colombo and the short section of highway from Rome to Fiumicino. As he roared up the Rampa delle Tre Fontane, he shot a fleeting glance at the rusted ferris wheel of the Luna Park, a monument to his childhood and to a time that was there, frozen, as if that city hadn't known how to progress past its own ruins, but only to stack one set of ruins atop another.

With the back of his glove, Malatesta cleaned the bloody ooze of mosquitos and gnats off his visor, a result of the off-ramp to Tor di Valle. Someone had decided to build Rome's new soccer stadium there. Who can say whether that was a good idea. He slowed down when he drew even with the Magliana neighborhood. There had been a time when that quarter, built below the level of the river by some genius of urban planning, was known as open territory under the control of organized crime. Maybe its inhabitants had gotten sick and tired of such a dark and, nowadays, unjustified reputation. And he wondered with a half-smile what they thought of the idea that had been circulating for a while now: to build a cable car to connect Magliana to EUR. A cable car. And why not a spa, and ski slopes with man-made snow, as long as they were at it?

He knew the scene of the crime like he knew his own pockets. His father used to take him to Coccia di Morto when he was a kid. In the afternoons, when he left the offices of the ministry, outside Rome, at EUR. He'd take him there to see the airplanes. He'd made no secret of his dream that one day Marco would captain one of those aircraft. Poor Papa! Marco had put him through so much shit. He'd hated his father. He'd ruined him. And only long after it was too late had he realized how unfair he'd been to him. He'd been a real bastard.

The thing that told him he'd arrived was the stench. The lime-encrusted wreckage of the Smart Car was floating on a murky carpet of mud, water, and fire-extinguishing foam that hadn't yet congealed.

He braked the motorcycle to a halt a hundred yards or so from the crime scene tape that isolated the perimeter of the blaze. He tilted it on its side kickstand. He took off his helmet and slowly strapped it to the motorcycle seat with the cargo net. He stuck his gloves into one of the two leather saddlebags. He bunched up his jeans around the thigh, to diffuse the heat from the engine block. And he slowly walked toward it. He'd learned to do this, with the first corpse that he'd ever had to recover, a Chinese man in the drainage canal of a clandestine tannery. It had become a habit, or perhaps a superstitious ritual. He needed to walk at a measured pace before ushering himself into the presence of death. He showed his badge to the squad of territorial police that had sealed off access to the pine grove, and noticed that Captain Alba Bruni broke away from a small crowd of RIS officers in white overalls and hurried in his direction.

"Colonel . . . "

"*Buongiorno*, Captain."

"RIS has been working on it for a while now, but it seems like a fairly complicated thing."

"Things are never simple."

"Sorry, what I meant to say is . . . "

He watched her blush. And he felt a stab of chagrin for her. There was so much, too much left unsaid between them. The aftermath of a brief and very recent fling that died as he was gripped by the urge to run that unfailingly seized him whenever an affair seemed to be turning into "something serious."

Alba was young, determined, and desirable. But she was in love. And for Marco, that was a problem without a solution. Keeping an emotional distance, when it was someone you worked with at close quarters, can be a form of torture. But hurting Alba with a long-term strategy of deception and illusion would just have been cruel.

He turned his gaze to the charred wreckage of the Smart Car and waved for Bruni to follow him. A sheet covered the driver's seat. Slowly, Malatesta lifted a corner of it. The stench of flesh and plastic fused together hit him. He guessed from the skull and the upper portion of the rib cage, neither of which the flames had had time to fully devour, that he was looking at a human being. The fire had destroyed everything else.

"It isn't even clear whether this is a woman or a man," said Bruni.

"And in the surrounding area? Have you taken a look around?"

"RIS has bagged some evidence: three human teeth, over by the trunk of that pine tree."

Bruni pointed to one of the RIS technicians who was collecting shreds of bark, much of it charred, from what remained of a tree a good thirty feet away. Malatesta went over.

"Lieutenant Colonel Malatesta, anticrime section, Special Ops, *buongiorno*. Aside from the teeth, what else do we have here?"

"The area around the car is full of footprints, but we don't know yet if they have anything to do with what happened. The odds that they'll tell us anything are about the same as winning the lottery. The fire department made a tremendous mess putting out the blaze and the water they sprayed on it is going to make any work we might do pointless. It's a swamp now. Anyway, they managed to put out the fire in time to save one of the plaques on the chassis. If we're lucky, we should at least be able to track down the name of the registered owner of the Smart."

"And did you find the teeth around this tree?"

"Affirmative. And to go on a preliminary visual examination, I'd say they belong to the corpse."

"So we can at least say that this wasn't a car crash or some junkie who fell asleep in his car with a lit cigarette, right?"

"Affirmative. I'd say this has all the trappings of a murder. We ought to have results in a reasonable period of time."

Malatesta nodded slowly.

"Somebody must have really been pissed off," he whispered.

Still walking very slowly, he headed back to his Bonneville, followed by Alba. He reached for his cell phone and dialed the number for General Thierry de Roche.

"Well, Marco?"

"Let's just say that the drive out here wasn't in vain."

"Do you think it's worthwhile to keep this case for ourselves or should I leave it to the territorial police?"

"I'd say let's keep it. At least for the time being, General."

"Is there anything I need to know immediately?"

"Nothing urgent. We're still on the opening credits. We don't even know if it's a man's or a woman's body."

"Then I'll see you back in the office."

"At your orders."

"Oh, I was forgetting . . . As usual, on the Sapone incident, you decided to disregard orders . . . "

"If you'd been in my shoes . . . "

"Look, I was trying to pay you a compliment, not dress you down."

He flicked the red button to end the call and then turned to Bruni, who was standing about ten paces away.

"Lunch?" he asked, pointing at the motorbike.

"I don't have a helmet."

"What, are they going to pull us over?"

Bruni smiled. She delicately wrapped her arms around the colonel, taking a seat on the soft, low saddle of the Bonneville.

"A pastry at Sisto's in Ostia?

"A pastry at Sisto's."

Marco pressed down on the starter button and yielded to the sensation of her small breasts pressing against his back.

## V

A few days after the death of the Lithuanian woman, Sabrina had received a phone call.

"Are you the girl who was with the Honorable the other night?

"Who wants to know?"

"A friend."

"Yes, that's me."

"Listen up and listen good, you whore. There was no night, no Honorable, no dead whore. Have I made myself clear?"

"Yes, but . . . who is this?"

"I told you, a friend. You just forget everything that happened and live your life in peace. Start getting any funny ideas and I'll send you to sleep with your girlfriend . . . Did I make myself clear?"

"Crystal clear."

"Good girl. Keep it up, just like that."

Sabrina was a practical girl.

At age seventeen, she'd already had to retake two classes at the vo-tech business school. Books just turned her stomach. She needed to invent something, or before long she'd wind up looking like that shapeless potato sack of a mother of hers, a loser who busted her back soaping the heads of decrepit old bitches for forty euros a day, under the table, without benefits. But where to begin? When she looked around her, in the neighborhood, at school, among her girlfriends, all she saw was apathy and misery. As for her boyfriend at the time, Sandro, a guy from Quarto Miglio—need we say more than that?—even though they hadn't gone any further than a little bit of protected sex, he was already raving about getting married, children, eternal fidelity, and all that line of bullshit. Another loser ahead of his time: the only reason she hadn't dumped him was because of the paycheck he brought home as an apprentice carpenter. It wasn't much, but enough for a pizza out and a joint, which was always better than nothing.

No. She couldn't go on like that.

She had to turn things around.

And sure enough, things turned around.

It happened the night she turned eighteen. Sandro had thrown a party in her honor at the Palacavicchi, the megadiscotheque outside of Ciampino. Which meant: a table in the row furthest from the dance floor, the kind of table the waiters tend to turn up their noses at—with a couple of friends of his—complete assholes—the man was a construction worker, the woman, she wasn't surprised to learn, was a shampooist, and there was prosecco in plastic cups and a stick of hashish that looked like shoe polish to end the evening in a blaze of glory.

On the verge of despair, Sabrina wandered away from the little group with some excuse. A guy who was leaving the inaccessible VIP lounge guarded by the inevitable steroid-swollen bouncers had given her an interested glance, and then had suggested they go someplace else and get something to drink.

She had accepted the invitation. Anything, as long as it wasn't that evening's absurd party. Someplace else turned out to be the guy's villa in Grottaferrata, outside Rome. His name was Enzo and he was a broker for a pool of insurance companies. They fucked, pumped up by a line or two of cocaine. That was the first time Sabrina had ever tried cocaine. She liked it, but it scared her a little bit. Anyway, in the end, Enzo handed her a couple of banknotes.

Sabrina turned the money over in her hands, baffled.

"Okay, okay, you're right, beautiful, maybe I was a little stingy. Here, that makes three hundred, but don't ask me for a penny more, business is going bad these days . . . and maybe next time, you could float me a discount, what do you say?"

Sabrina could have burst into tears. Or she could have burst out laughing. The guy had taken her for a whore. Sabrina could rebel against the idea or just treat it with chagrin. The choice was hers.

Sabrina understood, at that exact instant, that the merciful hand of fate was lifting her out of misery and offering her a dazzlingly bright future. That was when things turned around. This was her calling.

"I'll give you my cell phone number. Call me when you want. And if you have any friends you want to send my way, I'd be happy to meet them."

That's the way Sabrina's career began. Her nom de plume, so to speak, was Lara, and she was one of the most sought-after escorts in Rome.

But Sabrina was a practical girl.

She certainly didn't plan to grow old turning tricks.

Her life plan called for ten years or so as a working girl, no more than that, because this line of work, in the long run, hollowed you out, and there's nothing sadder than a faded hooker trudging down sunset boulevard, and maybe even—horrible to think of it—back out on some actual street, and not just the metaphorical one. Another three years and she'd be done, finished, over and out.

She'd open up a little place all her own. A bar. One of those fancy, understated bars where people with Corso Trieste faces go to enjoy their happy hours, playing a game of foosball and maybe snorting a line or two. Or maybe a beauty shop, why not. And she could even install Mama at the cash register.

But now, forget about it.

The guy on the phone had been clear. Very, very clear.

Malgradi had pulled his levers. Spadino was out of his mind if he thought he could blackmail the Honorable. Should she have warned him? But why would she have bothered? Spadino was a piece of shit like all the rest of them. The only smart thing left to do was keep quiet.

And what if that wasn't enough? What if they decided that she was still too dangerous?

Sabrina took down her website, www.larasecrets.com, paid a Romanian to set up a prepaid SIM card, destroyed her cell phone, cut her hair, and dyed it blonde.

Would that be enough of a metamorphosis?

And in the meanwhile, how was she supposed to run a business?

Sabrina had a girlfriend. Teresa was one of those working girls who had exited the profession at the height of her success. She wasn't like the other ex-call girls: she hadn't turned into a cloistered nun, she didn't pose as a respectable middle-class matron, she hadn't cut herself off from all her old girlfriends. She had a weakness for Sabrina, but not just for her: what with all the time she'd spent around men, she'd learned to loathe them. Women were quite another matter. Women—they were, and always had been, sisters.

They met at the fitness center in the Tuscolano quarter, an establishment that Teresa ran with an iron fist. It served only women.

"No, but Sabrina, just get out of the business entirely, right? There are no more pimps, who'll complain?"

"I can't. I don't have enough money set aside to afford it."

"Set up another website."

"I was thinking of something a little more discreet, a little more confidential. I told you, I can't explain why, but I have to stay under cover."

Teresa took a sip of her fresh juice, an apple-carrot blend, and thought it over. When she leaned forward, she'd delicately brushed her girlfriend's breast, as if by accident. Sabrina let it ride.

"You ought to find a way to get into a left-wing social circle, Sabri'."

"What? Communists? Those guys hate us!"

"To hear them talk, sure, but trust me. I'll let you know."

Teresa leaned over again, but this time Sabrina jerked clear of the "accidental" caress. She wasn't at that point yet.

# VI

In spite of the darkness, the black sand of Ostia Ponente was still warm. It took Number Eight a certain degree of effort to get over the fence that surrounded the last kiosk operating on a municipal concession before reaching the wharves of the tourist marina. He set down his heavy Technisub duffle bag and looked up at the sign that read PETER PAN, painted in all the colors of the rainbow in lively cursive. He stared at the small stamp at the bottom right. "Municipality of Rome. District XIII. Social Cooperative for the Public Good. State Concession no. 24—May 8, 2007, exclusive beach use, for the benefit of children, minors, and the differently abled."

Retards and kiddies, sure! Cooperative, sure!

Rights to beach access were no joke. That half a mile of beach, closed off to the north by the jetties of the tourist marina, were gold. Solid gold. Like every square foot of beach from Ponente to the gates of Capocotta. Was there or wasn't there a good reason why, in Levante, the last asshole in line was now willing to pay up to six million euros for a three-year beach concession? Was there or was there not a fucking reason why the beaches of Ponente shouldn't belong to the bosses of Ponente? Are we or are we not masters in our own homes? Was there or wasn't there a reason to hold tight to that beach, like the priceless treasure that it was?

There was, there was, no doubt about it, *there was*.

"Waterfront."

The Waterfront, Samurai had explained to him with a broad smile.

"Ostia is going to be Rome's Waterfront. *Boardwalk Empire*," he had mouthed in English. "Atlantic City, Italy. Think, try to think. Force yourself to rise a little higher than the sidewalk, every once in a while. At least an inch or two. I know that it's practically impossible for you, but give it a try. I'm not saying every day. But now and then."

"*Uoter* what?" he'd recoiled; after all, he barely spoke proper Italian, forget about English.

Samurai, the way he always did, had glanced at him with a look of compassion, which rapidly faded into a sneer of disgust. And then he'd translated, the way you do with an illiterate.

"Casinos, hotels, restaurants, health clubs, yachts, shops. That's what Waterfront means, you brain-dead fuck."

Number Eight was as touchy as a gorilla. A lunatic who caught fire over nothing. But he'd taken the abuse because of the respect he owed Samurai. And for the money that shit was promising to bring in. "Just think, uncle, this time I'm going to give you the gift," he'd said, warming up as he talked to Nino in prison, repeating like a pet parrot the word he didn't even understand, *uoterfront*. "I'm going to get you *er uoterfront*, uncle!"

But on one condition: that the beach be cleared of outsiders. Because the Communists, during their time running the city, controlling the city council on the Campidoglio, the Capitoline Hill and the seat of Rome's city government, had done more damage than a hundred flood tides. "The sea belongs to everyone—sure, boom!" they had said. And they'd entrusted six lots of beachfront—six, not just one—to a handful of bums. Cooperatives, they called them now. What kind of fucking cooperatives, though? Of a bunch of damned *zecche*; ex-hippies, leftists, Commies, dope smokers, collectively known as *zecche*, ticks.

It had taken a while to get things back the way they belonged. Number Eight had begun supplying cocaine, free of charge, to that human vacuum cleaner and whoremonger the Honorable Pericle Malgradi who, God bless the souls of his fucking ancestors, snorts more coke than oxygen. And sure enough, the bet had paid out. Now he had him by the balls. Things had changed. The Communists were out of power, and there was a new law, which stated that the concessions would be renewed only for those who had "proven that they knew how to successfully and efficiently run a socially crucial service such as bathing services on the coastline." Words that were music to his ears. And in particular, they were a signal that it was time to get busy.

Because, let's just say that, heaven forbid, the beach establishment were to burn to the ground on you, whose fault is that? Yours, because you were incapable of "running it successfully and efficiently." And if someone else, an ambitious person, happens to have the cash and is willing to lay it down, and is capable of "running it successfully and efficiently," then it's only fair that he should nab the concession. It's the free market, no? And that's what the law says, anyway. As for the "socially crucial service" for little kids and the handicapped, they were as capable as anyone else of putting in a slide, a merry-go-round, and a rubber swimming pool. But where *they* decided. A good way off from the beach, where they wouldn't get in the way. After all, what difference did it make to them?

And so, one after another, the kiosks had burned down. And it was all his doing, Number Eight's. Because it was his responsibility. One kiosk a week. Always at night. Always with the same gasoline and the same rudimentary triggering mechanism, placed in the electric panel of the beach establishments. The rest went without saying. Dried out by the briny air, huts, beach umbrellas, and gazebos went up like newspapers. In a second. And the spectacle of blazes on the beach had become a regular appointment, almost as popular as dogfights, which were a magnificent draw you could set up in a garage. People came from all over Rome to watch pitbulls tear the flesh off each other by the chunk. Okay, it brought in a few euros, too, but that wasn't the point: nothing was as good as a show.

He looked at the dial of his Rolex Oyster Perpetual. The hands said it was past midnight, and he needed to get moving. PETER PAN: this was going to be between the two of us.

He texted Robertino, one of the guys who'd been working with him since he was a kid. "Let's go."

The first firework, a whistler, rose straight into the air over Piazza Lorenzo Gasparri as he started tampering with the electric panel of the Peter Pan center. The second firework, a rocket that burst open into a weeping willow of green, white, and red sparks, illuminated the gas tank that he emptied over the kiosk. For a moment he stopped to watch the fireworks bursting into the air from the terraces of the barracks in Piazza Gasparri and Via Forni, the geographic heart of Ponente. Nuova Ostia, his Ostia. An idea of his own, because, as Uncle Nino had taught him: "If you want to count for something, it's not enough to do the despicable crime. You have to make sure that people know who did the despicable crime."

He'd left Peter Pan for last. It was a beachfront establishment where little kids actually went; the work of destruction would demand a few hours of overtime. The seven-foot slide, built like some medieval castle, and all the toys, tractors, and spring-mounted plastic horsies, stacks of buckets and sand molds, boogie boards, Gormitis and Pokémons . . . in other words, a nasty job that had to done by hand, and all before flicking a lighter.

He found the axe next to the fire extinguishers. Factory new. Perfectly balanced, too, with the original edge on the blade. With a light, hardwood handle, and a red axe head. He grabbed it with his right hand and raised it high, about even with his ear. Then he staggered toward the slide with a voice that he forced to be that of a falsetto, bowlegged, like an ogre in a Saturday morning cartoon.

"Oh children, my darling little children, Captain Hook is here, he's he-e-e-ere! Tick, tock, tick, tock."

In less than ten minutes, he'd demolished the dream castle with methodical fury.

"Oh, oh!" *crack.* "Oh, oh!" *crack.*

He accompanied every blow of the axe with a clever phrase and a smile. Then the time came to devastate the play area, with its tractors, bouncy horses, and surf boards. At last, he fished a cigarette out of his jumpsuit and flicked his burnished metal Zippo with the silhouette of the Duce into flame, twice. First for the cigarette. And then for the Peter Pan.

The gas fumes and the glow of the flames enveloped the kiosk in a second as he walked back down the waterfront promenade and tossed his duffel bag into the back of the Hummer. He revved the enging and pulled out as a lilac-colored fountain of fireworks concluded the display in the sky over Ponente.

The Off-Shore, realm of Number Eight, wasn't far away. It was right on the beach of Coccia di Morto. Eleven thousand square feet of wood and glass overlooking the water. Just a sample of what "*er uoterfront*" would be in Ostia. The name Off-Shore had been chosen by Number Eight, in defiance of Samurai, who said that he was an ignorant as a bag of hammers. Forty-five hundred square feet of bar criss-crossed on a perpendicular by a counter in the shape of a Fascist lictor's staff. A gym with five treadmills overlooking the beachfront, a boxing ring, and an assortment of weights that would be more than sufficient to keep a team of Olympic contenders in shape. In a corner, near the storeroom where they kept the liquor and, when needed, the gats, and which was secured behind two armored doors that opened with a combination, he'd also set up a tribal tattoo center, Er Geko, with little waterbeds for the clients. And, of course, he'd carved out the space for three darkrooms that seemed like a collection of bedrooms out of Scarface. The Seashell, the Hammock, and the Merry-Go-Round.

That little plaything had cost him plenty. But not in terms of materials or labor, because people worked for him free of change. No, it cost him in terms of the cash needed to grease the hand of a general in the municipal police, a fucking animal. A piranha fish. A hundred thousand euros right away, in stacks of ten euro bills. A Romanian whore all tricked out for a "full-service" party for his son's eighteenth birthday, and a rubber dinghy made available all summer long in the Canale dei Pescatori, with Yamaha outboard motors, 250 HP each.

But he was all set, at least, with his permits.

It was three in the morning, by this point, and the Off-Shore was packed. Number Eight stank. Of wood, burnt plastic, and sweat. He tossed the keys to his Hummer to Albin, the Romanian parking lot attendant who was rolling himself a joint the length of his hand.

"If they get it dusty, you're fucked."

He slipped into the Conchiglia and found Morgana snorting a line, bent over the glass coffee table that sat right in front of the huge bed in the shape of an oyster shell. Such a nice ass on that girl. Pert, petite, snug. She was twenty years old and she was the only female from Ponente that he had accepted into his crew. But not because he was screwing her. Because out on the street she was cruel as a witch, and in bed she was as docile as a geisha. He slipped a finger between her ass cheeks, laughing as he whirled his tongue around in her ear.

"I'm looking to relax. But not now, later. Let me get a shower and then I'll see you in there. Who's here?"

"Just about everyone. Even Rocco."

"Anacleti?"

"Yeah. He came with that rat Spartaco."

"The journalist?"

"That's right, Liberati. He told me he hadn't been by to say hello in too long."

"He must want money, that scab."

Morgana emerged. He took a quick shower, massaging for long minutes his neck and his chest, upon which the face of a joker laughed, beneath the chest hairs. He put on a white shirt, snorted a couple of lines, and headed over to the bar.

Rocco Anacleti, Spadino's boss and the chief of all the gypsies in Eastern Rome, came toward him, arms wide open, struggling to push his way through a swamp of coked-out teenage girls, lawyers, doctors, and the occasional cleaned-up street thug from Fiumicino, and gave him a bear hug. He'd dressed himself up with a pink shirt and a pair of white-linen pasha pants that made him look shorter and fatter than he really was. It seemed like a sincere hug. Obviously, he knew nothing about Spadino. Nothing at all.

"All good?"

"All good."

"I've been waiting for you forever."

"I had a lot of things to take care of. I don't know who else to hit."

"Tell me about it. Cinecittà is turning into a circus. Everyone wants to be the boss. Even the damn *zammammeri* think they can do whatever they want," he said. "All of 'em, gyspies, fuckers from the east, Arabs, junkies. It's just unbelievable."

"It's a freak show out there."

"Speaking of which . . . have you seen Spadino?"

Number Eight pretended he'd been caught off guard.

"Me? No, why?"

Rocco gave him a funny look.

"He said he was supposed to have a meet with you."

Number Eight started hearing an unsettling background noise.

"With me? When?"

"I dunno, yesterday, I think. Anyone, no one's seen him. And they say someone found a burnt corpse in the Pine Grove."

"Yeah, I heard about that . . . But what does that have to do with Spadino?"

"The burnt corpse was in a Smart. And Spadino drives a Smart."

"So what can I tell you? Try asking around. Oh, I see you brought Spartaco."

"And guess what that guy wants?"

"What does he ever want? Money, right?"

From the bar where he stood sipping a mojito—cadged for free, no doubt about it, thought Number Eight—Spartaco was waving his arms in a Judas Iscariot greeting. He was a former Fascist comrade now in his mid-fifties, with a history as a two-bit kick-boxing champion that had ended early and badly. He had been expelled from the Federation for putting an adversary into a coma. He had crushed the man's cranium with a kick while he was flat on the mat. Then he'd ventured into the radio business, and everyone now knew him as Spartaco the journalist. The voice of Radio FM 922, "the year of the March on Rome, for Christ's sake."

The journalist. Oh, sure. Spartaco was a puppet, dancing on the strings of anyone who paid him. A lapdog owned by Samurai, who had known him since he was a kid, during the war with the Communists. Money, money. That was the only word he understood. The only thing he was seeking. And in fact, money was what he was there for.

"Fabulous this Off-Shore. Looks better every day," he said.

"Spartaco, I don't have time. Just tell me what you want."

"No, nothing, it's just that I'm running a little low with my sponsors. Maybe, if you can spot me ten thousand, I'll run your Off-Shore on the radio for a month or so. Maybe, you could be interviewed a few times, live, what do you say?"

"A thousand. And don't show your face around here again."

"You're a pal."

He didn't even bother to reply. He grabbed Morgana by the wrist, dragging her away from some guy who'd been drooling over her for a while.

"Now I feel like it."

# VII

I'm Teresa's girlfriend."

"*Ah, Teresa, Teresa, perché sei tu, Teresa?*" He sang the words of an old song, then segued into a courteous greeting. "Come right in, make yourself comfortable, don't linger in the doorway. And you are?"

"Justine.

"The Divine Marquis's Justine or the little fox of a Jewess in the *Alexandria Quartet*? But what does it matter? Come in, come in, my dear."

In his day, the Professor had been famous, very famous. So famous that even Sabrina had heard of him. Just a few days before they met, Sky TV had broadcast an old movie based on one of his hit novels. The Professor played himself in it: an absent-minded intellectual, half a philosopher and half a comedian, who could make you laugh at the miseries and paradoxes of life.

Huh, thought Sabrina as he welcomed her into his large apartment on Via Nomentana, huh, look how he's aged! The salt-and-pepper man in his fifties with the deep blue eyes had been transformed into a bent, quavering old man who had to stop and brace himself against some piece of furniture every couple of steps to keep from losing his balance. On the walls, framed production stills winked down mockingly, portraying the Professor at the height of his success. The hallway they walked down to reach a vast living room that opened out onto an enormous terrace was lined with books tidily stacked in bizzarely shaped bookshelves. There were incomprehensible paintings and unsettling sculptures.

"Pascali . . . Bacon . . . Tano Festa . . . "

The Professor rattled off a string of names that Sabrina had never heard of. The tone of voice in which he described his treasures was weary, resigned, and vaguely ironic. As if to say: but why am I wasting my breath on you, seeing that you're ignorant as a goat?

"Just wait for me here a moment, my dear. I'll finish getting ready and I'll be right with you. I imagine that Teresa must have told you what this is all about . . . Justine.

"I know everything, Professor. You can count on me."

"Trust is a serious matter," the Professor psalmodied, suddenly grim-faced.

Then a cunning smile appeared on his yellowed, parchment-like face, and the Professor started singing an old advertising ditty: "Galbani, Galbani, Galbani means *trust!*"

Teresa had warned her: "He's a little odd. He lives in the past. He just hates it that the film crowd doesn't give a damn about him anymore. But he's filthy rich, and he's nice enough in his way. If you know how to work him . . . "

Filthy rich. Well, the place he lived was promising enough. Sabrina jotted down a few notes on her iPhone: the names of the artists that the Professor had mentioned. Later, she would look up the market prices on the internet. Maybe it would turn out those scribbles were worth thousands of euros.

"Well here I am, darling. Do you mind calling a taxi?"

"Are you sure you're not forgetting anything, Professor?"

"Ah, yes, of course, so sorry, my dear, I apologize, you must forgive me . . . we said eight hundred, I think, isn't that right?"

"Yes, Professor."

"Uncle Mimmo, my dear, to you I'm just Uncle Mimmo."

So if he was Uncle Mimmo, she was the niece from the

country who was studying Economics at the Roma Tre University in Ostiense, and she was staying with him temporarily until she could find accommodations more appropriate for a young college student. That understanding had been the reason for her chaste blouse and the non-designer jeans, the little red jacket with an unostentatious brooch, the minimal amount of makeup, and the flat, sensible shoes.

"No slit skirts and no four-inch heels, no pushup bras, and keep your tattoo covered up. Remember: you're a leftist." Teresa's words of wisdom.

But Teresa was overstating things. The first glance that Sabrina got when she and the Professor made their entrance into the penthouse apartment of the producer Eugenio Brown didn't strike her as all that devastating after all. There were male Communists in jacket and tie or scarf, but there were also plenty in Merrell sneakers and deconstructed linen by Etro. There were female Communists that were modestly attired in unrevealing clothing, though still with a touch of skillfully applied makeup, and there were young things in dizzyingly short skirts showing off scraps of sexy intimatewear, who were happily teetering on skyscraper heels. In other words, there were individuals there who wouldn't have looked out of place at a party thrown by Malgradi's friends, and others who wouldn't have made it past the first glance of the line of bouncers. If she'd dressed up the way she usually did, with that aggressive, whorish array that constituted her second skin, she would have avoided seeming like what she looked like right now: a pallid, insignificant glass of water.

The perfect country niece.

The Professor introduced her to a few people. They all greeted her courteously but without warmth, and there was no lack of ironic eyerolls. Oh, sure, the niece, those glances eloquently stated. Hey Professor, give us a break! You're out of date, no doubt about it, but still, you're one of ours, so we willingly accept these little peccadillos of old age. Still, you could have chosen her more carefully, this young niece of yours.

Once they had made their way through this first round of helloes, the Professor collapsed into an armchair "designed by poor old Sottsass in '73" ("Sossas, armchair , '73?" Sabrina diligently jotted down on her iPhone), and started telling his usual round of anecdotes. Four or five losers listened to him, sincerely delighted. Or, perhaps, who knows, they might have been faking it: out of pity, or who knows why. Sabrina was sitting next to Uncle Mimmo, and she laughed when the others laughed and let the old man distractedly stroke her thigh when he thought that no one was watching. Eight hundred euros was still eight hundred euros, after all, but what a pain in the ass! It was obvious that the heart of the party was elsewhere. Maybe out on the terrace that overlooked Piazza Vittorio. In the heart of the Esquiline quarter where Sabrina took great care never to set foot, a hotbed of shit-kicking immigrants that, however, the Professor and his friends found "charming, irresistible, so authentic and alive, the genuinely multiethnic Rome . . . "

What the fuck? Around here you can't find an Italian for love or money. They're all Chinese, and that's how it is.

At last the Professor felt the urgent need for a quick trip to the bathroom. Sabrina took advantage of the opportunity to scurry out onto the terrace. It was a clear night in late June, but she had other thoughts in her head. The Professor was just a passport to left-wing parties like this, but she'd rather have a nail driven into her head than face another evening's entertainment like this, so it was time to get your ass in gear, Sabrina.

She started wandering around among the knots of people standing around, she went over to the tables. Everywhere people were talking, talking, talking. They were talking with such passion and determination that they seemed to be deciding the future of the world.

"We've got to convert to the zero-mile diet, it's all about being locavores. Absolutely."

"I couldn't agree more. I've started drinking only fair-trade, *vino libero* wine. No more sulfites. They're a plague. Do you have any idea of how much poison they can legally put in a bottle of wine these days? Up to eighty different components, can you believe it?"

"I adopted a cat. Poor little thing, he'd been meowing outside my door for a week. It broke my heart to just leave him out there, all alone and abandoned. And after all, it only cost four hundred euros for the vaccinations, the veterinarian, and the castration."

"Four hundred euros? That's what Luisa charged me to take the cycas plant to the botanic hospital. It needed treatment, she said."

"Ah, and how did it go?"

"She managed to kill it in just six months."

"Cycas? Huh? Sidekick? What's a sidekick plant, someone they take with them to parties? And how did she get sick, this poor sidekick plant?" Sabrina wondered to herself.

Biting into a chili pepper-flavored tarallo, a bald man, just like the bouncers you see at Malgradi's parties, sighed and said: "I'm reading *American Pastoral* by Roth. A masterpiece."

"You'd like to write something like that, wouldn't you, my friend!"

"I've give ten years of my life."

"Do you think anybody wants ten years of your life?"

"I hear that Matteo Garrone is planning to make a movie about Fabrizio Corona, the photographer . . . "

"You got that information at the freezer counter, sweetheart. Matteo lives downstairs. He thought about it for a good long while, then he decided to drop it."

"Too bad. No doubt, he found Corona just as disgusting as everyone else."

"The thing is that Corona represents the television, the bunga-bunga parties, all those things, and those things are the horror, and the horror can't be depicted. Not even Fellini knew how to do it, back in his day."

"The terrible thing is that none of this ever seems to stop!"

"It's our fault as much as anybody else's, my dear. We're just too soft. We stopped putting up any opposition long, long ago."

A short, fat, bearded guy launched into a sermon about politics.

Sabrina was tempted to yawn. She was drowning in boredom.

They were talking about all sorts of abstruse things, and even when they did say something you could understand, they did it in a way that . . . as if it were only and exclusively *their property*. And the whole rest of the world could take a hike! For that matter, none of those she'd approached to strike up a conversation had made the slightest effort to involve her.

Teresa had warned her.

Teresa had brooked no discussion on the point.

"That's an exclusive circle. They're all little comrades, I don't know if you get the picture. Getting in is almost impossible. Say the wrong word, and you're out on your ear!"

And that was the exact impression she was getting. An exclusive circle. Sabrina found herself missing the crude cheerfulness of Malgradi's social circle. There, surrounded by that herd of satyrs intoxicated on Viagra, at least she'd never felt out of place. They were welcoming, warm, protective. Certainly, the first chance they got they'd dump you and wave a hasty goodbye. But in the meantime, it was thanks to them that she'd gotten as far as she had. And without them, she felt lost.

But when it's all said and done, where the fuck have you wound up, Sabri'? Holding hands with some toothless old man for eight hundred euros?

She jammed her hand in her purse with a nervous gesture. A line of coke, that's what she needed right now, to put up with the stress and the disappointment. But Teresa had been categorical on this point, too.

"Forget about the coke. It's not as if there's not a little of it going around, but if the larger circle is, so to speak, closed off, the sector of the nostrils is absolutely impenetrable!"

Which means, Sabri', deal with it, and let's just smoke ourselves a nice fat ciggy.

"May I?"

Sabrina practically couldn't believe her own eyes. Someone had finally noticed her. Before her loomed the tall figure of Eugenio Brown, owner of the house. In his hand was a lighter, already aflame.

He was a handsome man. In his early fifties, tall, salt-and-pepper hair, in an Armani suit. A producer. A word that exerted an unquestionable allure over Sabrina. Producer meant film. Maybe television. Why not? She had a fine figure, she'd never had any hesitations. So why not? She wouldn't exactly be the first girl to pass directly from the bed to the soundstage. Why not?

Eugenio Brown. If you're going to sell yourself, might as well do it with someone who's at least somewhat attractive.

"Thanks, I just couldn't find my lighter."

"Are you getting bored?"

"No, it's just that . . . "

"There are times when my friends manage to be completely detestable."

"The thing is, I don't know anyone here."

"I understand you. Beginnings are always so difficult."

Sabrina flashed him her most seductive smile. Eugenio Brown put a hand on her arm.

"Do you like this place?"

"It's a little jewel box."

Eugenio Brown smiled at her. This was the first time anyone had described the 2,400 square foot penthouse as "a little jewel box." He stared at her with increased interest.

He was decidedly a good-looking man.

She sensed the desire in him.

But he didn't seem to be making up his mind to make the first move.

Sabrina felt a surge of impatience. She laid a hand on his. She amplified the seductive effect of her smile.

Eugenio Brown's lips parted.

A hairy-looking individual in a checked shirt grabbed him by the arm, forcing him to turn around.

"Sorry. Eugenio, Signora Baldini is looking for you."

"Yes, I'm coming. Until later, then, Signorina . . . "

"Justine."

"Justine, right."

The producer vanished, striding with a lithe step toward a tableful of people concealed behind a lush banana tree.

Checked-shirt lit a Tuscan cigar. Sabrina would gladly have chewed him up and spat him out, the asshole. He'd carried off her prey just at the crucial instant. She turned around to go back to the Professor, but Checked-shirt barred the way. He was smiling, the damned vulture.

"May I have a word with you, Signorina Justine? Or should I say . . . Lara?"

Sabrina looked around. It seemed as if no one was paying them the slightest bit of attention. She raised her hand and was about to sink it into that self-satisfied face. She wanted to leave a mark on him, a scar on that animal. Yes, a visible scar, maybe. After all, at this point, it was clear that the situation was irremediable. But instead he took her hand, lifted it to his lips, and planted a tiny, damp kiss on the back of her hand.

"Don't worry. I'm not dangerous. I like men. Come on, let's get something to drink, I need to talk to you."

There was a curious delicacy to the guy, which somehow she found disarming. She followed him, docile, over to the liquor table. He poured a couple of whiskeys and then steered her into a deserted little corner of the terrace.

His name was Fabio and he was a screenwriter. He was gay, which is how the people on the left say that someone's a faggot, and he had recognized her even with her short, dyed hair.

"And how did you recognize me, excuse me?"

"From the website. You were the girl on www.larasecrets.com, right?"

"Sorry, but if you're a faggo . . . if you're gay, how did you . . . "

"Ah, but I'm essentially a libertine."

"Which means?"

"I like everything that has to do with sex."

"And so?"

"And so I wanted to talk to you about Eugenio Brown."

"What, him too?"

"No, quite the contrary, Eugenio likes women very much."

Sabrina heaved a sigh of relief and admitted that, if nothing else, she had to admire his style. For Malgradi and his men, there was no such thing as women. There were only pussies.

"Well?"

"He was recently widowed," Fabio started over again. "A long and painful disease carried her off. They were a very close couple. Eugenio is one of the few film producers left who still believes in a quality product."

"Yes, but what's that to me?"

"He's a fine person. And he's very fragile. Don't hurt him. That's all."

The hairy screenwriter withdrew with a smile that was meant to be friendly but that also clearly stated: I warned you, as a friend, but I could easily turn into an implacable enemy. Oh, man, as if she had anything to be scared of from that orangutan. Sabrina tossed back the whiskey and was swept with a wave of excitement. A fragile man. Fragile men can conceal major surprises. Fragile men fall in love. Fragile men can easily pass from the role of customer to that of lover.

Eugenio Brown was walking toward her.

But now Sabrina wasn't feeling impatient. Now she knew that she'd soon have him in her grip. This was the time to play a little hard to get.

She rushed inside. She found a notebook and a pen, tore out a page and wrote down her cell phone number. Then, seeing that no one was paying any attention to her, she searched the place until, atop a narrow spiral staircase in a little loft, she managed to identify the master bedroom.

She left the sheet of paper in plain view on the bedcovers with their Indian motifs and went back downstairs.

The Professor had fallen asleep. A stream of drool was oozing down his scarf. Sabrina gently awakened him, called a cab, took him home, and put him to bed, just like the good little niece she was supposed to be. That was part of their deal. The only extra that she conceded him was a quick squeeze of her tits. The Professor gratefully peeled off a 200 euro note.

Now she only needed to wait.

She didn't have to wait long.

Eugenio Brown called the next day, in the morning.

# VIII

The Anagnina district had the unmistakable, sickly sweet odor of those places where the stench of humans and cement has not entirely overpowered the scent of the countryside. It reminded Abbas of his Teheran. Certainly, seen from Via Mongrassano, the Castelli Romani were not the Alborz Mountains, and the green terrace on which you could just guess at the location of Frascati had neither the power nor the dark elevation of Mount Tochal. But the air, the air was the same. Especially now that it was summer. It gummed up the mucous membranes of the mouth like sand. It dried out your nostrils. It scratched at the throat with that aftertaste of carbon monoxide and pitch, veined as it was with a reek of rotting carrion and garbage.

His shop was at the corner of Via del Casale Ferranti. It was beyond the last station of the A Line of the Rome metro. Where the sheep had been driven by their hunger for cubic feet. That little hole of a shop must once have been a parking spot, but the fence he'd bought it from swore that it was registered as an "artisanal workshop." Abbas had made do. He'd lined the wall with cartons and newspapers to insulate it against a perennial and detrimental humidity. The work bench was an old butcher's counter standing on rusted saw horses. In a cheerful disorder, the blocks of marble served as bases for counters in unfinished cherrywood, holm oak, and the strips of ebony upon which he practiced the art that had belonged to his father and his grandfather. He'd been carving since he was a boy, and those hands of a pianist, with the long graceful fingers, reminded him every day of his good fortune. Even now that, at age sixty, his grip on his mallets and chisels had become less sure and his brown skin had become like onion paper, throwing veins and tendons into relief.

He'd never been able to figure out whether his customers valued his skill or the cut-rate prices he set. But it never seemed as if anyone gave a damn about his sketches. For instance, with that Rocco Anacleti, the one who lived in the Romanina quarter, the one whom everyone in the quarter greeted with all the humble deference you give to a tyrant, things hadn't gone especially well. With a certain pride Abbas had displayed his grandfather's sketches on parchment, sketches that he kept lovingly arranged in a leather album.

"And what are these supposed to be?"

"Persian floral motifs."

"And you think I'm going to put this piece of faggotry on the headboard in my bedroom? This is Rome, we're not at your house. What I do in bed is I fuck."

He'd made do with a well-endowed satyr in relief.

"I want it made out of wenge. And it better smell like it's old," Rocco had ordered.

But then when he'd seen the finished product, he'd gone out of his mind.

"What am I, a nigger? Do you see my face? What color am I? Am I a nigger, to your eyes? Brighten up this fucking wood. And right away!"

Abbas had been forced to start over. Using bleached holm oak, this time. The cost had spiraled. To dizzying heights, considering the startling vulgarity of that boiserie. A thousand euros. Money he still hadn't seen. Though he never tired of asking for it. At first, courteously, on the phone. Then he'd gone so far as to send a registered letter to Rocco Anacleti, with a flood of Sirs and capital letters, pointing out that, "in the absence of the courtesy of a reply," he'd be obliged to contact the lawyer of his artisan's guild.

At the stoplight at the end of Via Tuscolana, Max pressed the gear shift of his Triumph Street Triple with a gesture of intolerance. The *clack* as it shifted into first always gave him a subtle rush of pleasure. Because it was the nerve signal of what was yet to happen. It was horribly hot for nighttime. The exhalations of the 108 horses between his legs made his jeans stick to his thighs, the ski mask under his helmet had been reduced to a sponge drenched with sweat, and inside his red sneakers his feet were sizzling like two grilled cheese sandwiches. The Castelli Romani loomed ahead of them. Max detested the Castelli Romani. They had always seemed to him like a dam erected precariously atop an anthill. A few evenings back, on Radio FM 922, Spartaco Liberati, the Voice of Rome, had come out with a riff on his nostalgia for the *ponentino*, a beloved local westerly wind. And we just don't have the winds we used to have, it's all suffocated by the buildings, taller and taller . . . Ah, the Castelli Romani, the *ponentino* wind . . . the kind of horseshit tour guides love to foist off on you.

The truth was that he felt uneasy.

Rocco Anacleti had told him that there was a matter to be settled with an Iranian. Rocco Anacleti was on edge. That would normally have been a job for Spadino, but Spadino had disappeared. Rocco was on edge and he started coming out with some strange things.

His assignment: to stand watch, and guard Paja and Fieno's backs.

He didn't like those two. He didn't like this job. He didn't like Rocco Anacleti.

Soon he was going to have to make some decisions.

The meeting had been scheduled out front of the Centro Sperimentale di Cinematografia. Just past the glass-and-cement rectangles where the Ministry of the Interior had moved the executive headquarters of the anticrime section, the political police, and the highway police. Max rode in second gear until he heard the bike begin to scream, and as he passed the big electrically operated gate surmounted by the escutcheon of the ministry, he beeped his horn as he always did. How could he forego the fun of mocking that cluster of besieged cops in a quarter where they controlled nothing?

He recognized the black BMW convertible parked at the corner of Via delle Capannelle. Paja's blonde ponytail and Fieno's black hair, shaven to the nape of the neck. Those two were a pair of rabid dogs who wouldn't live to be twenty-five. A few years younger than him. Two pieces of shit coked to the marrow. And, just like him, raised in Cinecittà. They'd started out selling pills to schoolkids, when the Neapolitans ruled the roost. Then they'd started wagging their tails around the Anacleti family, the gypsy clan as ancient as the Colosseum, who were pushing every single gram of coke and hashish between Tor Bella Monaca and Piazza Tuscolo, between the Casilino quarter, Cinecittà, and Via Appia. People parked on a mountain of cash, and the only thing about them that was still *gitano* was their history, the occasional clown act in costume, their over-the-top weddings, their greed, and a herd of children, cousins, nephews, and grandchildren all registered with the city under the same name.

Rocco Anacleti. Paja and Fieno's boss. Max's boss.

Or at least, that's what he thought.

Paja gestured toward Max with his forearm sticking out of the BMW's window. His face betrayed all the jolly enthusiasm of a patient just sitting down in the dentist's chair for a procedure.

"Hey, Nicce, you made it. You see, Fieno? The philosopher bothered to show up."

Nicce. The Roman pronunciation and spelling of Nietzsche.

That nickname, Nicce, was supposed to come as a compliment, it should have reminded him that the thesis he'd written on Kant was done out of love as well as a favor to his widowed mother who, luckily, was no longer alive to see him now. Instead it made him see red. It reminded him that out on the street, they were all the same. More of the bullshit he had to pretend he believed. He replied to Paja with a nod of his helmet and pulled out, following the BMW for the short stretch of Via Tuscolana, up to the intersection with Via del Casale Ferranti.

Abbas liked to work at night. The only thing he hadn't gotten used to in all these years in Italy was the idea that work should correspond to routine office hours, to city regulations and not, instead, to the rhythm of the body and the needs of the business. He'd left the shop's metal security shutter halfway up, and he'd worked for hours next to the little stereo that had been a gift from Farideh, his baby girl who had become too pretty and too grownup. He often thought, when he looked at her, of when her mother had died. Of how she had pressed close to him in the morgue of the Regina Elena Hospital, as they had looked down at the rigid body of the only other woman in his life. That day, Farideh had whispered to him that they'd make it, they'd survive. And that promise had become a prophecy. Farideh was his whole life. His anchor, his roots, his future. And that was why he always let her have her way. Even now, when she had started listening to the CDs by Plastic Wave and Kiosk, the dissident rock bands banished from Tehran. A music that he didn't understand, but that Farideh loved. And that was too loud for him to be able to hear the noise of the car and the motorcycle that had pulled up in the street outside his shop.

Max just lifted the visor of the helmet and took a step

toward Paja and Fieno as they were pulling ski masks over their heads.

"Well?

"We're going in. You stay here. If anything happens," Fieno muttered through the ski mask, "find a solution. You're the philosopher, right?"

The two men pulled soft leather gloves out of their jeans pockets. They put them on with meticulous care. In every gesture, in every nuance of their voices, they were doing their best to imitate their great hero. Rocco Anacleti. They had been born slaves, and slaves they would remain for the rest of their lives. Samurai had taught him that a real man has no boss. A maestro, perhaps, but never a boss.

Paja and Fieno walked into the shop and pulled the metal security shutter down behind them, almost all the way to the ground. Max sat down, arms crossed, on the trunk of the BMW. The best place to keep an eye on the street.

Abbas found himself unexpectedly face to face with them. Paja slammed his right fist into Abbas's face and broke his front teeth, flooding his mouth with blood. The Iranian sank to the floor, slamming his temple onto the pavement. His vision went dim. Still, he could glimpse the other man in a ski mask; he watched as the man pulled a grease-stained rag out of his cotton jacket. When he felt that rag being forced down his throat, he decided it was all over, and he tried to fight back with what little strength he could muster.

Completely pointless.

Paja dragged him over to one of the shop's walls, next to some visible plumbing, tying his wrists to a pipe with a hemp cord. And it was at that point, flat on his back with his arms outspread like the Christ to which the Romans prayed, that Abbas began to understand.

Paja went over to the stereo and turned up the volume. And

as the notes of *Autotomy* by Plastic Wave transformed the workshop into a sonic hallucination, Fieno bent over Abbas. The faces of the two men were practically touching, and now the old man could smell the stench of his torturer's sweat and nicotine through the ski mask.

"Okay then, you fucking Iranian, you say you want your thousand euros, eh? Why, do you think that money belongs to you? Listen, remember you're nothing but a *zammammero*. And we don't have to pay *zammammeri*. Got it?"

Abbas's pupils dilated, as his neck stretched in the spasm of what was meant to be an affirmation.

"What? You understand? No, you don't understand. You asked for your money, you Moroccan. You sent a letter. You brought the lefties into it. . . It seems to me you made a mistake. What do you think, did you make a mistake? What? I can't hear you! Speak a little louder, asshole, I can't hear you!"

How long were those two going to take?

Max heard the volume of the music spike louder, and he could no longer restrain himself. To hell with Rocco Anacleti. He left the street and ducked into the shop.

Paja was holding a wooden board in his left hand. In his right, he was gripping a mallet that he'd found in a tool chest. He gestured for Fieno to sit down on Abbas's supine body, to prevent it from shaking and to restrain any unexpected jerking of the legs. Then he squatted down next to the old man.

"All right, now you tell me, you fucking Iranian, where are we going to start? With the left hand or your right? Which hand do you prefer to use for your shitty work? Which hand do you use to grab the money when you ask to be paid? I didn't understand you. Did you just say that it makes no difference? It makes no difference? Then let's start with the right hand, because when has anybody's left hand ever been good for anything?"

Max lunged at Fieno.

"Leave him be! He's just an old man!"

Fieno tumbled to the ground, caught off guard by the sudden violence of the attack. But he was immediately back on his feet. He extracted the gat he had tucked in his belt at the base of his spine and aimed it right at Max's forehead. Right between the eyes.

"This is a .38, asshole. Just try breathing and I'll open your fucking head on your shoulders!"

Max stepped back to the security blind, putting his hands in the air. Fieno turned to Paja.

"Let's make this little faggot watch the whole performance, from start to finish."

Paja arranged the wooden board between the palm of Abbas's hand—and now the old man was grunting like a beast being butchered—and the pipe to which his wrist was tied. He lifted the mallet over his shoulder and then brought it down one, twice, three times, five times on the craftsman's slender fingers, on the knuckles, on the fingernails. Until all he was looking at was a purplish paw of swollen flesh.

Abbas passed out.

Paja turned to look at Fieno, who was still holding the pistol aimed right between Max's eyes.

"Should we call it a night here?"

"I said the whole performance."

"But the Iranian is out cold. He can't see a damn thing."

"He'll wake up. And what he sees when he wakes up is what matters most."

"All right."

Paja threw the blood-smeared mallet across the workshop, damaging a preliminary carving that had been begun on a slab of ebony. Then he started rummaging again through the Iranian's toolbox.

"And what do you think of this?"

Fieno nodded.

"And turn off that music, nobody's going to be doing any more screaming."

Paja snapped the blades of the pincers shut several times. As if to test their power. He grabbed Abbas's right hand and continued his work, turning his back on Max and Fieno.

"This guy's not going to be able to use his hands to even pee anymore."

They took off their ski masks and left the shop drenched in sweat. Fieno slipped the gat down the back of his pants and pointed his forefinger at Max.

"We'll settle up with you later."

Max heard the BMW take off at low speed, and then he took a few steps toward Abbas's body. He loosened the hemp bonds knotted to the pipes, freed his wrists, and arranged the old man's arms along his sides.

All this was too much, even for him.

He had chosen the streets at a certain moment. Or maybe the streets had chosen him.

But this wasn't the streets. It couldn't be.

He lifted the old man's head from the floor. Then, slowly, he also raised his torso, leaning him against the wall. He freed him of the rag and duct tape that was gagging his mouth, to prevent him from suffocating in the mucus and blood. And only then did he manage to appreciate the dignity of his features, though they were contracted in pain. That olive complexion crisscrossed by deep creases, the cheeks sunken hollow by hard work and fatigue and highlighted by a fine layer of white whiskers.

He felt pity for that old man. He would never have admitted it, but he felt pity for himself, as well.

He strode quickly out to the street and his motorcycle. Just in time to cross paths with a white Chevrolet Spark that was pulling over toward the lights of the shop, with the security shutter now open. He slowed down, stopping a hundred yards or so down the street, to see who it was.

A young woman. She was talking on the phone. And laughing.

"Look, Alice, I'm going in to see my father right now. Yeah, yeah, he works at night, too. All right, I'll tell him . . . Of course."

Max held his breath as he watched her. She possessed a magnetic beauty. A fleshy mouth, the eyes of a doe, and long, shiny black hair that tumbled down her back. A walking dream.

"Okay, Alice, I need to get off now. I'm going into Papa's shop."

It was time to go. He accelerated to 55 mph in first gear. In time to avoid seeing her walk into the shop. To keep from hearing the demented screams at the sight of her father's horror. To reach Via Tuscolana and from there run every red light until he reached the Arco di Travertino, where he came to a halt not far from a couple of trannies who were smoking, crouched on a low wall by the IP self-serve gas station.

"Ciao, dark and handsome!"

"Not today."

He took off his helmet and leaned the bike over on its kickstand. He rummaged through the pockets of his cotton Belstaff jacket, in search of his dedicated cell phone. The one that called only one person and took calls from one person only.

Samurai answered on the second ring, even though it was one in the morning.

"What's going on?"

"I have a problem. Or maybe you have one, too. I need to see you."

"Now?"

"Yes."

"All right. On Corso Francia. In twenty minutes."

Max stuck the cell phone back into the jacket pocket and strode a few steps closer to an Alfa Romeo Giulietta that he had noticed parked with the lights off when he'd first pulled into the gas station.

He knew that car. It belonged to the Carabinieri Marshal Carmine Terenzi. He went over to the driver's side, just in time to see a stubby, hairy hand with a wedding ring on the third finger grabbing a hooker's bleached blonde hair. The head was pumping up and down like a mannequin, and the swine was leaning back with his head on the seatback, mouth open, tongue lolling.

Max took one last drag on his Marlboro and stubbed it out on the side of the Alfa. Terenzi shot him a smile through the car window as he came.

Max turned his back on him.

Crooked cop. That's what the streets had turned into, too.

Samurai, as always, was punctual to the second.

"All right, can you tell me what's so urgent it calls for you to interrupt my meditation, Max?"

"The Anacletis, Maestro."

Max told the story in a rush. Samurai listened without the slightest reaction. The young man was upset. Samurai could detect the acrid odor of anger emanating from him. And a saccharine whiff of pity that he didn't like one bit.

"Go smoke a cigarette," he ordered, at last. "I need to think. And if you don't mind, make sure you're downwind. You know how I detest the smell of tobacco."

Max stepped a short distance away. Samurai sat watching the nighttime traffic on Corso di Francia. All that electric frenzy churning in the night, that senseless busy to-and-fro of homunculi.

Samurai was fifty-two years old, tall, with close-cropped gray hair. He always dressed with sober elegance, and his favorite color was black. Under his Kiton jackets, he loved to wear stretch T-shirts that showed off an agile and natural musculature. He never snorted coke, he didn't smoke cigarettes, and only on rare occasions did he indulge in a finger of pure malt whiskey.

Samurai was a slave to nothing and no one.

Samurai allowed himself to be controlled by nothing and no one.

He was the one who controlled everything. He was the boss.

He had grown up surrounded by the myth of a Fascist national revolution; he'd made his bones by beating up reds in high school, then he'd graduated to armed robberies to finance the group, he'd ambitiously dreamed of a coup in Italy, seizing power, exterminating Jews and Communists. One day, he'd watched his best friend be shot full of police lead. He'd managed to survive by some miracle. But the cops tracked him down. An informant had ratted him out. Samurai happened to find out about it through a fellow Fascist who frequented the same gymnasium as certain members of the police SWAT team.

He prepared himself to die with honor.

But the days continued to pass. And no one came looking for him. He thought about turning himself in. The wait was killing him. At last, someone got in touch. An officer of the intelligence services. He offered Samurai a deal. A few dirty little jobs in exchange for protection. Samurai told him to go to hell.

The cops, as was to be expected, came back looking for

him. This time, they came in force and large numbers. Armed and pissed off. They were looking for a firefight, a chance to kill him at last. The best outcome for everyone. The obscene pact that had been offered him could be buried with his corpse.

Samurai put up his hands and let himself be handcuffed with a mocking smile.

At his trial he never opened his mouth. He was given five years. In prison he read Pound, Céline, and *The Decline of the West* by Oswald Spengler, and exercised regularly to keep from succumbing to the boredom. They took him for a hard guy, an uncompromising political prisoner, and they let him be. He said hello to everyone and was friends with no one. He got a six-month reduction of his sentence by behaving like a model prisoner.

But politics had nothing to do with good conduct. Not anymore, anyway. Samurai was disappointed. Prison had forced him into regular contact with his fellow men. He had seen and recognized human beings for what they really are. There was no hope. Impossible to awaken their benumbed consciences.

It really seemed that the society he wanted to change was dead set against being changed. It really seemed that he had chosen the wrong life.

His meditations culminated in the decision to commit suicide, in the same way the writer Yukio Mishima had done.

He'd act a week before being released from prison. That way the meaning of his extreme act would be quite clear to everyone: disgust for the modern world, revolt against the mediocrity of the masses, contempt for the miserable and the weak. Better a heroic death than to live on as a slave.

A few days before the date he had set, they suddenly transferred him to a different cell. His new cellmate introduced himself as Dandi. He was also about to be released, a big young man with an ironic smile and an affable personality, and he boasted that he had put together the most powerful and invincible gang in Rome. He hadn't done it all on his own, he made clear, but with "certain friends you really ought to get to know."

"My time is done, Dandi."

"Really? But how old are you, excuse me? Twenty-five? And you're talking like my grandfather?"

"It's not the age that matters, is what you're carrying inside you."

"And just so I understand, why don't you tell me what you'd be carrying inside you?"

The guy was likeable, and he seemed trustworthy. Samurai decided to trust him. The solitude was slowly killing him. He told Dandi everything. It didn't take much time. He had just started spouting out a quote from Julius Evola's *Revolt Against the Modern World* when Dandi interrupted him.

"Okay, now I see. So you're saying you want to kill yourself because this shitty world doesn't deserve you."

Samurai nodded: a crude summary but, he had to admit, an effective one.

"You know what you remind me of? One of those Japanese guys in the movies . . . the ones with the curved swords that are always sitting around scheming how to crack open some enemy or other's head, probably over some slight to their honor . . . what do you call them, come on, help me out here . . . "

"Samurai."

"There, right, that's it. Do you know who you are? You're a fucking samurai. And don't take this the wrong way if I say it to you, but seeing that you're going to kill yourself anyway, it's just words anyway . . . but the way I see it you don't have the slightest idea how things work in this world."

"And who's supposed to explain it to me, you?"

"Look, do whatever you think best. But tell me one thing:

you go ahead and kill yourself, and do you think that the world gives a good goddamn? Sorry, you know, but if they didn't care when you were a politicized armed robber, do you think they're going to get scared at the sight of your corpse? So now turn out that light, because now I need to get my eight hours' sleep, or tomorrow I'll have bags under my eyes, and if there's one thing I can't stand, it's having bags under my eyes."

Samurai tried not to pay too much attention, but the words of that cleaned-up street thug had opened a crevice inside him that widened day by day. He let a little time go by before returning to the topic.

"So listen, all things considered, what do you think I ought to do?"

"What's chapping your ass is this idea you have that the world has screwed you. Then why don't you pay the world back in the same coin? Screw the world. Screw everyone. You'll see how much better you feel, afterward. Just like after a good thorough fuck, trust me on this, Samurai."

Who knows. Maybe Dandi had a point. And maybe there was more truth in his words than in all the books that had opened his mind when he decided to abandon the main thoroughfare his parents had chosen for him, the law degree, his father's law office, an office that had belonged to his grandfather before him, and his great-grandfather before that, and even before that . . .

Or maybe, quite simply, Dandi had told him what he wanted to hear.

Suicide was put off for some other day. Dandi and Samurai left the penitentiary of Regina Coeli together.

Dandi introduced him to his friends.

Samurai joined the gang.

But that was a long time ago.

Dandi was dead.

Libano was dead.

Lots and lots of others were dead, too, a few had turned informant, a few others were just doing their time and keeping their mouths shut, dreaming of when they could start over, maybe with some modest little office job.

Samurai was still around. His old nom de guerre meant nothing more than abandoned dreams, at this point. Dandi was the one who had pinned that name on him, but he'd done his best to live up to it.

And power—that was concrete, alive, and real.

Samurai was the top, the number one.

Even though, whenever anyone reminded him of the fact, he preferred to reply, with one of his enigmatic smiles: I'm just the first among equals.

That way, no one ever took offense and business could continue. It was all the fruit of his instincts. It had all begun with the boys from Il Bagatto, and the harvest from the seeds sown there had been a rich one. The network extended over the whole city. Unbreakable ties of loyalty.

Certainly, there was no longer anything heroic, by this point, in that drab, gray Rome he had inherited from the days of daring and ardor. The loansharking that he had once scorned as beneath him was now his daily bread. And maintaining his iron grip on the government of the night was a high-wire act that forced him into continuous concessions to worms devoid of heart, guts, and brains.

But that's the way things go in this world, right, Dandi?

Samurai gestured for Max to come over.

The young man stared at him with eyes that could still ignite with passion. There was once a time that he too . . . Perhaps that was why he saw in Max the person he'd been back then. Or maybe, if destiny had allowed him to bring a son into the world, he would have wanted him to be like Max. Different from the pieces of shit in Ostia and Eastern Rome. With the fiber and the nature of a boss. Still capable of catching fire. And even of making mistakes. Like that other one, the one he had betrayed so many years ago.

"Tell me that pity has nothing to do with the story of the Iranian, Max."

"He's just a poor old man, Maestro. What the hell could he ever have done to the Anacletis to make them unleash those two animals on him?"

"Nothing, in fact, to tell the truth, they're in the wrong. They failed to pay a debt."

"And so . . . "

"And so pity too has to be kept out of this and all other stories, Nicce."

"Achilles, too, was moved by the tears of Priam, and gave him back Hector's dead body."

"That's a comparison that's out of place here, my boy. That wasn't pity. That was respect for a valorous enemy. The code of war. And in fact, after that the Greeks entered the palace and slaughtered all the Trojans. Or did you forget that part?"

The young man bowed his head.

Samurai continued, in a soothing voice.

"We don't like the Anacletis, but we need them. We have to permit them a certain amount of brutality. It's a way to keep them under control. Still, we are in agreement. Those two troglodytes, Paja and Fieno, have gone too far. But don't you worry about it. I'll take care of things."

Samurai sensed that his explanation hadn't persuaded Max. Oh well, he'd understand in due time. Before dismissing him, he slapped him affectionately on the back.

"I have great plans for you, Max. Important things are going to happen in the next few days, and I want to be able to count on you. But leave your pity at home. This world doesn't know what to do with it, believe me."

## IX

H ello? Spartaco?"

"Yes, who is it?"

"It's me, Pippo . . . "

"Ah, Pippo . . . but listen, I don't remember: do we know each other?"

"Of course we do! I'm Pippo from the Fidene borgata. What, don't you remember? We met at the opening of that bar in Trigoria, it must have been right before Easter. Pippo, the tall guy who brought the kid with the captain's jersey that you autographed for him, 'Spartaco, Heart of Roma' . . . "

"Hey, you know what I say, Pippo?"

"No, what do you say?"

"That I owe you an apology. E-e-eh, it happens, I just forgot . . . it must be the passing years . . . "

"What are you talking about, Spartaco, you don't age, you're immortal."

"Or else, it could be this heat that's eating us alive . . . "

"It's killing us, Spartaco, it's killing us!"

"Or maybe the thoughts whirring around in my head, and let me tell you, I've got plenty of those this morning."

"Well, forget about them, Spa', you're still the best."

"E-e-eh, forget about them? easier said than done . . . Oh well, Pippo, what did you want to tell us?"

"I was listening to the news about this new trainer . . . this kid . . . But who did he ever train before? What has he won?"

"Nothing, Pippo, nothing is what he's won. At A. S. Roma they always hire the rejects."

"Hey, couldn't they find anything better on the market, though? They say they want to make the club great again, but if you ask me, I'd say that . . . "

"That everyone's good at talking, right? The Americans, the Russians, the Arabs . . . yeah, we've seen it all here, under the dome of St. Peter's . . . Oh, what? Excuse me a second, Pippo."

"Of course, Spa'."

"What?"

"I said: of course, Spa'."

"No, I was just talking with the director . . . Oh, sure, the sponsor . . . well, you could've thought of it earlier, couldn't you? Sheesh, we're all working hard here, what do you think . . . Come on, guys, step it up, get busy . . . Pippo? Are you still there, Pippo?"

"What do you think, when I finally get you on the phone, I'm likely to let you go so easy, Spa'!"

"Right you are, Pippo. We need people like you. Big hearted people like you! Listen, Pippo, can I ask you a question?"

"Ask me? Of course you can, Spa'."

"Does law and order matter to you, Pippo?"

"Oh, what are you kidding? When you take away someone's sense of safety, you've taken away everything."

"It couldn't be any more obvious. Well, all of you who care about law and order, all of you who go off to work each day and leave behind you, at home, your wife, your girlfriend, your mother, your sister, your daughter . . . all you who no longer want to live in the fear that without warning some gypsy might break into your home—and I say gypsy just to name one possibility, because none of us here at Radio FM 922 are racists, but it's a well-established fact that when there's a burglary in an apartment, an armed robbery, a home invasion, you can beat about the bush all you want, haggle over the details, but in the end it's always them . . . So, to make a long story short, all of you who want to live in peace, then guys, I'm not kidding, at least once you have to drop by Rubinacci Armored Doors and Locksmiths, on Via di Tor Marancia number 77 B, let me repeat, number 77 B, where you'll find the answer to all your . . ."

Alba Bruni entered without knocking. Or maybe, actually, she had knocked and Marco Malatesta just hadn't noticed, concentrating as he was on the words being spouted on the A. S. Roma soccer fans' favorite radio station. He lowered the volume and invited the captain to have a seat. Out the plate glass windows of the anticrime section, on the third floor of an office building that was . . . how to describe it? functional? . . . they enjoyed an enviable panoramic view of the Ponte Salario. The Torretta dei Crescenzi—a historical tower house and the last remaining memory of a once-glorious past filled with passions that were forgotten for good now—could barely be glimpsed behind the wall of—how to describe them? functional?—buildings that had turned the ancient suburb into an unsettling slice of modernity. When all is said and done, Marco Malatesta thought to himself, a perfect picture of our condition as servants of the state besieged by the filthy products generated by many of the very people we are supposed to be serving.

"RIS made a call."

"Hallelujah!"

He grabbed the freshly printed sheet of paper that Alba had just handed him, focusing just an instant too long on the fact that their fingers brushed. Alba, Alba . . .

"Identification almost certain."

"They traced it back from the Smart Car, in fact. Now they're going to cross-check it with the mother's DNA, but still, they're pretty confident."

"How pretty confident?"

"You know what RIS are like. There are times when they can be exasperatingly slow, but all in all, we can rely on them. Let's just say that they were willing to go out on a limb. The charred corpse from Coccia di Morto is this Marco Summa."

They went over to the terminal and checked him out together. Alba smelled of apples, just a hint, nothing intrusive. How the hell do women do it? There was a scorcher of a summer waiting in the wings, the air conditioning was working one day and broken the next, and she, and all the others, every last one of them, seemed to have just stepped out of a beauty center.

"Can we concentrate on work, boss, please?"

"Sorry. All right then, let's see . . . "

Marco Summa had a criminal record for small-time drug dealing, as well as a criminal complaint, charges that were later dropped, for pimping and aiding and abetting prostitution. On the screen there appeared a fairly recent identification photo. A ribald pose, eyes that were struggling to appear grim, and perhaps awe-inspiring, but which actually just looked dull and blank. They'd seen hundreds—the colonel and the captain had—of faces just like that one, out on the street, in the police station interview rooms, in the dock during trials, during investigative interrogations in prison. Young men with no heart and little if any brains. The cannon fodder of small-time criminal enterprise. Maybe Marco Summa, AKA Spadino, as his file stated, had tried to make the qualitative leap to a new level and had come face to face—he, pathetic mouse that he was—with some crueler, hungrier rat.

"On top of everything else," Alba pointed out, "he appears to have gone missing a few days ago."

Well, this took care of that matter, no doubt about it. But bit by bit, as they worked their way through the documents on Spadino—arrests, case reports, tips—his cop's intuition shifted his focus away from routine bureaucratic matters to the code red of more serious matters. Deadly serious.

"He died outside of his district, Alba."

"Right. It says here that he was arrested twice by the Carabinieri, Cinecittà precinct."

"And someone burned his body in Ostia . . . I'm catching a whiff of broken boundaries. And when someone like Spadino crosses a boundary, someone might get royally pissed off."

"Mhm . . . And then there are a few other details worth

taking into account. I've done a little sniffing around. At the Carabinieri station in Cinecittà something seems to have happened. In just the last year, two colleagues taken off the force for actions unbefitting an officer, a lance-corporal and a brigadier. Two kilos of cocaine and twenty, let me repeat, twenty kilos of hashish gone missing. The entire staff of the station has been reshuffled."

"So who's in charge now?"

"A certain Terenzi. Maybe we should summon him to come in."

"Let's go see him in person. Right now," Marco decided.

"I need an hour," she said, "I need to finish my report on this Spadino."

Once he was alone, Marco went back to listening to Radio FM 922. Spartaco Liberati was still pontificating. On the other end of the line, there was a new interlocutor, a certain Gino from Ostia.

"You've got a point, Gino. Rome isn't what they say, the wise men writing in the newspapers, the big names . . . people who don't even know Rome, who have no idea of what the streets really are."

"And you've got a point, Spa'."

"Now, you take this corpse they found in Ostia. Now they're trying to paint Rome as if it was Al Capone's Chicago. A city full of criminals, a city without law and order . . . but you know who they really are, the people saying these things, Gi'?"

"They're the same as they ever were, Spa'."

"Of course they are! It's the leftists, communists, and they can't stand the fact that they've lost city hall, so now they think they're white knights defending law and order! But, my dear gentlemen, you should have thought twice before handing the city over to the gypsies and the *zammammeri*! So now, Gi', you know what I say to you? That maybe that poor sucker in Ostia was just smoking a cigarette and he dozed off and set himself on fire. And even if there was, let's say, a murder . . . well, we can't keep everything under control, can we? You know the way these things are."

"Hey, Spa', you're the greatest."

Yes, Sports fan radio is so relaxing, thought Marco Malatesta, with a smile.

But it's also so useful. This was something he'd kept from Alba because, aside from General Thierry, no one knew anything about his past. Sports fan radio acts as a barometer, giving you a read on what's happening in *le curve*. And *le curve* are the barometers of what's happening on the street. The megaphone of those who are excluded from the communications networks belonging to the people who count, or at least think that they count. Fan radio is the voice of a silent mass that navigates on a wavelength all its own. A wavelength that is impenetrable to the usual instruments of analysis. For example: the fact that Spartaco Liberati should be dedicating such a substantial chunk of time to the dead man in Ostia is a fact that makes you stop and think, Colonel. It's not just an old Fascist activist lending a hand to the right-wing majority. It signals concern, let us even say, uneasiness; and someone wants to strangle that uneasiness as it is being born. It's an oration aimed at "whom it may concern" at the behest of someone has been tuned to that famous frequency since the earliest day. Understand who. And why. That was the task awaiting him and Alba.

A chain of events had swung into motion, and the trigger had been Spadino's charred cadaver.

Marco was perusing Terenzi's personnel file when Captain Bruni burst into his office. A little ahead of schedule.

"Nothing doing for today, Marco."

Terenzi had taken a personal day off. The mission was postponed until tomorrow.

"Then I'm going to pay a call on an old friend instead," said Marco.

At that exact instant, Rocco Anacleti was receiving a phone call.

The dead man in the pine forest had been identified. Without the shadow of a doubt, it was Spadino.

The gypsy intoned in a low voice, "I travelled and travelled far and wide . . . " *Gelem Gelem*, a Romani dirge that evoked the extermination of the Black Legion. It was dedicated exclusively to his people.

Spadino wasn't born a Roma, but he was as close to a Roma as a *gadjo* could ever hope to be. And he had died like a dog, massacred and then burnt. His soul would long struggle, in the afterlife, to reassemble the pieces of his violated body.

Anacleti experienced a brief moment of heartbreak. Then, natural and unrestrainable, the thirst for revenge burst forth.

Spadino, goddammit, was one of his men.

Rocco Anacleti sent a text.

Number Eight was awakened by the tune of *Faccetta nera* playing on his cell phone. He shoved aside Morgana, who'd been sprawled at an angle over his hairy, manly chest, and read the text.

"Get ready for a funeral: your own."

There was no need for a signature. Rocco Anacleti had made himself known.

Number Eight formulated two thoughts in quick succession.

Well, it was bound to happen sooner or later.

It seems to me I fucked up good and proper.

Then, exhausted by the effort, he shut his eyes again. The coke surged. And at last he saw.

*Er uoterfront.*
The light of sundown was caressing Ostia so you felt like

licking it. And the silhouette of the monumental four-story casino overlooking the waves was reminiscent of that mountain in Brazil, what the fuck was it called? . . . Oh, yeah, *er Pandezzucchero*. Sugarloaf Mountain.

*Mamma mia*, look how beautiful, the casino.

And what a beautiful name they'd given it.

Armageddon.

Which means something like . . . oh, Apocalypse, that kind of thing. Cool, though. They'd even put in a ski slope, with artificial snow. And a chairlift that ran from the pine grove all the way to the top.

Number Eight was enjoying the view from the top. Piazza Gasparri and the waterfront promenade, all glass and cement. An elevated parking lot stretching out over the water that made you think you were in Dubai. And they say that without a few palm trees you don't live as well. Oh, sure.

*Er uoterfront.*

How wonderful.

Number Eight twisted around on the jumpseat on the chairlift and looked behind him. The Via Ostiense cut through the center of an expanse of cement that stretched as far as the eye could see back to Rome, illuminated by the lights of the shopping centers, by the building complexes, both working class and intensive and deluxe. Raphael Park, Michelangelo Park. Leonardo Park. Donatello Park. As if those parks represented the Teenage Mutant Ninja Turtles. And after all, goddammit, they could have come up with some names that were more modern for those anthills selling for six hundred fifty euros per square foot. I don't know, Off-Shore Park, just to fit in with the local establishment.

Uncle Nino was waiting for him when the chairlift reached the top, on an expanse of pink deep-pile wall-to-wall carpeting.

How elegant Uncle Nino was. All off-white, head to foot.

With a young girl squeezed into a red latex tube dress rubbing up against him.

"You see, Uncle, what your little Cesaretto has been up to?"

They hugged and then walked into a wooden chalet built on the casino roof, surrounded by fir trees and boulders from the Dolomites. It really did feel like being in the Alps.

From there, the view of the plain was magnificent.

Seven hundred million cubic feet of cement. A variant on the zoning plan, they'd called it. What kind of a variant were they talking about? This was a certainty. The New Ostia for a New World. Their world.

They didn't even know what to do with the money anymore, where to keep it, they'd hauled in so much. They'd taken in a ten-fold return on the investment. A couple of hundred million just for the Adamis. And he had bought a yacht like the one that Russian who owned Chelsea, Abramovich, sailed around in. With a helicopter on the deck. *Roma*, he'd christened his yacht. What was there to argue about? It was black, made of carbon fiber, and he kept it moored at the wharf in front of the casino. The kind of thing the Arabs could just drool over.

Saliva on his pillow woke up Number Eight, along with the noonday heat.

The bed was empty. His temples were pounding. His tongue was chained to the roof of his mouth.

He reached out and grabbed his cell phone and reread the text from Rocco Anacleti.

Who the fuck cares, the gypsy will just have to deal with it.

# X

Samurai was a man possessed by his rituals. Marco Malatesta had learned that quickly. Long before he ever put on a police uniform. The locations, the times, the manners of his presence in the city were punctuated by a sort of compulsively repetitive routine that was designed both to reassure and to strike fear. An obsession transformed into an instrument of his rule.

Whether in broad daylight or in the dark of the night: Samurai was there.

And he, Marco, intended to remind him that he was back.

For that matter, this was a propitious occasion. If it made any sense to start asking around a little bit on how Spadino had died, well, then, Samurai was the right place to start. And whether or not he had actually had anything to do with the pyre in Coccia di Morto was of minimal importance, right then and there.

Malatesta pulled up at the end of Corso di Francia on his Bonneville around noon. He prepared to wait a hundred yards or so from the last gas station before Via Flaminia. Though it was true the quarter had changed—between the Collina Fleming and the Milvian Bridge a mushroom patch of clubs and gourmet restaurants had sprung up that ought to have erased whatever soul those streets had ever possessed—it was every bit as true that that slice of the city with its "black" Fascist heart was and remained the property of Samurai.

"Once a day, he stops by there. The same gas station. The

one where we used to get gas for our mopeds when we were kids, before going to the soccer stadium. Someone even told me that he'd bought the place, along with half of Corso Francia," a friend from the old days had once confided to him. And Marco had no reason to doubt his word.

In spite of the distance, Malatesta recognized him immediately. The minute he got out of the Smart Car that he'd pulled over onto the concrete apron of the carwash. And he smiled when he saw a small crowd of smooth-cheeked young hoodlums move toward him with the muted respect due to a pack leader. Samurai hadn't changed. A few gray hairs. A tailor-made suit designed to make him look like the businessman that he wasn't. Otherwise, he was identical to the Samurai he still remembered from that night at Il Bagatto. Malatesta lit a Camel and walked over to the gas pumps. As he walked, he took rapid-fire photos with his iPhone: among Samurai's numerous obsessions, privacy and secrecy topped the list. The only photographs of him now in circulation dated back a quarter century. To have a few more recent ones of him could prove invaluable.

"*Buongiorno.*"

Even though he had come up behind him, the stentorian tone of voice in which Marco had formulated his greeting hardly seemed to surprise him. Samurai turned around slowly, without moving a single facial muscle, while with a broad sweeping gesture of his arm, he put a quick end to the burst of apprehension among the young men surrounding him.

Marco decided not to give him time. He'd learned, at his own expense, that you must never give Samurai that advantage. Never.

"Any chance we can talk in private, or do you still need an audience to perform in front of?"

Samurai put on a serpent's smile and dismissed his entourage.

"I remembered you as impetuous but well mannered. And, if I may say so, a few pounds lighter. But maybe time and your new profession have been poor teachers. Colonel, am I right?"

"Lieutenant Colonel. And after all, I've only ever had one poor teacher. Someone you know."

"Thanks for coming to see me, but the news of your return to Rome had already reached me. Welcome back. What pushes you to this part of the world, Marco? Nostalgia for the good old days, no doubt?"

"Pure curiosity."

"Aaah . . . "

"Marco Summa. Does that mean anything to you?"

"No. Should it?"

"Maybe you knew him as Spadino."

Samurai's smile blinked out in a sneer of disgust. It was a good way to conceal his chagrin and uneasiness. News travelled fast, in Rome. Rocco Anacleti had only just informed him of Spadino, and here you are, the Carabinieri, ladies and gentlemen. Nasty story. The flames could get out of hand.

"I'm sorry, but that name means nothing to me."

"Imagine that! You know, they found him dead in Coccia di Morto. Charred. All that was left were his teeth."

"My God, what a horrible thing. But I don't know anything about it. You're wasting your time, Colonel."

Marco bestowed a smile of commiseration upon him.

"You haven't changed. You're still the same piece of shit you always were. You're still pushing drugs, coke, smack, all that filth that churns up kids' brains. You've even brought crack to the city."

"You're barking up the wrong tree, Marco."

"Bullshit. Spadino was a pusher."

"That's not my problem." Samurai took a step forward and shook his head. "I don't know who your informants might be, Colonel. But you ought to try to get some better ones. Take a look in the corporate registry. You'll find my name, along with the names of all my companies. I'm a businessman, understand? A businessman. I have nothing to do with that other stuff now."

"Tell it to someone else. Maybe you can tell the four punks who wait for you every day in front of this gas station."

Samurai pointed his forefinger toward Malatesta's temple.

"You ought to do something about your temper, Marco. You've never been able to conceal it. At age twenty, that's understandable and forgivable, and I did forgive you. But by now I'd hoped to see you behaving in a more mature manner. And you know, when you lose your temper, your scar starts pulsating. It's a clear warning sign of your fragility. That's an advantage you can't afford to concede. To anyone."

It was predictable. Samurai fished freely in their shared abyss. But he'd miscounted his cards. Marco massaged his temples.

"I have some bad news for you, Samurai."

"What's that?"

"I'm fond of this scar, you know that?"

"Let me guess: the ladies find it exciting?"

"Women have nothing to do with it. The fact is that this scar reminds me of something I still need to take care of."

"Vendetta isn't always a noble sentiment."

"I'm not looking for vendetta, Samurai. That Nazi garbage has nothing to do with me now."

"Oh, nothing to do with me either, you should have realized that. I don't take revenge. I simply see the way things are and how they change and I recognize it. And if necessary, I do my bit to help them change. I control destiny, Marco. I don't live with rancor, because I make sure there's no cause for it. You know that. That's always been your problem, Marco. You want to change the world. But you can't change the world. You can only manage it."

Marco smiled.

"You know what, Samurai? You've become pathetic."

"Let's not exaggerate."

"When I was swallowing the bullshit that you tried to foist off on us at Il Bagatto, you had some appearance of humanity, or at least you tried to put one on. Now you're just an old serpent about to molt its last skin."

"You could also say that I was and I remain a generous man. After all, the fact that you're still alive is entirely due to me. I could have crushed you like a cockroach, but I chose not to. Never forget that."

"You were wrong not to settle that account, Samurai. Because I don't intend to be generous. I'm not repaying any favors. I owe you nothing."

Samurai sighed.

"I don't think we have anything left to say to each other. And I have a pretty full schedule today. So I'm afraid we're going to have to put an end to our enjoyable conversation right here and now. Even though I have to admit I'm sort of sorry. Because I imagine it's going to be our last."

"You imagine wrong. In case you haven't figured it out, this is just the beginning. But I feel sure you understand that, right? If I were you, I'd find out a little more about this Spadino. See you around, Samurai."

Marco turned on his heels and headed back to the Bonneville. Samurai's voice caught him like the lash of a whip.

"Forget about the motorcycle. You're too old for that now, Marco. And Rome is a dangerous city."

## XI

E ngineer Laurenti made his decision at the very instant that the director of the Cassa di Credito e Risparmio, Prati branch, Rome, on Piazza dei Quiriti, handed him the brochure of the financing company.

"Here you'll find the answer to your problems, Engineer."

He responded with a faint, false smile, and then underscored it with a firm, vigorous handshake.

Laurenti looked him squarely in the eye with a surge of disdain that the other man didn't even bother to perceive.

"All right," he said, getting to his feet, "it's all clear."

"You'll see, things will shape up," the other man encouraged him.

The engineer nodded, suffered through another handshake, and finally walked out into the open air.

His son Sebastiano was waiting for him, as rigid and tense as he'd left him, twenty minutes earlier.

"How did it go, Papa?"

"Fine, fine, son. It's all taken care of, it's all under control."

"Well then, Papa, maybe I'll go . . . "

That's only right, thought the engineer. He has his life. He's impatient to live it. I've been a lucky father. Sebastiano is a sensitive young man. He understands that something's not right and he insisted on accompanying me. Now that I've reassured him, he's in a hurry to be rid of me.

But then he couldn't make up his mind to let him go.

"You feel like getting some ice cream?" he suggested,

impulsively. "How long has it been since we got ice cream together, the two of us?"

Surprised, but also flattered, Sebastiano immediately said yes.

They turned off down Via Cola di Rienzo and took a table at Il Piccolo Diavolo. They ordered two large bowls of ice cream: fruit flavors for the son, creams, the richest, fattiest flavors possible, for the father.

The greedy delight with which Sebastiano plunged his spoon into the ball of strawberry ice cream brought a stab of sorrow to his heart. He thought it through again. He had palmed off a pious lie upon him. But wouldn't it actually have been more honest, fairer, to have told him the truth?

Then Sebastiano started telling him about the trip that he and Chicca had planned to Alaska.

"In Juneau, you catch a seaplane and you can ice skate on the glacier. If we're lucky, we'll see a polar bear hunting seals. And there's a chance to spend a night or two in a tent on small islands surrounded by icebergs. You sleep right there, you understand? And before you do, they make you sign a release, because there's no guarantee you'll survive it."

The engineer regretted having thought it through again. Let's just consider it like this, he said to himself, in a flash of the clear-minded vision that so many times before had come to his aid in the harsher moments of life: I'm giving him a few more moments of carefree existence. He'll remember it till the day he dies, and maybe he'll be grateful to me for it. The memory of these last instants together will stay with him in the dark hours that await him. Sebastiano: the pure one, the innocent one. I'm the one who made you like this, son. I taught you a love for adventure because it is only right that a man should always wish to go beyond his limits, forward, ever forward, where no man has ever ventured before. And I raised you in the cult of a respect for one's fellow man; I explained to you the ethics of hard work, which in the end rewards the just and punishes the undeserving; I spoke to you about the effort of making something, the only authentic metric of value for a life worth living.

They really did make a lovely picture, the two of them. They emanated a pleasing sense of strength and confidence. A father in jacket and tie, in spite of the heat, fifty years old but looking much younger, a tall, noble figure, and then the son, likewise tall, the slightly conceited demeanor of someone who has just emerged from adolescence, and deep in his gaze a gentle insecurity that time would take care of erasing soon enough.

You'll understand soon enough, son. And you'll curse my name. Because I've ruined your life.

After the gelato, they indulged in an espresso.

"Tell me something," the father suddenly said.

The son, with an instinctive gesture, looked at the old Donald Duck Swatch on his wrist, a wrist covered with the soft sparse goose down of youth. Of course, of course, he probably has an appointment with Chicca, with some friend or other, it's hot out, they're going to want to go to the beach, didn't he just get a fine A plus-plus in Mathematical Finance? Why should I inflict my presence on him any longer?"

"Okay, let's say goodbye here. I'm heading over to the metro. I have some business to take care of."

The engineer paid the check, quickly embraced his son, and strode off with a confident step for his last journey.

He hesitated in front of the civil courthouse on Viale Giulio Cesare, hemmed in by the usual crowd of lawyers and shady businessmen who were eagerly offering empty hope to a legion of bankrupts who'd been crushed by the recession. But there really was no hope.

He did everything properly, without haste. He went into the Lepanto metro station. He purchased a ticket at the automatic

vending machine. He took up his position on the platform facing the oncoming train.

He had no second thoughts.

He hadn't worked like a slave for thirty years, he hadn't
built a solid business structure out of thin air, he hadn't built
houses that were the setting for the charming cries of newborn
babies and the frantic moaning of young lovers, houses destined to stand for centuries, he hadn't done all this only to
wind up in the clutches of a gang of goddamned loan sharks.

If there was no more future for Luigi Laurenti, well then, to
hell with it all.

And forgive me, son, forgive me for having taught you a
vast array of nonsense. Perhaps you'll just hate me. He thought
back to the signatures that he'd asked his son to add when he
still believed he could get out of it.

A long blast of the horn and a buffeting gust of wind
announced the subway train's arrival.

Engineer Laurenti closed his eyes and with a courageous
leap, he left the platform.

But since, after all, fate doesn't give a damn about pride,
none of the numerous commuters riding the A Line of
Metroroma that day were able to enjoy the privilege of being
eyewitnesses to the self-sacrifice of a decent, respectable man.
A suicide without witnesses, without a farewell note, without
even a last text of explanation, is no suicide. At the very worst,
it can be written off as a "mishap," due in this case to an "accidental loss of consciousness or control." Or else, to use the
words of Don Filiberto, the elderly parish priest of the church
of the Redeemer, due to the omnipresent, unquestioned, and
unquestionable "will of God."

And Sebastiano, who instead knew, was forced to swallow—
in the coils of a disgust that was actually stronger than his grief
and sense of guilt—the grueling mantra of a post-mortem

eulogy from which the cursed word—suicide—had been rigorously banished.

A few rows further back, sitting among the incredulous friends of the victim and the families of the employees, who were anxiously worrying about the uncertainties the future held, was another one who knew. He was a young man Sebastiano's age, named Manfredi Scacchia, and he was the son of one of Rome's most celebrated loan sharks, that very same Scipione Scacchia who, along with his good buddies Dante Pietranera and Amedeo Cerruti, formed the trio of bastardly buzzards better known in the circuit as the Three Little Pigs.

"May he roast in hell, why wouldn't he have killed himself, the engineer. He had more debts than hairs on his head."

In response to old Scipione's comment, young Manfredi had retorted with a polite skepticism. He knew them well, the Laurentis, both father and son. He'd sat next to Sebastiano for the five interminable years of high school at the prestigious Convitto Nazionale. Now they were attending the same university, both in the department of economics, and they were both doing equally well. They were great friends. It had been none other than old man Scipione who had mapped out for his only son a future different from his own.

"You need to rise in society, boy, you follow me? You need to climb the ladder! So, don't behave like a dickhead, mix with these upright citizens and learn from them. We need to climb, got it? Climb."

Manfredi was a wise and obedient son. So he refused to believe his father's words. The engineer was a model businessman, a respectable person, one of the few still in circulation. So what the fuck are we talking about here?

"Listen, handsome, you study because you need to climb

the ladder, but on certain things, trust your papa. Listen, let me tell you something. Before he let that fucking train scatter him in all directions, the man went to beg a bank director, and a friend, for help. And this friend of his suggested he turn to . . . you want to guess?"

"To you?"

"That's right. You see, when you really try . . . The apple doesn't fall far from the tree, does it? And I'd already drawn up a debt reduction plan and everything. But that asshole, God rest his soul, let himself get carried away by his foolish pride. Well, amen."

Manfredi was working his way up the procession toward the ritual's critical moment; the handshake and embrace with the orphaned son. If his father was right, thought Manfredi, the son would suffer the consequences of the father's misgivings. And another step forward would be achieved.

When Sebastiano greeted him, with a heartfelt embrace, the loan shark's son whispered to him, along with a brotherly "you need to stay strong," another phrase, which the circumstances at hand deprived of its real meaning: "You can count on me."

The real meaning became clear to young Sebastiano a couple of weeks later when, in the lurid office that old Scipione stubbornly kept just a stone's throw from the old Monte di Pietà, the religious pawn shop that had been the center, for six hundred years, of the piazza of the loan sharks (*what can I tell you, son, I'm just sentimental like that*), the debt left unpaid by the late Engineer Laurenti was taken over by the Stella d'Oriente investment company. Sebastiano could have gotten away with just forfeiting his inheritance, if only his father had kept him out of it. But Sebastiano had signed, and now he could no longer get clear. He was therefore officially the owner of companies that had been boiled clean. He was personally responsible for the debts. And so it was that young

Sebastiano Laurenti, so recently a promising young talent of the Roman economy, became—thanks to another half-dozen signatures at the bottom of complex contracts—the personal slave of his fraternal friend Manfredi.

# XII

Ten o'clock. The time is now, thought Tito Maggio. This evening's guests were arriving.

On Via dei Banchi Nuovi, in the heart of the Baroque quarter of Rome, through the glass front door, the chef and proprietor of La Paranza, "the restaurant serving live seafood for those who want to feel fully alive," saw a metallic gray BMW 7 Series with flashing roof lights. The driver hurried around to open the rear door, holding out his arm to the prelate as he stepped out. Tall and elegant in his clerical attire, he was accompanied by a man who must have been around the same age. A little over sixty. His hair was fluffy and white, and he was wearing a three-piece summer Tasmanian wool suit, an immaculately white shirt with a high, stiff collar and a polka dot tie with a minuscule Vatican coat of arms.

Maggio executed one of his most energetic bows. He brought the prelate's highly perfumed hand, adorned with the episcopal ring, to his forehead. Then he extended his own hand toward the second guest, who clasped it in a flaccid, sweaty grip.

"Welcome to La Paranza."

"Thank you," the man replied. He then proceeded to introduce himself and then the prelate.

"I am Benedetto Umiltà, pleased to make your acquaintance. Allow me to introduce His Excellency Monsignor Mariano Tempesta."

Tito gestured for his two guests to follow him to the private dining room, which he indicated with a broad sweep of his arm, stepping to one side as did so. Tempesta and Umiltà were welcomed into a circular room with a wine cellar on the wall, illuminated by the gentle light of the table lamps and redolent with the scent of the fresh flowers that, every morning, Tito Maggio ordered in, in exchange for two pounds of marinated anchovies, from a conniving employee of the municipal cemetery division.

"Are we still waiting for him?"

"Why of course. Though, as you may already know, other friends are expected to be joining us."

"Certainly. No one's chasing us. The night is still young."

The prelate's contemptuous sneer filled him with terror. Tito retreated toward the kitchen, bitterly regretting that last wisecrack. What on earth made you think that you could crack funny with a priest? What if these people complained? Why had he thought it was a good idea to turn on the charm with that Vatican crow, oh what an asshole he really was!

Once he entered the kitchen, he unleashed tension and discontent on his employees.

"What the fuck! You really are a dickhead, aren't you! *Madonna mia*, Mustapha or whatever the fuck your name is, these little Toledo swords are supposed to be inserted in the prawns from the ass up, and not from the head down, do you understand that or not? If you do it that way you're going to ruin them, you stupid fuck. Do you know what the English phrase *finger food* means, goddamn you and your ancestors to hell? It means that if I charge fifty euros for a plate with a couple of raw prawns to eat with your hands, you shouldn't have to bring the customer a pair of gloves to keep from spraying themselves with the juice that drips out. I mean what the fuck! Come on, right?!"

Mustapha was a baby-faced Egyptian young man that Maggio

had tracked down in a pizzeria on Via Giolitti, behind the train station, I Due Briganti, where he had always worked as a dishwasher for ten Euros a day. He simply nodded his head without having the strength to say so much as yes. Mustapha pulled the two king prawns off the "Spanish" swords that Maggio bought, obviously counterfeit, in Gaeta from a guy that everyone knew as The Chinaman, and repeated the same operation from behind this time. His two comrades at the burners were silent. One of them was named Gianni, a guy with a long rap sheet, originally from Catanzaro, about fifty or so, with convictions for aggravated property crimes and attempted multiple homicide; Gianni had a pair of arms the size of planks with a shark tattooed on one and a killer whale on the other. The other kitchen worker was Hari, an Indian in his early thirties who detested seafood and whose true calling was selling DVDs of the greatest hits of Bollywood in a hole in the wall on Via Foscolo, at the corner of Piazza Vittorio.

Tito was just about to resume his tirade when Gianni pulled the cigar stub out of the corner of his mouth and brusquely informed him that the Three Little Pigs had arrived. Tito Maggio, sniffing and wiping his nose, left the kitchen.

Benedetto Umiltà delicately lifted a bottle of water and filled the bishop's glass.

"I'm so happy you can be with us this evening, Your Excellency."

"I believe it was important, no?"

"Fundamental, I'd say. But we are men troubled with our small, foolish worldly concerns. What is absolutely crucial for us, is hardly as compelling to pastors of souls like Your Excellency."

"Even pastors have their earthly needs and their reasons for impatience, my dear Benedetto, as you know full well."

Tempesta smiled, displaying a perfect set of teeth. And

Umiltà recognized that grin he knew well, a grimace halfway between a sneer and an obscenity. The first time it had assaulted him had been on the eve of the 2000 Jubilee. All of Christian Rome was opening itself to the brotherhood and the wallets of the world at large. Hundreds of thousands of pilgrims from the four corners of the world. A pact would have to be made with the city's pagan soul. Benedetto Umiltà was the right man for the job. He was operating at the highest level of public works.

He and Tempesta had understood each other immediately. Don Mariano had not yet been ordained a bishop, but he was already studying to be a cardinal. And in that year of grace, His Holiness the Pope had named him envoy aross the Tiber for the public works of the Jubilee. Umiltà had certainly known profiteers in and around the curia in his time, but what had struck him about Tempesta was that he had method. Method. He was weak in the flesh and in his appetites—and there was nothing new about that—but he experienced sin as a resource, an opportunity, not a shame. And he had understood him, in fact, in that same year of grace, at Porta Pia, in the offices of the Ministry of Public Works. They'd signed one of the protocols of an agreement that released the financing for the construction of the last section of the underpass of Porta Cavalleggeri. Tempesta, after laying down his Montblanc pen on the long table where the papers had been signed, had smiled that very same smile. Then, he'd placed that palm of his right hand on the back of Benedetto Umiltà's left hand.

"Rome, our Rome, once the cradle of a sublime beauty, will become even more beautiful."

"No doubt about it," Benedetto Umiltà had replied, practically lost in other thoughts, uncertain whether in that context he should already unfurl the title of "Excellency" that was generally expected to be in the offing for Tempesta.

The monsignor had tightened his grip and looked him right in the eye.

"But the one thing for which we should never stop thanking the Almighty," he'd added in a gentle whisper, "is the beauty of His incomparable works. First and foremost, the human body."

Benedetto Umiltà had blushed and then he'd returned the gaze.

At that very instant, they had told each other everything.

Benedetto had fled, appalled. He, who had always felt he was being stalked by sin as if by a relentless ghost, had been profoundly mortified and struggled mightily to break free. He stopped answering the monsignor's phone calls, stood him up, entrusting their appointments to colorless substitutes, he even considered requesting a transfer to some other office. One evening he'd found himself unexpectedly face to face with him, in the foyer of a concert hall where they had both just attended a recital of works by contemporary composers from Eastern Europe.

"Don't you think it's wonderful how our brothers from the East, even as they struggle under the heel of a pitiless dictatorship, still benefited from the power of such a courageous, radical spiritual elevation?"

Benedetto Umiltà had mumbled something, once again trying to make his escape.

The monsignor had put his hands together and shaken his head. And on his sharply honed face that smile had appeared, at once so gentle and so tremendous.

"You're ready, Benedetto. But you lack the courage to admit it. I have my car right outside."

And that had marked a liberation. A revelatory ray of sunshine which, from that day forward, would illuminated things with a different light. If Benedetto Umiltà now experienced desire as a gift, that was thanks to him, Mariano Tempesta.

Sure enough, the Jubilee and that meeting had projected him into a completely different dimension. Not only of the flesh. He had ventured into the Big Time. The contracts for the Jubilee had made him rich. And in the years that followed, his bank account with the IOR had swollen to eight figures. Between one ministry and another, he'd survived the various coalition governments, both left-wing and right, that had taken turns running the country with no more difficulty than it took to change his shirt in the morning. And for that matter, what the dickens, he was just a technician, after all. A civil servant. With the support, naturally, of Tempesta, who, as a bishop, had proven to be, if possible, even more ambitious in his appetites. In his new position, the monsignor oversaw and administered a considerable slice of the real estate holdings of the Holy See. Magnificent homes and apartments, in the heart of the historical center of Rome, rented out as residences or as sexual playgrounds to a plethora of political barons and boyars, managers, journalists, and mistresses of the world of political patronage, with Umiltà acting as both their guarantor and their blackmailer.

And now the game was rising to an even greater level.

Under the table, silently, his hand reached out for Tempesta's, which responded, promptly.

Tito Maggio shut behind him the sliding glass door that separated the aquarium of the open kitchen from the dining room. Smoothing it with both hands, he pressed the chef's toque down on his head, checking to make sure that his irremediably greasy hair hadn't already stained it. He checked the time—10:30 P.M.—and tried to suppress the shortness of breath that made his diaphragm pump like a bellows. It was a nervous tic, actually. He blamed it on the excess fat and the weight that he carried with him wherever he went, but it was just an indicator of the anxiety attacks that regularly swept over him. Samurai was a maniac when it came to punctuality. Being that late wasn't like him. He just hoped Samurai wasn't about to jilt him entirely. That was his night. The evening of Tito Maggio's resurrection.

The Three Little Pigs were sitting at the usual corner table. Not indoors—*'cause with this air conditioning you're going to give us all sciatica*—but in the garden rather, which the wood-lined, barrel-roofed dining room strung with fishing nets overlooked. Right under the lemon trellis, with its terracotta vases he hadn't finished paying for yet. Better that way: at least they were out of sight, where they wouldn't disgust the chic clientele.

The Three Little Pigs. His great misfortune. Dante, Amedeo, Scipione. Three cousins, people said, but who knew if it was true, after all. They'd fattened up when Dandi was ruling the roost at Campo de' Fiori and they'd grown up shining Secco's shoes. Taken together, they were two hundred years old. Old, ugly, nasty, immortal, like the loans they made out of their gold-buying operation on Piazza del Monte di Pietà and on Viale Trastevere. Shops that never close, where business is always good, like graveyards. Tito was in debt to them for five hundred thousand euros. Too many ill-considered expenses, too many crazy deals, too much cocaine. Five hundred large. With sixty percent annual interest. And even though he'd raised the prices on the menu like a hot-air balloon, he couldn't keep up with them. Also because he'd made up his mind to sacrifice all sorts of things, but not cocaine. Of course, he subsidized the white powder in part by peddling it, too—but not much, just twenty or thirty grams a month, strictly for his friends—and in part with the lavish arrangements of raw seafood that he delivered punctually, at noon every God-given day, including Sundays, to Villa Marianna, the state-subsidized clinic run by Professor Temistocle Malgradi, the Honorable's brother. In that clinic, Ciro Viglione, the king of Casapesenna, was under hospital arrest. He was healthy as a horse, Don Ciro, and Christ could he eat. But still, poor Tito, it wasn't enough. It was never enough. The deeper he slid into the shit, the more he snorted. And the more he snorted, the deeper in the shit he was submerged.

He'd even thought of going back to the porn industry, where in another life he'd been an actor much in demand. But now, the shape he was in, somewhere between Oliver Hardy and the fat musketeer, what was his name again . . . they wouldn't even have hired him for a costume drama! Anyway, the Three Little Pigs were regular guests at La Paranza. Lunch and dinner. Antipasto, pasta course, entrée, desert, espresso, and after-dinner drink. Once they had eaten their fill, they ordered a round of Avernas and summoned him to the table. They'd point him to a chair with them and pull out one of those graph-paper Pigna notebooks, greasy-paged and dogeared, full of numbers scrawled in that loopy handwriting that is typical of illiterates.

"Tito, don't think for a second we're trimming a penny. You're still going to have to pay us the five hundred thousand."

"Then what are we doing?"

"When a person eats well, he's not in so much of a hurry. And we're eating very nicely here, Tito. That's what we're doing. We're forgetting about our hurry."

He was stuffing them with food like three sausage skins, just so he could push the edge of the cliff a little further along. But, God be praised, all this was about to end.

As she came walking past, he grabbed Natasha, the Russian college student who made ends meet by turning tricks and whispered into her ear not to mention the special of the day to the Three Little Pigs. That special was meant for the rosy little mouths of those who were destined to yank him out of the frying pan. Just then, Amedeo spotted him and waved him commandingly over to their table. Tito sent Natasha on ahead, but was obliged to tag after her.

"*Buonasera*, Signori, have you decided?"

"Wow, look who's here, the Russian girl! Listen, honey, why don't you bring us some of that German wine, there. What the fuck do you call it? Ge . . . Ge . . . "

"Gewürztraminer."

"That's right. To eat, we'll take three hot appetizers . . . You know the ones, with the little pieces of toasted bread and octopus on top, right? The usual, are we clear? Then you can bring us three seafood carbonaras. And then . . . what do you have that's fresh?" mumbled Scipione, as if the whole thing cost him an intolerable effort.

"Everything we have is fresh."

"Oh, sure, of course it is. Yesterday I burped up swordfish until lunchtime. Let's do this. Bring us a turbot with potatoes."

"Baked?"

"How else? Boiled? Hey, do you even eat fish, or do you just write it down?"

They laughed with gusto at the wisecrack.

"Hey, hey, Tito! Tell the Russian girl not to be as stingy as she usually is. Bring us heaping portions, not those usual faggoty servings."

Nothing new under the sun. They always read from the same tired script, these filthy pigs, and every time it chapped Tito's ass. How it chapped his ass!

"Come on now, Tito, don't make that face! You know we love you like a brother!"

Amedeo got to his feet, wobbly on his short legs, and tried to come over and hug and kiss him. Tito took refuge in a half smile. He would gladly have kissed the Three Little Pigs, if they were laid out cold on a slab. Cold on a slab. Still, he thought, as he cast a gaze around the dining room, tonight it would be difficult to find any of those sitting at the tables who were actually paying for the meals they were enjoying. For the most part, they were freeloading just like the Three Pigs. There was that troglodyte Roberto Gerani, a former bricklayer who now demanded that he be addressed as Engineer Gerani, who had renovated the place for him. He was out a hundred thousand clams with Gerani, and he made sure to drop by and eat on the cuff regularly. There was that prosecuting magistrate who seemed to be bronzed all year round, and who never talked about anything but sailboats. Every time, he came in with a different piece of pussy. Then there was that nasty pig from the Passport Office, Dario Bernardi, with his little boyfriend from the Viminal, i.e., Ministry of the Interior, a couple of queens that you wouldn't believe. In a burst of desperation, Tito had even thought he might try throwing himself on their mercy. He'd tried it, too, one night a couple of weeks ago. But there had been no mistaking the upshot.

"Am I interrupting, sir? Might I break in for just a brief moment?" he had whispered, bowing low at an almost perpendicular angle to Bernardi's table.

"Why would you even ask, Tito? Tell me, after all you're the proprietor."

"Exactly, sir, that's precisely the problem."

"What problem?"

"The question of who is the proprietor."

"But it was just a manner of speech, you must have misunderstood."

"No, I mean to say . . . I have a bit of a problem with this restaurant. In the sense that I'm in the middle of a situation . . . "

"Tito, now I'm the one who has to interrupt you. Forgive me, eh, but I'm going to interrupt you, it is I who's doing the interrupting!"

The faggot's voice had gone into a shrill falsetto.

"Heaven forbid. I've made myself clear, haven't I?"

"Absolutely. Loud and clear, you've made yourself clear. But I have to tell you I have no influence over the health inspections."

What a piece of shit. Everyone in Rome was well aware— even the rocks and the trees seemed to know—that he was at the end of his rope with the shylocks. Health inspections, my ass. Maggio dropped the subject then and there. He'd backed away from the table with another bow, asking the two faggots if they'd care for a second round of oysters. And when they'd nodded, he'd stuck his head into the open kitchen and whispered to Mustapha to offload that shipment of mollusks that smelled so foul they'd had to park them out in the alley.

But it had to come to an end. It was coming to an end.

Out of the corner of his eye he saw that the front door was swinging open, and he abandoned the Three Little Pigs then and there and hastened to welcome the new arrivals.

Not two minutes later he was breaking into the silent intimacy of the private dining room, generously pushing a majestic wheeled ice bucket in which stood proudly planted the first bottle of Dom Ruinart Blanc de Blancs Millesime Brut Champagne. He'd personally arrange for the reinforcements, when the time was right. Only the best, for his guests, the best and with the finest presentation.

"Here are the other friends you were waiting for. Be my guests, gentlemen, come right ahead."

They were two gentlemen in their early sixties, well, if quite predictably, dressed, stuffed into dark suits and announced by a whiff of cologne and aftershave. Benedetto Umiltà leapt to his feet as if his chair was springloaded.

"Your Excellency, may I introduce you to Ciro Viglione and Rocco Perri?"

Tempesta, smiling, decided there was no need to get to his feet, and with a gentle movement of his hand he allowed the two men to pay proper homage to his ring. Umiltà went on with the boilerplate courtesies.

"These are the businessmen I was mentioning to you, Your Excellency. The South that is determined to survive. Dottor Perri is Calabrian, from Cirò Marina. Dottor Viglione is Campanian, from Casapesenna."

The bishop nodded, allowing Umiltà to continue, while Viglione and Perri took their seats at the large round table, rummaging in the bread basket as they did.

"I can assure you, Your Excellency, that Dottor Perri is a visionary. Everything he touches turns to gold. Because he can see gold where it seems that nothing is glittering. And thanks to this particular talent he is one of the best funded entrepreneurs in Rome. Oh lord, the last thing I'd want to do is count the cash in someone else's pockets, but if an honest businessman doesn't begrudge me the speculation, I'd say that nine hundred million can't be far off the mark. Am I right?"

Chewing an olive oil-drenched chunk of bread, Perri nodded and dispensed a few pearls of wisdom.

"My grandfather taught me that you need money to make money. So there's no such thing as too much money, isn't that right, Your Excellency?"

"The works of man are works of God. And after all, what is money if not a work of man?" Tempesta said wittily.

Viglione expressed his support of the observation by raising his champagne flute.

"You were lucky to have such a wise grandfather, Rocco. I owe everything to the Jesuit fathers of Caserta. They showed me the way."

"And what a way it was," twittered Benedetto Umiltà. "Just think, Your Excellency, this gentleman's family built Latina. And *this* gentleman brought us the tunnel of Porta Cavalleggeri, the Holy Bypass. You do remember, don't you, our very first meeting?"

"How could I ever forget?" Tempesta replied with a smile.

Viglione drained the champagne from his flute, savoring his evening out of the rooms and hallways of the Villa Marianna, where he had been under hospital arrest for more than a year now, but where his business affairs had never once stopped prospering. He left the clinic and returned as he pleased. He knew people, Viglione did. And after taking one look at the monsignor, he knew he was in good hands. The man asked no questions, and that was a necessary prerequisite. In fact, it was the first rule of business. Never ask *dove maronna aggio truvate i suorde*—where the money came from. He had a mountain of cash, as much as and more than Perri, who himself hardly knew what to do with the money he made from cocaine, slot machines, online gambling platforms, restaurants, and clubs. But Viglione also knew that he'd continue pulling in mountains of cash if Samurai wasn't just talking bullshit. Every euro he pulled in with the coke wound up in his construction sites. Between the fifteen-story tall mushroom-shaped restaurant Il Fungo at EUR and Caserta, not a brick, a bulldozer, or a cement mixer moved without his say-so. And now, if they brought the benediction of God Almighty into the picture, then fucking hell was all he could say.

"Why, what important people, isn't this all too much for us?"

The voice of Counselor Davide Parisi made the guests all turn to look at the door to the private dining room. He had arrived with Michele Lo Surdo, an accountant who was Parisi's partner. They were both about forty-five years old. And they were both marionettes dancing to Samurai's strings. Samurai had first met them when they were just kids in a chapter headquarters of the FUAN, the youth organization of the extreme right. They were both dressed in cushy pinstriped Cenci suits. Lo Surdo was a shrewd and reckless accountant.

He was little more than a straw man at the center of a network of offshore companies that he started up, shut down, and moved around like tanks in a game of Risk. He controlled a couple of paper mills that he used for Samurai, of course, but also for the large clientele of tax evaders who were constantly around, and who needed false invoices like they needed the air that they breathed. He lived in a villa in Grottaferrata, had an obsession with escorts, and was basically Parisi's natural appendage.

Lo Surdo was well acquainted with Parisi's extraordinary professional mediocrity. Born into the profession. And what a profession, seeing that his father had become famous defending Dandi. "Davide Parisi? The criminal lawyer who doesn't know what the penal code even is and who studied courtroom maneuvers in the Monte Mario tribune at the Stadio Olimpico," as Lo Surdo often liked to say to him, in open mockery. But still he admired Parisi's absolute ruthlessness and recklessness, knowing that even he couldn't come close; and to a certain extent he admired his sheer guts as well. Parisi was a no-talent slob, but he would stop at nothing. And that's why Samurai protected him and was going to introduce him to the client of his life. Rocco Anacleti.

They were all there in part on account of that gypsy. And the people sitting at that table, starting with Viglione and Perri, meant that the thing really was about to happen.

Parisi made a rapid circuit around the table, shaking hands with all the other guests, until he finally came to a halt looking down at Tempesta with a broad smile.

"I told the colleague who represents that mutual friend of ours at the Roman Rota that we have an understanding concerning that problem: we're going to proceed with the annulment for failure to consummate," Parisi said to the bishop.

"I'm glad you did, Counselor. Just think, I'd been informed

they intended to proceed with a suit for *impotentia coeundi*. But how could they think such a thing, I explained to your colleague. That lovely boy there. Come, come."

Lo Surdo took a seat next to Benedetto Umiltà.

"Please don't forget, Dottore, to come by my office sometime this week, so we can settle the matter involving Cyprus. That way we can move forward with that block of transactions concerning the IOR. You know, we can't hold that issue in abeyance indefinitely."

Umiltà nodded and checked his watch. Eleven o'clock. Samurai was running late. Tito Maggio was on a low boil.

"We'll wait for him to get started, naturally," he repeated to the assembled crowd for what might have been the tenth time, with his usual anxious urgency. And when he received a chorus of confirmation, he decided to show off his skills.

"A lobster tartare, while you're waiting? Otherwise, perhaps a nice platter for the table with a salad of razor clams, marinated scampi, an octopus compote, king prawns Toledo style, grouper sushi . . . "

"Do you have oysters?" asked the bishop.

"I didn't dare to include them in the list, it struck me as obvious. I normally bring oysters along with the bread and the water. I have my own way of doing them."

"Which is how?" the bishop's salivary glands had flooded his mouth.

"We serve them with Beluga caviar and a rockfish tisane."

Perri raised the forefinger of his right hand.

"That wonderful illegally caught fish from the last time, what was that?"

"We have it again tonight. The carpaccio of porgy from the protected marine reserve of Ponza."

"That one!" confirmed the Calabrian with a wink.

Benedetto Umiltà, beaming, mimed an applause by softly putting his hands together.

Maggio hastily stuck his head into the open kitchen and handed the order to the three men working the burners.

"Mustapha, just try and fuck up this order and I'll serve you sliced tomorrow at lunch."

But why was Samurai running so very late? Tito Maggio felt a shiver of terror. Could he have dumped him too, just like all the others? Was he going to have to resign himself to living out his days as the Three Little Pigs' personal slave?

Samurai was displaying his customary icy, phlegmatic demeanor, but in fact he was seething with rage. The clock in the Mela Stregata on Corso Vittorio Emanuele II read close to eleven o'clock. Rocco Anacleti was running more than an hour late. Years back, he'd set fire to that place, when the left-wing activists used to go there for their aperitifs. What a waste of effort. He shot a glance at Cellini's angel, at the center of the bridge that led to Castel Sant'Angelo. He liked Cellini. He felt a little like him. Part bandit and part artist.

He shoved across the counter the cup of green tea he had ordered to kill time.

"I asked for a cup of tea, not a vegetable infusion. And I'd asked to have it served lukewarm."

The young man behind the bar withdrew the cup with a shiver. He'd never seen such ferociously expressionless eyes as the ones on that customer dressed in black from head to foot. Even though what finally broke those interminable seconds of silence was the arrival of the person whom the customer seemed to have been waiting for all this time.

"Ciao, Samurai."

"Punctuality tells you all you need to know about a man."

Rocco Anacleti shook his head with a grimace. Samurai grabbed him by the arm and they walked out into the street together, turning toward Via dei Banchi Nuovi.

"You're right. You're completely right. My fault."

"They've been waiting for us at La Paranza for the past hour. And I didn't ask to meet with you ahead of time."

"I'll say it again, forgive me. But I'm out of my mind. Out. Of. My. Mind. You know what I'm talking about?"

"What's the problem?"

"Spadino."

"Dead men are never a problem."

"Dead men aren't. Killers can be."

"Do you know who killed him?"

"Number Eight. And I wanted to warn you that that piece of shit from Ostia is now a dead man walking. I'm going to have him butchered, as the Madonna is my witness."

"How can you be so sure that it was him?"

"I wouldn't be telling you what I'm telling you now."

"You know, right, how much I detest errors?"

"I'm not wrong on this."

"That's not enough."

"It is for me."

"It's not up to you. It's my decision."

"Spadino was my man."

"That's of no consequence. Unless you're willing to tell me why Number Eight is supposed to have killed him."

"I don't know why. And I don't care, either."

"You ought to, though. You're just an asshole in a rage. Who maybe doesn't deserve to have a seat at the table that's waiting for us."

"Business is one thing, Samurai. Our street business is completely different. That's mine and I'll take care of it."

"I thought you were starting to look like an actual boss. But in spite of your age, you're still just a thug. You know who Number Eight is, right? You know how much weight Ostia swings in what we need to do, right? No, I don't think you do know, Rocco. If we want to bring this deal to a happy end, we need peace, not war. We've already heard from the Carabinieri.

Are we really going to flush it all away when we're this close to the finish line?"

"Revenge is sacred to me, Samurai."

"There will be plenty of time for that too."

Anacleti clenched his fists and took a deep breath. Samurai's expression turned grim.

"Don't give me your scary faces, Rocco. And don't make me have to tell you a second time. In fact, let me give you one more piece of advice. Avoid putting on your scary face with the poor old Iranians you order beaten within an inch of their lives."

"What the fuck are you talking about now?"

"Pay that old man. Immediately."

"Who told you about it?"

"And who told you about Number Eight?"

Anacleti dropped his head. By now they could see the entrance of La Paranza.

"All right, Samurai."

"All right means you do what I tell you. That you forget about Number Eight and you pay the old man. Is that clear?"

"All right," Rocco conceded.

That was a promise tossed into the wind, obviously. Like all promises that any Roma chief makes to a *gage*, a non-gypsy. Yes, certainly, he was talking to the great Samurai. But Samurai himself was just a gage. And, most important of all, Samurai thought like a gage. Vendetta isn't the sort of thing you can give up so easily. Vendetta is a chieftain's blood, his heart. That means, Samurai, that you're just going to have to resign yourself.

At the front door of La Paranza, Tito Maggio welcomed Samurai with a hug from which the other man recoiled in disgust.

"You stink. And I haven't had dinner yet."

"Forgive me. But you know, I'm so happy to see you. And after all, this magnificent evening out . . . "

"I've already told you, you just make sure you satisfy the demanding palate of the bishop and his faggoty little boyfriend. Do that and I'll take care of your problems. There's no need for you to wrap your arms around me and smear your smell of sauce on my clothes."

Preceded by Anacleti, Samurai entered the private dining room, interrupting the antipastos. For the first time, the bishop got to his feet. Samurai gripped both his forearms and looked into his eyes.

"Your Excellency, you are our shepherd and this is your family. With your blessing and your involvement, ours will be acts of pure goodness."

"I am here to listen," the bishop nodded.

Samurai gestured to all the others to continue eating. Everyone except Losurdo and Parisi.

"Pull out the plans, the sketches, the estimates, and the documents with the proposed variants on the zoning plan. And explain to His Excellency and Dottor Umiltà just what we're thinking about when we say social housing and Waterfront."

# XIII

He'd given them explicit instructions, their boss had. A job done right. Two, three, four . . . In other words, pop as many caps as it would take. No fuckups. No shooting their mouths off. Silent as clams. With everyone. And leave not a trace. The gat had to be clean, and the "horse" to ride into the pasture would need to be clean too.

Naturally, Paja didn't have the slightest idea of why the Anacletis had decided to rub out Number Eight. Did Spadino have something to do with it? Maybe. But wasn't there a pact of some kind with the people from Ostia?

Who knew.

You know what, though? Who cares, he'd said to himself. And not merely because it was out of the question to argue or ask questions when the order came down from Rocco. But because, as his grandfather used to say, thinking just makes you anxious. To say nothing of the fact that, sometimes, the work could be fun. Like this time. Why not. Number Eight had been overdoing it for some time now. A buffoon who was always fucking other people in the ass. Like his uncle who was locked up, just for starters. But also Denis, his good buddy. Lord knows, another two-bit lunatic. But there was no comparison. Denis was a real man, with a pair of balls. And a pair of balls isn't something you can buy at the supermarket.

He had it in for Number Eight himself. Old disagreements about girls. At a certain point, Number Eight had got it into his head that he had some kind of special right to screw them before anyone else. Even if they were his friends' girlfriends. Even if his friends really cared about them. That's how things had gone with a girl that Paja was crazy about. Vanessa. Number Eight had laid his foul paws on her, and when Paja had objected, Number Eight had just laughed in his face.

"What are you talking about, Paja, when you say we aren't supposed to lay hands on our friends' women? When have we ever been friends?!"

Right. Exactly. He'd arranged for the gat. A Slavic-made Luger 9 x 21 mm., just brought in from Bar, the open port of Macedonia. The guy who had procured it for him, an ex-con who lived in Mungivacca, on the far side of the Romanina district, had left it for him in a hut behind the Ikea. Because it wasn't a good idea for them to "lay eyes on each other." As for the motorbike, Fieno had borrowed it from a young doctor over in Quadraro, one of those guys who was so precise and courteous it made you want to vomit. Coked out of his skull. If he'd ever guessed what the black-and-yellow BMW 1200 GS Adventure he was so proud of was going to be used for . . . but then again, when the nostril is running dry, you always think of your old friend Fieno, don't you?

Then it's time to pay your debts, Doc.

You couldn't even breathe on Piazza Lorenzo Gasparri. It was one of those nights without a breath of air. The sea smelled like an open sewer, and it lay motionless. Not even the junkies in Largo delle Sirene, the drug-dealing piazza they controlled, had bothered to show up. Crushing a mosquito on his purple-and-yellow Los Angeles Lakers jersey—*go fuck yourself, you look like a bumblebee*—Number Eight thought back to how poisonous it could be. He was sitting with his ankle on his knee on the trunk of an Alfa Romeo Mito parked a hundred yards or so from the Caffè Italia. And he continued massaging his right ankle, swollen like an old man's—*don't tell that I'm already starting to get varicose veins, what the fuck.*

That evening he'd told Moira—the tattooed bartender who'd been around, a little past her sell-by date—that she could close up early. In that heat, not even the slot machine junkies had shown up. He thought the chance to quit early would make her happy, but instead the change of program seemed to throw her off. It was only when she'd pulled down the bar's security shutter, revealing the garter belt under her red skirt that was squeezing her big ass tight, that he'd understood. And in fact a 220-pound Romanian in his early fifties had come over and given her a kisss on the cheek. Just take a look at our poor Moira. Since the days when Uncle Nino used to take her for a ride, she'd slid down the slope to these horny Slavs without a penny to their name.

On the bypass, Fieno hit 100 mph almost without noticing it and, decelerating with a brusque downshift as they came up on the off-ramp for Via Cristoforo Colombo toward Ostia, he lifted the visor of his helmet to speak to Paja, folded over on himself in his denim jacket, inside which he was holding the Luger.

"Sure enough, these fucking Germans are just phenomenal. Hey, Paja, have you heard what this boxer engine sounds like? Forget about Japanese bikes. Japanese bikes can kiss my ass. This thing, you open her up and she takes off."

"Sure, okay. But wait until you go in for your registration renewal, then you'll laugh."

"Why, do you renew your registration?"

"No."

"So?"

"It's just something I said. To say it."

"There's times I don't understand you, Paja."

"What's there to understand."

"Don't get mad, eh. But sometime you really strike me as an asshole."

Through the jacket, Paja let him feel the Luger, pushing it up against Fieno's back. Almost at the center of the Dainese logo that covered it.

"You see you got pissed off right away?"

"Fieno, I just don't have any imagination. Try to understand."

"What did I even say. I'm just joking around. What, are you on edge?"

"I'm looking to get done with this job we have to do."

"Hey, Paja, if it was your first time, I'd understand. But we've been in the middle of these tarantellas for a lifetime now."

"What do you think I'm talking about, Fieno? For me, beating someone up is like making a bowl of pasta all'amatriciana. I was nineteen years old when I whacked my first man. Just think. But if you're going to make a pasta all'amatriciana, you have to make it right: makes sense, right?"

"Now you're making me hungry. What if we stopped for a panino or something? You work better on a full stomach. There's a nice kebab place at the first turnoff for Casalpalocco."

"What is there?"

"A kebab stand."

"Oh just go fuck yourself. Open her up, get going. Otherwise we won't get there in time."

Number Eight was talking on his cell phone. He was politely explaining to the manager of a club who was two months late with his "enrollment fee" that spending the rest of what life was left to him in a wheelchair wasn't a particularly bright prospect, so he should pay, and waste no time doing so. As he was speaking these words, the motorcycle carrying Paja and Fieno rumbled slowly down the Lungomare Duca degli Abruzzi, Ostia's waterfront road. Fieno downshifted to first gear, keeping a steady speed of 20 mph, with his left hand gripping the clutch handle. Paja lifted the visor of his helmet to get a unobstructed view. The coast was clear. He noticed the security blinds of the Caffè Italia were down.

"Just take a look at that. Why is the place shut? And where the hell's that asshole?"

The imprecation caught in his throat. A sudden surge of adrenaline reached his brain at the sight of the guy in the yellow tank top sitting on the hood of an Alfa.

"Here you are, handsome. Here you are now. Now you're done running the show."

With his left hand, Paja gave Fieno a light tap on the ribs, who slowed down even more. Thirty yards. Twenty. Now Paja could make him out clearly, Number Eight. He'd just tucked his cell phone into his pocket. Paja clinched the grip of the Luger, pulled it out of his jacket, extended his right arm. He fired the first shot when the BMW was right in front of the target. The bullet blew the Alfa Romeo's rear window to smithereens.

Number Eight threw himself to one side, falling onto the asphalt between the Alfa and a Volvo parked next to it. He started crawling on all fours while Paja's semiautomatic continued vomiting fire. He could no longer tell how many shots had been fired. Lying prone as he was, he was only aware of a stabbing pain to his eardrum and a shower of broken glass bouncing off the backs of his hands as he tried to cover his head. He didn't even hear the shout that preceded by a fraction of a second the roaring acceleration in first gear as the motorcycle took off.

"Go! Go!"

But his eyes. His eyes were still good.

He slowly got to his feet, staring at the tail of the motorcycle as it veered to the left, heading down toward the water. He impressed on his retina the image of the passenger riding pillion. The piece of shit who had just shot at him.

A long blond ponytail hung out of the helmet. And he knew that ponytail well.

They remained silent until they reached Axa. There Fieno slowed down and raised the front of his full-face helmet.

"That guy's not getting up again, is he, Paja?"

"I don't think so."

"You don't think so?"

Paja said nothing.

Something told him that the driveby had gone wrong. But he lacked the courage to admit it.

Marco and Alba arrived half an hour later. The territorial police and the white-jumpsuited officers from RIS were already onsite. Two sleepy-eyed local crime-beat reporters were jotting notes. The assistant district attorney on duty, bored out of his skull, was chainsmoking.

The cast of the scene of the crime, arrayed in their full glory, in other words.

Well, maybe full isn't the word. The victim was missing. The blood. The witnesses. And the audience.

"Someone shot someone else but didn't get them," the lieutenant who commanded the Ostia Carabinieri barracks confided disconsolately, "and that's all we know. Otherwise, a total fog. We recovered eight cartridges, but there might be more. No one saw a thing, no one wants to say a word."

"It's nighttime," Alba commented, stifling a yawn.

The lieutenant shot her an ironic glance.

"It's Ostia," he replied, pointing around at the shuttered windows, the deserted streets.

"True," Marco confirmed, "it seems there aren't a lot of rubberneckers around here."

The lieutenant smiled. His name was Nicola Gaudino, he came from Naples and there was no mistaking how he yearned to get back to the shadow of Mt. Vesuvius. The geography of the Camorra clans, complicated though it might be, seemed much more reasonable than the rigorous omertà of Ostia.

Between one bureaucratic requirement and the next, day had dawned. The assistant district attorney went back to Rome. RIS broke camp. The first early morning wayfarers poked their heads out, shot a vaguely curious glance at the police barriers and the vehicles bearing unmistakable marks of gunshots, and then continued on their way.

Sisto was just opening. An old waiter recognized Gaudino and offered to make everyone a nice piping hot black coffee.

They sat down at a small café table still damp with the cool night dew. The lieutenant spoke to the waiter.

"Did you hear anything last night, Giova'?"

The waiter spread his arms wide, in a gesture of resignation.

"I see all the usual faces at the tables, Lieutenant. And maybe I might even hear what they're saying. But I mind my own business. Certain names are best left unsaid."

"But why?" Alba butted in.

"Eh, my dear Signora," the waiter sighed, "you all come out here, you take a look around, you might even do a little something. But then you leave, and I have to go on living here. So, certain names are best left unsaid."

"The Sale clan. An old criminal aristocracy, if aristocracy is the right word. And the Adamis," the lieutenant went on wearily, "the real boss is the uncle, Nino, but he's in prison. He's left all family business in the hands of his youngest nephew Cesare, who goes by the name Number Eight on account of the fact that his head is bald as a billiard ball. He runs a club, the Off-Shore, with a few other nutjobs just like him. We suspect he does a little of everything. Drugs, construction, even some arson of the beach establishments that won't fall into line."

"Murders?" Marco put in.

Gaudino grimaced in bafflement.

"They rubbed out two old and powerful bosses a couple of years ago. Cases that were never solved, of course. But for some reason, I think that with those two killings the Adamis and the Sales made a clean sweep and became the bosses of the place. To find proof of it, though, you'd have to be a shrub in the shadow of the Hanging Tree."

"The Hanging Tree?" asked Alba curiously.

Marco heaved a sigh. Ah, the historical memory.

"It's the heart of the pine grove of Castel Fusano. There's a bench. In the old days, the gang members used to go there."

Gaudino broke in.

"Yes, but nowadays it's for a different reason. They go there because there's no cell phone reception. And anyway, that Cesare is capable of anything. In any case, the people aren't going to talk."

"Oh, but it's not like we're in Scampia here, for the love of Christ!" Alba snapped. "We're practically in Rome. Not twelve miles from the Colosseum."

"Captain, I'm sorry to have to tell you this," Gaudino interrupted her, "but the truth is that here it's the bad guys who take care of the have-nots. They give jobs and a scrap of hope to those who have neither. Here, if someone steals your moped, you don't go to the Carabinieri, where we sit behind locked doors, safe and warm. You go around the corner, to Piazza Gasparri. And the thing is that when they go to the bad guys on the piazza, the bad guys get their moped back for them, while all we do is take their complaint. After all, what's a criminal complaint? Words on a piece of paper. Around here, the ones they love are the bad guys, Captain."

"That's the same story they always used to tell in Corleone," Marco cut him off brusquely. "But then at a certain point that came to an end." Speaking to Gaudino, he ordered him to organize, and immediately, a roundup. "Yank them out of bed. The Adamis, the Sales, their hired hitters, their young thugs, their small-time dealers, their wives, their sisters. All of them. Take twenty men, no, take thirty. If you need men, I'll send some over. Load them into paddy wagons and haul them in to the barracks, to give them a bracing new view of things. Serious interrogation sessions and search their homes with a fine-tooth comb. Let's give them the idea that we're breathing down their necks."

Gaudino, who would gladly have given him a bearhug, limited himself to snapping to attention.

Marco thought it over for a minute, then added his final instructions.

"And I want you to ask everyone, and I mean everyone, about Samurai. Act vague, as if you didn't really care about it, just a routine investigation."

Both the lieutenant and Alba stared at him in bafflement. Marco realized, to his horror, that that name, Samurai, meant nothing to them.

The problem with those kids was their youth. The lack of historical memory, to be exact. They lived in the present. It was up to him to bring them up to speed with past events.

With a sigh, he started telling them the whole story.

# XIV

In the basement premises of the Carabinieri station on Viale Marco Fulvio Nobiliore, in the heart of Cinecittà, a short, powerful, hairy man sat on an unsightly, off-kilter chair, in the interview room. Facing him stood a tall young woman, a full five foot ten, with chestnut hair and jutting cheekbones. A red satin top revealed a generous 38 cup, while a skimpy green skirt sheathed long legs that were perfectly waxed. And while her attire unmistakably declared her profession, you had to look much closer to see that she wasn't really a woman at all. Her official name, in fact, was Jesus Fernandes da Silva Pereira. She—or he—was born in Recife, in the poorest part of greater Brazil, but now her professional name was Lorena. After traveling around most of Europe as a working girl, fate had brought her to the boulevards of Eastern Rome. She'd been working in the area for no more than a couple of weeks when the Carabinieri had stopped her in a routine check. As for the fireplug of a man sitting across for her, he was Carabinieri Marshal Carmine Terenzi. Since Lorena was new to the quarter, Terenzi, conscientious commander of the territorial police that he was, had taken it upon himself to explain to her the rules of the game.

"Do you work at home or out on the street?"

"For now on the street, Senhor. For a home, I need more money, maybe some other day."

"How much did you make last night?"

"Not much. There is recession. It's so hot out."

"How much, I said."

"Hundred."

"You want me to believe you?"

"I swear it on my mother's head, I only made hundred!"

"Give me your purse."

Lorena clutched a sparkly dingus to her bosom, a handbag she'd probably bought for five euros at the street market on Via Sannio, and grimaced in consternation.

"Why you so mean to me? I can make you so happy . . . "

"Give me that fucking purse!"

"Hundred fifty, Senhor. I swear on my sister. I made only hundred fifty."

Terenzi got to his feet, with a vague smile on the round moon face dotted with patches of stubble left over from a half-hearted shave, and without a word, grabbed Lorena's genitals and started to squeeze.

"Ouch! You're hurting me!"

"And that's nothing, my girl. Come on, the purse."

Prophylactics, lipstick, a vibrator, and, there it was, three hundred euros. The marshal shook his head, in a display of chagrin.

"What a sly little person you are, eh?"

"Excuse me, Senhor," Lorena whimpered, "I never tell any more lies."

"All right, I want to believe you because you seem like a likable girl, Lorena . . . but this money's confiscated."

"What am I supposed to do, I have to pay my debts! How can I do that?"

"Then get busy, you have all the goods you need, sweetheart."

The marshal pocketed the roll of banknotes, then gestured for Lorena to sit down. The tranny obeyed.

"Well, now that we know each other, let me explain how it works. As long as you're out on the street, you take a block and make it yours . . . do you understand me when I talk to you?"

"What is 'block?'"

"You have a point there, I ought to make things simpler. You choose a section of the street and you don't move from there. You work, you pick up your customers, you do your business, and no one will come and bust your chops. Clear?"

"Clear."

"Fine. And everything you earn, half goes to me."

"Half, Senhor?"

"Yes, I know, you have a point, I'm being generous, but what can I tell you, I'm just in a good mood today. Don't overdo it with the gratitude, eh?"

"*Grazie*, Senhor."

"What are you doing, getting smart?"

"I? No, never in life, no, no."

"All right. For the payment, here's how we do: I'll come by, or one of my men will, every Tuesday. No, Tuesday's no good, that's when the Moldavan girls are at the gas station . . . Let's say Thursday, all right?"

"All right. Can I go now?"

Terenzi unzipped his pants and walked over to Lorena.

"What, in such a hurry? Now that we've become friends, let's have some fun."

Just as things were at their nicest—no doubt about it, trannies have an extra gear or something, the marshal was thinking to himself between one moan and the next, it's no surprise they've chased the regular whores off the street, it almost seems like the trannies actually enjoy it, they're not like those fucking refrigerators from Eastern Europe—right when things were at their best, someone knocked on the door.

"Marshal?"

The guard. Brandolin. An asshole from Friuli, a new recruit.

An idiot like all Friulians. Oh, he'd fix him good, later. Two weeks cleaning toilets, at the very least.

Lorena stiffened, and loosened her grip.

"Keep going, who the fuck told you to stop? Yes? What is it? I told you I didn't want to be disturbed!"

"Marshal, you'd better come immediately."

In the tone of his underling, Terenzi perceived the nuance of urgency that heralds an impending pain in the ass. It would be an error to underestimate it. After all, it hadn't been long now since they'd entrusted him with that "reputationally challenged" Carabinieri station, and business was gong splendidly.

He put a hand on Lorena's head, heaved a sigh of resignation, and got himself together.

"We'll finish up with you later."


He went to open the door. He found himself face to face with young Brandolin's beet-red face, as well as a guy with longish hair who looked like a bona fide son of a bitch, and a stunning blonde who was worth ten Lorenas. Two well-heeled citizens. Probably someone had burgled their apartment and they were here to file a complaint. Their appearance had intimidated Brandolin, who felt shy about collecting their testimony all on his own.

Terenzi put on his finest military demeanor and addressed the unfortunate guard in a peremptory tone of voice.

"Brandolin, I've told you a hundred times that civilians aren't permitted in this wing of the station."

And that was when something astounding happened. The guy who looked like a bona fide son of a bitch stopped Brandolin with a decisive glance just as the young officer was about to offer an excuse, took a step forward, came to a halt in front of Terenzi and, eyeing him arrogantly, with a gaze between the amused and the defiant, asked a question.

"Why, Marshal? Is there something you don't want people to see in there?"

This was simply out of this world! Who the hell did this little asshole think he was?"

Terenzi saw red.

"How dare you? I'm the commander of this station! Brandolin, the IDs of these two individuals."

With a slow and studied gesture, the two civilians handed the marshal their badges. Terenzi turned pale. And snapped to attention. Lieutenant Colonel Marco Malatesta, Captain Alba Bruni. Fuck, from the ROS.

"At your orders, Colonel, sir! At your orders, Captain, ma'am!"

Brandolin, in an effort to stifle his laughter, let out a sound that was somewhere between a gasp and a sob.

Lorena chose that exact instant to materialize on the threshold of the interview room. She let her long forefinger with its enameled fingernail slide along Terenzi's forearm and, in the most nonchalant voice imaginable, said: "Well then, Senhor, I'll be going."

Marco stared at Terenzi.

The marshal cleared his throat.

"A . . . normal territorial roundup, Colonel, sir."

"Well, Marshal, is there any reason to detain this lady any further?"

"Go ahead, go," Terenzi muttered, on the verge of hysteria.

Lorena cleared out, swinging her hips.

"Territorial roundup," Marco observed sarcastically, once they were alone in the Carabinieri station commandant's office.

"He was screwing her," Alba pointed out.

"My compliments on your finesse."

"Ah, the air smells of shit in this place."

"I can't say you're wrong."

Terenzi reappeared. He was carrying four file folders with yellow covers. Now the marshal was all smiles and bows. He was acting the jovial host. As he was gathering the documents they had asked for, he had taken a few minutes to get in touch with a colleague from the old school, someone who knew the ins and outs of the entire command chain.

This had been their exchange: "Malatesta? You're in deep shit, Carmine. That guy is a tremendous pain in the ass."

"But I have no beef with him, and vice versa."

"Just as well. But watch your step. I've heard that he's half crazy."

"And he had to come pick on me of all people?"

"Be careful. He's one of Thierry de Roche's men."

"Well, that's great news!"

The colonel hefted the file folders.

"Is this everything?"

Terenzi shrugged his shoulders.

"I thought I'd made myself clear, when I asked you for everything you had on Spadino and all the other subjects with ties to him."

"Well, this is it, Colonel! There's nothing else, in the whole barracks."

Marco and Alba split up the files and started studying them. There were three files—he had been brought in for questioning once and arrested twice. But they already knew that from the computer records. The police reports were much more interesting. On two occasions, Spadino was in the company of a pair of individuals whose identities were included in the report, right down to their noms de guerre: Zuppa, Dario, AKA Paja, and Scavi, Luca, AKA Fieno. No doubt about it, the Roman underworld remains true to form, eh! From another report, Paja and Fieno appeared to have been detained along with a certain Max. His moniker: Nicce. Pronounced like the philosopher. So who is this supposed to be? The intellectual of the group?

"Spadino . . . Paja and Fieno . . . Nicce . . . what do we know about these people, Marshal?"

"Well, what you see written there . . . "

This time it was Alba's turn to address him.

"Excuse me, Marshal, but you attended the police academy, didn't you?"

"Of course I did, Captain!"

"And during the courses you took didn't they teach you that the most important things aren't what's written in the report? Come on, don't waste our time: what do we know about these people?"

Terenzi, still obsequious, tried to minimize.

"But, no disrespect intended, I would rather call them stray dogs. Two bit thugs . . . small fry . . . that's right, small fry . . . "

Terenzi was sweating. Marco felt himself fill up with the exhaustion of the night spent chasing ghosts in Ostia. He didn't like Terenzi. And nothing was adding up.

"Now listen to me, and listen carefully, Terenzi. You say: small fry. Let's say you're right. All the same, put together lots and lots of small fry and you have a sizable catch, a major haul. A full school of fish. And every self-respecting school of fish has a pilot fish. The one who sets the course and assigns the tasks. Now, let me ask you this: who is the pilot fish right now in Cinecittà?"

Jesus Christ, Colonel, what do you have, a crystal ball? The sweat by now was designing alarming dark rings under the armpit of Terenzi's shirt. Oh, sure, the name, you can find it for yourself, this fucking name, I have no interest in winding up eaten by dogs, personally speaking!

"Colonel, sir, on my honor. This is a quiet beat. The last murder around here was a year ago, and it was about some guy's wife cheating on him. There's no protection racket because, with the downturn, everyone knows, the fishing isn't good, if you know what I mean. Sure, the occasional street fight among third-world immigrants, but nothing much. You know, they're always the ones who cause the trouble, the *zammammeri*. Ah, and then, if I'm going to say it all, there's also the occasional *zecca*, goddamned ticks, grubby lefties, roaming around, they congregate at an occupied movie house, the Arcobaleno. They say that these are theater people, but to me, they're just *zecche*, plain and simple. In any case, I've got a couple of infiltrators, the situation is under control. Trust me, Colonel, sir: *zecche* and *zammammeri*, they're always the ones who cause trouble, but otherwise . . . "

Marco Malatesta didn't move a muscle.

"On my honor . . . ouch!"

*Zecche* and *zammammeri*. The same language used by Spartaco Liberati. The same culture. The same fear. The Carabinieri Corps was preparing to celebrate its two hundredth anniversary. And it still couldn't rid itself of miserable wretches like Terenzi.

And the problem is that many, far too many, continued thinking the way that the various Terenzis did.

*Zecche* and *zammammeri*. And all the rest was just fine, Madame Countess. Maybe they might have a more sophisticated way of conveying it to you, but that was the culture.

A putrid, tenacious culture, hard to kill off. Marco knew it all too well. Because for far too many years, it had been his culture too.

And at times, Marco had had to call on all the resources of his personal belief system to keep from succumbing. Because there was another thought that was bothering him. That the miserable wretches might actually be the majority, while he, and a very few others, were just hopelessly outnumbered, a tiny minority. The clean face that they liked to show off at official ceremonies but that they ostracized and shoved aside when the going got tough and real interests were at stake.

But he couldn't let himself give in to pessimism. Pessimism

is just a byway to death. Marco was increasingly convinced that he had his finger on the wound. A purulent wound that was infecting Rome. It was from here, from this outpost commanded by an officer straight out of an operetta, certainly unfaithful, probably corrupt, it was from here that they would have to set out to put a halt to the contagion. That is, unless it was already too late.

He jumped to his feet.

"All right, Marshal. Alba, get the files. We'll hold on to them for further examination. Is there anything we need to sign?"

"Of course not, Colonel, sir!"

"Good. Keep your eyes open, Marshal, it's important."

"At your orders, Colonel, sir!"

Terenzi escorted the officers to the exit, all the while offering a profusion of smiles and prostrations. He stood there for a moment to contemplate the lady captain's imperially fine ass—*I'd give odds of ten to one that the colonel is screwing her, then they come out here to preach moralistic sermons, these assholes*—then he went back into his office, turned the air conditioner up to full, and from his extension made a call to Rocco Anacleti's private cell phone: a Swiss SIM card registered to a nonexistent shopping center.

"The ROS are getting upset about this thing with Spadino," he began, without any preamble.

"I don't want any pains in the ass, Tere'."

"Which is why I'm here."

"Good boy. And make sure you behave the way you're supposed to."

"That's why I called you. To tell you to be on the lookout."

"Did you mention any names?"

"What do you take me for?"

"For what you are: a piece of horseshit crushed underfoot by the master's boot," he replied, in Romansh.

"But if you talk in Gypsyish, I can't understand you, Rocco."

"I said: for the monthly payment, let's take care of it tomorrow, okay?"

"That's fine."

At that exact instant, Marco and Alba, in a little bar just five hundred yards from the Carabinieri station, were sitting in front of cups of steaming hot coffee and promoting, in the field, the young Giordano Brandolin from Tolmezzo to the rank of "special agent."

His first duty: to surveil Terenzi, observe, report everything, even the most seemingly insignificant detail.

Brandolin had just left the bar when Lieutenant Gaudino phoned. The roundup in Ostia had turned out to be a very good idea. The clever bastards had obviously gotten rid of all compromising material, aside from two grams of cannabis destined to be filed away under "personal use." And that, in and of itself, was suspicious: as if they were expecting a raid, from one moment to the next. Which means that not only did they know about the ambush, as was predictable, but they'd certainly been involved.

"And what do they say about Samurai?"

"Nothing. Lips sealed, awkward expressions, the occasional faint smile."

But that wasn't the news.

"Cesare Adami, Number Eight, him and none other, the boss. He looks like he's lived through a tsunami."

"Where is he now?"

"Here with me."

"We're on our way."

Alba stifled a yawn, ran her hands through her hair, and followed him.

The bandits were going back to their bad old ways, Marco

mused when he found himself face to face with Cesare Adami, AKA Number Eight. Ugly, dirty, and nasty. An anthropological profile, you might have said. The thing they needed to do was restore the old boundaries, he decided, draw them in a sharp, clear manner, and make them impregnable once again. There's us and there's them, so we have to know, listen, and see. And act, above all, we have to act.

Nonetheless, while Number Eight swore up and down that he knew nothing about ambushes and shootouts, and that the marks he had on his face and arms were nothing more than the result "of a lively night with my girlfriend, Morgana is her name, give her a call and she'll confirm," he found himself evoking the mocking, and in its manner stern, image of Samurai. Could it be that any link existed between the chilly boss and this brute? It was possible. In his day, Samurai had preached a holy alliance between the aristocracy and the horde. Could he have succeeded in putting that theory into practice? In that case, who was Number Eight, actually? The small-time boss he claimed to be, or yet another marionette dancing to Samurai's strings? Or somewhere in the middle, between the two? Or had Samurai really left the scene, as he claimed? In that case, was it the new recruits that Marco ought to be concentrating on?

Us and them. Us and them. How much of this filth is a result of our weakness? From our desire to be like the ones we say we're trying to combat but whom we actually admire? And what is it about them that we admire? Their freedom? Their ruthlessness? The shitty lives they lead? There was a dynamic that he knew all too well. After all, until he made up his mind to get out, that had been his own story.

He realized that Alba and Gaudino were both staring at him, waiting for him to make a decision. Number Eight, too, was scrutinizing him, and behind his mask of obtusity, Marco was able to decipher without difficulty the features of a lucid, animalistic ferocity. Suddenly, the truth became clear to him.

Number Eight had killed Spadino. Or, in any case, that was what the people who tried to rub him out believe. Spadino was one of the Anacletis' men. Ostia attacks Cinecittà, and Cinecittà hits back: the war has begun. A Mafia gang war. Because you had to call things by their name.

"You may go, Signor Adami."

With Alba and Gaudino's help, Marco drew up a preliminary report in which he laid out the conflict now brewing, prophesying more violence and more deaths unless decisive action was taken. To ward off the worst, he was requesting wiretaps, tails, stakeouts, men, listening devices, and resources. Overwhelmed by his lack of sleep, he personally deposited the report with the secretariat of Dottor Manlio Setola, the prosecuting magistrate who supervised investigations into organized crime.

The answer reached him the next day, in the afternoon.

Nothing. The prosecuting magistrate wasn't inclined to authorize a thing on the basis of what he described as an investigative hunch without any solid supporting evidence.

"Idiot!" he snarled, while talking with Alba. "This isn't some cop's intuition. These are facts! I can't wait to see what he says when they bring in the next dead body, this Dottor Setola!"

On one point, however, you had to admit that the magistrate was right.

Wars usually break out for some substantial reason.

And so far, Marco had failed to identify that substantial reason.

## XV

B randolin phoned Malatesta.

"At your orders, Colonel, sir!"

"Brandolin, you're the only one I know who can convey the idea that a word is in capital letters over the phone."

"Pardon me, what did you say, Colonel, sir?"

"Nothing, never mind. Let's skip the formalities. Any news?"

"The marsh . . . I mean, *he* has organized a public safety operation for nine o'clock this evening."

"Is there a demonstration planned?"

Brandolin lowered his voice.

"Not exactly a demonstration, Colonel, sir. It's actually more of a meet-up. You know when they spread word on the web and then they all make an appointment?"

"I live in the present day, my dear boy."

"I apologize, Colonel, sir!"

"Don't worry, I apologize to you. And just what is this meet-up about?"

"I don't know, Colonel, sir. He just said that we had to maintain public order."

"But that's normally a job for the State Police."

"Colonel, sir, I don't know what to say. The command came down ten minutes ago."

Things were starting to look interesting.

"Well, you go, and tell me everything you see."

"I can't go, sir."

"What do you mean, 'I can't go?' This is an order, Brandolin!"

The voice came over the line, broken, as if the other man were about to burst into tears.

"Sir, with my utmost respect. I'm on guard duty all day long."

"Well, get someone to replace you."

"The marsh . . . The duty is for the rest of the week. It's a punishment. For . . . what happened the other day."

Marco felt a surge of fondness for that young man, as if he were a big brother. He had to take it easy, with Brandolin. In any case, he could force him to obey. His superior rank afforded him that option. But why expose him to further retribution from Terenzi? Better keep him covered as well as he could. Terenzi was a genuine bastard. If he so much as suspected that the young man was spying on him, he'd make his life a living hell.

"I'm very sorry, sir, but I really don't know how I can get out of it."

"You're doing fine, Brandolin. Keep your eyes open like you're doing. Where is this meet-up?"

"At the Arcobaleno, the occupied movie house."

"I'll go."

"Colonel . . . "

"Tell me, son."

"I think that he's looking for an excuse to . . . to do something."

There were a fair number of young people standing in front of the Arcobaleno. They were milling around in the little plaza outside the front doors, all of them rigorously equipped with regulation solo cups of beer. Clouds of smoke from hand-rolled cigarettes wafted over the knots of young people who emitted, from time to time, bursts of laughter. There were also a few mothers with toddlers in tow, and there was a small group of middle-aged gentlemen with bright faces and curious expressions: neighborhood faces, who had happened to turn up—who knows how—in that little mob scene that was just waiting for the signal to start the meet-up.

And there were twenty-four men in full riot gear, with helmets and shields.

Terenzi's boys.

But what was the point?

In the afternoon, Marco Malatesta had made a few phone calls. The movie house had been a squat for more than a year, ever since the old owner had shut the place down and word went around that it might be converted into a bingo hall. The occupation had been spontaneous, not managed by any group, large or small, at least none that had been clearly identified. There had never been incidents nor had there been reports of any "sensitive" activities. The occupying activists did theater for kids, organized petitions for public water and against nuclear power, staged book presentations, willingly made the stage available to bands and theater troupes, and held courses in popular music. Actors and playwrights who were generically "politically engaged" had passed through there. From a contact of his at the police court he had learned that no forcible evictions had even been ordered.

So Terenzi was playing dirty.

If, as the good officer Brandolin had theorized, he was looking for a clash, then only afterward, once matters were settled, would he inform whomever it might concern. Maybe after cracking a few skulls, he'd write on the report: "intervened to disperse a seditious assembly . . . " And in any case, Terenzi had taken great care to avoid all personal exposure. He'd sent his men, the worm.

Whatever the case, it was a provocation.

He wondered whether he ought to intervene.

But, for the moment, it was better just to observe.

The situation, all things considered, seemed pretty manageable. The young people were quite calm, they merely shot the cops ironic glances and innocuous mockery. If worst came to worst, Marco could always pull out his badge. He waded into the small crowd and made his way to the entrance. A poster, actually a broad, handwritten sheet of paper, set forth the evening's menu:

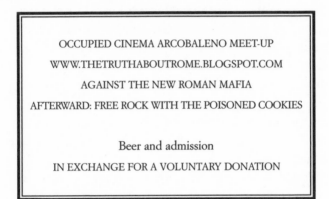

OCCUPIED CINEMA ARCOBALENO MEET-UP

WWW.THETRUTHABOUTROME.BLOGSPOT.COM

AGAINST THE NEW ROMAN MAFIA

AFTERWARD: FREE ROCK WITH THE POISONED COOKIES

Beer and admission

IN EXCHANGE FOR A VOLUNTARY DONATION

Marco couldn't repress a smile, a blend of exasperation and tenderness. The truth about Rome. There was an Eldorado he'd stopped trying to track down for some time now. The truth ... if he'd ever had a blog, he would have called it "TwoOrThreeThingsForABetterLifeInRome." A small thing, admittedly, but perhaps a more reasonable one. And among these two or three things, no doubt, would be to wipe out those Mafioso bastards. Apparently, the same objective as the organizers of the meet-up. Anyway, this certainly looked like it might be interesting.

He went in. The lobby was like that of any ordinary movie house, and it too was jam-packed with young people. On the walls were posters for movies old and new, *Once Upon a Time in America*, *The Cayman*, *The Lady from Shanghai*; there was also a large mural, a cartoon of three of the Beagle Boys, only with the faces of famous political leaders.

From both the left and the right, just to keep from being unfair to anyone.

In front of the auditorium, which was closed off by a red curtain, there was a young woman guarding two glass vitrines half filled with change and small bills.

"Ciao. Are you new? You can donate whatever you like."

Marco rummaged through his pockets, pulled out a twenty euro note, and dropped it into the glass vitrine. The girl seemed uneasy.

"I can give you change for that, if you want."

"I'll just have a beer in there, okay?"

She smiled and waved him in.

The Arcobaleno must have been a parish cinema once. You could tell from the wooden seats, from the small rectangular screen mounted on a stage along which were lined up three microphones connected to a central amplifier. And from a shrine to St. Rocco that no one had dared remove from the wall that housed it.

Nearly all the seats were full. A rough guess, Marco thought, was about a hundred people. If you counted the people waiting outside, maybe twice that.

Terenzi was out of his mind. How did he think he was going to manage an operation in that setting? Was he looking for a massacre?

Marco stayed at the far end of the auditorium, close to the exit. Ready to take action.

A young man with a ponytail walked out on stage and took possession of the microphone. His voice was battling against the piercing whistle of the amplifier. A rasta began making desultory attempts to fiddle with the cables.

"Hi everyone. I'm Dario, from the Rebel Dragons. I'll just

ask for a few more minutes of your patience, Alice Savelli is on her way. In the meantime, if you want to tell the people outside to come on in, we'll be starting in no more than five minutes."

Dario from the Rebel Dragons stepped down off the stage. Soon all the seats were occupied. More people kept coming in. The young people laughed, they exchanged greeting from one end of the auditorium to the other, they drank and, respectful of the prohibition, they didn't smoke. Marco perceived an unusual, positive energy. They seemed combative, but the violence in the air that he remembered from his own younger days was absent. They wanted to change the world. But how? All that energy, all that hunger for change, all that—why not, revolutionary—anxiety, where was it headed? He had opted for the uniform, which was his way of feeling he was at war. But those young people? What did they really have in mind? Just peace, love, and music?

He felt someone brush against him. His eyes focused on a seedy looking young man with a scraggly beard.

"Colonel," he whispered, softly.

Marco recognized him, in spite of the disguise. Ferrero. He'd been a student of his, a few years ago. A kid from Turin with a lot of energy and ambition. The infiltrator Terenzi had mentioned.

"What's going on, Ferrero?"

"We're about to go in, Colonel."

"Come with me."

Marco grabbed him by the arm and dragged him out into the street. Terenzi's boys had lowered the visors on their helmets and were massaging their thighs with their nightsticks.

"Would you care to explain, please?"

"Marshal Terenzi's orders."

"The reason?"

Ferrero seemed uneasy.

"Well, actually, he . . . "

"Come on, let's hear it, son."

"He told us to find something."

"Ah! He told you to find something. And what, exactly? Weapons? Drugs? Subversive propaganda?"

"Anything, sir."

"Let me understand this, Ferrero. You're a regular here, so you might know where to find it, this something."

Ferrero dropped his eyes. Marco felt a frigid rage surge within him.

"Where did you put the shit, Ferrero?"

"Colonel, it was an order."

"Now, I'm going to give you an order. No, make that two. First: send those dickheads immediately back to barracks. And then come back here."

He waited for the platoon to withdraw in an orderly fashion, then he went back in, followed by a contrite Ferrero. The stage was still empty. The buzz of the crowd was scarcely drowned out by the notes of a blues song that the loudspeakers were broadcasting. No one paid them any mind. Ferrero led them to a little room to the left of the stage. On a rough wooden table, two girls were making sandwiches and the desultory rasta was rolling himself a joint. Ferrero exchanged a vague wave of greeting with the girls and then headed over to the icebox, opened it, and pulled out a little black backpack.

"Thanks for holding onto it for me," he joked.

He was not given so much as a glance or a reply.

They went back out into the main auditorium. Marco grabbed the little backpack.

"What did you put in this?"

"Nothing, really, Colonel. A couple of Molotovs."

"This bag weighs too much for a couple of Molotovs, son."

"A . . . a little shit."

"What kind of shit?"

"I don't know. A white bag. Half a kilo, I think."
"Go on, get out of here!"

At last the buzz died down and silence fell.

Two women were walking into the auditorium. One was a petite brunette with curly hair, a grim, angular face and determined, intelligent eyes, perhaps under thirty; the other was taller, younger, with long raven hair, a perfect oval face, as proud as an eastern goddess.

They were taking turns pushing a wheelchair. Crumpled in it was an old man. His face was puffy and his hands were bandaged. From what you could tell from his features, there was a clear resemblance with the young woman. Her father, Marco said to himself. They're foreigners, he decided.

All three of them climbed up onto the stage. The petite brunette took the microphone and started talking. She had a nice voice. Warm, courteous, intelligent.

"For those of you who don't know me: I'm Alice Savelli, you can find me on my blog, "thetruthaboutrome." I want to tell you a story that affects us all. You see this man beside me in his wheelchair? His name is Abbas Murad. Thirty years ago he fled Iran. He was given political asylum because he was being persecuted by the regime of the ayatollahs. He came to this land, driven by desperation, with his wife and a toolkit containing the instruments of his trade. His only wealth. Abbas is a wood carver. An artist. The heir to a tradition a thousand years old. And today Abbas is an Italian citizen. So is his daughter Farideh, who brought him here today. It would have been right for Abbas to tell us his story in person. Unfortunately, as you can see, that's something he can't do. And do you know why not? Because first someone shattered his hands, so that he can no longer work, that's right—those artist's hands. Then that same someone broke his jaw. To keep him quiet. But what can Abbas have done to deserve all this?"

Alice handed the microphone over to the younger women with black hair. Absolute silence reigned in the auditorium.

Farideh grabbed the microphone and introduced herself. Her hands were shaking.

"I . . ."

"You can do it, Farideh."

"I can't. You go ahead, I'm begging you!"

Now the audience was captivated.

Alice took back the microphone.

She told the story. The work Abbas did. How Abbas asked to be paid. The arrogant contempt of the customer.

She named names.

"The Anacleti family. Silvio Anacleti. Emanuele Anacleti. Antonio Anacleti. Rocco Anacleti. You know them, don't you? Don't pretend otherwise, ladies and gentlemen. All of you know them, we know them. They call themselves gypsies, but they dishonor their ancient and noble people . . ."

The auditorium exploded in indignation. A guy raised his hand and asked to speak. He said he was a journalist. He mentioned a blog no one had ever heard of. Alice invited him to speak. The journalist cleared his throat. Did Alice have proof of such a serious statement? No, but she knew. Even if that *I know* that Pasolini had pioneered had by now become a tiresome refrain. Did she authorize journalists to report those names? Certainly. But she knew they would never dare. Did she realize she was exposing herself to the risk of lawsuits? A lawsuit would be manna from heaven! At least that way there would be a trial.

"Because we've reported to Marshal Carmine Terenzi of the Cinecittà Carabinieri station what happened. And nothing has come of it. No one came to interview Abbas. No one contacted him at all. No one!"

Now it was all clear. Marco went outside to smoke a cigarette. His heart was churning. Alice Savelli had guts, heart, and courage. And now he felt a little less alone.

He finished his cigarette in peace, then he called Brandolin and ordered him to look for Abbas's complaint.

He already knew the answer, but still he had to try.

A taxi equipped to carry the handicapped picked up Farideh and her father, and vanished into the muggy night.

Max pulled his orange-and-black KTM into traffic and followed the taxi. Since he'd first seen her, that night at her father's workshop, he'd been unable to get Farideh out of his head. No one noticed him. Not even Marco. Alice appeared at the entrance to the movie house. With her was the Rebel Dragon and a couple of other kids. They were engaged in an animated discussion. Marco went over and introduced himself.

"A Lieutenant Colonel from the Carabinieri!" she said ironically. "What's going on, did you decide to wait for the meeting to end before summoning me to appear at the barracks? Am I under arrest?"

"I wanted to show you this," said Marco, and emptied the backpack.

The young people turned pale.

"What's this supposed to mean?" the Rebel Dragon cried indignantly. "We had nothing to do with that!"

"Of course not. You had nothing to do with it," Marco said brusquely, "it was our doing. Or certain among us. I sincerely apologize."

They looked at him as if he were crazy.

Marco held out his business card to Alice.

"I need to meet with Abbas."

He grabbed the backpack and walked away, without waiting for a reply.

# XVI

The vans arrived at the Anagnina station around ten. Every Monday morning. They unloaded Ukrainian, Moldavan, and Romanian woman. Some of them were scheduled to wash the asses of elderly dying women, while others were already working as whores. All of them, without exception, had only one thought in their heads: make money, make lots of money, and make that money as quickly as possible.

For the young man who was watching the scene with a look of disgust on his face as he sucked on a licorice root and leaned on his armor-plated BMW X6 SUV, money was also the most important thing. His name was Shalva Israelachvili, he was thirty years old, and he came from Georgia. Stalin's Georgia, just to make that clear. A compatriot who might have had his shortcomings, but if nothing else had known how to keep the Russians in line.

He was a Jew, and he'd become a Nazi. Because he believed in law and order, and that's how he saw himself: as a man of law and order. Women adored him. They said he was gorgeous. They lined up to jump into his bed. And in fact, with his long black hair, his fair skin, his oriental cheekbones, his deep dark eyes, a compact but not massive physique, and the innate elegance of someone accustomed to being around people, he was reminiscent of the early Sean Connery. But he was much, much more, Shalva was.

He was a boss.

At the age of fourteen, encouraged by Bekha, his beloved older brother, he had told the rabbis to go to hell along with all their paranoia and he'd gone back to his homeland, finally liberated from the longtime oppressor. For that matter, wasn't Georgia the most beautiful place on earth? Back home the story was told of how, when God was busy distributing lands to the humans He had just created, the Georgians were having one of their lavish and proverbial banquets. And so it was that the Georgians showed up too late and God, sorry but also a little ticked off, explained that there were simply no more lands to be given. At that point the Georgians said: yes, Holy Father, we are late, that is true, but it was because we were drinking to Your health. And so God, touched, assigned them the land that he had been keeping for Himself.

Georgia, my homeland!

Thanks to Bekha, the Vory v Zakone, the powerful Mafia of Thieves had welcomed him with open arms. He had grown up in his big brother's shadow, and when he left this world for good, *Sieg Heil* to his blessed soul, he had inherited all his contacts.

Officially a lumber importer, Shalva was the organization's representative in Italy. His Italian was perfect, only faintly inflected by the vague suspicion of an accent. He feared no rivals in the transportation business. His trucks came and went incessantly along the routes of the Balkans, transporting human flesh, arms, drugs, and everything that served to make the harsh existence of human beings a little less miserable.

Instead of fighting them and persecuting them, the government ought to bow down to people like him. They should put up monuments. It was people like Shalva who made the lives of so many good people actually worth living.

Once the aspiring whores and housekeepers had cleared out, a fat, sweaty guy broke away from the crowd of van drivers. He went over to Shalva and asked him, deferentially, if he had a light. His name was Stanila, he was Romanian, and he had been working with the Georgians for years. They spoke Italian. It was supposed to seem like a typical conversation between two strangers.

"The white Audi," said Shalva, flicking his lighter into flame, "across the way, three hundred yards, under that billboard."

"There's a new guy," Stanila whispered.

"Who vouched for him?"

"One of your men, Thaka."

"So what's the problem?"

"I don't know. I don't like him. He's too nervous."

"That happens on the first trip."

"If you say so . . . "

"You're not convinced, eh?"

"No. But you're the boss."

There was no doubt about that, and it was wise of Stanila to keep it in mind at all times. In any case, the Romanian was an experienced transporter. His sixth sense was something to be relied on. So was his sense of fear. Stanila knew that there was much to be gained from staying on the right side of things. He knew that in business trust is everything. He knew that if anything went sideways, they might all be suspected of betrayal.

And he knew that no mercy would be shown to traitors.

"All right. Tell him not to come."

"What about the package?"

"Tell him to take it back to whoever gave it to him. Is that clear?"

"It will be done."

"Now get going."

Stanila went back to the others. Shalva saw him in conversation with a tall skinny guy. The tall guy clearly launched into an objection of some kind. Stanila told him to go to hell. They guy shrugged in resignation and started off toward his van. The other drivers headed off, acting nonchalant, toward the white Audi where Thaka was waiting for them.

Shalva pulled out his iPhone with the Georgian SIM card, opened Viber, the Israeli app that couldn't be hacked, and called Samurai.

"Shalva, brother!"

"I need to talk to you."

"I'll be with you at noon."

Then he got in his SUV and took off, without laying down too much rubber.

Thaka was too far away to be able to judge his reactions. He wondered if he'd been right to trust Stanila's hunch. Maybe the Romanian was wrong, and there was an explanation for it all.

Still, it really was remarkable that the very same day he brought Thaka, one of the last arrivals, to do deliveries for the very first time, a new face should happen to have popped up. And the person who had vouched for him, it just so happened, was none other than Thaka. Two new developments taken together constituted an oddity. And Shalva wouldn't have gotten where he was now if he hadn't learned to be wary of oddities.

For that matter, the system that he had developed had been running smoothly for two years now. An eternity. Maybe the time had come to develop something else. Here's how it worked: Shalva had shut down one of his shipping companies. The delivery vans had all been sold at auction. All aboveboard. Except that they'd arranged to give preference, among the bidders, to those who were married and had children. The new van owners were approached with a clear and simple proposal: they could do whatever they pleased with the vehicle, provided that with each trip a "little package" was delivered to Shalva, or delivered at any rate to a trusted person indicated by him. Payment for each delivery: five hundred euros.

Shalva liked to boast that he was a generous employer. Everyone accepted, except for one arrogant young man who had put an end to talks by spitting in Shalva's emissary's face.

The next night, two men had broken into his house and raped his wife.

Was it clear, now, why Shalva didn't want bachelors without personal ties in his organization?

The young man had filed a complaint with the police.

That same evening someone had broken his arm.

The young man had withdrawn the complaint.

There had been no further problems.

Each package contained one or two kilos of refined cocaine. When he was in Rome, Shalva personally supervised the deliveries, but no one could ever testify that they had seen him handle the shit. The material aspects were taken care of by the young men who, from time to time, backed him up. They were the ones who took delivery of the packages and forwarded them. Shalva's percentage, after transporation costs and Samurai's share, was thirty percent. An arrangement that was not spectacularly profitable, but still reasonably advantageous, and above all, safe and secure.

At least, it had been until that morning.

While he was turning into Via Cassia, he wondered once again whether he was becoming paranoid.

And he concluded, well, if I'm wrong, I'll be out a couple of kilos of shit. And what does that really matter?

Samurai pulled into Trevignano at noon on the dot. Punctual to the second, and dressed in black, as always.

The two men embraced on the Georgian-style patio of the villa Shalva had had built on Lake Bracciano.

Every time he set foot there, Samurai was forcibly reminded of the unlikely origin of that piece of Olde England transplanted into the countryside north of Rome. It had been

Shalva himself who told him about the misunderstanding the architect, a well-dressed little dandy in a bowtie, had stumbled into.

"It's because when I said 'Georgian style,' he thought I meant like the English! So I threw him down the stairs."

"Maybe you could have gone over and taken a look at the job while it was under construction."

"What do you think, I have time for that? I trusted that piece of shit."

"That piece of shit did more than just build a house for you, Shalva. He did you a big favor."

"But he got everything wrong."

"And it's a good thing. As a result, instead of having a Moorish dacha with trivial marblework, you now have the residence of a true gentleman."

"You think?"

"Trust me."

Shalva was one of the very few people to whom Samurai allowed physical contact. He'd watched that boy grow up, and he knew that he could trust him. He knew how devoted Shalva was to him. Twenty years ago, Samurai had saved the eldest son, Bekha's life. In spite of the fact that he put on considerable airs, Bekha was nothing much. He'd landed in Italy convinced that he was bound to become the boss, and then he'd wound straight up in the Rome Hotel, as they called the prison, with a sentence of six years and eight months for international heroin trafficking. In prison, he'd stepped on the toes of a major Camorra boss, and Samurai had had to draw on every ounce of his power to keep prison from becoming a living nightmare for Bekha. Even back then, Samurai was thinking big. The disintegration of the Soviet empire had started moving the gears of a world too long crucified on the sterile and obsolete stand-off between East and West. Business horizons opened up that would have been unthinkable just a few months ago. The wheels started to turn again. At last they could play the game freely. Making a friend like Bekha was a far-sighted calculation.

But when Bekha got out, having served his time, he started acting every bit as arrogantly as before. And this time the Neapolitans had decided to reckon up the bill. Samurai had vouched for Shalva personally.

"Are you going to stay and have lunch with me, brother?" Shalva used the Italian term *colazione.*

"They say *colazione* in Milan, Shalva. In Rome we call it *pranzo.*"

"Well, stay and eat anyway. I can make you a nice *khachapuri.*"

"That fried panino filled with your stinky cheese?"

"Don't talk that way about our national dish!"

"The French have something similar. They call it a *croquemonsieur*. And it's every bit as disgusting. I'll settle for a cup of tea."

"My samovar is always on the boil and my heart is always warm for my friends."

Shalva served the hot drink in English Wedgwood porcelain tea cups. He added two cubes of ice to his own tea. Samurai furrowed his brow. There were certain violations of basic style that could irritate him boundlessly. He set down his cup and shook his head.

"You really refuse to become a proper citizen, Shalva."

"But I'm trying to stop smoking."

"All right," Samurai sighed, "I'm a little on edge today."

"Problems?"

"We're on the brink of full-blown war, brother."

Samurai brought him up to speed on the most recent events. Shalva said that sometimes war is inevitable. And it can even be useful.

Samurai knit his fingers together and raised his hands to his forehead. This was the pose he assumed when he needed to think. If Shalva could have, he would have held his breath.

What if it turned out the Georgian had been right? And what if Samurai chose not to intervene? If he just let them slaughter each other? After all, this could be the right time to do a little housecleaning. Get rid of the scum. Samurai was sick and tired of all those tawdry ignorant subhumans who infested the streets. But this wasn't the time yet, no.

"Let's forget about evil thoughts. You got in touch with me, Shalva."

"Do you think you could help me place a . . . a large quantity of cocaine?"

"How large?"

"A metric ton."

"No problem," Samurai whispered, unruffled. "Where is the stuff?"

"Folegandros, or Naxos. It hasn't been decided yet. There's an agreement with several cops on site, the Pugliese have arranged to grease the wheels."

"I don't like the Pugliese. They're treacherous chatterboxes."

"The Pugliese are powerful in the Mediterranean, Samurai. They've got this traffic covered. We can't cut them out."

"If they'll settle for ten percent . . . "

"I'll try to convince them."

"Don't just try."

"We'll need a boat."

"Consider it procured."

"And a skipper."

"I've got the right person. But we're going to have to bring the Neapolitans and the Calabrians in too. Let's just say we can get away with twenty percent. Just to keep them happy and not mess up the balance of power. Well, a hundred minus thirty makes seventy. Our deal is the usual?"

"Of course, of course."

That is, forty-five to Samurai and twenty-five to Shalva. Reasonable, advantageous.

Samurai sipped his lapsang souchong tea tempered with jasmine blossom. The scent of dirt mixed with the aroma of smoky wood. A perfect union of feminine and masculine elements.

"If the deal goes through, you'll get a fair amount of cash out of it, Shalva."

"Well, as you know, a share belongs to my countrymen, but when it's all said and done . . . "

"Do you already know how to invest it?"

"Are you about to tell me something important, Samurai?"

Samurai told him about Waterfront and the social housing project. Shalva listened open-mouthed.

"You see, now, why we can't afford a gang war right now? We're all involved, all of us. Me, the gypsies, the Neapolitans, the Calabrians, and even you, if you want to be."

"Me?"

"We're going to need a great many vehicles to transport workers from one construction site to another. And we'll need more for logistics and assistance. I can't let you have a piece of the earthmoving work, because that belongs to the Neapolitans, but as to the rest of it . . . you ought to put together a company and submit a bid for the contract. Naturally, strictly for appearances, the results are guaranteed. You just calculate that for an investment of, let's say, ten, you'd see a return of sixty, seventy times that . . . "

"Samurai, I swear it, you are my brother, my father, and my mother."

"No, leave out the mother, the mother is sacred, leave her to us Italians."

Shalva couldn't believe his ears. However much the tone was the usual, chilly and dry, this was the closest he'd ever heard Samurai come to actually making a joke.

"We need to drink a toast to this, Samurai."

"You know I don't like alcohol."

Samurai stood up to take his leave.

Shalva cleared his throat.

"Samurai . . . "

"What is it?"

"It's about the 'packages.'"

"Problems?"

"This morning I caught a whiff of a cop."

"I'll look into it and let you know."

# XVII

Number Eight slowly massaged his right ear. He brushed his forefinger over the rough scabs in the left corner of his mouth.

Fuck that Paja and fuck that Fieno: he looked like a leper.

Still, Silvio, the veterinarian who cared for Morgana's maremma sheepdog, had done a good job. He'd stitched up his lip and cheek with twenty or so stitches and staples. Which would start falling out in a week or so. A few more days and his face would start to look human again. But there was still the problem with his hearing. The buzz in his ears wouldn't quit. The only thing the bullets from Paja's pistol had damaged was the one thing that asshole hadn't been aiming at. His eardrum.

He had holed up in the hovel in Santa Severa that Denis had found for him. Not even Jesus Christ Himself would be able to track him down there. He'd gotten rid of the Carabinieri without difficulties: they'd caught wind of something, but they had no proof. Evidence: it'd be a great day when they came up with that one, Number Eight thought to himself.

He twirled the Marlboro Red in the cocaine in his cigarette case. In the milky midday light, he leaned over the balcony and gazed down on a shamrock-green sea below. A couple of kids fighting in the street caught his eye.

The one who looked to be older, maybe fifteen at the most, was straddling the other one, who was flat on his back on the asphalt. He was gripping a knuckleduster in his right hand, holding it half-raised in the moment before the first blow.

"You made me do this, you stupid asshole. I don't have any choice. You know yourself that I have to do it. Those are the rules. What the fuck am I going to say to everyone else, otherwise? After all, if I don't do it, you're going to."

Despite how high above them he was, he could hear the dull thud of the blow, and he saw the head of the punk flat on his back as it twisted to one side in the act of spitting out blood and what looked like teeth.

Number Eight smiled contentedly. He went back into the living room, turned on the DVD player, and restarted the porn flick from the point he'd left it at dawn. On the remote he pressed the mute button.

Things weren't over with Anacleti, not at all. And, no disrespect intended, but who the fuck cared what Samurai thought about it. After all, he wouldn't even know until it was too late. Certainly, he was going to be pissed off. But it would be wasted effort, as the saying goes. He too would have to come around, in the end. After all, they had a clear understanding. Samurai was supposed to keep his nose out of the business on the street. In part because now it was more than just a question of honor. Now it was a matter of survival. He'd drawn a wild card. There wasn't going to be another Piazza Gasparri, and he could thank the idiocy of Paja for that. Because you tell me how you can unload a 9x21 mm pistol at someone crawling on the ground without hitting him even once. Next time, the guys from Cinecittà wouldn't miss.

And after all, it wasn't as if he'd started this war. Who had authorized Spadino to take something he should never even have touched? Who was supposed to keep that vicious rabid dog on a leash? Him, or Rocco Anacleti? What, it wasn't like he'd picked up the phone and called Malgradi, was it? Or hadn't it actually been the Honorable who had begged and

pleaded? He didn't see a lot of alternatives. To persuade
Anacleti to put an end to it, to let it drop, they were going to
have to whack another one of his men. Paja. Or maybe that asshole friend of his. Fieno. But this time, right in his backyard.
In Cinecittà.

He froze the DVD on a scene of a threesome. Yeah. It had
to be something spectacular, a tarantella that would make people talk about it for weeks. And too bad if it meant they'd have
every cop in Rome on top of them. Weren't they after them
already? In Ostia, Morgana had told him, after the mess at
Piazza Gasparri, the place had been full of those cockroaches.
Plainclothes and in uniform. All of them wandering around
questioning everyone, even the kids at stoplights. As if they
didn't know that in Ostia people mind their own business.
And that means, no evidence, no-damned-ev-i-dence! For that
matter, what did one more or one less squad car change? The
important thing was that he had to stay holed up for another
little while. Until he had his normal face back and his ear was
working right. The others were going to have to take care of
business.

Denis made his way through the stacked Corona beer cartons. He'd taken the guns back to the Off-Shore after the
search. Because you never know. He'd kept them hidden in a
false wall in the beverage warehouse. Number Eight had
insisted on having nothing but the finest. Clean and top quality. Four Remington pump rifles, two Franchi SPAS-15 combat
shotguns, a Maverick 88 pump-action shotgun, three Uzi
machine pistols, four Kalashnikovs; two 7.65 mm and four
6.35 mm Beretta pistols, a VZOR 70 7.65 pistol, and five Smith
& Wesson .38 caliber revolvers. And something like two thousand rounds of ammunition. An oversized arsenal. The
toyshop of that idiot, Number Eight. The way that guy acted
as if he was the boss of all Ostia. It's true that they'd become a

heavy crew, but they still remained in the shadow of Uncle Nino. Number Eight raved and fantasized in his deliriums of grandeur, but the minute he lost his uncle's protection, they'd sweep him away. Denis had tried talking sense to him, but the guy just turned a deaf ear. As he was distributing weapons to Robertino and Morgana, Denis asked himself for what must have been the thousandth time whether he wasn't committing a grave error. But the two of them stared at him, full of hope, already intoxicated with the prospect of action. After all, it might just be the right thing. After all, the power relations might easily shift. After all, you only live once.

"We can get it done in an hour. We go and we come back. We'll take them out in front of their bar on Piazza Cinecittà."

"The Ferro de Cavallo?" asked Morgana.

"That's right."

"But that place is crawling with cops. Half the Ministry of the Interior is right around the corner."

"Exactly: an open insult. We'll do it late tonight. Paja and Fieno are always hanging around there. And today there's a match on Sky, too. Which means that sure as shooting we'll get them."

"But what if we don't find them?" Robertino ventured.

"I tell you they'll be there."

Morgana smiled. And she shouldn't have. Robertino was a rat but he was a perceptive one. Everything he found out he told Number Eight. Everything. Even what he'd had for lunch that day. And like all rats, he was constantly there, sniffing and nuzzling, looking with those small beady eyes, darting from one side to the other. Denis had warned Morgana about it the first time he'd taken her to bed. It had been at her place. One autumn evening. She'd called him with some excuse and when he got there, he'd found her naked and stoned out of her mind on the bed. Where she'd driven him crazy with desire and pleasure.

"No one can know. No one can figure it out. Not even by accident!" he had told her, as he said goodbye just before dawn. And she had laughed, miming the routine of the three monkeys: see no evil, hear no evil, speak no evil, running her tongue over her parted lips.

But Denis should have known. With a girl like that, things were by their nature bound to run out of control. They fucked like animals. At any time of the day or night. As soon as they could, and wherever they could.

One time, together, they'd taken the sucker she was cheating on to Levante to collect the vig from a guy they were shylocking. Morgana had given him a blowjob as he sat at the steering wheel.

He thought back to that one all the time. Him with both hands on the wheel and his eyes wide open, staring toward the front door that Number Eight had walked through. Morgana bent over his crotch, one hand grabbing the automatic gearshift of his black Porsche Cayenne.

That girl was one hell of a problem. He was going to have to solve it. But not that night.

Denis slipped a Smith & Wesson under the belt behind his back. Morgana zipped a Beretta 7.65 into her pink Mandarina Duck fanny pack. Robertino, after hefting them for a good long while as he made up his mind, chose an Uzi and the VZOR-70. As Denis was distributing the clips, Morgana laid out three lines of coke.

"What, you want to go to work on an empty stomach?"

They got in the Porsche Cayenne and drove to Infernetto. Without uttering a word. And for that matter, it would have been impossible, considering how high Denis had pumped the volume on *Velociraptor!* by Kasabian. They stopped just short of Casalpalocco proper. Not far from La Caverna, the club where Rocco Anacleti and old man Adami, a few years ago, had decided that there was plenty of room in Rome for everyone. Where they had signed a peace treaty, splitting up control of the clubs and bars. Back then, there were a dozen or so. Now there were four times as many. Denis pulled over under the pine trees and parked, making sure that he wasn't in a no parking zone.

How he missed Uncle Nino. He was more than a father to him. The last time he'd gone to see him in prison, he'd recognized all Nino's bitterness and regret for a love that he couldn't express the way he would have liked.

During their conversation, Nino had leaned closer, lowering his voice.

"You just have to be patient, Denis. Though I know it's not really your nature. Never has been, ever since you were a little kid. But from here I can't make a decision that, in reality, I'd already made the day you came into my home, to live under my roof. It's not your turn yet. Cesare is my nephew. You understand this, don't you?"

Denis had looked down.

"Believe me, I know he's an asshole. That it's not for him. But he's blood of my brother. That cannot be undone. At least not as long as I'm in this prison. To me you're like a son. Remember that."

They got out of the Cayenne and Robertino grabbed the bag in which he'd stashed the Uzi and a handful of clips. They looked around. They decided to steal a Mercedes-Benz B-Class parked about a hundred yards away. That was the right car to get them out to Cinecittà and back. They burned up the fifteen or so miles on the beltway in fifteen minutes. Just enough time for Denis to satisfy a curiosity. Asking about it point-blank, about what until then he'd preferred to push away into a shadowy corner of his mind.

"Morgana, tell me something. Have you ever whacked anyone?"

"What the fuck is it to you."

"Just something I want to know. It's important."

"Do you think I don't have the balls?"

"I'm just thanking God that you don't, but you do have a beautiful ass."

Robertino burst out laughing. Which Morgana didn't like.

"What the fuck are you laughing about, you miserable encephalitic."

Denis cooled her down.

"Oh, oh. Come on now. We're just kidding around. Why are you being so touchy?"

"I've fired a gun, if that's what you want to know."

"At a man?"

"I've fired a gun."

"Okay, I understand. Let it go. Let's do this. If things go sideways, just don't get in front of me."

They'd reached the off ramp for Via Tuscolana. They pulled off heading for Rome and only slowed down when, as they pulled onto Piazza di Cinecittà, they saw the signs for the Subaugusta metro stop, reflected in the huge neon sign of the Ferro di Cavallo. The stolen Mercedes rolled at walking speed past the bar's plate glass windows and Robertino got a chance to take a good clear look around the interior. There were just four losers sitting in front of the big-screen TV broadcasting the Sky network's post-game coverage.

"Paja and Fieno aren't there. No one's there. Just a few *zam-mammeri*."

The Mercedes went past the bar but, not two hundred yards down the street, it pulled a U-turn. Denis reversed until he came even with the Ferro di Cavallo and pulled over on the opposite side of Via Tuscolana.

"The two of you wait for me here."

He wanted to check in person.

Robertino grabbed him by the arm while he was opening the car door.

"What if we just toss a couple of molotovs?"

"Fuck off."

Denis barely made it onto the sidewalk that ran past the bar's plate glass windows when he sensed a presence behind him. Morgana.

"I told you to stay in the car."

"I didn't come all this way just to be a babysitter."

Denis took a few more steps toward the entrance of the Ferro di Cavallo. Just as the four men in front of the big screen TV were leaving the bar, completely bored. He turned and spoke to Morgana, looking at his watch, which now read almost midnight.

"Robertino is right. Paja and Fieno aren't here. And I'm definitely not waiting for them to show up. We'll come back tomorrow. Come on, let's go."

Morgana didn't move. Three of the four young Moroccan men they'd seen inside the bar emerged, chatting in Arabic, visibly revved up, high. One of them was holding a pack of MS cigarettes in one hand and came to a stop in front of her, gumming his cigarette. After a slight bow, he mimed the image of a lighter, and Denis pushed him away with a good hard shove.

"Get the fuck out of my face."

Then he turned back to Morgana.

"Well? What are we going to do? Do we want to spend the night here with this garbage?"

Morgana was still standing there motionless. As if in a cataleptic trance.

"You don't think you might have overdone it today with the coke? Okay, I'll wait for you in the car."

Denis turned to leave and started back across Via Tuscolana.

The last of the four Moroccans came staggering out of the Ferro di Cavallo and practically ran right into Morgana.

"Ciao, pretty princess."

He never got a chance to let the smile fade from his face. The 7.65 mm bullet caught him square in the mouth, rocketing through his cranium just above the back of his neck. A spray of cerebral material splattered against the bar's plate glass window, while Morgana, her arm still extended, emptied her entire clip in the direction of the entrance with short sharp movements of her wrist.

Denis shouted. He grabbed the Smith & Wesson that was jammed down the back of his trousers and, with the adrenaline practically making his temples explode, ran headlong toward Morgana. He grabbed her and dragged her toward the car, hurling her into the back seat while Robertino was struggling with the Uzi.

"You're out of your mind!"

The Mercedes ran all the red lights until the beltway. And from there to Infernetto no one spoke a word. Once they got to where they'd left the Cayenne, they split up. Denis ordered Robertino to get rid of the Mercedes.

"Take it to the Magliana wrecking yard." He grabbed his bag full of weapons and dismissed him. "I'll tell Number Eight about what happened. You mind your own fucking business."

Morgana got into the Porsche with him. Denis lit a Marlboro, slowly tooling down the last stretch of Via Cristoforo Colombo. He was waiting for just a single word to come out of Morgana's mouth, a sound that might help him make some sense, however partial, of what had happened. That execution, random and brutal, which not only did nothing to put an end to the war with the Anacleti clan, but actually turned their mess into a savage brawl among wild beasts that didn't bode well for anyone. Just more bullshit days and blood ahead of them. So he finally decided to make the first move himself.

"Tell me why. Just tell me, and I swear it'll remain between us. I'll tell Number Eight that it was me. That that nigger was working for the Anacletis and that that's why I whacked him. It was supposed to be a vendetta and a vendetta is what it was. That's what I'll tell him. But you, as the Virgin Mary is my witness, you'd better talk!"

Morgana looked at him with a distracted smirk. As if that question had nothing to do with her.

"Don't tell bullshit to Number Eight, that rat Robertino'll tell him everything anyway."

"Then try telling me what you're going to have to tell him. Why?"

"What did you ask me in the car when we were going to Rome?"

"I wanted to know if you'd ever killed a human being."

"No, that's not what you wanted to know. You wanted to know if I had the balls to do it. Well, I did it. And now you know that I've got the balls."

Denis fell silent. They'd reached Morgana's place. A garret apartment on Piazza Lorenzo Gasparri, in one of those modular structures made of flaking reinforced concrete that surrounded the piazza, pockmarked with dozens of satellite dishes and colored by patches of hanging laundry.

"Ostia is nice, but sometimes it makes me feel like I'm in Tirana," he told her.

Morgana opened her door.

"Are you about done talking?"

He followed her inside. They fucked till dawn.

## XVIII

Three days after the events at the Arcobaleno, Alice phoned Marco Malatesta.

"Abbas expects us at six."

"If it's all right with you, I'll swing by and pick you up, so we can go over together."

She gave him the address of a gym over near Villa Gordiani.

"Pilates?" he guessed, tossing out the first in a series of ill-chosen comments.

"I box, Colonel."

Marco showed up a few minutes early. Alice, under the stern gaze of a boxing federation instructor, was trading punches with a black woman twice her height and weight.

He tucked himself discreetly into a corner, to watch.

Wearing headgear, the two young women alternated elegant movements, practically dance steps, with furious hails of punches. It wasn't clear why they still avoided hitting each other in the face: whether it was to preserve the purity of their features, out of some kind of understanding, or a lack of technical expertise. In any case, that belligerent agitation of sweaty bodies had something both powerful and erotic about it.

But Marco decided to keep that thought to himself.

At the end of the third round, the instructor separated the two young women, distributed criticisms and compliments, then sent them both to the showers.

Marco left the gym. Three Camel Lights later, he saw Alice coming toward him.

She was wearing a red blouse and a long, close-fitting skirt of the same color. As he was handing her the spare helmet, Marco was struck by the aroma of citrus fruit that was emanating from her freshly shampooed hair.

The Triumph Bonneville ate up the empty summer roads, and the familiar sensation of a woman's body pressing against his back was a pleasurable curse. Marco told himself that he needed to take things slowly. One wrong word and the delicate web he had set out to weave would be inexorably torn apart.

Abbas occupied one of the two beds in a decorous little room in the Sandro Pertini hospital. Sitting next to him was Farideh. Alice made the introductions. The young woman explained that her father was scheduled to have another operation on his hands the next day.

"But now a little I can talk," the man mumbled, flashing a gentle smile that struck Marco to the heart.

The colonel decided to lay out his cards.

"I checked into it. At the barracks they say no complaint was filed."

"Farideh and I went in together!" snapped Alice. "We went to the commandant's office together."

"I believe you," Marco cut her off. "That's why I'm here."

And he showed Abbas the pictures of Paja and Fieno. Abbas shook his head.

"Their faces were covered, I don't . . . maybe the eyes, yes, certainly, the eyes . . . mean eyes."

"All right, Signor Abbas, thank you. I just needed to check."

"But there was another one," Abbas added, "one who was different. He threw himself against the one who was bigger of the other two. It seems to me that . . . he didn't agree . . . he wanted to help me . . . "

There were three of them, then. Alice hadn't mentioned

that fact at the Arcobaleno center. Three, and not two. And there was one who seemed different from the others. Paja, Fieno, and what was the name of the other one? Ah, Nicce, like the philosopher. The overall picture of the situation seemed pretty clear. Just to make sure, he asked the old man if the one who was playing the part of the good guy had a mask over his face too.

"Yes. But his eyes were different. Cold, but they were the eyes of a human being, if that makes sense."

"That makes perfect sense, Signor Abbas."

The effort of the conversation had left the Iranian exhausted, and he let out a moan of pain.

Farideh hastened over to lift his head, solicitously.

Marco called Brandolin. He dictated brief, rapid instructions.

"In half an hour a young Carabiniere will arrive here, his name is Brandolin. You, Abbas, repeat everything you told me just now, he'll write a report, and then you'll sign it. Do you think you're up to that?"

Abbas raised a hand, as if to impart a benediction, then his limb dropped sharply back to the bed covers.

Marco and Alice withdrew, both of them deeply moved and indignant. He offered to give her a ride back.

"How the hell did you know about all that stuff, eh, Colonel? The molotovs and all the rest . . . "

"If you'll accept an invitation to dinner, I'll explain."

At La Quaglia Canterina, a renovated farmhouse just a stone's throw from the Arco di Travertino, dinner was served on rustic tables set out under a trellis covered with Isabella grape vines. The proprietor was called Federico; he had a wild head of graying hair and he greeted Alice with a kiss on each cheek.

"He used to be an architect," she explained, as they were

sitting down at their open-air table. "Then he decided he was fed up and he converted to zero-mile cuisine."

Alice took off the red blouse, revealing a black stretch T-shirt that was pleasantly form-fitting. She wore light but well-applied makeup. The scent of citrus was delicate and fresh. The image of an orchid popped into his head. Lovely. Lovely and complicated.

"What did you do with that backpack? The one that you all planted at the Arcobaleno movie house?"

"Professional confidentiality," Marco smiled. Then, seriously: "Confiscated and deposited as official criminal evidence. Officially, on a tip from an informant."

"So you haven't reported Terenzi."

"No. But he's on the blacklist now. When the time comes, he'll pay. I'd emphasize the need for you to be careful. You've taken on the Anacletis. Expect a reaction."

"Should I hire a bodyguard?" she asked, provocatively.

"I'm thinking more about character assassination, if you'll allow me the expression. Slander, or else lawsuits for defamation, that kind of stuff."

"I'm used to it."

"You're a strange young woman."

"You're a strange Carabiniere. Why are you doing all this?"

"Because we're on the same side."

"You and me? Really?"

The ironic smirk on Alice's face faded as Federico appeared at their table. The menu, handwritten on loose sheets of paper, called for a deconstructed pasta with *amatriciana* sauce. Cold trussed rabbit with a medley of garden vegetables. A three-chocolate torte with a pomegranate heart. And of course, fair-trade, free wine. *Vino libero.*

"That is, without sulphites," Alice pointed out.

"Actually, right here it says: 'Contains sulphites,'" he pointed out, after pouring.

"Sure, of course, but much lower levels than you'll find in any other bottle of wine. And anyway, Federico's cooking is always better than the frozen precooked meals you'll get elsewhere."

Alice Savelli considered him, if not an actual enemy, something very close to that. He had to find a way to reassure her.

"I'm not an enemy, Alice. I'm not investigating you. I'm not spying on you."

"Are you trying to make me believe that you haven't gathered information about me?"

"Of course I have. I did what anyone would do. I read your blog. And I got an idea."

Federico served organic bread, focaccia made of Khorasan wheat, and basmati rice croquettes flavored with hillside-grown scallions.

"An idea about me? How interesting. Please go on."

"A person who is firmly opposed—"

"Ah, you can say that again."

"Opposed to rape and violence against women," Marco resumed, "opposed to welcome centers for immigrants . . . "

"Calling those filthy stables 'welcome centers' seems vaguely hypocritical, don't you think, Colonel?"

"I couldn't agree more. Ah, and opposed to the new Roman mafia."

"And what else?"

"And then there's one more thing that surprised me."

"And what would that be?"

"There's no politics."

Alice heaved a sigh of impatience, as if she were dealing with a foolish child. They dove into the deconstructed *amatriciana*, which proved to be less deleterious than expected. They ordered a second bottle of wine.

"Do you really think that the things I do, that so many of us do, aren't political?"

"Well, when I read your blog I found all sorts of things in it. For instance, I wasn't clear which side you're on."

"You mean left-wing, right-wing? That's old hat."

"You're not the first person to say that to me."

"Politics, the way it works now, with parties and assorted claptrap, is a filthy mess. We ought to load them all onto open boats and shove them out to sea, make a clean sweep. All of them. No one excluded. On the right and on the left. And then start over from scratch. Direct democracy, for instance. On the web. Did you know that the one percent of the wealthiest actually governs 99 percent of the world? Derivatives, subprime mortgages, hedge funds . . . bah!"

Heated, impassioned, rebellious, and fully alive. So different. Truly the voice of another world. How many years' difference between them? Seven, eight, or even ten? And Marco felt so furiously out of step, so out of time.

Suddenly she scrutinized him, grim-faced.

"Exactly what is it you want from me, Marco?"

"The same thing that you want, Alice. A better world."

They had shifted, without realizing it, to a first-name basis. Part of the credit for that went, no doubt, to the chocolate torte, made with pomegranate seeds and chocolate from Modica in Sicily.

For the first time, he heard her laugh. A laugh with the rich warmth of a youthful, impetuous force.

"This script isn't convincing me. I'm the one who's supposed to make the wisecrack about the better world. You're supposed to say: the world is the way it is, my dear girl, and neither you nor I can ever hope to change it. So let's be satisfied with what we have and stop trying to cause trouble."

His hand had come to rest, as if accidentally, upon hers. Alice stared him in the eyes and asked if he had a cigarette. Marco pulled out his Camel Lights. Federico served an artisanal grappa, "produced," he insisted on pointing out, "by a cooperative of ex junkies."

The junkies hadn't been kidding around with the proof on that grappa. That evening's alcohol content was on the verge of skyrocketing. Alice pulled her hand away.

Still, the ice had been broken. She explained to him that she'd become interested in those neighborhood stories when a tranny had commented on her blog.

"We became friends . . . well, maybe friends is too strong a word, but long story short, she's an interesting person. And in any case, she trusts me. She spread the word. Lots of people started writing in, from the neighborhood. And I spread their news. Otherwise, how could I ever have found out about Paja and Fieno, the Anacletis, and the rest of that freak show? Then Farideh showed up. That girl is a treasure, Marco, believe me."

"Has anyone ever mentioned a certain Nicce to you?"

"Nietzsche, you mean? Like the philosopher?"

"No, Nicce, just like that, Roman-dialect style."

"No. He's probably a Nazi."

"That's a safe bet."

"Anyway, word's going around in the neighborhood that Paja and Fieno beat a sixteen-year-old kid black and blue."

"Why did they do that?"

"Because he's gay, that's why."

"And is that a good enough reason?"

"There's no need for a reason if somone is different."

"That's something I can't wrap my head around. Personally, I prefer women, but I respect gay people."

"Oh, sweet Jesus, what a pathetic line. Just stop trying, Colonel."

"What did I say wrong? I thought I was being correct."

"After all, you are still a Carabiniere," she said, cutting him off, with another peal of laughter in which he thought he could detect an undercurrent of seduction.

At two in the morning, they were still together. It was her idea to wrap up the evening with some good music.

"The Niro is playing at Il Circolo degli Artisti."

"Wait, what? Now he's singing, too?"

"Not the actor, dummy. The Niro, he's a Roman artist. Very hip."

Sweaty young people, among whom Alice moved freely and lightly. Beers. A couple of whiskeys. Unfamiliar songs, vaguely surreal or declamatory lyrics. Marco felt like an alien. At a certain point, though, The Niro started singing a song he knew. Marco joined in the chorus.

"Hallelujah! Hallelujah!"

"Well, at least you knew one song!" Alice complimented him.

"Who doesn't know 'Hallelujah'?"

"Right. The great Jeff Buckley."

"Actually, the song's by Leonard Cohen."

"Who?"

"Jesus, Leonard Cohen, the Canadian poet. The one who sings 'Suzanne.'"

"But isn't Cohen kind of a . . . drag, really?"

Alice had made him feel like a dinosaur. He fished in his pockets in search of the last cigarette. His cell phone was vibrating furiously. Missed call, missed call, missed call. A text from Alba.

"Where R U? Fresh corpse in Cinecittà. Come now."

# XIX

S tate of Emergency As Crime Spikes in Rome." "Summer, Bloody Summer." "Ministry of the Interior: Extreme Measures for Law and Order Being Readied." "Slaughter of the Innocents." "The Sacrifice of Abdel." "That Dead Man Has a Lot to Say About Us."

The dead man at the Ferro di Cavallo had unleashed a lethal mix of understandable horror, two-bit rhetoric, and political opportunism of the lowest sort. The adhesive holding it all together: a firm determination to steer clear of the heart of the matter—the murder, the possible culprits—concerning which no one, and that means absolutely no one, seemed willing or able to offer the slightest shred of evidence.

Marco Malatesta stopped reading the papers, turned off Radio FM 922, and barricaded himself in his office.

He could see clearly now. And his hunch had paid off.

The massacre in Cinecittà confirmed of his theory. There was a war going on. No one could deny it, now.

General Thierry, not the type to hang back, went with him to call on Setola.

The prosecuting magistrate was an attractive man, deeply bronzed, with long wavy gray hair and the airs of an aesthete. In his office, where prints of historic yachts enjoyed pride of place, the Carabinieri General Rapisarda, commandant of the Custoza division, was waiting for them. A high-muck-a-muck to whom Thierry reported and whom he despised; moreover, the feeling was mutual. Marco had run into him only once, during an official ceremony. He had been left with an impression of arrogance and superficiality: the perfect cocktail for a careerist destined to rise to dizzying heights.

They got a chilly welcome. Marco laid out his theory.

And ran smack into a brick wall.

According to Rapisarda, the Moroccan had simply been the victim of a settling of accounts between drug pushers. The fact that he had no criminal record and hadn't ever even turned up as a suspicious character was of no importance as far as the superior officer was concerned.

As for Spadino, Setola saw it as nothing more than a "mere case of geographic proximity," and that investing the kind of resources Marco was advocating pouring into the case would "prove to be an authentic squandering of funds."

Once again, the request was rejected out of hand, and Marco and Thierry were summarily dismissed.

The general couldn't make head nor tails of it.

"Unbelievable!" he complained to Marco once they'd gotten to Ponte Salario. "What the hell do they need before they'll come around? A massacre? If things keep going like this, they'll have one."

"Hmm, yes, *una bella ammazzatina*, as the Sicilians like to say. It might even prove useful."

The calm irony in Marco's voice baffled Thierry. He was about to reply when he received a call on his cell phone. He listened in silence, then jammed his thumb down to end the conversation.

"Bad news?" asked Marco.

"Terrible news. You're off the investigation. Setola doesn't want you interfering. And Rapisarda agrees."

"I'm not surprised. Try to picture it through their eyes."

Rapisarda plus Setola equals Politics, he explained. A government that's being held together with scotch tape has no interest whatsoever in starting a law and order campaign in

Rome. They have more than enough trouble with the European Central Bank, the spread, and the Frankfurt stock exchange. They needed results. Rapid and, above all, "compatible."

"Compatible with what, Marco?

"With the phase, let's put it that way. A settling of accounts here, a minor case of drug dealing there."

"But I'm not going along with it!" Emanuele roared.

He'd write a scathing report to the district attorney. He'd brief the commander in chief of the Carabinieri. Respectfully, but firmly, he'd make his views known: by cutting out Marco Malatesta, their best man out on the street, they were committing a colossal error.

"General, if you truly care about me, don't do any of that."

Thierry looked stunned.

"You're joking, right?"

"Never been more serious in my life. You remember back in rugby days, Emanuele?"

Before flipping head over heels for A. S. Roma, Marco had been a decent fly-half. Not vicious enough to break systematically through brutal defense lines, but fast enough and sufficiently quick-thinking to be able to move the three-quarters in a game that he tried to pretend resembled, only distantly resembled, the legendary All Blacks. Thierry had been his trainer. He continued to repeat, obsessively, a mantra that was supposed to have something to do with the philosophy of life, or something similar: in rugby, if you want to go forward, the ball has to go backward in search of the support line. And there's no support line without a team, the collective team.

"Which means that now I'm going to take some of the accumulated vacation time I'm due," Marco concluded, decisively.

"You want to drop the case."

"I wouldn't dream of it. I'm just taking a step back. Defensive phase. Regrouping. As soon as we can find the support line, we'll start off again, all together. And this time we'll drive straight to the goal."

"Bullshit!" Thierry retorted.

Marco smiled. Thierry rarely lost his proverbial ironic composure. This time, he was beside himself.

"Bullshit!" he repeated. "The man who invented rugby meant to create a healthy, robust pastime for the gentlemen of the English countryside. But this is Rome, goddamn it to hell! Here, 'gentleman' is a curseword! You aren't going anywhere!"

"Trust me. It'll work."

It took him an entire evening to talk him into it, but in the end Thierry gave in. And the following morning Marco was on a flight for Palma de Majorca. Aside from his swimsuits and a couple of T-shirts, his tiny suitcase contained the latest novel by Haruki Murakami and a CD of *Me ne vado da Roma*, the immortal litany by the great Remo Remotti.

# XX

It was no walk in the park to explain to Number Eight the mess in Cinecittà. But less complicated than Denis might have thought. Basically, they'd whacked a *zammammero*. An unlicensed gas station attendant, twenty-nine years old—that's what they learned by reading the newspapers—who was called Abdel Salam and worked as a freelancer at the Erg self-service two hundred yards from the Ferro di Cavallo, picking up fifty-cent tips from people who didn't have the energy to get out of the car and fill their own tank of gas.

It was pure chance that he was in the bar, the article that appeared in *Il Messaggero* said. Cue sobs and tears. They'd interviewed the widow, a housecleaner who was wailing like a fountain. Obviously: she was thinking about how to get herself a nice fat pension. The journalists had gone to the elementary school that the fatherless daughter attended to collect the terrifying drawings that her little classmates had done. The mayor had summoned a camera crew to follow him and take footage of him from behind, head bowed, arms crossed, on the sidewalk where they'd scrubbed away the African's blood and brains and where he had placed a wreath of flowers from the city government. The Communists had stretched out a streamer: "Never Again." Oh, sure, of course not. In other words, the usual tarantella. And after all, nobody really gave a damn. Sooner or later the *zammammero* was going to have to die anyway.

And yet, there were problems. That Morgana had started the whole thing. That the police were furious as rabid dogs. That the whole thing with the Anacletis wasn't ending here. And that Number Eight wasn't born to think straight.

Denis understood that when he went over to see him in the studio apartment in Santa Severa where he was hiding out. Number Eight was wrecked to the gills.

"Nice, bro!" he said with an idiotic smile, weaving in the doorway in his undershirt. His hands were betraying a continual tremor.

"You took it well. I see you're nice and calm," Denis replied.

"When I heard that you'd hit a bullseye on some black, I'd have ripped your head off. But then Samurai called me. And he told me that we need to meet. That we need to talk."

"So is that a piece of good news, in your view?"

"Of course it is. It means that the Anacletis have decided to beg for pity. That they understand they need to kiss the tip of my prick. They're scared to death, is what, ha!" Number Eight let out a yell and pumped his fists in the air.

"What else did Samurai tell you?"

"Nothing. You know what he's like on the phone. You need pliers to pry words out of him."

"Exactly."

"Exactly what? You see, Denis, you don't understand a thing? You see why I say that you still need to get some experience? If Samurai takes action over this street thing, that means that he understands that we own the street. That this swipe of the lion's paw was badly needed. That they aren't going to try and come after me again. Wake up and smell the coffee, Denis."

"What does Uncle Nino say?"

"What do I know? Anyway, where he is, he's not running away. He'll let us know. And what do you think he's going to say? Do you think in my situation he'd have just done nothing?

Denis, I don't know about you, but I'm not going to just stand here with my dick in my hands."

"Don't you even want to know who whacked the nigger?"

"Doesn't matter to me. What difference does it make?"

"Morgana."

"Morgana what?"

"She's the one who did it."

"Pretty girl of mine. Mhm."

"I'm heading back to Ostia. You need anything?"

"Yeah, the candy striper. I still have some booboos. Haa haa haa! Haa haa haa!"

With a sneer of disgust, Denis shut the door behind him while Number Eight kept on laughing convulsively. He felt utter contempt for that man. And above all, he knew the blood of the gypsies. That was his blood too.

Via del Ponte delle Sette Miglia had all the sounds and the colors of the *zambra mora* being held by the Anacletis. On a large meadow, in the shade of enormous brightly colored tents, the festival of reconciliation marked the end of a feud among cousins. A shipment of coke, cut poorly and recut even worse. Rocco, in his official capacity as *duca* and with an unappealable verdict, had established the reciprocal cash reparations to be paid. The women had made dolmas, green peppers stuffed with rice, meat, and tomatoes. The children of the two families of reprobates plunged their hands into the trays loaded high with pita bread, the flour and water crêpes stuffed with ricotta and beets, potatoes and onions. Men and women danced to the melodies of a small combo's manouche swing, or gypsy jazz.

Paja and Fieno pulled the black BMW over to the side of the road and joined Rocco, who was sitting at one of the open air tables, set for a meal, with Max. The two men were engaged in conversation, which they broke off when Paja and

Fieno arrived. Rocco invited them with a gesture to take a seat, then he pointed to the pot of *bosanskibonaz* and plunged in a gigantic ladle. That stew, made of meat, green peppers, savoy cabbage, potatoes, and cauliflower, would be hard to digest in a blizzard. When it was ninety degrees in the shade, it was sheer torture. Paja filled his bowl as if he hadn't eaten for a week. Fieno took just a taste to keep from offending the host. They knew why they were there. Max's presence was a further confirmation. Nicce didn't come out for trivial matters. And then, they had nothing to do with the gypsy reconciliation. They needed to talk about vendetta, rather. The blood of the Ferro di Cavallo needed to be washed out in some way. Because the people from Ostia weren't looking for the *zammammero*.

His mouth crammed with that gypsy cement, Paja muttered as he chewed what were no doubt meant to be words of defiance.

"There's no need to even talk about it . . . We'll just go and this time . . . "

"You're not going anywhere. And you know what I'm talking about!" Anacleti said in a chilling tone.

Fieno had no idea whether Max knew about the disaster of Piazza Gasparri—hadn't the boss said that it was supposed to remain a secret from everyone?—so he said nothing. In fact, he kicked Paja under the table to make sure he kept his mouth shut, that is, assuming he even had the courage to open it to lodge an objection.

Max took the floor.

"It's the boss's decision. But I ventured to suggest we keep cool. Very cool. If we're going to take revenge, it can't be now. Too many cops out on the street."

Anacleti laid a hand on Max's shoulder.

"You have a good head on your shoulders, Nicce. You're a philosopher, and a real one."

Paja glanced over at Max with a look that oozed hatred. Anacleti went on.

"Nicce has a point. Now's not the time. And anyway, nothing before we know what Samurai wants. He called me. He wants to see me. And we have a few good reasons to be pissed off. He'll have to listen to us this time."

"We'll come with you. That way, if there are problems . . . " Fieno hastened to suggest.

The boss pulled a giant ladleful of *bosanskibonaz* out of the pot and dumped it in his bowl.

"The two of you stay here. Eat up and take a nice long nap. Come on, Max," he said. Then he got up from the table and gestured to Max to follow him.

Paja and Fieno started to leap to their feet as well. But Anacleti waved to them to remain seated.

"What did I just say? And after all, the dessert's coming any minute. The one you like best, Paja. Halva!" he shouted in the general direction of one of the women who were rummaging in the trunk of a black Mercedes sedan, the clan's make of choice. The woman came over with two silver platters on which steamed an oily polenta, covered with doodles of simple sugar syrup, dried fruit, and pine nuts. As he strolled off with Max, Anacleti smiled: "I'm counting on you. Clean the plate. Otherwise I'll take offense."

The sun deck of Il Tatami overlooked the countryside of the Parco di Veio. And for a moment, Samurai let himself be caressed by the warmth of the sunshine. Alone and naked, except for his mirror-lens Oakleys, he looked down and observed his waxed chest and legs. He took a deep breath, inhaling the essence of bergamot with which he had been imbued by Zelda, the Filipina shiatsu masseuse, a woman who seemed to have had her tongue cut out, which alone made him appreciate his contact with her. Il Tatami was an exclusive club, not some gym or fitness center, both of which recked off the masses. Luca managed it, a Fascist comrade who had returned home from Japan after twenty years on the run. He had come back only after the Italian Supreme Court declared that the statute of limitations had expired on old charges of armed conspiracy. He loved Luca, and Luca loved Samurai. What they had in common was a hatred of bad smells. And a love of rare things, tradition, and the search for the self.

He reached over and picked up an iced glass of centrifuged kiwi juiced from the bamboo side table next to the anatomical lounge chair on which he was reclining. He had asked Luca to shut the club for the afternoon.

"I'm expecting friends."

Luca had nodded. Without asking questions.

In fifteen minutes those rabid dogs from Ostia and Centocelle would be there.

Samurai stood up from the lounge chair and slowly walked the length of the path of scalding stone that led from the sun deck to the showers. He allowed the soles of his feet to become hotter and hotter, feeling the stab of pain that comes just before third-degree burns. Then he quenched the heat in a basin of 40-degree water. The effect on his peripheral blood circulation was instantaneous. A tingling that announced a beneficial awakening.

Feet and head, he thought.

He opened the chromotherapy Hidrobox, and a powerful jet of 98-degree water that changed constantly between indigo blue and emerald green began to relax his neck muscles and his dorsals, running between his legs in a triumph of lotus-scented foam. With slow, circular movements, he massaged the nape of his neck, and then his temples. He dried off with ten minutes in the sauna, which was aromatized with lemon-balm.

Samurai wasn't sure that it was the right thing. Lower himself into the gutter. Plunge his hands into that sewer of a feud between Ostia and Cinecittà. Why not just let them take turns exterminating each other, like scorpions in a bottle? But the truth is that he didn't have much of a choice in the matter. Things couldn't continue as they were. He would soon enjoy the Schumpeterian moment in which creative force is released from destruction. But not yet.

Feet and head.

He needed them. And he wasn't the only one. The Calabrians under Perri needed them. The Neapolitans under Viglione. That buffoon Malgradi. The project of Waterfront and the working class housing had a single sine qua non. And that condition was that peace reign uncontested between Il Fungo at EUR and Lido di Ostia, between Casalpalocco and Romanina. At least until the city council approved the resolution that would upend the nature and direction of urban development between the city and the sea. Rome couldn't continue to burn with the short-sighted fury of a band of psychotic coke hounds. It was time to put an end to it. Immediately. Now.

Submerged under a luxuriant bougainvillea hedge, Il Tatami's electric gate swung open at the second honk of the black Hummer's horn. The car stopped under a cane overhang in the interior courtyard, and the silent Zelda appeared, ready to lead the man who stepped out of the car indoors. Number Eight was alone. He walked into the club's outbuilding, a perfect reproduction of a *katei*, a Japanese house. Legs crossed, Samurai, dressed in a black linen suit, was sitting on a mat in the center of a large room, with a minimalist decoration in cypress, iron, and bamboo. With his hands, he was slowly lifting to his lips a porcelain cup of lukewarm green tea.

Holding his hand, Number Eight started to walk closer.

"You wouldn't happen to have a chair, my back is a wreck . . . "

Samurai held up his hand to block him, and pointed to the floor.

"Sit."

He lowered himself onto the cushions, sensing a loss of control over his sweat glands.

"Fucking hot . . . You can't catch a breath today," he blurted out.

"We're not here to talk about the weather."

"Tell the truth, I don't know what you want to talk about, Samurai."

"You don't know?"

"No."

"You know what I can't stand? People who think they can make a fool out of me."

"Hey Samurai, what are you joking around? I really have no idea."

"I'm going to ask you one more time. And this is going to be the last. Do you really not know why you're here?"

"Okay, I know why. But we're not the ones who started this tarantella."

"Really? And you think Spadino just died because he nodded off? Explain that one to me, I'm curious. He fell asleep with a cigarette in his mouth in the pine grove?"

"Spadino was a piece of shit and you know it yourself."

"If I look around I see nothing but dung."

"What?"

"Dung means shit."

"Ah . . . anyway, Spadino had taken it into his head to blackmail Malgradi, Samurai. He was going around telling anyone who would listen that his time had come. That alliances aren't forever. And then Malgradi reached out and asked me to help him out."

"What was he blackmailing him for?"

"Because a prostitute died in his arms, and Spadino had given him a hand with the cleanup. That's what he told me."

So that was the reason. Animal lust. Samurai was nauseated.

"Spadino wasn't just any ordinary junkie. Spadino was Anacleti property. You knew that, right?"

"Of course I knew that. And that's why I had to whack him. How dare the Anacletis come and eat out of my bowl without permission? With them, I've always respected their bowls. So you want to know something? Look at this."

Number Eight held his BlackBerry out to Samurai, the phone with the text that Anacleti had sent, condemning him to death.

"They came looking for me in Ostia, Samurai. You tell me, what was I supposed to do?"

The door of the Japanese house swung open. And with a faint hint of a bow, Zelda ushered in Rocco Anacleti and Max.

Number Eight leapt to his feet and started to reach his hand around behind his back.

"Don't try it."

Samurai's voice hadn't increased a bit in volume.

Number Eight took his seat on the floor cushions once again.

"I don't like surprises."

"Neither do I, right?" said Samurai, addressing Anacleti.

Anacleti didn't say a word and just clumsily let himself drop onto the floor, along with Max, who greeted Samurai with a brief nod of the head.

Samurai reported what he had learned from Number Eight. Anacleti was furious. That was just so much bullshit. He had never tried to fix Malgradi. And anyway, even if Spadino had wanted to subject the Honorable to a treatment, that had been on his own individual initiative. The family had had nothing to do with it.

"Exactly!" Number Eight crowed. "So you ought to thank me, because I crushed the serpent's head!"

"A rat with a rose tucked behind its ear is still just a rat," the gypsy murmured softly in his language.

"So what are you talking about now?" Number Eight jibed at him, provocatively.

"Nothing. I was just praying for the soul of poor Spadino."

Samurai let an interminable minute of silence go by. He sipped his green tea with his eyes fixed straight ahead of him.

"Do any of you troglodytes know what Abdel Salam means?" he asked.

Number Eight opened his eyes wide, the way he did whenever his instinct was no longer of any help to him.

"It means *zammammero*. Isn't that the black from Cinecittà?"

Rocco Anacleti shot back at him: "That's right, you fucking dickhead. And you don't know how much he's going to cost you. You'll have to beg me for pity, slithering on the ground like a worm."

Samurai turned to look at Anacleti.

"Right, because you know something about worms, don't you? Aren't worms people who make promises they don't keep? Aren't worms people who take it out on poor old men?"

Anacleti tried to backpedal.

"Listen, Samurai, I . . . that Iranian . . . You see, I mean . . . Plus, that night I told you . . . "

"Shut up." Samurai rephrased the question. "Do any of you know the meaning of the Arabic name Abdel Salam?"

Max replied, carefully enunciating the words. As if he wanted to savor to the fullest that moment of complicity with Samurai.

"Servant of peace. It means 'Servant of peace.'"

Samurai smiled, with a nod.

"Thanks, Max. Abdel Salam. Abdel Salam. Would you mind repeating after me. In a loud voice."

In disbelief, Number Eight and Rocco Anacleti muttered out that name. Once, twice, three times, ten times. Like a prayer. Until Samurai gestured to stop.

"You need to know how to read fate, and chance. A Servant of peace is dead. And now, the two of you will take up his mission. Is that clear?"

Number Eight and Rocco Anacleti looked at each other. They were probably both thinking the same thing. But they both knew they weren't there to negotiate. Samurai wasn't done.

"I'm not going to tolerate any more impulsive moves. This is going to be a zero-tolerance state of peace. And there will be no appeals on the sentence against anyone who fails to respect this peace. Oh, and I forgot. That old Iranian is going to be paid for the work he did. I don't think we have anything else to talk about. Now shake hands and repeat that name one last time, Abdel Salam."

Max struggled to restrain a smile. The two pieces of shit had gotten what they deserved.

Number Eight scratched his bald head.

"But, excuse me, for real, Samurai . . . now that we're at peace . . . and I say this to you too, Rocco . . . I hear that a Carabiniere has showed up and he's busting people's balls . . . don't you think it would be a good idea to whack him?"

Samurai looked at him as if he were a filthy louse. In spite of himself, Number Eight dropped his gaze.

"No shooting cops. Not these days."

"Look, if it's a matter of courage, it's not as if I'm short of it, eh!" Number Eight retorted heatedly.

"We don't shoot them because it's in nobody's interest. There are other ways of neutralizing an annoying enemy. And I've already put them into play. The question is closed."

Samurai got to his feet, turned to Max with an almost affectionate wave and, before leaving, issued the final order.

"You're going to leave here separately."

Number Eight nodded. And he followed him out, not a minute later. But not before turning and looking one last time at Anacleti and his man.

"Nice going, Max, you've become a boss. You've climbed the career ladder."

# XXI

Before giving in to the courtship of Eugenio Brown, Sabrina dangled him on the cord for a while. A technique known as the perfumery: spray a nice seductive scent in the air to whet the animal's appetite, and then come to a halt right on the verge of the thing, or *illu ché*, as her maternal grandmother, Pugliese from Andria, used to put it.

Playing the part of the aspiring girlfriend was an amusing sideshow. But Eugenio Brown, however well-mannered and self-controlled he might be, was still a man. Sabrina couldn't afford to let the producer's initial enthusiasm begin to chill. She had to take care not to overdo it with the shy act. And so, on their third date, she took the initiative and took him to bed.

As a lover, Eugenio Brown proved to be the classic individual identified by the abbreviation GFE. That is, the Girlfriend Experience, as described by the phrase current in the escort network. When a male pays good money to fool himself into thinking he's making love to the girl he's going to take to the altar. Kiss and penetration, in other words, were taken for granted: after all, it's never pure chance when you find yourself turning somersaults naked in the cabin of a 79-foot Maestro 82 yacht in the waters off the exclusive marina of Cala Galera. But for everything else, it seemed necessary to ask some sort of special permission.

"Can I kiss you there? Is it okay with you if we turn over? I'd like to . . . I don't know if this is something I can ask you . . . But you can always tell me no . . . I mean . . . "

Sabrina soon got used to it, alternating sensual languor with simulated embarassment, and only from time to time letting slip tiny hints of the shameless technique that had made her so popular in her field of endeavor.

It was a good thing she hadn't inserted her tiny red diamond into the appropriate aperture.

"All in due time, Euge', because we've got plenty of time ahead of us, don't we?"

And it was precisely because she had made up her mind that her affair with Eugenio Brown was going to be a long-term one that she decided to lay out her cards face up, and level with him in full. Over the years she'd been a very busy girl. There was always the risk of being unmasked, as had already happened once with the gay screenwriter. And so, better to be completely transparent. And do it now: a man fully macerated by recently consummated sex is in the right state to take in a moral blow.

And so, when he returned to the cabin after a short swim, she served him the usual chilled Grechetto, asked him to sit down next to her, and told him: "I'm not who you think I am. My name isn't Justine, it's Sabrina. And I make my living as an escort."

A phrase that, in the original version she'd formulated, was supposed to ring this way: "Until I met you, I made my living as an escort." Sabrina had opted for a more unassuming version. She had no idea of how Eugenio Brown might react, so it was probably best to keep a few aces up her sleeve, to be played as needed.

There was no reaction of any kind.

Eugenio tossed back a gulp of wine and invited her to continue.

Sabrina told him about her drunken, abusive father. About her rape at age thirteen at the hands of a classmate. The son of a wealthy family who had arranged to cover up the incident.

She said that when her father heard about it, he'd beaten her black and blue.

She'd run away from home. She'd started to steal, here and there, and she'd been picked up by the cops and returned to her parents. Her father had taken her out of school and sent her to work as a housekeeper. The son of the family where she worked had molested her, and so had the head of the household. The lady of the house had decided that the only thing she could do was fire her. For two years, she'd developed a junk habit. She'd managed to kick it thanks to a kind-hearted nun who had rescued her when she'd been on the verge of jumping off a bridge. At age eighteen, she'd found herself alone, desperate, penniless. She'd started hooking it. Her young life had been one long procession of the wrong men, wasted opportunities, rapes, and filthy mishaps of every sort.

"Then I met you. And here I am now. Now, you do what you want. I can leave immediately. If that's what you want."

Eugenio Brown took her hand and smiled.

"I don't want you to leave. I just want you to stop telling me lies."

Sabrina's feelings were hurt. As she'd been telling her story, she'd gotten so worked up that she'd started to believe it herself, that tissue of horseshit.

"So you already knew?" she whispered.

"Yes."

"Who told you? Was it that faggot Fabio . . . was that who it was?"

"It doesn't matter if it was him or someone else, Justine. But you were straight with me. At least in your intentions. And that made me very happy. Only . . . "

"Only?"

"At least pretend that you love me a little, okay?"

It hit her like a punch to the gut, a smack to the nape of the neck, a gob of spit between the eyes. Hey, no, that's not the way you do, Eugenio Brown, what the fuck! What's with all this sweetness? What is "pretend that you love" supposed to mean? Are you surrendering yourself into imprisonment, Euge'? Tied hand and feet to a mistress like me? With her many years of frequenting whoremongers, Sabrina was convinced she'd long ago erased all feelings of tenderness toward men. If she'd paid any credence to the voice that had just insinuated itself into her heart, she would have stood up, gotten dressed, and dumped him then and there. I'm not made for a man like you, Eugenio Brown, find yourself a better woman than me. Why, what the hell kind of . . .

And yet. And yet no matter what the heart might tell her, it wasn't easy to give up a penthouse apartment on the Esquiline Hill, an eighty-foot yacht, the weekends of the present and, presumably, of the future. How do you say no to a hunk with the money and the power that Eugenio Brown could boast?

Sabrina tilted her head to one side, ran her tongue over her lips, sniffed, the way you do if you're struggling spasmodically to suffocate the tears that are surging up from the center of your chest, but you're determined not to appear weak, and with a tiny voice that cracked with emotion, she said:

"So . . . you're not sending me away?"

Eugenio Brown delicately set the glass down on the night-stand, lunged at her, and fucked her savagely.

Afterward, he told her that he'd always call her Justine.

"Sure, my love, Sabrina sounds a little low-class, doesn't it?"

"No, my love, it's because of the literary origin."

"The litera . . . oh, right, that thing about the two Justines . . . the Professor told me the same thing . . . but it's not like I really understood . . . "

They were on the bridge of the yacht, docked. They were watching the evening procession of the beautiful people of Rome up and down the wharf. From time to time someone would exchange a greeting with Eugenio. That's right, go ahead and look, look and die of envy, you assholes!

"Now I'll explain it to you," Eugenio said as he lit a Cohiba.

As far as Sabrina was able to piece it out, one of these two Justines was a sort of slave in a series of sadomasochistic games. Sabrina had a friend or two who worked in that line. Girls who were willing to let themselves be tied up and insulted for a thousand euros. Or else they had to dress up as frisky, bare-assed maids and serve their masters topless and wearing stiletto heels. Others, for an extra fee, were willing to let themselves be used as ashtrays, and others still, the most expensive ones on the market, as toilets. Filthy stuff that she'd always steered well clear of. As for the other Justine, she must have been a wealthy lunatic who hopped from one bed to another, and men went crazy over her. So what makes her so special! Ah, and then there was also a writer who killed himself because he couldn't have her all to himself.

"He committed suicide? Over a woman? Come on!"

"Does suicide scare you, Justine?"

"No. It just seems like a dickhead thing to do, Euge'!"

Eugenio went on recounting the exploits of these two papier-mâché heroines. He had a nice voice, maybe just a little monotonous. The evening breeze was caressing Sabrina's naked shoulders, causing a series of pleasurable shivers. She snuggled close in the producer's arms and shut her eyes. Sleep was about to carry her off. It had been a truly unforgettable day.

Eugenio gave her a gentle lick on the ear.

"Still, you know, sweetheart, I really ought to thank the Professor."

"For what?"

"If it hadn't been for him, we would never have met."

"So send him a bottle."

"He wants me to produce a film for him."

"And are you going to?"

"Maybe."

Sabrina sat up straight, suddenly alert.

"Do it. Produce this film. And give me a part. That way I'll know I really am important to you."

Upon their return from the weekend in Argentario, Sabrina moved into the penthouse on the Esquiline Hill. She called Teresa and thanked her for the tip that was promising to change her life.

"Really? That's wonderful! I'm so happy for you, Sabri'! Hey, now, don't forget you knew me when, eh . . . because around here, it's not like things are going all that great . . . "

"Don't worry, Teresa. I know what gratitude is."

Oh, sure, of course she did! Just for starters, the first thing to get rid of was her old phone number: if it was going to be a new life, it needed to be new from top to bottom.

Eugenio obtained an audition for her with the director, Bellini. They costumed her as a maid. Her role was to walk onto the set and say: "Madame, the eggplants are burnt."

The director, an old hack worn down by years and years of professional frustrations, threw in the towel.

"Eugenio, forgive me, but she's a hopeless case."

"Give it another try, you know how much I care about this."

"Euge', when an actress says it four times four different ways: eggsplants eggplant eckplants explant . . . "

"Maybe she was just anxious . . . "

"Listen, my friend, trust me. She comes from too far away. You'll never be able to make it work with her."

Eugenio decided to give her a personal coach. Carlo was his name, and he tried to teach her the correct pronunciation of the vowels, the correct tone with which to say a line.

Sabrina put her all into it.

In the meanwhile, she cleared matters up with Fabio. It turned out that somebody else told Eugenio. She and Fabio became something like friends. Someday, he told her, I'll have fun narrating this love story of yours.

"Love story strikes me as excessive, Fabie'."

"Then let's tell him that you're like Eliza to his Higgins."

"What is that, another book?"

"A play, actually. It's an updated version of the ancient myth of Pygmalion, in a modern version by the Irish playwright George Bernard Shaw."

"You leftists all talk so difficult."

"Well, of course you'd think that, considering the fine gentlemen you used to spend your time with."

If anyone else had dared to speak to her with that tone of voice, Sabrina would have scratched their face off. But she liked Fabio. So she asked him to tell her the whole story.

"Pygmalion is a sculptor who carves a statue that is so beautiful that he winds up falling in love with it. So he goes to the goddess Aphrodite and asks her to make the statue human. The goddess agrees, the statue becomes a woman, and they lived happily ever after."

"Well, well! And what about the play?"

"A professor takes in a commoner, educates her, and turns her into a sophisticated lady. Then she marries a lord, and they lived happily ever after."

So that's what Eugenio Brown was doing with her. He'd picked her up off the street, so to speak, to turn her into a fine lady. Sabrina started to feel a certain fondness toward him. Gratitude, perhaps, was the most appropriate word to describe it.

She redoubled her efforts, subjecting herself with a brave smile to the murderous sessions with Carlo.

But after even the personal trainer threw in the towel, Eugenio took her out to dinner at Sette, on Via Settembrini, in

226 - C. BONINI & G. DE CATALDO

the Prati quarter, and over a dish of Tagliolini allo Scorzone di Volterra he told her in no uncertain terms that she was never going to become an actress.

The working-class fury, so long repressed, exploded as she threw a liberatory scene.

"So what you're saying is that, as far as you're concerned, the only thing I'm good for is blowjobs!"

The couple at the neighboring table turned around, horrified.

Eugenio tried in vain to placate her.

"I never thought anything of the sort, my love. It's just a matter of finding something better suited to your inclinations."

"Bullshit! I'm no worse than all those sluts who work for your friends at RAI. I know how these things work. All you'd have to do is pick up the phone and they'd write me a contract!"

"No, my love."

"What do you mean by no? That you don't want to do it, that's what you mean. You're just a piece of shit! And cut it out with all this 'my love.'"

"I'm Eugenio Brown. I've been fighting those guys who, as you say, just pick up the phone all my life. And that's why they respect me, do you understand that? In any case, this conversation is over. Now try to calm down."

Sabrina threw the half glass of Brunetto, Brunone, whatever the fuck that 100 euro-a-bottle wine is called, right in his face and stormed out.

Convinced that she'd just lost Eugenio Brown once and for all, she headed back to the Esquiline and started packing her bags.

It's better this way, Sabri'.

Left-wingers. Pieces of shit. Eugenio Brown was no better than all the rest. He'd bought her and paid for her. Just like all the others. But at least those others, once the trick was turned, paid cash, and generously too, and then it was goodnight, been good to know you. All this mental masturbation about the theater, the drama, I'll turn you into this, I'll turn you into that, Pygmalion . . . Pygmalion my ass! You want to know the cold, hard truth, Sabri'? Men like Malgradi are happy to have a hot fuck, and that's fine. But men like Eugenio Brown want to change your soul. But I'm still me.

As she was filling her suitcase with everything that belonged to her—and also, as a form of reparations, a few little souvenirs, like the Rolex sitting on the bathroom counter and a couple of small paintings, no more than 6" x 12", which might seem small and insignificant but were worth amazing amounts of money, or so Fabio the faggot had sworn to her—footage of the Sky TV midnight news broadcast was streaming on the HD screen of the immense television set in front of the king-sized bed.

Out of the corner of her eye she caught a glimpse of a scene that struck her as somehow familiar. She put down the black cashmere dress that had belonged to the late Lady Brown, picked up the remote, and turned up the volume.

> Horrible discovery in the heart of the Marcigliana nature reserve, just outside of Rome. The corpse of a woman, in an advanced state of decomposition, was found this morning a little after ten o'clock by a citizen who was out walking his dog. The body was partly mutilated, probably by the wild animals that live in the forest . . .

Vicky.

They'd found her body.

What was it that guy had said on the phone? I'll send you to sleep with your girlfriend . . .

Eaten by dogs!

Suddenly, Sabrina turned lucid again.

She was on the verge of an unforgettable fuckup.

There are people who can't afford their pride, Sabri'.

She furiously unpacked her suitcase.

Eugenio Brown came back a little past midnight.

She rushed into his arms.

"Forgive me, forgive me, forgive me, I didn't know what I was doing, forgive me, my love, it will never happen again."

Eugenio Brown was stunned.

Sabrina let the purple La Perla negligee slide to the floor. She stood naked before him. She turned around. For the occasion, she had dusted off the famous red diamond.

Eugenio Brown forgave her.

# XXII

The Honorable Pericle Malgradi called Spartaco Liberati and informed him that "a select independent jury of municipal authorities" had named him winner of the Golden Pen Award, "which is assigned to the Roman journalist of the year who has most greatly distinguished himself in freely giving voice to the issues and concerns of the city, as well as defending the rights of the citizenry." Then he cut straight to the chase. He knew perfectly well that with that cynical fraud there was no need for a foolish preamble.

"No, say it isn't so, Your Honor. I won? That's crazy. At last, the reward for a lifetime of sacrifices."

"They're called blowjobs, actually, Liberati. Blowjobs."

"If you say so. But you have to admit, Spartaco Liberati, journalist of the year. That's unbelievable. How does it sound, Your Honor? Do you know how many sponsors we'll get on the radio, now?"

"Look, I don't have a lot of time to waste. I just wanted to tell you a couple of things. First thing. Don't show up without a jacket and tie, or they won't even let you in. Much less give you a prize."

"Your Honor, don't worry. I'll make you proud of me. The only thing is, excuse me, you understand . . . Well, just out of curiosity . . . Would there by any chance be a check that goes with the pen?"

"What a question, Liberati. Of course there is. What's a

prize without cash? Five thousand. We're not at some Communist street fair, here."

"Of course not. That's just what I thought."

"The second thing. I'm not going to tell you to write a speech, because I don't even want to try to imagine what would come out of an illiterate like you. I just ask you not to make any gaffes."

"What's one of those?"

"Winding up with shit on your face, Liberati. Winding up with shit on your face."

"Of course not."

"Let me say, in reference to blowjobs, that I'd prefer you not come out with the story of the paid interviews with city commissioners or councilmen."

"And why should I, Your Honor. Those are private matters, between us."

"With you I never know what to expect. And anyway it's possible that a real journalist attends the awards ceremony. And he might even think of asking you a nice, easy question."

"What question?"

"For example, why is it that a guy like you, who only ever talks about A. S. Roma, suddenly starts shooting off his mouth about municipal politics."

"Well, it's obvious. I can answer: 'Because the Monte Mario grandstand is full of politicians.' Good one, right, Your Honor?"

"There, you can see for yourself. Here's what you do. You keep your mouth shut. When they call you to the stage, I want you to say: '*Grazie.*' Or, if you really must: '*Grazie*, I'm deeply moved,' even if no one believes it. Then you put on a nice big smile for the photographers. You shake hands with the mayor while he gives you the case with the pen and the envelope with the check. And then you go back to your chair and sit down. Is that clear?"

He was beaming as he ended the call. See you on the Capitoline Hill. Who's going to miss out on those five thousand euros?

All he needed to do now was get his hands on a suit for the ceremony. And he tried with the usual crooked barter that involved a free mention on the radio.

"The way it works is you sponsor me with a nice suit and I'll get you half the south curve at the stadium as paying customers."

First he swung by Zara, then he went to Gap. But by the second fuck you, Spartaco Liberati had had enough. So he drove up Via Casilina, to the Giardinetti district. To Elegance, five floors of apparel for hoodlums from the outskirts of town trying to clean up their act, fat men, and cheapskates. The guy at the cash register, Mimmo, was a friend. One of those nutjobs who listened to FM 922 on the air and then again on the podcast, as if it were the Holy Gospel, and who went to the prefight celebration at the Ace of Spades.

"Hey Spa', what problem is there? I'll make you look fabulous. And I'll even give you a 50 percent discount. You have no idea the stuff that's come in lately."

"I can just imagine."

"Come on."

Mimmo had put him in the capable hands of Danila, a redheaded sales clerk who looked about twenty with a nice ass, cat eyes, a piercing on her bellybutton, another on her right eyebrow, one in the middle of her tongue, and another, he imagined, where he unfortunately couldn't see it.

"Size?" she asked.

"I'd say an L."

"Oh, sure. Thirty years ago. I doubt you'd even fit into an XXL."

"Listen sweetheart, try not to be such a bitch, or I'll tell Mimmo to kick your ass out on the street."

"I'm fucking Mimmo on a regular basis."

"Oh, all right. Let me see this XXL."

The clerk came back with a pleated suit in shimmering rainbow hues like the scales on a trout fished out of a mountain stream. And if that thing had even 10 percent cotton fibers, it was a miracle.

"And where did you get this, at the circus? I'm supposed to go receive a major award, not pull pigeons out of a top hat."

"It comes from Albania."

"Exactly. I'm not going to a wedding for illegals."

"Try it on. If you ask me, that's your color."

He pulled back the curtain in the fitting room and was overwhelmed by a cloud of stale air. He held his breath the whole time he struggled into that mulletskin suit.

"What do you say?"

"Perfect. Now I'll bring you a white shirt, socks, and shoes."

"And a tie in a color that goes with it . . . No, wait. I've got the tie. The navy blue tie from the A. S. Roma team suit."

The shirt was made of cardboard. As were the shoes, for that matter. A badly rendered copy of a pair of Saxons, which they had imitated right down to the trademark that emblazoned the faux-leather insole: Sagsun.

Mimmo had a few things to say at the cash register.

"Nice piece of ass, eh?"

"You should have told me that was your woman. I came off looking like a dickhead."

"What are you talking about, 'my woman.' She's a temp. She's dating the owner's son. I screw her every once in a while."

"Now I feel worse. Okay, how much for this garbage?"

"Hey, Spa', now I'm going to get offended . . . this is guaranteed stuff."

"Guaranteed how long? Half a day? Anyway, tell me."

"Fifty euros for the lot."

"What about the discount?"

"I gave you the discount. I don't get it, you want this stuff for free?"

"I don't have any cash with me. Tell you what, I'll take it off your bill at the boxing gym. Go, magical A. S. Roma, Mimmo!"

And so the big day finally arrived. His big day. Spartaco Liberati climbed the steps up to the Campidoglio in the velvety light of seven in the evening, with setting sunlight that bathed the Palazzo dei Conservatori in pastel hues. He looked around. He spat out a fragment of lupine bean that had gotten stuck between his teeth.

Freedom of the press, sure. Independent journalism, my ass. The watchdog of liberty, yeah, yeah. The facts. What facts? The truth? My grandfather's ass: the only truth is what you get to say on the radio.

That healthy cynicism—*realism, re-a-li-sm*—gratified him. But yes, what mattered most in life was hitching your cart to the right guy. And when he'd given you what you needed, goodnight nurse. A kick in the ass and it's been good to know you. Another horse and another ride. And that hot air balloon, Malgradi, who did he think he was?

The Honorable couldn't imagine that with the Golden Pen he was about to slip into his breast pocket, he was going to be transformed from the red mullet he was into a shark. What, was there just one Honorable in Rome? And after all, how long could this Malgradi last? He had only one boss: Samurai.

He was on time. Around the statue of Marcus Aurelius, he noticed two Carabinieri in dress uniform flanking a general deep in conversation with Malgradi. A guy with a face as smooth and chubby as a toddler's ass, remarkably short and apparently bent under the weight of the stiff dress cap with a great deal of gold braid and the embroidered eagle of the joint command. On his chest was a battery of medals and ribbons, and on his arm was an elderly harridan dressed as a scarecrow. Surrounded by an entourage of rubberneckers, clearly there for the award ceremony, the youngest of whom was sixty.

He thought to himself: Where on earth am I? What is this? Did they evict everyone from the geriatric wing at San Giovanni's hospital? Now, you tell me!

With a wave of his hand, Malgradi gestured to Liberati, waving at the clock. It was time to go in.

The Hall of the Horatii and Curiatii rapidly filled up with the band of senile old men and teased-out witches who clearly cared nothing about him or the prize. All they cared about was the uniformed fireplug, Malgradi, and the mayor, who was standing in the middle of the great hall, planted there stiff as a stockfish next to a plexiglass podium with a narrow gooseneck microphone at the center. The mayor brushed the microphone with the palm of his hand.

"Good evening everyone, and thanks so much for being here tonight. Good evening to the civil and military authorities who have been so kind as to be with us tonight, and in particular His Excellency General Mario Rapisarda, commandant of the Custoza division of the Carabinieri Corps, whom I see here in the front row with his lovely lady by his side."

Oh, sure, call her a lady. Lucky you, if you can see that as a lady.

"In the name of the city I have the honor of presiding over as first citizen, I would like to welcome all of you to the first edition of the Golden Pen award, with which this year the city government of Rome intends to honor the most noble of professions, journalism, and one of its finest practitioners, namely Dottor Spartaco Liberati, the free, independent, and tireless voice of Radio FM 922. A nice round of applause, please."

Holding the A. S. Roma team necktie against his chest, Spartaco sketched out a bow as he rose from his seat, while the audience full of old people skinned their hands raw with clapping.

"Dottore, Dottore."

Why is he calling me Dottore? I didn't even go to college.

The mayor went back to the microphone.

"Of course, I could add a great many things, but I'll keep my own counsel and leave the details to the Honorable Pericle Malgradi, who has consented to grace us with his presence and who is the father of this prize, along with his foundation 'Back On Your Feet, Rome,' and the Association of Restaurateurs and Wine Purveyors. If you please, Your Honor . . . "

The mayor took a seat in the front row facing the podium. Malgradi cleared his throat.

"It is difficult, in this hall where the Treaty of Rome was signed in 1956, furnishing the cornerstone of the European Union, it is difficult to keep from thinking about just what the stroke of a pen can and cannot do. A word can unleash a war. A word can place the final seal upon a prosperous and lasting period of peace . . . "

General Rapisarda's wife leaned over and spoke into her husband's ear. This Malgradi was such a good speaker!

"It is difficult, observing in this hall the history of Rome as it is told to us through these seventeenth-century frescoes by the marvelous artist, Giuseppe Cesari, also known as the Cavalier D'Arpino, to think about what we would be if man wasn't the sum of what is passed down from generation to generation. Look now, let us look together."

Malgradi solemnly turned his gaze to the ceiling of the hall.

"The Discovery of the She-Wolf, the Battle against the Veientes and the Fidenates, the combat between the Horatii and the Curiatii."

Spartaco was rapt. He hadn't understood a single word of what Malgradi was saying. Baffling.

"Man has lived on news since the dawn of humanity. But

what is news? The Discovery of the She-Wolf is news. But is it also news to know who that she-wolf chose between Romulus and Remus? You may say to me: the Honorable is taking a long running start at this thing. But I reply: No! I tell you that it's about us, about our time, that I am talking. News is responsibility. That's right. Re-spon-si-bi-li-ty. There are those who say that there is no news, there is no journalism unless there's a *scoop. Scoop.* That's an English word, just like the English word *gossip*, like the Italian *pettegolezzo*. A treacherous word. *Scoop* means 'to dig.' That's right, to dig. And what are they looking for, those who dig? They're only looking for garbage, my dear friends, ladies and gentlemen. They're looking for muck. Those who dig are rummaging through the things that people have chosen to forget for the good of one and all. Those who dig are seeking to discredit their innocent victims. Journalism is something else. It's responsibility as truth. Remember that. Responsibility as truth. That is the motto that I have chosen for my prize, the engraving on the 24-karat solid gold fountain pen that our friends from the Association of Restaurateurs and Wine Purveyors are awarding today to Spartaco Liberati for the luminous testimonial he has provided for this approach to his chosen profession. Thank you."

The various arthritics struggled to their feet, in a prolonged burst of applause, while Spartaco, obediently, limited himself to a thank you. To the hasty photo pose with the mayor and the clamshell case containing the check and the pen that he insisted on pushing into his hands. A horrendous gold-plated suppository with a cap—*what 24-karat solid gold, fuck you and your ancestors, this thing was made in China!*

Then a small brigade of municipal envoys in livery materialized, wearing white gloves and circulating with gigantic silver-plated pewter trays that, hoisted high in a carefully studied and adroitly synchronized movement, revealed to the watery eyes of that audience of diabetics towering stacks of tea sandwiches as imposing as Mayan tombs, buffalo mozzarellas from Caserta, made by the Saverio Viglione & Sons cheese-works, spicy *'nduja* pork sausage, and compositions of stuffed mignon panini.

Spartaco put up with the monarchistic litany that one of the horrendous harridans who had witnessed the ceremony was inflicting upon him; she had introduced herself as the Baroness Farneti, last-born daughter of an officer of the royal guard of Humbert II of Savoy, "the King of May, as you'll remember . . . "

He was convinced, as far as that went, that only by putting up with Belfagor the Demon would he be able to obtain the cell phone number of the only halfway decent woman there that evening. The granddaughter who had accompanied the Baroness there tonight. A cute blonde denizen of the opulent Parioli quarter, dressed like a nun, but with the smirk of a girl who knew more than she was saying, and a tiny heart tattooed on the inside of her wrist.

"You know, Dottore, my little girl would so like to become a journalist. And maybe a person like yourself could serve to break her in."

From where he stood, Spartaco noticed how Malgradi and Rapisarda were deep in consultation, standing in the shelter of one of the hall's three great, carved walnut-wood doors. And once again, he was struck by the air of extreme familiarity that the two men were displaying. It was not some mistaken impression.

Rapisarda was a Calabrian from Reggio, about sixty. His father had been a companion of schooltime snacks and later, of dubious clientelism, with Malgradi's father. Both of them Fascists, both of them baronial powermongers at the university school of medicine. The sons grew up together. And then went on to follow different paths in life. So to speak. Malgradi had worked his way across the entire political spectrum, managing to leap onto the winner's bandwagon only seconds before the catastrophe.

Mario Rapisarda had made his career by fancy footwork in the halls of power. By immediately learning a basic lesson: Right-wing, left-wing, it made no difference, as long as there was a payoff. Even though he had never stopped fostering, in his heart of hearts, an anthropological and, at the same time, aesthetic anti-Communism, in line with what his father had taught him. As a freshly appointed second lieutenant in Naples, he had learned that there was a thin line that ran between the arrest of a Camorrista and a ticket for a grandstand seat at the Stadio San Paolo for a city commissioner or councilman, and that that line marked the difference between the obscurity of a brief entry in the crime pages and the dazzling and concrete experience of ten, or a hundred clean, sweet-smelling hands to clasp in less than two hours. As a result, first as a major and later as a colonel, he had feathered his nest in Rome, thanks to his marriage to the daughter of an Undersecretary of Defense. A woman who was ugly as sin, but as useful as a life insurance policy. He had worked his way through the schools, the logistics units, the exhausting social minuets in the drawing rooms that count. Thanks to all this, he had become the unfailing protagonist, the perennial guest of every television talk show about crime.

At general headquarters he was a punchline. "The Carabiniere on Horseback," they called him. But he didn't give a damn about those pathetic losers. Undaunted, he would pontificate before audiences of cosmetically enhanced women, stick figures, bee-stung lips, and botoxed dowagers, concerning scenes of the crime, weapons, and motives—all of them topics he had never bothered to learn the first thing about. But that's where junior officers came in useful, the ones who were working out on the street.

Now they were together once again, he and Malgradi.

Where destiny had fated them to be. But both of them, the one and the other, lacked a final step to their career. Malgradi dreamed of becoming a cabinet minister, Rapisarda dreamed of becoming a commanding general. They could help each other out.

Spartaco had finally gotten rid of the demon Belfagor and now he could smell the whiff of lily of the valley from the young granddaughter who was jotting down her cell phone number on the palm of his hand with the Chinese pen. He went back to observing Malgradi and Rapisarda.

The Honorable was gesticulating with a certain emphasis. The general was nodding with a worried gaze, running his hand from time to time over his greasy combover.

Spartaco tried to figure out what the two men were saying to each other.

"You follow what I'm saying, I hope, General. This return to the city might prove to be a serious problem. I'd say even a source of embarrassment for the Carabinieri as a corps, in fact."

"That Malatesta is a good cop, but maybe a little overenergetic. Don't worry, Your Honor."

Malgradi took his leave of Rapisarda, walked a few steps, and dragged Liberati over to the far side of the hall.

"Now you listen to me, and listen good. You've taken the prize, you've taken the money. Now do what you've been told to do. Start that campaign on the radio. And hit it good and hard. The way you know how to do when you have a good topic. Don't make me sorry I did this. Is that clear?"

## XXIII

S amurai was proceeding slowly in the direction of Ostia. He planned to arrive right as the ceremony he had no desire to attend was drawing to a close. Sitting at his side, silent as always, was Max. Diligently puttering along in the endless lines of deep-summer traffic, they were listening to *Soccer on the Brain*, the radio show that had made that sewer rat Spartaco Liberati famous in the Roman demimonde.

Well then, dear radio audience, we are presented with yet another left-wing mystification. The violent death of an immigrant in Cinecittà turns into another opportunity to shout about the Mafia. What Mafia? What are they yammering about? A bloody settling of accounts among foreigners—which is what we're talking about until proven otherwise—and what do they go and turn it into? An execution, a burgeoning gang war. Gangs? What gangs? Do you want to get it through your heads that Dandi, Freddo, and Libano are dead and buried? It's over and done with! *Fi-ni-to!* Is that clear?

Spartaco knew what he was doing, Samurai had to admit. The disinformation campaign had begun and was going great guns.

And yet there is a but, unfortunately. And here I really am left speechless. There's some girl in Cinecittà who's called Savelli. The first name is Alice, I think. A *zecca*, just to be clear. Well, you know what she's dreamed up? She's decided to go around slandering half the neighborhood. Respectable people. And the incredible thing is that the Carabinieri are letting her do it. Do we see what this is the prelude to? The Communists defame, and the Carabinieri stand by and watch. How could that be? My friends, if you'll just be patient, you'll see that yours truly is going to get to the bottom of this story. And it strikes me that when I do, we'll all have a good long laugh. Ah, yes. And now, R.E.M. with *Leaving New York*.

Here, Samurai thought to himself, Spartaco was slightly off target. He explained to Max that, from what he'd been able to figure out, Alice Savelli couldn't technically be described as a "Communist." If anything, one of those confused idealists who nattered on and on about changing the world without bothering to take reality into account. People like Samurai considered them so many medieval millenarianists. Utopians dreaming of a world without banks or bosses, where there's no left and no right, a flat gray wasteland devoid of beauty where all that matters was that insipid title, *citizen*, which meant everything and nothing. It was citizens who condemned Socrates to drink the hemlock, and it was citizens who chose—by a majority vote, actually—between the prophet Christ and the thief Barabbas, opting for the latter. What offended him about these people was the total absence of any aristocratic impulse, whatsoever. In a certain sense, it was the flip side of the coin from Number Eight and all the other street thugs: primitive elements that had to be maneuvered, in the best cases, and almost always eliminated, eventually. Nonetheless, they grew in number at an unsettling pace. Their rejection of the old political order was taking root. Among their ranks, there were also recycled reds. As proponents, in any case, of a strong ideology, they were bound to succumb to herd mentality. Samurai foresaw a phase of convulsions with outcomes that were, in any case, predictable. All moderation was bound to be swept away by the impetuous gusting winds of the conflict. And in the end, the final showdown would be between us and them. For that very reason, he'd started to think again, after so many years, in terms of "us." And from time to time he had again started teaching the young men whom Luca gathered in his restaurant, Il Tatami. Still, this wasn't a rekindling of his old love for a cause long since dead and buried. It was just a precautionary measure before the ineluctable battle. A form of preventive, legitimate self-defense. His ideas were clear, indeed, far too clear. For that reason, his ties with the millenarianist Alice Savelli needed to be nipped in the bud. For the moment, their countermeasures had proven effective and Malatesta had been neutralized. But the ensuing peace was too precarious. They had to move quickly. Malgradi had to take steps.

The music faded into a commercial break and the first few houses of Ostia appeared on the horizon.

The parking area in front of the church of St. Mary Queen of Peace was overflowing with good citizens. Mixed in with the crowd, the punks from Ponente that Denis had disguised as legionaries stood out in particular. Their name, too, the Cavaliers of Constantine, had been Denis's idea. He thus showed that he'd actually read a book or two in his lifetime.

Number Eight, for once dressed like a Christian, in a cream-colored three-piece suit with a pearl-gray vest and white shoes, threw his arms around Denis in a burst of enthusiasm.

"Hey Denis, there are ten thousand of us, hey-ho, hey-ho! We're the curve of the Stadio Olimpico. Everyone has to see that we're in charge around here! In fact, I'm in charge!"

Denis nodded. For once that dickhead had it right. Monsignor Tempesta had called for a solemn *Te Deum* "so that peace might return, reigning over the tortured lands of Ostia," but the real meaning of that ceremony was unequivocal: around here, we're in charge, and now the war is over.

The bishop appeared on the church courtyard and started showering benedictions on the crowd.

"Hey, Denis, we're making a movie here, Denis."

But Denis had hurried away in haste and fury. Number Eight saw Denis cut through the crowd, which withdrew respectfully as he appeared, to deliver to the monsignor a large sword with "The Cavaliers of Constantine" engraved on the blade.

In short, a triumph.

Number Eight smoked an indeterminate number of cigarettes while waiting for the crowd to thin out, and then, at a gesture from the Honorable Malgradi, he walked over to the knot of people at the center of the piazza where Tempesta enjoyed pride of place. With him were not only Malgradi, but also Benedetto Umiltà and Denis.

"Your Excellency, let me introduce you to Cesare Adami. The pride of Ostia, if I may say so. Living proof that the sins of the fathers do not and cannot fall upon the sons. A pillar of the community."

Number Eight smiled. The bishop undressed him with his eyes, then extended his hand with the ring—*jeez, what a sparkler!*

"So tell me, my son, are you truly a believer, and I mean deep down?"

"Your Excellency, let's just say that I know exactly how deep and how down priests can be."

Malgradi rolled his eyes in vexation. But the bishop cut the tension with a burst of frank laughter, in which the Honorable joined after a moment's hesitation. Denis locked arms with Number Eight and led him away.

"I see that hilarity reigns sovereign here today," said an icy voice, from behind them.

The bishop and Malgradi turned suddenly serious. Samurai and Max took a step forward.

"Even though I don't see any reasons for being so cheerful, do I, Your Honor?"

Pericle Malgradi ran a hand over his forehead, suddenly aware of the atrocious heat of that summer morning.

"I'll take that as a joke."

"It might be more accurate to call it an observation," threw in Samurai, lunging for the kill.

"I'm doing everything I can."

"Really?"

"The regional government has approved the housing plan, now it's just the municipal government that needs to move forward with the variant on the zoning plan."

"That's what I'm talking about. The whole thing is blocked."

"I don't understand."

Samurai swiveled to speak to Monsignor Tempesta, intentionally turning his back on Malgradi: his physical gestures were meant to help make the humiliation more effective.

"You must forgive me and you must forgive us, Your Excellency, but I'm accustomed to keeping faith with my word as given. And I made you some promises."

The regional zoning plan allowed for the possibility, in the quadrant between EUR and Ostia, of multiplying the existing cubic footage in terms of built or permitted structures to a level at least five times greater than the limits established by the zoning restrictions. There was one condition: That for every 700,000 cubic feet a house of worship is built. That was the *benefit* for the area beyond the Tiber that they had discussed during their dinner at La Paranza and that had so delighted the fellow diners. They had decided to rebaptize the "housing plan," calling it instead the "churching plan." That was the single crucial reason why Monsignor Tempesta and his little boyfriend Benedetto Umiltà were members of the crew. The deal was clear. The churching plan, along with the allied primary urban planning works that accompanied it—roads, lighting, water, natural gas—would open the door for Waterfront and social housing. But in fact, what was crucial was the variant to the city zoning plan that Malgradi had taken for granted, but which now clearly wasn't quite as obvious a thing as it had seemed.

Tempesta turned conciliatory. And he set out, in a comforting, mellifluous tone, to soften Samurai.

"You see, Dottore, I have appreciated and I continue to admire your pragmatic approach. But if I can say a word on behalf of a more measured attitude, I don't want to believe that our friend the Honorable has kindled flames of hope in our hearts so powerful that, how shall I put this . . . he remains unaware of the catastrophe that he would face if he were to fail to live up to our expectations. Am I right, Your Honor?"

Pericle Malgradi nodded like a primary school pupil whom the teacher has just given an extra question, a second chance. Tempesta went on.

"Let me add something. I'm so convinced that things will right themselves that just yesterday I had a conversation with my friends at the IOR, and they assured me of the utmost collaboration on the financial aspects of the project."

Tempesta handed Samurai a business card on which were printed the names and phone numbers of the executives with whom he would be talking in the Bastion of Nicholas V, the historic headquarters of the Vatican bank, the IOR. A crucial step. The IOR was needed to disguise and launder the cash that was going to be pumped into the project by Perri, Viglione, the Anacleti clan, and Samurai himself. Once safely in the Vatican, that frightfully huge mass of liquidity which had to be invested—more than five hundred million euros, according to their prudent estimate—would flow back into the transparent circuit of two of the largest credit institutes in the country, to finance Waterfront and social housing, just as spring water feeds a mountain stream.

The monsignor lunged in with a move that no one was expecting.

"Actually, gentlemen, I wonder and I ask you whether our concerns shouldn't be factors other than the timing of a vote in the city council. I see too much unacceptable violence. And I wonder whether mankind can ever hope to build anything upon the rubble of death. What happiness can we evince in such grim and frightful darkness? I wonder whether it is within your power to disperse such a bewildering fog."

Samurai felt a stab of pain to his hypothalamus. Taking a scolding from the bishop was too much even for him. Perhaps he should have been tougher on the Anacletis and Number Eight that afternoon.

Max seized the moment and broke in.

"Your Excellency, allow me to put in a word. We haven't met, but I believe that . . . "

Tempesta smiled and nodded, as if he already knew all about him. Encouraged, Max went on.

"Well, Your Excellency, I can tell you that the fog will disappear. I can guarantee it personally. People from the street only know the language of the street. And the language of the street, no matter how hard I try, is my language."

Magnificent. He hadn't been wrong about that young man, Samurai decided. Tempesta had challenged him, hurling him down from his pedestal to the miseries of the street. And Max, without needing to be asked, had taken on the burden of those miseries. Max's words had put the bishop back in his place. Or perhaps, he should say, they had put matters back in their place. Everyone involved in this matter, quite simply, would take care of what lay within their purview. Enough said.

Tempesta underscored that message with a hieratical gesture of benediction.

That same evening, Max and Farideh made love for the first time.

He had introduced himself a couple of weeks earlier, walking up to her as she was translating Persian poets, seated at a table at the Caffè Necci, in Pigneto.

He had told her everything that could be revealed about himself. They'd gone out for a while. They'd held hands. There had been a few chaste kisses. He was hooked. Practically overwrought. He desired her. But he also wanted to protect her. Stay with her. And change his life. As if that were still possible.

He suggested they go to the beach at night. She agreed.

He took her to the outskirts of Capocotta. Seated on the raised back seat of his Triumph Street Triple, like the heroine of a Manga cartoon, Farideh wrapped her arms around Max ecstatically. She was convinced that she knew everything about that strange young man who had suddenly become part of her life. After all this time, she was finally happy. Blindly, instinctively happy.

Under a moonless sky and in a windless night, the sea was one vast black patch. Still as petroleum. They sat on a dune, remaining in silence for a while. Until Max finally burst the bubble.

"I was right, wasn't I? It's beautiful, don't you think?"

"You're not tricking me, are you?"

"What are you talking about?"

"Are you what you seem to be?"

"Why would you ask me that?"

"Because, after what happened to my father, I've lost all trust. All that violence . . . "

Max felt guilty. He held her close.

"Violence is a part of life, Farideh. A philosopher once said that even philosophy is violence, and suffering. Because it isn't possible to think decently without causing yourself pain."

"But you'll never hurt me, will you?"

Max ran the forefinger of his right hand over her lips. Slowly. He kissed her. And he kept on kissing her until she relaxed in his arms.

And while he was inside her, he heard her repeat one last time the question that had made his brain explode.

"You'll never hurt me, will you?"

# XXIV

Sebastiano Laurenti, the orphaned son of the engineer who had killed himself, started working at Luxury Cars, at kilometer marker 13 on Via Salaria. It was a car dealership owned by Scipione Scacchia, one of the Three Little Pigs. His job consisted of handling the official bookkeeping and accounting, which concerned the purchase and sale of clean vehicles. All the rest—that is, the shylocking, the family's principal and most profitable business—was handled by Scipione personally. When necessary, Sebastiano was to fill in as a salesman. That happened when they had to handle customers of a certain level, for the most part professionals, soccer players, people in show business. In those situations, Manfredi, the old man's son, lost the roguish confidence that he loved to show off as if it were a trademark of sorts. Prospective customers were left aghast by Manfredi's ceremonious unctuousness, as he shrilled out favorable prices in a querulous voice. Many of them dropped the discussion entirely midway through, revolted by a handshake that thought it was hale and hearty but which, in reality, translated into a slimy contact.

"Study, that's what you ought to do," old man Scipione admonished his son wisely, "this isn't your field. Let the young engineer do it, it's clear he's got a feel for it."

Yes, certainly, Sebastiano had a way about him. He spoke the same language as those arrogant assholes, they got along famously, he was able to obtain the most favorable treatment and terms, business was going swimmingly, and so on, and so forth. Still, though, it gnawed at Manfredi. He didn't want the role of heir apparent, the rich kid who had grown up in the lap of luxury. He had much grander ambitions. One day, that dealership would belong to him, as would everything else. But in the meantime, he didn't want to sit idle. And so, when Sebastiano was working a client of that sort, Manfredi would stay close, studying his methods, making an effort to imitate his gestures, memorizing phrases and intonations. He felt a little sorry for him, of course—that young man with such great expectations who had once had the world in his hands but now was left with nothing. But that pity wasn't entirely separate from a certain feral pride: Sebastiano would always be indebted to him, because without Manfredi's help he would be homeless. Sebastiano had to live up to the gift he had been given.

In any case, yes, Manfredi still had a great deal to learn.

And so, toward the end of the month, he moved into the penthouse on Via Chinotto, technically still the residence of the sole survivor of the Laurenti family but actually already the property of Sor Scipione, and before two weeks were up he wound up in bed with Chicca, the little sweetheart who was sick and tired of being the girlfriend of a loser like Sebastiano. Poor girl: it wasn't her fault if her boyfriend was now penniless and the trip to Alaska had had to be postponed.

Old man Scipione disapproved.

"You've overdone it, Manfre'. And a girl who puts out like that, in such a hurry, is at the very least a slut."

"It's not like I have to marry her, is it?"

"Be careful. Women bring trouble and nothing but."

What Scipione was trying to say was that stirring Sebastiano's resentment hadn't been a very smart move. There could be dangerous consequences. The young man might begin to nurture a lurking rancor that could easily explode someday. He might as well just strip him of everything he owned, and do it immediately, without indulging in this farce of a friendship that, deep down, was no good to anyone.

"Trust me on this one, son. That guy hates you!"

"Hey Dad, he's already gotten over it, believe me."

"I'm going to get rid of him, Manfre'."

"That's out of the question. Sebastiano is a friend of mine."

"He's a friend and you screwed his girlfriend. Just think how you'd feel about him: and what would you do in that case, wouldn't you stab him when you got a chance?"

Scipione, still full of doubts, took Sebastiano out to eat at La Paranza. The young man practically left his food untasted.

"Go on, eat something, you're skinny as a rail!"

"I'm not much of an eater, Signor Scipione."

"But you don't know what you're missing! Tito Maggio may be a piece of shit, and I can guarantee to you that he is one, but put him in front of the burners and he's an artist!"

Still, he'd emerged from that dinner feeling reassured. Sebastiano didn't really give a damn about the fact that his son was sleeping with his former girlfriend. That was an old story, buried now, Sebastiano had explained as he poked at a carrot and the old man gorged on roasted amberjack, we're still good friends. Understandable. The young man wasn't a member of the circle, the kind of guy that was capable of stringing you up over a piece of ass. He was born rich, and that's the way it is among those people: you slept with my girlfriend? Well who gives a damn. We can still be close friends. You can lose your money, but good manners stick to you like the plastic upholstery covers in a brand new SUV. So long as they don't stick to your ass when you stand up!

Scipione let loose a filthy raucous laugh of self-satisfaction. A fishbone went down the wrong way. He started to cough and splutter. Imperturbable, Sebastiano handed him a chunk of bread, waited for the old man to chew and swallow it, and once the coughing stopped delivered a formidable slap to the man's back. No more coughing. Scipione appreciated it. He dismissed with an impatient gesture a worried Tito Maggio who had rushed over to help, and promised the young man a raise.

If Manfredi wanted to have some fun with the engineer's son, he had the green light. As far as he was concerned, the matter was closed.

Then he asked Sebastiano to drive him over to the gas station on Via Anagnina, where they picked up a tranny, and he treated himself to a fitting conclusion to the evening.

Sebastiano declined Scipione's generous offer to partake, waited for the old man to get dressed, took him home, parked the SUV in the garage, and went off to sleep in his rented room on Via Rodi, not far from his old family home. A reminder that they had robbed him of his life.

And they would pay. Sooner or later, they'd pay. In the meantime, in the solitude of his narrow room, Sebastiano was training himself in the school of hatred. He realized that he'd be able to learn a great deal from old man Scipione.

## XXV

Rocco Anacleti was waiting, sitting at the corner table in the Ikea restaurant, in his home neighborhood of Romanina. He hated it. He hated the colorful, cheap lamps. He hated those who flocked to the place like it was some temple erected to the god of consumption, he hated the meatballs with the lingonberry sauce that an impertinent waitress had served him so rudely. But most of all, he hated to wait.

Terenzi never changed. He still hadn't understood that when a matter was urgent, he had to move his ass. Right away.

He was just on the verge of leaving when, even before he saw him with a bowl of spaghetti with tomato sauce on a tray, he recognized the whiff of two-bit cologne in which he must bathe every morning. The marshal was in plainclothes. As he was every time they were forced to meet in person.

Terenzi sat down alone at the table next to Anacleti's. He loosened his tie. He tucked the paper napkin into his shirt collar and leaned forward over the plate of pasta.

"You finally made it, Marshal."

"I had to take care of something."

"There's just one thing you need to take care of, before I get royally pissed off."

"What's that?"

"The vans that deliver the caregivers."

"Since when have you given a fuck about the caregivers?"

"I'll ask the questions. You're not paid to be curious."

"What do you want to know?"

"If there's an investigation."

"Into the caregivers?"

"If you sit backward on a horse, that horse will always be backward," Rocco sighed, in Romansh.

As usual, Terenzi stared at him with a stunned expression. And as usual, Anacleti translated after his fashion.

"Sorry, I meant to say . . . find out if they're looking into the movement of the delivery vans."

"I'll try."

"'I'll try isn't enough. 'I'll tell you tomorrow' already works a lot better."

"It won't be easy."

Anacleti stood up from the table and leaned over close to Terenzi's ear.

"I don't give a flying fuck whether or not it will be easy. Those two Brazilian hookers you beat up the other day? I had to take them into the emergency room myself. Fucking maniac."

Anacleti headed over to the restaurant's cash registers. And Private Brandolin instinctively turned away, hurrying over to the vacuum-packed herring counter.

They hadn't seen him. Neither Anacleti nor Terenzi. He waited until first the one then the other vanished into the crowd at the exit. He pulled out his cornflower blue Nokia. The one with the oversized numbers and keys that his mother had given him the day he took the oath, forgetting to tell them at the phone store that the cell phone was for her son and not for her.

"Colonel Malatesta?"

"Brandolin. What's going on?"

"I'm at Ikea."

"Should that be of any interest to me?"

"I was looking for a set of recycling bins, and came over after the end of my shift."

"Christ, Brandolin."

"Forgive me, Colonel. The bins are just a pretext. Truth be told, I came to Ikea with Terenzi."

"Have you made friends?"

A horrified whimper, an almost animal lament, came from the earpiece, triggering an immediate sense of guilt in Malatesta.

"Sorry, kid, it was just a joke. Come on, tell me the rest."

"Terenzi had a meeting with Rocco Anacleti."

"What kind of a meeting?"

"Terenzi came in. Anacleti was sitting at the restaurant. He was waiting for him. They talked for a while. Heads together, busy busy."

"Could you understand what about?"

"No. I was terrified that Terenzi might see me."

"He didn't see you, did he?"

"No."

"And did you really need a set of recycling bins?"

"Yessir."

"Buy the most expensive kind. Consider them a gift from me, Brandolin."

"At your orders, sir."

Marco set his cell phone down on the wooden folding table that occupied the tiny space between the two lounge chairs in the first row on the *playa grande* of the Hotel Formentor. Now it was a matter of breaking it as gently as possible to Carmen. Explain the situation to her without hurting her feelings.

"Carmen, I have something to tell you."

The lovely Catalonian blonde with whom he had, so to speak, established a bond over those unforgettable ten days on Palma didn't even look up from the latest novel by Javier Marías.

"You going back home, *caballero*? That's no surprise. It's not like we were going to get married."

The little speech he was planning to improvise stuck in his throat now. He found himself grinning like an idiot, once again admiring the endless surprises that were women. With a hint of uneasiness he couldn't exactly pin down: certainly, this hadn't been the love of his life, but what the hell, with all this looseness in relations between the sexes . . . It's true, men had been acting this way for millennia. The new development was that now women were doing the same thing. He wasn't sure how well he liked this new development. He ought to talk about it with Alice. But his thoughts were elsewhere. The phone call from Brandolin was the signal that he'd been waiting for.

Something was starting to stir.

And soon they'd be seeing the effects of it.

The defensive phase was coming to an end.

This was the time for a counterattack.

He'd have to start with a series of little steps.

In the meantime, he'd have to go back to Rome.

Then gather information. Aggregate data. Arrange for discreet surveillance systems. Focus his intelligence. Lay out the nets and yank them in only at the right time.

The game was starting up again. Just as he'd expected.

He bid Carmen farewell with a kiss, he boarded the evening's last flight on a very expensive first-class ticket and, the minute they set down at Fiumicino, he fired off a text to Thierry: "Phase Two: urgently need line of support."

# XXVI

Rocco Anacleti summoned Paja and Fieno to come meet him at the Casilino 900, where the city washed up against the beltway. He had a chop shop there, to convert stolen cars and motorbikes into marketable spare parts for the black market in such things. Another flourishing business that was a part of his empire, and as ancient as the noble art imparted to him by his grandfather, the art of stealing.

Rocco Anacleti arrived in the industrial shed slightly ahead of schedule. And there to welcome him was Zorro in his grease-stained mechanic's overalls. He was a Croatian in his early forties, and his real name was Vilim. Too complicated, too hard to say, he had thought when he first met him, newly arrived in Cinecittà after the end of the civil war in the Balkans. A better name was "Zorro," which if nothing else was a perfect description of the horrible ragged scar that ran the entire length of his upper lip, to the base of the nose. A souvenir bestowed upon him by a Serbian knife blade, during an interrogation session. Silent as the masked man, right? And for a job like the one he was doing in this industrial shed, silence was a fundamental prerequisite. He paid him a fortune by the standards of the sector, fifteen hundred euros a week. But his generosity had purchased the man's loyalty and, with the passage of time, the two men had even become fond of each other. Even though Anacleti knew that, like any wounded beast, one day Zorro too would turn explosively savage.

Anacleti acted out an embrace, taking care not to get dirty.

"Everything all right?"

Zorro pointed to the skeleton of a BMW Adventure GS 1200 in a corner of the shed.

"I was just finishing that one there. I still need to pound out the frame. This week went well. It's the fifth one we've chopped in three days. And we still have lots of orders. We're a little behind with the cars."

"How far behind?"

"I have two Jeep Grand Cherokees and a Nissan Qashqai that have been here for a week. I need to get busy."

"All is good, then."

"Not really, boss. There's the usual problem."

"Which is?"

"That filthy pig Dottor Renato came by. He said that the shit we're giving him isn't enough anymore."

Renato Festa was a tick who worked at the Department of Motor Vehicles. A guy in his early forties that Anacleti had gotten to know at the Ferro di Cavallo, where he normally purchased his five grams of coke for the weekend. He had soon realized that the man was in rags because of the cost of his unfortunate habit, and in the end the exchange struck him as obvious at the very least. For his weekend coke blizzards, free-of-cost, and for the occasional extra, like the trannies that Anacleti would send around to see him at his home every first Tuesday of the month, Festa would slip Zorro the spread sheets of newly registered SUVs and superbikes, complete with license plate, name, and address of the owner. And Zorro would send a couple of pint-sized acrobats who used to work in a circus in Zagreb to pay a visit to those apartments. Two artists capable of climbing up any cornice and squirming through even the narrowest grates of any french window. After all, with the new generation of anti-theft devices, the only way to steal cars and motorcycles was with their actual keys. And you had to get into the owner's home to get them.

Anacleti pretended he hadn't quite understood what Zorro had just said.

"The shit's not enough? Is that what the little motherfucker said?"

"That's what he said."

"Then you take care of it. In your fashion."

"I'll mix up some acid. I love to watch an asshole's face sizzle."

The Croatian's raucous laughter brought a nod of approval from Rocco Anacleti. He liked Vilim. A lot. And one day—he felt certain—Vilim too would rise at his side through the family's hierarchy. And Vilim would become his lieutenant. Like Paja, Fieno, and Max. For that matter, the contamination of gypsy blood with what the street had to offer had transformed a band of thieves and Fascist hitters confined to that corner of the Romanina quarter into a heavy crew. These days there was no counting the lines of tough kids hoping for jobs as couriers or lookouts for the narcotics trade. And the Saturday night brawls between punks in their early twenties in the clubs of the southeastern quadrant of the city had become a gymnasium where you could go any time you pleased to select the young blood that would flow into the ranks of the armies that now effectively conquered the opposition of even the fiercest soldiers in town. How many of them were there? A hundred, a hundred fifty, he would have guessed. And the fact that he'd lost count only made him proud.

The laughter of Paja and Fieno made Rocco Anacleti swing around, jostling him out of his thoughts. They'd arrived.

"What the fuck do you have to laugh about?"

The two men apologized and stood, arms folded, a stance they assumed when they knew they were about to be given orders.

"Now listen to me, and listen good. I want you to go to that

fucking Iranian's workshop and put this down on his table."
Anacleti pulled a wad of bills in different denominations out of
his pocket. Hundred-euro notes, fifty-euro notes, twenty-euro
notes. "I don't even know how much this is. Definitely more
than the thousand euros that beggar was pestering me for. Give
him the money, tell him that this is from me, and this marks the
end of it. That if they ask him about it, he has to deny everything. No, wait, even better, tell him that he has to go in to see
the Carabinieri, and tell them that nothing happened at all. Is
that clear?"

As always, Paja couldn't restrain himself.

"Why?"

"Why, what?"

"Why can't he just go without us giving him all these euros?
I can convince him without the cash."

"Paja, you know something? I can't stand to look at you
anymore. Do what you're told or I swear, as God is my witness,
if I hear you ask just one more question, I'll crack your ass
open with my own hands."

The two men spun on their heels in unison, like a pair of
cops, and then screeched out of there in their black BMW
toward the Tuscolano quarter, Via del Casale Ferranti, the *zammammero*'s workshop.

In spite of the wheelchair, Farideh had agreed to accom-
pany him every morning to his workshop, where Abbas
remained alone for hours until his daughter came back to get
him. Seated, virtually immobile. In contemplation of everything that his hands would remain unable to do for many
months yet to come. Or maybe never again. They had already
operated on him twice to reduce thirty or so fractures and
insert the first of two pairs of titanium plates that—according
to the doctors—would never restore the sensitivity of his hands,
but might at least give him back that smidgen of mobility

necessary to put food in his mouth, get dressed in the morning, get undressed at night.

Paja and Fieno walked in on him while he was deep in the study of an album of sketches by his grandfather.

"*Buongiorno*, can I help you?"

The two of them hadn't seen the old man since that night. And the courteous nature of that greeting caught them off guard. What, was the old man sick in the head?

Fieno did the talking, because of the two he was the one whose voice Abbas hadn't heard the night of the punitive expedition.

"These are for you."

He tossed the wad of cash on his workbench, under Abbas's inquisitive eyes; those eyes immediately filled with tears, while a sudden tremor started shaking his body.

"Don't worry, old man. It's all over."

Abbas nodded. Mechanically and repeatedly. As if an electric discharge was jolting through him. Incapable of uttering a single word. While a jet of urine drenched the crotch of his trousers. Fieno went on.

"There's just one last thing you have to do. Get someone to take you in to see the Carabinieri, and tear up that sheet of paper you signed. You'll do that, won't you?"

Without bothering to wait for the answer they took for granted, the two men left him in his filth and with that wad of cash he could look at, but couldn't even hold in his hands.

On his way out of the workshop, Fieno touched a couple of ebony miniatures.

"These little dolls are nice. Do you make them?"

How many hours went by after that, Abbas couldn't have said. But when Farideh arrived in the workshop, she found him just as Paja and Fieno had left him. First she stared at him, then at the money on the workbench. She raised a hand to her mouth and started weeping. At first quietly, then sobbing in despair. Without the strength to get closer to her father and put her arms around him, her father who reeked of sweat and urine and who was sobbing like she was.

There was no need to explain anything to his little girl. Farideh had understood. And now, he, her father, had to decide.

"Don't do it, Papa. Don't accept."

Abbas shut his eyes, and his memory of the night when he had seen Teheran for the last time, thirty years ago, became clearer. He felt the eyes of the two *pasdaran* in khaki jumpsuits on him, at the airport border checkpoint. He saw once again the hairy hands of the elder of the two. The man was turning over and over in his hands the passport that a cousin in the revolutionary council had miraculously managed to obtain for him. It said that he was a newly graduated student traveling to Rome for a semester of specialized studies at the medical school there. The pasdar had shut the document and then he had looked at his hands gripping the handle of his suitcase. His entire life was in that suitcase, along with the savings in foreign banknotes that his father and mother had entrusted to him, in a final act of protection. Two thousand dollars.

"And you're supposed to be a doctor?"

Abbas had nodded.

"What kind of a doctor?"

"Surgeon," he had muttered, betraying the trembling of his lips.

"With those hands? You're a surgeon and you have those hands?"

He'd shut his eyes. It's impossible to rub away the calluses from working with chisels and woodcarving knives. The pasdar had repeated the question.

"With those hands?"

They'd dragged him into a dirty little windowless room. They'd made him open his suitcase.

"Dollars. Congratulations to our talented little surgeon with his golden hands. You know you could be hanged for this, doctor. You know that?"

The two *pasdaran* had split the banknotes in uneven shares. Fifteen hundred to the older man, the rest to the younger.

They'd given in when he begged them.

"Please, please, just take the money."

Abbas opened his eyes again. Farideh was still standing motionless in front of him. She'd stopped sobbing. Now the tears were running down her cheeks, gathering in large welling drops on her chin.

Thirty years ago, he'd allowed himself to be humiliated by his jailers. He'd purchased his freedom for two thousand dollars. That same freedom that had brought him, first, a new homeland, and then the joy of the marvelous creature now sitting across from him. That roll of euros from the Anacletis wasn't really all that different from the dollars he'd handed over to the *pasdaran*, after all. His daughter's life and serenity were worth another humiliation in the face of his latest tormentors. Even at the cost of her contempt. One day, she too would understand.

"Farideh, please, put that money in my pocket and take me to see the Carabinieri."

# XXVII

The morning following his return to Rome, a furious burst of ringing from his doorbell caught Marco off guard in the middle of one of his recurring dreams. He was in a green meadow, densely carpeted with tiny white blossoms, and lots of little dogs with brown spots were frolicking around him, chasing each other happily, blithely indifferent to the troubles of the world. According to the female psychologist from Seattle he'd spent a few days with, between conferences at the 1999 World Social Forum, that dream was an indication of some deeply buried yearning for innocence. Maybe there was some truth to that, but the fact remains that whenever he bent over to pet the puppies, they disappeared as if by magic, leaving him in the throes of a melancholy sense of abandonment. As for the psychologist, their love story had come to a brusque end. Largely because, in the face of her impassioned attempt to analyze him, he had retorted with a sarcastic and exquisitely Roman, "And who gives a fuck!"

In any case, it was a little past nine.

Who could be looking for him at that time of the day?

General Thierry, maybe?

But for the general Sundays were sacred. It couldn't be him. Unless something serious had happened.

He grabbed the Beretta lying in plain view on the nightstand and walked toward the front door.

"Yes?"

"Ah, you're here. It's Alice. Open up. I need to talk to you."

Alice. Only then did he realize that he was completely naked.

"But how did you find out where I live?" he asked, stalling for time, as he struggled with the first item of clothing he had been able to lay hands on, a tattered terrycloth bathrobe that had once been red but now verged on an unsettling drab pink.

"You gave me your card, Sherlock!" she retorted drily.

He opened the door.

When she saw him appear before her in that odd getup, she couldn't help but laughing.

"I give up," she said jokingly, putting her hands in the air.

Marco stuck the pistol into the pocket of his robe and invited Alice to come in.

"Two minutes. The time to take a shower and I'll be with you."

Alice looked around with a certain uneasiness at the furnishings of the small apartment on Via Monte Bianco, in the heart of the nondescript Talenti quarter. It looked like the set of a movie from several years back. A place where time had stopped. The little living room with the good sofa and the mahogany table surmounted by the sideboard with the porcelain service for twelve. The green-and-white flowered bathroom tiles in majolica. A corner shower flush with the floor, enclosed in a shower curtain on sliding hooks that featured a lithograph of the crucial scene from *Psycho*, the one where the deranged Anthony Perkins dressed as Mother Bates lifts the kitchen knife high to strike his blonde victim, Janet Leigh.

Her uneasiness derived from the sense of normality that the whole place inspired. A normality both petty and bourgeois, solid, that emanated a sense of goodness. Of bonds that do not shift due to self-interest.

Fate hadn't been so kind to her. Her folks had eaten away at each other for years, engaged in an unsustainable trench warfare, until the definitive abandonment of that marriage, a divorce that had left its mark on the troubled adolescence of their only daughter. Once they'd come to a separation agreement, they'd handed Alice off to Grandma Sandra, her sole bond with the filthy world. Alice had played out her brief alternative existence in perfect freedom. A bad period, something she'd tried to forget. For a little while, she'd fallen prey to furious panic attacks. People who've never experienced them have no idea, but a panic attack is something very close to being at death's door. It unfailingly happened to her when she was wrestling with a major life decision. She'd liberated herself by taking up boxing. When the decisions involved are: either hit, or be hit, it becomes immediately clear to you that there are no right decisions and wrong decisions. The decision is always right, and it's always the first one. It can go well or it can go badly, but that is no longer within your own control. At that point, the panic attacks vanished. She'd learned to seize and discard opportunities without thinking too hard about it.

Marco reappeared. Black T-shirt and jeans. Wet hair, freshly shampooed. He smelled good. Wonderful, to tell the truth.

"Here I am. Sorry, I wasn't expecting you, to say the least. And also, I'm not very coherent first thing in the morning. And . . . should I make you a cup of coffee?"

"Sure, thanks."

He seemed emotional, less self-confident than she remembered him, Alice thought, as he bustled about preparing an old Moka Express coffee pot.

Was she the reason for that effect?

Alice felt attracted to Marco. In some inexplicable way. And that attraction frightened her. They were too different for anything good to come of it. She could have told him the news with a phone call, and that would have been that. But the thing was, over the past few days, she had frequently caught herself thinking about him. And wondering: why not?

Alice started looking around the bedroom. A few pieces of Ikea furniture, an unmade futon with an A. S. Roma poster over it, a gigantic Yamaha stereo system lodged in a messy combination of cubic shelves where Marco kept his collection of two thousand vinyl records.

Then, in a surprising contrast, signs of a globetrotting existence: the head of an Burmese Buddha, a Ganesh with a mocking expression, a Balinese batik with a scene of the battle between the Pandava and the Kauravas, a statuette of a laughing peasant in a Maoist uniform.

"I spent a few years in the MSU, the support unit for the foreign diplomatic missions. I can say 'I like you' in a considerable array of languages, both living and dead," he smiled, appearing from behind her with a tray and espresso demitasses.

"I just love this Buddha. It imparts a powerful sense of peace," Alice murmured, as she caressed the statuette.

As they were drinking their coffee, Marco told her about the souvenirs that he couldn't put on display. His memories: The sneer of opportunist politicos. The impenetrable masks of the dictators for whom he'd had to act as a bodyguard. The handshake with which he'd said farewell to the secret agent who'd become his blood brother in Iraq and who had been cut down by friendly fire as he was using his body to shield a hostage he had just liberated. The Afghani child bride he had torn out of the clutches of her husband/owner. His memories of those years abroad.

"We'd been given orders not to intervene. But disobeying orders is sort of a specialty of mine."

"And how did you do it?"

"I did it, that's all that counts."

"Did you have to . . . kill?"

Marco didn't answer. She took his hand.

"While you were talking, you didn't seem like a Carabiniere."

Marco smiled.

She released her clasp.

She told him everything in a rush: how Abbas had been paid by the Anacletis, the sarcastic grin with which Terenzi had greeted her and Abbas's daughter at the Carabinieri barracks when they had come in to file their complaint, the libelous campaign undertaken by Spartaco Liberati, who had called her a tick and a Carabinieri spy. She also added that the neighborhood locals had even stopped sending in the usual number of tips to her blog.

"They're afraid, that's clear."

"They've stopped trusting me, Marco."

He tried to comfort her. The fact that the criminal complaint had been withdrawn didn't mean a damn thing. The investigation would continue anyway.

"I really doubt that," she shot back, spikily. "You know what's going to happen? Even if I decide to take this thing down to the bitter end, Abbas won't show up at the trial to identify his assailants and torturers. And even if he does show up, he'll just say he was mistaken. You see what'll happen as a result? And don't tell me that you don't know that."

"I do. I know it, Alice. And that's why I'm going to keep going."

"Down the wrong road," she said, needling him.

Marco threw his arms wide in a gesture of helplessness.

"I don't know any others."

"Because you're a part of the system," she pointed out, "and maybe you represent the best part of it."

"What's that supposed to be, a compliment?"

"Still," she went on, ignoring the question, "when a system is rotten to the core, you can't change it from within."

"The famous revolutionary shove?"

"I'm not a violent person, Marco. And I'm not a visionary lunatic. It's going to take time, I know that. But things are going to change. It's in the air that you breathe, change is every-where. Look around. Look at what's happening. The world is full of people who can't stand another minute of this world order. Go online and google certain key words, like Occupy, or Zuccotti Park . . . "

He looked at her with a mixture of tenderness and exas-peration.

"Zuccotti Park, Occupy . . . you think you're the first per-son to come up with this, Alice, Jesus fucking Christ! Go tell that story to Rocco Anacleti, Paja and Fieno, Adami Cesare AKA Number Eight, oh, and tell Spartaco Liberati while you're at it, of course . . . In any case, with or without your help, I'm moving forward on this. Even though, with you," he added, softly, "it would be so much nicer . . . "

Alice sealed his lips with a kiss.

What the hell, sure, maybe she'd even waited too long for that.


To comply with Rocco Anacleti's demand—was there or was there not an investigation underway into the caregiver ring?—Marshal Terenzi turned to a friend in the immigration office. His name was Polillo, an inspector with a long career behind him and a regrettable weakness for cards and Nigerian hookers. And it was in fact in the waiting room, to describe it euphemistically, of Queen Elizabeth, a Junoesque women who stood 5' 11" and had a generous 44-inch bust, that Terenzi waited, his nerves increasingly on edge, while the inspector consummated the thoughtful *cadeau* that Terenzi had so gen-erously bestowed upon him.

Still, how long was this guy going to take? He'd been sitting on that sofa with his legs splayed, smoking cigarettes, listening to every excruciating detail of the Nigerian's stagey moans of pleasure and the rutting grunts of his interservice cousin from the State Police for too long. Even though Terenzi had been perfectly clear with the negress: something quick, because afterward I need to talk to this guy about serious matters.

Clearly, though, Polillo had some catching up to do after a dry period. Or maybe he'd just overdone it with his daily dose of Viagra.

At last the inspector emerged, his face lit up by an idiotic smile. Behind him was the bored expression of Queen Elizabeth.

"Hey, it's true what they say, negresses really do have a fifth gear, Tere' . . . Oh, I really owe you on this one, you're a real friend, you are."

"Oh, sure, a friend . . . do you think I cashed in my weekly chit with her for your pretty face? You want to get something to drink, Poli'?"

"What I need, the shape I'm in after that, is a crate of Gatorade . . . you ran me ragged, beautiful!"

"And you come back to visit when you like, sweetie," the Nigerian tossed out mellifluously.

Sure, but at your own expense next time, you cheapskate, thought Terenzi to himself, locking arms with the man. They wound up in a pub on Via di San Martino ai Monti, and over a beer Terenzi reminded Polillo about "that little favor."

"Oh, right, of course, the caregivers. But why are you interested in knowing, sorry?"

Here he is, the cocksman. Now he was even acting suspicious.

"Because Anagnina is my territory, Poli'. And after all, if something's going to happen, it ain't right for the State Police to take all the credit."

"You have a point! There is a little something . . . "

Polillo knocked back a gulp of beer and leaned forward, lowering his voice.

"But it's not ours. That shit belongs to the COS."

Terenzi nodded. He hated those smartasses from the

Central Operations Service every bit as much as Polillo did . . . They were cops with hard horns, those guys, people willing to get their hands dirty, more than smartasses.

"There's a guy who's spilling the beans, an informant, I hear," Polillo went on. "He says that behind the traffic in caregivers, there's a coke-dealing ring. They haven't weighed in yet because they want to work their way up the chain. But in the next few days something big's supposed to happen."

"Wow, Poli'! This is dynamite!"

"Oh, I never said a word to you, eh!"

"We never even saw each other," Terenzi said brusquely.

He walked out of the bar, leaving Polillo with the check. The least he could do was pay for that.

## XXVIII

Marco took Alice out to La Paranza.

It was only right to show her the kind of human beings that might disgust generous-hearted utopians like her but that, in the flesh, she'd never before encountered.

"The unctuous and over-courteous character who obtained this wonderful secluded table for us, from which we can survey the comings and goings of the capital's gilded youth . . . "

And he went on with a description of Tito Maggio, followed by abundant laughter.

"Those three fatsoes who are scraping all the flesh out of the lobster and spraying crustacean juice thirty feet in all directions. People call them the Three Little Pigs . . . old shylocks. Just think, one time, one of them . . . "

And then he trotted out the story of when the nastiest looking of the trio, the one in the middle who looked like an even more obese Oliver Hardy, yeah, that's right, him, while getting fellatio from the wife of a guy who owed him, aboard the inevitable SUV, but hers in this case, to save on gas, had actually been rear-ended by a drunken truck driver and came very close to losing the family jewels.

"Excuse me, though, but how do you know these things?"

"Wiretaps."

"Ah, so that's what they're for. Then the people who want to outlaw them are in the right!"

And more laughter.

Marco went on.

"That's not all that wiretaps are good for. For example: you see that distinguished-looking gentleman holding court at the table with the soccer players? He's a prosecuting magistrate. And he's in debt to the tune of a hundred fifty thousand euros with the Three Little Pigs. On account of his gambling habit."

"And he takes cash in exchange for trials!"

"We don't have proof. But we're keeping an eye on him."

"And what is he doing with the soccer players?"

"Look, that man has only one good quality. He's a die-hard A. S. Roma fan."

"Well, well, well."

"You just really can't stand soccer, can you?"

"No. If it was up to me, I'd make it illegal."

"I can see our future cohabitation is going to be problematic."

"I'd make cohabitation illegal too. And especially families."

"That there is something we might agree on."

"In other words, from what you're telling me, it's a sort of latter-day version of *The Sound of Music*. Everyone singing from the same page."

"Sure, but don't let yourself be taken in by this typically Roman display of fellow feeling and bonhomie. Half of these people have some horrible skeletons in their closets. And the other half is ready to cut each other's throats to get their hands on them."

"Get their hands on the skeletons or the closets?"

"Both. Around here, nothing is thrown away, as long as it has some market value. This is Rome, sweetheart."

"And that guy who just came in?"

"The guy who's all out of breath, as if he'd just emerged from a bout of torrential sex? Sorry, I don't know him."

"Well, I do, so there."

"You do?"

"Yeah. His name is Pericle Malgradi."

"That name rings a bell."

"He's an Honorable, from some right-wing party, or maybe a center party, I don't know, but anyway all home, family, and whores."

"Now I'm the one asking you the question: how do you know that?"

"I saw it with my own eyes. He brings carloads of them to a downtown hotel, La Chiocciola. A sort of high-end sex parlor. I went there with Diego. You know that the rooms are named after famous actresses?"

Marco reacted with a smirk.

"Diego from the meet-up? The Rebel Dragon?"

Alice didn't respond.

"Our room," she went on, "was called the Anna Magnani Suite."

He was on the verge of letting go with a bitter zinger. But he decided not to humiliate himself. Retroactive jealousy would be a form of surrender. Better to keep that to himself. She smiled at him, openly ironic.

"La Chiocciola is just a stone's throw from where my grandmother lives. Have I ever told you about Grandma Sandra? She was the one who raised me, after my folks broke up. She's ninety-five years old and she lives in a world all her own. But she's a force of nature."

"Introduce me to her."

"Only if you prove worthy of the honor."

It was all going fine. There was the kind of lighthearted back and forth that Marco desperately needed. It was all going fine.

Then, just as Marco and Alice were getting ready to dig into a Scorfano Imperiale all'Acqua Pazza, or poached scorpionfish, a young couple came through the front door of La Paranza. The young woman looked around, spotted Alice, and her pure and finedrawn face lit up. Dragging the young man behind her, she hurried over to their table.

"Alice!"

"Farideh! What are you doing here?"

"To tell the truth, I've never been here before, but he really insisted . . . This is Max, we're an item. Max, this is Alice and Marco, you know, that nice Carabiniere I told you about . . . "

The lieutenant colonel stood up and politely shook the hand that Max was extending to him.

"Why don't you join us?" Alice suggested.

Marco and Max exchanged a glance, and in that brief instant, they said everything that needed to be said.

"Gladly, but some other time," the young man explained courteously, "we're expecting friends."

Farideh tried to object. What friends was he talking about? Hadn't they discussed an intimate evening together, just the two of them? Marco gestured to Tito Maggio and called him over. The chef hurried over to take Max by the arm, piloting him toward another table.

As he steered Max past Malgradi, the Honorable started to say hello. Max ignored him intentionally.

Alice noticed that Marco was continuing to follow the young couple with his gaze.

"Are you interested in that young man? Are you less of a troglodyte than you seem? Am I going to have to change my opinion about your much-touted virility? Still, he's not a bad-looking kid."

"Why do you ask?"

The sudden seriousness in his voice surprised her.

"Has something happened, Marco?"

"That young man is a member of the crew that beat the hell out of Farideh's father."

"Are you kidding me?" she reacted, suddenly alarmed.

"His name is Max, AKA Nicce."

"The philosopher."

"That's right. And to tell the truth, he's the one who tried to defend the old man. But that doesn't take away the fact that he was there, with Paja and Fieno. He's one of the Anacletis' men. Farideh sure chose herself a nice boyfriend."

"Are you sure of that?"

"I don't have proof. Yet."

Alice, her eyes blazing, threw her napkin down on the table.

"I'm going over to talk to her."

Marco restrained her.

"Not right now."

"Farideh is a friend of mine."

"Please, not this second. Tomorrow. Call her on the phone. Go over and talk to her. But not yet. But here's another thing . . . I'm going to have to do a little research into this Malgradi."

"Now how does Malgradi fit in?"

"When Max walked past him, Malgradi tried to say hello. Max pretended not to notice. Curious, isn't it?"

"Don't try to change the subject, Marco. The fact that I went to bed with you doesn't mean that I'm at your orders."

"But I never . . . "

"I'm talking about Farideh. Listen to me, and listen good. I'm going to say it this once, and I won't say it again. I will never do anything that might hurt that girl. Promise me that she won't get dragged into this thing. Whatever it is that you have in mind."

Marco said nothing. That was a promise he wouldn't be able to keep.

A bad-tempered silence settled between them.

Max was uneasy. The presence of the Carabiniere complicated everything. Samurai had ordered him to send the Honorable over to see him, and on the double.

"Excuse me for a second, Farideh."

Max headed for the bathroom but, at the last minute, after checking to make sure that the Carabiniere wasn't watching him, he ducked into the kitchen and grabbed Tito Maggio, whose hands were busy with a large oval platter of seafood pasta with tattlers and octopus: Paccheri ai Totani e Moscardini.

"In exactly ten minutes, go over to Malgradi's table and tell him that Samurai is waiting for him on Via della Giustiniana. Tell him to get his ass in gear and get over there pronto."

"Consider it done, Max. And when you see Samurai, tell him that I bow and take his feet, no, better, I'm under his feet. Since he spoke to them, the Three Little Pigs have stopped busting my chops. That man is a genuine boss, let me tell you."

"Okay, okay, but just get going now, go . . . "

The message reached Malgradi in the midst of a full-court press as he courted an aspiring starlet, a peppery young thing who had her heart set on the role of the Countess of Castiglione in a period costume picture imminently slated for production. When he told her that unavoidable party business would be dragging him reluctantly away, she flew into a rage. Malgradi promised her the part, and her rage was transformed into honeyed smiles.

"Come on, I'll take you home, I have to get on the road," he said brusquely. And maybe, along the way, a little something would drop into his lap.

Samurai was waiting for Malgradi at the gate. He didn't ask him in, and he wasted no time.

"You have a week from today to get the resolution approved."

The Honorable tried to stall for time. The political situation was degenerating. The government was struggling to restore its credibility and reputation. Not a day went by anymore without some bastard prosecutor from the hall of justice launching a new investigation of some pillar of the political community.

The tide of hatred was rising. They had to move cautiously, or there was a serious danger of utter collapse.

"Social hatred has nothing to do with all this. The truth is that you're shitting your pants because of Spadino and the murder in Cinecittà. But it's all your fault. Actually, the blame all goes to your peerless cock. I'm wondering whether the right thing to do might just be to slice it off."

"Samurai, please."

"Malgradi, I restored the peace. But it's a very precarious peace. And with every day that passes, it grows more precarious. So you've got a week."

"I'll do my best, Samurai, I promise you that."

"Promises are smoke, Malgradi. Just remember that everyone is replaceable. A good player," Samurai concluded, "always plays on more than one table."

# XXIX

What was it Samurai had said to him that afternoon at Il Tatami? Servant of peace. You will be a Servant of peace. But what kind of peace? And what's more, why? Had anyone ever seen a boss like him, always bowing his head and doing what he's told?

Number Eight, as always, trusted in his animal instincts. Because it didn't matter whether you understood things. It was enough just to sense them. And he'd understood everything the first time he went back to Morgana after the ambush.

He'd gotten all dressed up. With a pair of black leather pants and a white cotton sweater. In his pocket was a five-gram cellophane-wrapped ball of white powder. The very finest. When he rang the buzzer to the apartment on Piazza Lorenzo Gasparri, Morgana had opened the door without even asking who it was. In the stale air of the studio apartment, he'd detected a hint of something pungent in the air. The smell of recent sex. And not his.

Morgana was half-naked. A black T-shirt, extra large, barely covered her pubic area and her magnificent derriere. She was already completely wrecked. Number Eight tried to take her, but all he got for it was an obstinate and hostile rejection.

"Do you mind if I ask what the hell's the matter with you?" he asked, shaking her roughly.

Morgana stared at him with a gaze that combined defiance with commiseration.

"I don't like men who hide."

"And who's hiding?"

"You are. Ever since they shot you, you've been running like a rabbit."

Number Eight hauled off and gave her a tremendous smack across the face. She fell on the bed and burst out laughing. He frantically yanked out the little ball of coke. He laid out two lines on the coffee table and snorted them both with a hundred euro bill. The shit went straight to his brain, giving him the pleasant sensation of heat dissolving the fog. He opened the door. He turned around one last time and looked down at the big bed.

"You've given me an idea. You bitch."

Number Eight went back to the Off-Shore. He stepped into the shower, the prisoner of an uncontainable rage, but also filled with certainty. It was time to become a boss again.

Midnight had come and gone. He dialed Paja's cell phone number. Paja didn't answer until the fifth ring.

"Who the fuck is this?"

"Are you sleeping?"

"Who is this?"

"I'm the guy you couldn't kill."

"I have no idea what you're talking about."

"Oh, come on, Paja. It's all taken care of, don't sweat it. I'm just kidding you."

"I don't like it when you kid around."

"And in fact, I'm calling you because I want to work together again, just like in the good old days."

"What are you talking about?"

"We need to straighten out a guy from Casalpalocco who thinks he's Scarface, he's starting to become a nuisance. He's been telling everyone that he doesn't take orders."

"So if you've got a problem why don't you solve it yourself? What do we have to do with Ostia?"

"Because it has to be clear to everyone that we've started working together again. And isn't that what Samurai wants, after all? Peace, no? You put this piece of shit from Casalpalocco in a wheelchair and all of Rome will know who's in charge now."

"Have you talked this over with Rocco?"

"Don't sweat it. He gives his blessing to this thing, too."

"For sure?"

"Why would I tell you a fairytale? What's in it for me? Check it out, if you want."

"Okay, I will. Anyway, I'm not coming out to Ostia alone."

"Then bring Fieno with you, no? The two of you can work him over better, anyway."

In Paja's prolonged silence, Number Eight understood that he'd done it. Paja wasn't going to check things out with Rocco Anacleti in the middle of the night. He'd fallen for it with both feet. And even if Paja called his bluff, well, there would always be another chance. It was decided now.

"When are we supposed to come?"

"Right now."

"Where?"

"The Ostia roundabout. When you're there, I'll come get you."

Number Eight wanted to do it all on his own. Because alone was the only way to do it. And because he'd imagined a thousand and one times just how and where. This was so much better than the *zammammero* in Cinecittà. Rome wouldn't stop talking about it for days. Even Samurai would be forced to come kiss his ass. And that slut Morgana would have to go down on her knees and beg him to forgive her.

He was going to do for Paja and Fieno at the Idroscalo, at the beach in Ostia. That's right, at the Idroscalo, like that other guy, what was his name, the one who made dirty movies . . . Ah, that's right, Pasolini. And he was going to do for them the same exact way. A slick piece of work: maybe even Samurai would appreciate it.

He didn't have a lot of time. But all the same, he got ready with great care. Eyes closed, naked, flat on his back on the bed, he relaxed the muscles of his neck and back for a solid fifteen minutes. He snorted just the right amount. Then he got into his F. C. Barcelona track suit and concealed the Smith & Wesson .38 in a black fanny pack. From the bar at the Off-Shore he grabbed an iced bottle of Veuve Clicquot and three champagne flutes that he arranged in the cup holders in the driver's side armrest in the Hummer. He turned on the engine and adjusted the temperature and humidity of the interior. He checked the level in the apple-scented air freshener. He fastened his seatbelt and drove the few miles separating Coccia di Morto and Ostia at a speed that never went over the legal limit, listening to "My Heart Will Go On" by Céline Dion, from the *Titanic* soundtrack. How he had loved that movie. Forget about Pasolini, he'd watched *Titanic* three times.

Paja and Fieno's BMW had sailed straight down Via Cristoforo Colombo with the car windows wide open.

And it had been a strangely silent journey, because Fieno's nose told him there was something not right about that late-night phone call from Number Eight.

"Hey, Paja, do you trust this guy?"

"I don't know. But what does it matter? If there's a guy to beat bloody, good. If there isn't, and Number Eight's being an asshole and starts getting funny ideas, there's always this."

Paja pulled open the black bouncer's jacket that he'd put on before getting in the car, revealing the butt of a Beretta 7.65. Fieno flashed a smile that looked more like a grimace and, instinctively, fished around in his pockets for the chrome-plated steel knuckleduster with skulls in relief.

"Did you talk to the boss, though?"

"Number Eight says that he talked to Rocco himself."

"Sure he does. And you trust him?"

"I pretended I did when I was talking with him. Anyway, I tried calling Rocco. The phone was turned off. I left a message."

"You'll see, he'll call back. And anyway, if he's pulling some bullshit, this time, as God is my witness, he won't live to tell the tale."

When the BMW pulled over on the right side of the Ostia roundabout, the Hummer was already there. Number Eight got out and walked over to the driver side window.

The three men looked at each other in silence for several long seconds. Number Eight smiled.

"So you decided not to wear helmets this evening?"

Paja didn't blink.

"Where is this guy we're supposed to take care of?"

"My guys picked him up and they're waiting for us. Want to get in and ride with me?"

"Why should we get in your car?"

"Because I know where he is. And I don't like processions of cars in the middle of the night."

Paja looked at Fieno, who nodded his head yes. They parked the BMW and got into Number Eight's SUV; the car started off along the waterfront, heading toward Ponente.

Sitting in the back seat, Paja carefully watched the road. Fieno, in the front seat, captivated by the control panel of that oversized jeep that glittered and glowed like a Christmas tree, continued to crack his knuckles and flex his right hand, opening and closing it so that the knuckleduster fit the hand nice and warm.

"Isn't this the way to your house?" asked Paja.

"Ah, I see you know where I live."

Fieno interrupted him.

"Do you or don't you understand that you're not funny?"

Number Eight lifted a hand off the steering wheel in a gesture of surrender.

"I get it, I get it. I give up. I won't do it again. *Mamma mia*, hey . . . you want a drink?"

The bottle of Veuve Clicquot and the three champagne flutes made the rounds of the SUV. Number Eight lifted his glass till it was level with the rearview mirror.

"And just try telling me that this ain't peace! To your health."

Paja and Fieno lifted their glasses without excessive enthusiasm. But they drank to the last drop, and came back for more.

"So where did you have Scarface taken?"

"To the Idroscalo."

"Nice shithole that is!" Paja pointed out.

Number Eight nodded theatrically.

"Right you are. But once the city graders have finished their work, you can bet on how beautiful *er uoterfront, er front* . . . how the fuck do you say the name?"

A few months ago, the graders had already plowed under the shacks of forty or so illegal squatters. The story they'd told to explain their actions was that the whole area was going to become the nature reserve of the Tiber delta. "A small patch to be restored to the enchantment of nature, in order to repopulate the avifauna of sea and lakes." And why not after all, the nature reserve of my testicles, Number Eight had laughed to himself as he watched the graders crushing drywall roofs and walls. He'd told an old ex-con to go to hell when he'd begged on his knees, pleading with him to spare at least his shack from destruction.

"Next time, don't vote for them."

The Hummer rolled to a halt on a broad expanse of sand and dirt, flat as a pool table. The work of the bulldozers after that of the graders. Number Eight pointed out to Paja a wilted patch of low vegetation that had miraculously survived the demolitions, wedged in among the heaps of rubble and garbage. It could hardly be seen in the darkness.

"Denis and Morgana brought the asshole out there. They tied him hand and foot and told him they were going to call the police, and that he would be taken home. Now you two go over to him, introduce yourselves, and give him a nice thorough beauty treatment with the compliments of the Sales and the Anacletis. Do a good job now. I don't want him ever to be able to walk again."

Paja wasn't even slightly convinced.

"You want to explain the reason for this whole production? Couldn't we just lay him out on the sidewalk in front of where he lives, this asshole?"

"We can do our work here without anyone bothering us."

Paja looked at Fieno. And leaning forward from the back seat, he grabbed Number Eight's shoulder.

"All right, let's do this another way. I'll get out alone and I'll go behind those fucking bushes. Fieno can stay here and keep you company. If you're fucking with us, it'll be the last thing you ever do. Eh? What do you say? Seem fair?"

Number Eight smiled.

"That's fine. If that's how you want it, Fieno and I will just watch the show. Lights, camera, action!"

Number Eight turned on the Hummer's headlights, Paja got out of the SUV and started walking toward the patch of vegetation lit up by the headlights. Fieno watched his partner from inside the car, not yet sure whether to be alarmed or to settle down to watch him take out his fury on that miserable wretch from Casalpalocco.

Paja took a few steps on the dirt surface, then he felt his cell phone vibrate in the rear pocket of his jeans. He grabbed it with his right hand and automatically raised it to his ear. He recognized the voice of Rocco Anacleti, distorted and breathless.

He was shouting.

"Where the fuck are you? Where are you?"

"At the Idroscalo, with Number Eight."

"It's a trap. It's a trap!"

In the chilly light of the dazzling xenon headlights, Number Eight saw Paja turn slowly around toward the Hummer with the cell phone held to his ear. Number Eight silently opened the fanny pack he was holding between his thighs, and pulled out the .38 caliber handgun inside.

Fieno felt its muzzle against his temple and heard Number Eight's voice.

"Don't even try to move."

Holding his right arm extended toward Fieno's temple, Number Eight started the engine. He put the Hummer into low gear. He jammed his foot down on the accelerator, steering with his left hand. The automatic transmission launched three tons of Hummer straight at Paja's silhouette. He screamed as the nose of the SUV hit him full on, just above the shoulders, decapitating him then and there. Ripped off of the body, the head with its ponytail landed somewhere in the darkness.

Fieno vomited onto the dashboard. The whole time, Number Eight never lowered the straight arm that held the .38 against his temple by so much as a degree.

"What the fuck! You've got puke all over my upholstery. What an asshole you are. This is leather. How the fuck am I going to get rid of the smell now."

As he said it, he pushed down the electric button of the right front window, which slid silently down. A faint sea breeze caressed Fieno's cheek, drying a rivulet of bile at the corner of his mouth. And that was the last thing he ever knew. The .38 caliber bullet pierced his cranium, dragging a puff of cerebral matter behind it, which trailed out over the Hummer's passenger door.

Number Eight doused the headlights, opened the passenger door, and tumbled Fieno's corpse out onto the dirt. He got back behind the wheel and raised the right-hand window. He put the Hummer into reverse and crushed Fieno's body into the ground. A three-metric ton press to finish the job with a flourish. Then he turned on the courtesy light inside the cockpit. He observed the lake of vomit and blood that had spattered even the Hummer's sun roof. He shook his head in vexation.

"Anyway, I was going to have it washed, this car."

# XXX

An ID card, miraculously found under a crushed shoe, made it possible to identify both of the corpses. The document belonged to Zuppa, Dario, AKA Paja, ex-convict, born in Rome on 9/3/1980. If that's the way things were, given the fact that where you found Paja you inevitably also found Fieno, the other mortal spoils could not have belonged to anyone while still alive other than Scavi, Luca, AKA Fieno, ex-convict, born in Rome on 7/12/1981.

Otherwise, the crime scene was one huge mess.

Lashed by an implacable wind blasting in off the salt water, immersed in the murderous dankness of the autumn night, caught in the light of the lamps that illuminated the bare dirt of the Idroscalo, the white jumpsuits of RIS seemed to give life to a dance that was as clumsy as it was surreal.

Wrapped in their windbreakers, shivering insistently, Marco, Alba Bruni, and Lieutenant Gaudino from the Ostia Carabinieri station were battling the cold, trying to make heads or tails out of a crime scene compromised by a surge of incongruous tracks. But it was difficult, if not impossible, to find their way in that welter of footprints, filthy rags, cigarette butts of every type and shape, and construction trash.

There was only one witness: that of the illegal occupant of a local shanty. It was his dog, a likable mut with a rascally way about him, that had found the bodies about three in the morning. But concerning the murders, or really, the brutal murders, because it had certainly been an outright slaughter, the man had been unable to provide any useful evidence.

The only thing that was unmistakable, after a first visual examination of the corpses, was the presence of an SUV. Both Paja's decapitated torso, and Fieno's shredded body—the RIS technicians concluded while waiting for the autopsy—presented in fact clear marks of having been run over or in any case impacted and crushed by large automobile tires. That vehicle, was the subsequent and fairly obvious conclusion, could only have belonged to the killer or killers, and the two victims must have arrived aboard it. In fact, the black BMW registered to Dario Zuppa had already been found at the Ostia roundabout.

The two corpses on the ground were Rocco Anacleti's hitters, as Malatesta explained to the prosecuting magistrate whose shift this was, and who had arrived at the Idroscalo after an hour or so.

"Paja and Fieno? But isn't that a kind of pasta?"

Marco stared at Bruni. They both rolled their eyes, then they turned their gazes to this young prosecuting magistrate who had introduced himself by the name of Michelangelo de Candia. At the very most, he might have been thirty years old; he was tall and distinguished, with small eyeglasses and a carefully groomed, blonde goatee. An unequivocally musical singsong in his speech betrayed his southern birth. The son and grandson of magistrates, he had a head full of pandects, and absolutely no street experience. The umpteenth ballbuster to come along. Marco unloaded him on Alba with a few phrases of formulaic courtesy and indulged in another, pointless round of inspection. No more than fifteen minutes or so. He'd seen enough. And he needed to get out of that place in a hurry. The deceased Paja and Fieno notoriously belonged to the inner circle of the Anacleti clan, so this murder now belonged to the district anti-mafia directorate. Which meant:

Setola, the magistrate who had ordered Marco dismissed from the force. Marco had no desire to cross paths with that idiot. The plan he had devised called for clandestine legwork behind the scenes and no open clash. The greatest possible caution and, when the time was right, rapid and unscrupulous action. It gave him an immense surge of pleasure to savor it in advance, that moment. The important thing, of course, was to make it happen.

He had just started over to his Bonneville motorcycle when, with a wailing siren and screeching brakes, an armor-plated Alfa Romeo Alfetta blasted onto the scene. Out of the rear door, which the driver had obsequiously hurried back to pull wide open, none other than Setola emerged. He must have spotted Marco during the ostentatiously brusque parking maneuver, because he strode toward him with a broad smile of false friendship.

"Colonel! What a pleasure to see you again. You were just leaving, I imagine . . . "

Which, translated from the Setolese, was a way of saying: beat it, this is my investigation.

Marco nodded, responding with a faint, hypocritical smile—after all Setola wasn't the kind of guy who could even detect certain subtleties—and picked up his helmet to put it on.

Michelangelo de Candia came over, accompanied by Bruni. The two investigators exchanged a fairly hostile glance.

"All right then, partner. Unless you have some objection, I'll just keep working here," said Setola dismissively.

The other man eyed him skeptically.

"Has the district attorney already assigned you this investigation?"

Setola jerked, startled.

"What does that have to do with anything? It's obvious, isn't it? This is our case, it belongs to the anti-mafia.

"There's only one thing that's obvious here, partner," de Candia retorted with determination. "I'm on duty and I'm running the investigation of this crime scene. If you want to keep me company, I have no problem with that."

And here, with a nod to Bruni, he turned his back on the sharp cutting edge of the Rome district anti-mafia directorate and went back to his work.

Marco stood there relishing Setola's angry frustration, then he put on his helmet and rode away on his motorcycle.

Well, well, well, we have a bad boy in town!

Could he have been wrong about de Candia?

Yes, he'd been wrong.

And he'd been completely wrong.

This became clear by mid-afternoon, when Michelangelo de Candia summoned him to his office, a cubbyhole stacked high with paper on the fourth floor of building C of the district attorney's office, and politely handed him the report that, a few weeks ago, when it was first written, had been mocked and dismissed by the higher-ups.

"Did you write this stuff?"

"It has my signature, I believe."

"It strikes me as interesting. It offers an interpretive key to recent events that might also come in handy in the investigation into the death of those two guys. The pasta chefs. Paja and Fieno."

"Your colleagues don't seem to see things the same way, Dottore."

De Candia took off his little round glasses and placed his hands together, as if in prayer.

"Even the best of us get things wrong sometimes."

Marco thought he detected a twinge of irony that he didn't mind one bit. He decided to lay his cards out on the table.

He explained to the prosecuting magistrate, in the same ironic tone, that he owed it to that very same report that he'd been kicked out. Evidently, the idea of a gang war wasn't considered compatible with the hoped-for outcome of that investigation.

"What about you?"

"What do you mean, what about me?"

"How did you react?"

"I went to the beach."

"An excellent decision," de Candia said with a laugh, "the iodine is good for the brain."

Then the prosecuting magistrate suddenly turned serious.

"I've opened an investigation targeting parties unknown. I just signed an authorization for the ROS. What I'm saying is that I'd like you working beside me. Well, will you give me a hand, Marco?"

"Where do we start?"

"Are you familiar with the expression 'carte blanche'?"

# XXXI

The infrared security cameras that the Anacletis employed to keep an eye, day and night, on a vast urban swathe with Via Zumbo at its heart provided advance warning at around 9:00 P.M. that night of the onrushing procession of ROS squad cars. But those same cameras couldn't prevent the damage that occurred. Those cameras did ward off the very worst, though—or at least so the Anacletis believed. As soon as they caught a whiff of cops on the way, the women of the clan hurried to the fireplaces that were always kept aflame, summer and winter alike, to burn a couple of kilos of cocaine.

The doors were knocked down with axe blows. The Carabinieri came in waving search warrants and shouting that they had a right to a lawyer.

With them was de Candia.

"This little courtesy call on the Anacleti family is something I really don't want to miss," he'd confided to Marco.

At that exact moment, another team was turning the Off-Shore and the homes of the Ostia crew upside-down and inside-out.

Coordinated operations. And violent ones.

Villa Anacleti was an immense embattlemented construction, embellished, on the upright structural pillars, by copies of Doric columns in polychrome Carrara marble. With the moon riding high in the night sky, it looked like something out of *Arabian Nights*, as filtered through the style of a

Disney cartoon. On the parking area out front, as if it were some high-end auto dealership, there were at least a dozen SUVs, a Porsche Carrera, two Bentleys, a Jaguar, a Lamborghini Diablo, and countless other high-performance vehicles.

On the patio of the villa, dressed in a pair of red silk pajamas and with a pair of green velvet oriental-style slippers on his feet, Rocco Anacleti was wide awake, surrounded by an assorted array of loudly garrulous sisters, cousins, and grandchildren. The execution of Paja and Fieno had thrown him into a trance state, interrupted only by sudden explosions of rage. He had refused to change his clothing and had summoned his entire clan around him to announce unspeakably savage retaliation. When Colonel Malatesta handed him the search warrant, his pudgy face took on a gummy consistency. He tried to mutter something, but the colonel, accompanied by his men, headed straight back into the bedrooms.

It was a sort of Ali Baba's cave. A triumph of carved marble, brasswork, damasks, and fine watches.

In Rocco's bedroom, a ceiling mounted stem lamp, reminiscent of a bush full of fluorescent thorns, illuminated a giant king-sized bed covered with a heavy bright-orange quilt. Over the bed hung a wood carving in bleached oak. A small satyr contemplated his own immense and erect phallus.

The colonel recognized the hand of poor old Abbas. At one of the extremities of the boiserie, he felt a thickening in the slab. He pried it open with a gold fork he'd found in one of the vitrines in the living room.

It proved to be a hidden compartment, which gave up a folder full of tracings, floor plans and area reliefs, maps, lists of specialized earth-moving companies, scale models of intensive affordable housing, an enlarged copy of what appeared to be sheets of the municipal zoning plan for the western sectors of the city, between EUR and the sea.

Clutching that stack of papers in his hands, he went back

into the living room, where Rocco Anacleti was sitting in an armchair, watching the Carabinieri come and go. When he saw the colonel, he started berating him.

"You haven't found a fucking thing, isn't that right?"

Malatesta walked over to him menacingly.

"Excuse me? What did you just say? Did I not hear you clearly?"

"I said you haven't found a fucking thing, Carabiniere."

"You think not?"

With a nod of the head, he gave two of his men the go-ahead to raise their axes and start splintering the cherry-wood wainscoting that lined one of the long ends of the immense living room.

De Candia raised an eyebrow. Marco shot him a reassuring glance: he knew what he was doing, de Candia should just trust him.

That's when Rocco Anacleti lost it. He lunged at the two Carabinieri, kicking one of them in the back. He was pinned to the floor and, in a chorus of shouts of pain, handcuffed. Malatesta kneeled down and, with his face practically grazing the floor, pushed the papers he'd found under the nose of the patriarch of the Anacleti clan.

"And just what are these supposed to be, you dickhead? Eh? Have you started studying to become an architect? Didn't you used to just be a thief and a pusher? Answer me, asshole. Why do you have these papers? What are you doing with them? Maybe if you answer me, you can help me figure out why they murdered your guys Paja and Fieno."

"I don't talk to cops. If you want, you can talk to my lawyer."

Malatesta stood up and, turning to a guy in his early thirties who seemed to be a member of the clan and who had watched the scene, frozen to the spot, he gestured for him to come over.

"Who are you?"

"Anacleti, Silvio. I'm the nephew."

"You can go ahead say the first name before the last name. Because I haven't sent you to prison yet. And anyway, your uncle is right. You need to talk to a lawyer, because I'm taking you in for resisting arrest and insulting an officer."

"I've already called Parisi. He's on his way."

"That's better."

Rocco Anacleti, in pajamas, slippers, and a loose tweed overcoat, was loaded into an ROS Subaru.

Malatesta used his cell phone to call Alba. In Ostia, the usual: a little hashish, no weapons.

Once again, they'd had the time to clean things up.

It wasn't even eleven yet. Everything had happened very quickly. While his men were starting to inventory the material they'd confiscated, Marco told the prosecuting magistrate that they could consider that night's work finished.

"Shall I have you taken home, Dottor de Candia?"

"So early? I don't know about you, but I feel like listening to a little music. What do you say, you want to come with me?"

Sure. De Candia really was an odd duck, Marco said to himself. But as long as they were on the same side . . . And then, he concluded as he was telling him yes, he was curious to know just how far his strangeness extended.

De Candia took him to a little club in the historical center.

"The cellar is a little private space for friends," he explained, "the proprietor is a friend and when I ask him he lets me use it."

There were a dozen or so people of all ages, though for the most part in their thirties and forties. Bourgeois faces, quite respectable. De Candia introduced him as an old friend. He got him a cold beer and a table next to the upright piano. Then, accompanied by a burst of friendly applause, he started to play. So he was a musician, too. And a good one. With great composure and inspiration, de Candia dominated the instrument, alternating angry cascades of notes with pauses dense with an uncertainty that you might have called poetic. Marco recognized a couple of pieces: a perky version of Thelonious Monk's "'Round Midnight," the anthem of the elite and slightly crazed masonic network of jazz musicians, followed by a bit of Abdullah Ibrahim and lots and lots of Michel Petrucciani. But all of it reinterpreted, revitalized, and personalized, in some cases to excess. A tour de force of character, power, and delicacy. The show lasted close to an hour. In the end, de Candia, to a shower of enthusiastic applause, joined him at the table.

"I'm speechless!" Marco commented.

"I admit that this is what I would have wanted to do with my life, Colonel. Unfortunately, I was born into the wrong family in the wrong city, and so I've had to accept a few compromises."

"I could teach a seminar on compromise."

"But I'm not complaining. It's fine the way it is. I do my job and when I can, I indulge in an evening out with my friends."

More unfiltered craft beers arrived, accompanied by the inevitable platters of Sienese Cinta pork salami and mountain pasture cheeses. They talked about jazz, about the legendary bad temper and violent magnetism of Michel Petrucciani. A toast to jazz, then.

"To jazz!"

Marco's cell phone vibrated. A text from Alice: "Even if you're a perfect idiot, I still miss you." He typed an impassioned response and emerged with a stupid smile.

De Candia studied him with his clear, ironic gaze.

"Is she pretty?"

"How the hell . . . "

"Oh, you're right," he said, shifting nonchalantly to a more informal tone. "I might ask: is she interesting? Is she well-read?

Is she sweet, feisty, sharp-edged, docile, intelligent, independent, or protective? There are twenty thousand adjectives to define the object of our desires, but we men always and inevitably come up with the same one: Is she pretty? Is she pretty? They're right when they tell us that we're limited and mono-maniacal. You're head over heels, aren't you? I was watching you, earlier, while I was playing. That languid demeanor, especially during the most melodic sections. I'd say we have a romantic on our hands."

"I wouldn't want to be questioned by you," Marco retorted.

"I'd like to meet her."

"I'll see what I can do," Marco replied, vaguely embarrassed.

De Candia cleared his throat and changed the subject.

"But you tell me: what on earth is a criminal like Rocco Anacleti doing with those subdivision plans? Don't you wish you knew?"

# XXXII

When Ciro Viglione asked him for the keys to the red Mercedes SLK, Dr. Temistocle Malgradi turned pale. "There's an inspection scheduled for today, Ciro."

"Doc, I don't give a fuck about that. I have to go out. And right away."

"So what am I supposed to tell the cops?"

"Just invent something. Aren't you a professor? Now, Professo', come on, give me those keys."

"Ciro, you shouldn't push things too far. This would be the third inspection you've skipped. I wouldn't want some over-zealous inspector to start gettings some strange ideas."

"Nothing will happen, stop worrying, Professo'. In any case, if they start busting our chops, you just pay them off. There's a little cash in the cabinet, the one to the right of the bed."

But Temistocle Malgradi kept stalling. What if they send new personnel, let's say, for a surprise inspection? They say that a new prosecuting magistrate has arrived in the district attorney's office, a hipster from Lecce who's got who knows what into his head. Wouldn't it be better to put this off a little?

"Now you've busted my balls long enough, okay! The keys!"

The doctor put his hands together as if in prayer and finally spat out the truth.

"Ciro, don't lose your temper . . . The Mercedes is in for repairs."

"Eh?"

It had been a damned piece of bad luck. A really unfortunate coincidence. Temistocle had borrowed the car to make a good impression on a young girl working toward her degree, a spectacular beauty, a genuine rosebud, and on their way back from a lovely evening out, you know how these things go, a glass of wine too many, a sudden swerve at an intersection . . .

"But it's just a scratch, eh, Ciro, and I swear to you that you'll have it back just like new."

Ciro stared at the chief physician. A flash of something glinted in his watery eyes. Malgradi shivered. He'd fucked up this time. Certainly, Ciro and the other guys needed him. Ciro did in particular, seeing that in his gilded suite in the finest clinic in Rome he was practically serving out his jail term free of charge, at the taxpayers' expense. For that matter, everyone needed everyone else in the game they were playing, but still, Ciro was a stone criminal, and when you're dealing with criminals you never really know.

But now Ciro had started laughing, and his eyes looked a little calmer.

"Not just like new, Doctor. New, period."

"Ciro."

"Ciro my ass! Tomorrow I want a new SLK. Red, no wait, this time I want it blue. And I want it parked downstairs. Right now, though, I'm in a hurry. What kind of car do you have?"

"You . . . I?"

"Do you see anyone else in here? Right now, Doc!"

With a sigh, Temistocle Malgradi held out the keys to his Audi Q7.

"Take care, Professo'."

Half an hour later he was parking in the piazza in front of Samurai's little two-story villa.

As always, the gate was wide open, there were no bodyguards in sight, and there were no security cameras. According to Samurai, a boss's best defense is pure charisma.

"A couple of stray dogs who'll shoot you in the back for a hundred euros are easy to find, Ciro. And once someone's sent them to get you, any attempt to defend yourself is futile. The problem has to be taken care of at the root. You have to be powerful enough to nip in the bud even the thought of doing you any harm. Have I made myself clear?"

"Sure, why not, Samurai! But you just go on down to Casapesenna, and try telling them that! And then we can all have a nice fat laugh!"

Ciro Viglione had known Samurai for a lifetime, and he'd detested him for the same amount of time. His Japanese obsessions were intolerable. His attitude of superiority made him see red. And his diet of a constipated queer, well, that was enough to turn his stomach.

But he had to force himself to like Samurai.

Business demanded it.

And in business there are no such things as liking someone or disliking them. In business there is only coexistence.

Ciro Viglione was fifty years old, and for the past thirty years he had been traveling in business class through the underworld, cleverly picking his way through larger and smaller Camorra wars. As the pill-addled *guagliuncelli* exterminated each other with commendable vigor out on the street and underbosses stabbed one another in the back, he shifted from one side to another with agile nonchalance. Now he was the wise man, now he was the seething lunatic. He took the best from this one and that, never even grazed by a bullet, protected by his natural propensity for treachery and his innate street sense. When things got too hot for him in Naples, he'd moved bag and baggage to Rome, and there he had begun to prosper in the shadow of his mentor, Trentadenari. He'd gone into business with Libano's boys, and when Trentadenari had decided to turn informant, selling human flesh by the pound in exchange for a bowl of lentils, he'd done his time behind bars in silence and dignity. When he got out he realized, to his surprise and above all to his infinite delight, that he was now the only Neapolitan of any heft left standing in Rome. Stitching his old alliances back together proved to be child's play. Now he, Perri, and Samurai formed a sort of triumvirate, as Samurai had defined it. The man really never missed a chance to bust people's balls. As if book learning had ever filled anyone's belly.

At any rate, Rome belonged to them.

And that's the way it had to stay.

Samurai came to meet him halfway, descending the white marble staircase with the step of an SS officer. Well, he was a Nazi after all, the asshole, wasn't he?

He was wearing a loose black kimono, and when Ciro noticed the white scorpion stamped on the back, he couldn't help but laugh.

"Samura', look out, scorpions sting!"

"This one is tame," the man retorted with the usual detached tone of voice. "And even if it tried, it wouldn't live long enough."

Ciro Viglione searched in vain through his limited arsenal for an adequate response, and finally just decided to drop it. On that terrain, there was no beating Samurai. Better to think about more serious things.

"I'm in a hurry, Samura'. What the fuck are you up to?"

"A good cup of tea tends to clear the brain." Samurai cut the conversation short, and headed inside. Ciro followed him, reciting an imprecation over and over under his breath.

Samurai poured cold green tea from a carafe with a curious elongated shape.

"It's called Gloria del Diamante," he explained, "the Diamond's Glory, one of the most refined products of the ancient glassmaker's craft of Murano."

Ciro Viglione wondered whether Samurai not only ate like

a queer but was one. He refrained from any comment. That wouldn't be a good idea. He knew a professional killer who had chosen to confess to twenty-five murders rather than admit to his own homosexuality.

"All right. But now can we talk, please?"

"There's been a little unrest between Ostia and Cinecittà," Samurai said in an icy tone.

"You call this a little unrest?" Ciro said, starting to get heated. "This is a historic clusterfuck! Dead people in all directions, shootouts, those fucking Carabinieri breathing down our necks. And you're sitting here drinking this fucking green tea!"

"The situation is under control, Ciro."

"Bullshit, Samura'. It seems to me that there are too many people around taking care of their own business instead of thinking about the welfare of one and all. You need to do something, and you need to do it fast."

Samurai sighed. Ciro wasn't entirely wrong.

He tried to explain to him that the problem still remained unchanged. Having to deal with primitives. Necessarily being forced to rely upon their savage force, reserving their control, let's even call it, their manipulation, for yourself, and running the risk of unpredictable outbursts.

"Because in the final analysis, Ciro, we need these motley crews. They're our labor. The proletariat from the street. We need to toss them a scrap now and again, and rein them in when they've run away with themselves. We can't do without them. *Unfortunately*."

Samurai seemed very sure of himself. With respect to him and Perri, Samurai had an advantage: he was a local. The indispensable indigenous player without whose decisive assistance no organization worthy of the name can seriously hope to sink roots in foreign soil. All the same, even he recognized that the street was seething. To what extent would

Samurai be able to keep that street under control? Would his word be sufficient? No disrespect intended but frankly, at this point, Ciro was fucking sick and tired of all this charisma, as he put it.

"Samura', listen to me: these are just words!"

"The deeds will follow."

"What do you mean?"

"That I'll put an end to it, all this unrest."

"But how?"

"Once and for all."

Okay, at least this was a concrete commitment. As long as he wasn't just trying to stall for time. But, for that matter, everyone had the same interest in the game going well, they all had the same stake in this thing.

And Samurai, clearly, had something in mind.

"All right. But don't take too long about it, okay?" Ciro said, at last, getting to his feet.

Samurai walked him down to the courtyard. Ciro called a taxi and gave the address.

Samurai pointed to the Audi.

"What about your car?"

Ciro told him the story of Malgradi.

"So now, we're going to play a nice practical joke on the professor. You call up the Anacletis and tell them to make this car disappear. That way we'll teach this asshole Malgradi to play tricks on me!"

"Does that strike you as an intelligent thing to do, Ciro?"

"Who the fuck cares if it's intelligent or not! It's a prank, Samura'. What, don't you understand the word? Prank?"

Once he was alone, Samurai parked the Audi in the garage, then went down into the basement, lifted a couple of partition walls, and triggered the mechanism that released the spring of a tiny trapdoor concealed beneath a tile that was identical to all the others in the floor.

Inside was an oily rag, wrapped around his beloved Mannlicher.

Samurai knew that he would have to get rid of it.

He was sorry about that.

But it was time for the Mannlicher to let its song be heard once again.

# XXXIII

De Candia had nailed the point neatly.

The plans that had been confiscated from Rocco Anacleti, with the cryptic annotations in the margins of stenciled maps, were perhaps the first piece of concrete evidence to surface since the slaughter had begun between Ostia and Cinecittà.

It didn't require an expert to figure out that someone had a Great Project in mind.

But how did the Anacletis fit in? Their presence didn't fit the picture.

Or maybe it justified it.

If a venerable old dynasty of thieves and pushers decides to go into real estate, it's because it's found a good reason to do so.

Marco questioned Rocco Anacleti.

"Well? What's so strange about that? I want to build a beachfront villa. I can afford it, you know?"

Sure, a beachfront villa! Those maps covered a huge area stretching from EUR to the province of Latina, by way of Ardea, Pomezia, and Casalazzara with plenty of detailed illustrations of the Ostia coastline.

A villa. Or maybe, a city.

Rocco Anacleti building a city? And what if that was it?

An idea was starting to take shape. And it reeked of real estate speculation.

On the bottom left of every confiscated sheet of paper was the logo of Mailand & Partners. One of the most prestigious architectural studios in the world. They were working for the Anacletis, those illiterates from Romanina? And just for them?

He thought about asking Mailand & Partners about it directly. But he decided not to. Without a signed warrant, they would have claimed client privilege.

But a warrant was predicated on a criminal accusation. And, until proven otherwise, there had been no crime.

Still, the stench of something rotten was getting stronger.

Marco concentrated on the territory marked out on the maps. Ostia. He made phone calls, he ordered archived reports. Ostia. Six cases of arson along the Ponente coast in the past few months. He got in touch with Lieutenant Gaudino.

"Yes, I'd mentioned that to you, Colonel. They're punishing the ones that don't fall into line."

But was it just part of a protection racket? Something didn't add up. All of the bathing establishments that had been targeted by the arsonists were run on a state concession by social cooperatives. They'd been burned to the ground. And after the fire, they'd all lost their state concessions.

He asked for help from an old acquaintance who worked in the municipal offices. He was given access to the files that interested him. The concessions had all been conveyed to the same individual. Michele Lo Surdo. A legendary business accountant tangled up in a thousand murky deals: in point of fact, the number one consigliere of the Roman underworld.

The picture was starting to take shape.

Gaudino was wrong.

They were burning the bathing establishments to clear rights to the beachfront.

And they were clearing rights to the beachfront so they could begin construction.

And since not a leaf rustled on a tree in Ostia without the permission of Number Eight, Number Eight had to be part of this.

In that case, why were the maps in the possession of the Anacletis?

Because they'd caught wind of the business opportunity and wanted in, and perhaps they'd been turned down and that had led to a gang war.

Or else, because they were in on the deal with the rest of them, only at a certain point things had gotten off balance and a gang war had erupted.

If the maps pointed in the right direction, then the entire area could be considered open for construction.

Marco pictured the scenario.

Millions of cubic yards of cement, no doubt. And a raging river of cash. Unless, without warning, the various Anacletis, Adamis, and Sales hadn't found a philanthropical calling.

And in that case, was it plausible that Neapolitans and Calabrians weren't already waiting in the wings?

To pass such a zoning plan would require the approval of a resolution by the city council, he reasoned.

He searched the official websites. Not a hint. There was no such resolution on the agenda. It wasn't hard to figure out why: those directly interested were eager to avoid publicity. The resolution would pop up out of nowhere. And by the time it did, it would be too late to organize any opposition.

So why hadn't it happened yet?

Because they hadn't struck a final deal yet.

To put the final touches on a pact of that scale, a great many hungry mouths would have to be fed and a great many thirsts would have to be slaked.

An unquestioned authority would have to be brought to bear. No, make that two. One to control the street. The other to marshal the halls of power.

Who controlled the street? Samurai.

But the street was being rocked by a gang war.

Did that mean Samurai had failed? Or had he actually retired, the way people were saying?

Marco couldn't believe that. People like Samurai never changed.

What about the halls of power? Who was the institutional sponsor?

As long as the war raged, such a figure had no incentive to come out into the open.

Which brought us back to square one.

Why the shooting if such a colossal business opportunity was in the offing?

Someone hadn't stuck to the terms of the agreement, and had chosen to overturn the table.

But neither Spadino nor Paja and Fieno seemed important enough to unleash a gang war.

There had to be something else at stake.

Marco copied everything and headed off to Alice's place.

He barged in on her, catching her off guard while, in the center of the living room of the two-bedroom apartment not far from Piazza dei Re di Roma, she was working the heavy bag. Glowing with sweat like that, in a tank top and boxing shorts, she sent a wave of blood to his head. And, fortunately, she put up no resistance at all.

Afterward, he told her that he needed her help to start playing dirty.

And Alice was more than willing.

# XXXIV

Manfredi gave Sebastiano a gift of a .38 caliber revolver and took him on vacation with him, to the area around the Gran Sasso.

"It's a clean weapon . . . well, maybe not 100 percent clean. But in any case, it knows how to do its job."

"So what am I supposed to do with it? I don't even know which end is which."

"What do you think we're doing here, anyway?"

They moved into a handsomely furnished mountain refuge which Sor Scipione had extorted from its rightful owner in the normal routine of his duties as a shylock: a doctor from Prati had gotten in over his head with Texas hold 'em. They practiced shooting early in the morning and at sunset. Sebastiano was a quick learner, he had a good eye and a steady hand, and to make a long story short, with each day that passed, he was looking more and more like the right candidate for what Manfredi had in mind.

The last night they were up there they went out to dinner in a trattoria crowded with young men in camo and combat boots.

"My father told me that up here the whole place used to be overrun with paramilitary camps. You know, that whole thing with people who were nostalgic about Il Duce and wanted to bring back Fascism, who were storing rifles and bombs to overthrow the state . . . "

"And are these guys," whispered Sebastiano, pointing to the other guests, "their children?"

"Nooo," Manfredi chuckled, "these are just a bunch of knuckleheads who play war games on weekends. You get the kind of buffoons you run into, Sebastia'?"

"So listen, Manfredi. The pistol, the target practice . . . are you looking for a bodyguard, is that it?"

The loan shark's son decided that the time had come to show his cards.

"No, we're just going to make a withdrawal," he said. "Don't worry."

"A what?"

"We're going to pick up a guy who owes us some money and we're going to bring him around," Manfredi explained.

"You've gone completely crazy!" Sebastiano objected, pushing away the ravioli with mutton sauce, that, actually, he hadn't even touched yet.

"It'll be a piece of cake, child's play. No one's going to get hurt."

"Don't look at me."

"Not even if Papa gave you a break on fifty percent of the principal?"

The engineer's son took his head in his hands. A monster. Manfredi was a monster. He'd taken away his home, his prosperity, his girlfriend, his dignity. And now he was taking what was left of his life. A slave, that's what he was going to become. A slave.

And when has a slave ever had a choice in the matter?

In any case, looked at clinically, there was something attractive about the offer.

"I want a written guarantee, Manfredi."

"We'll go to the notary. I'll take you to the notary's office, brother."

"Then, okay."

The loan shark's son leaned forward and, with a conspiratorial air, started telling him about it.

\*

They returned to Rome in the middle of the night, and took action at dawn. The guy they needed to convince was an accountant from a good family, with the face of someone from the Parioli neighborhood, fancy clothes, and a penthouse apartment in the Flaminio neighborhood. But he'd ruined himself with his coke habit. His wife had thrown him out of the house, and he'd indebted himself up to the neck with Sor Scipione. He was out to the tune of thirty large. Thirty thousand euros that, since he hadn't been willing to pay when pressured with gentler methods, would now have to be recovered with a more brutal approach.

"Because Papa is just too goodhearted," Manfredi commented, "so I have to take care of things. Or, actually, you and I do, brother."

Now the rat had holed up in the lair of a friend of his who was a tranny, Letizia, also known, for reasons that weren't hard to guess, as "platinum tongue," in a sort of attic apartment in the Tiburtino district. When they burst into the place, after kicking the door in, they were overwhelmed by the reek of sweaty bodies and stale cigarette smoke, and by a concert of moans and grunts that their sudden arrival brusquely silenced.

"Jesus, what a pig sty!" Manfredi muttered.

The accountant was a short, fat, bald man. The loan shark's son and the engineer's son had caught him with company: Letizia, a tall job with unmistakably masculine features, and a small woman about thirty years old—less than five feet tall— with curly hair and oversized breasts.

While Manfredi started searching the place for coke, cash, jewelry, and anything else that could be used to pay back the debt—with accrued interest of course—Sebastiano kept the little trio covered.

It was to the young man that the three hostages appealed, in rapid sequence. Each of them had their own tale of woe, which they recounted in distinctive tones of querulous lament. And each of them ready to rat out the others.

The accountant shouted that the busty bitch was to blame for the whole thing. She was the one who'd ripped off the cash. And so he, cunning as a fox, had lured her here, into a trap. To make her sing and to get the money back.

The big-bosomed midget with curly hair, known to the world as Luana, reacted venomously. Me a thief? That bastard is the one who's been walking around boasting about how he ripped off the shylocks. As for the shit and the cash, they were splitting it with Letizia.

When Letizia's name was mentioned, she volunteered that the two of them, the accountant and the little whore, had offered to go into business with her to sell their shit in the circuit of the trannies and the well-to-do clients who rented them out for their exotic evening entertainments. She added that the accountant had financed the purchase of the first shipment of coke with the very same thirty thousand euros that the two "segnori" were looking for.

Manfredi declared that the search was over. He held up a baggie full of coke, another baggie full of tabs of ecstasy, and two thousand euros.

"You look like you've been through the mill," he commented sarcastically.

That unleashed a flood of tears. The accountant swore on the heads of his three children that he had never meant to, that the cocaine had taken over his mind, that he'd pay Manfredi back to the very last penny, but that first he had to get that monkey off his back. The very next day he'd go into rehab. They had to take pity on him, poor wretch that he was.

The tranny cursed the brutal slum she'd come from. She had sixteen brothers and sisters to support. She'd work for them for free, if they'd only let her go.

Luana turned on the waterworks. One day she'd lost her

way, and she didn't even know why. Maybe because of her sick daughter, her dead father, the job she couldn't find. But she would pay them back. It was just a matter of time.

Manfredi thought it over. He hadn't expected this kind of a mess. He didn't know exactly how to handle it.

Sebastiano stood there listening to the three of them, and little by little an unfamiliar feeling began to steal over him. It was a mixture of anger, cruelty, and indifference. In those three unfortunates, he was unable to glimpse the victims of misguided impulses, the wreckage of lives cast adrift. Instead all he could see was three cunning bastards, pathetic sons of bitches who'd screwed the pooch and were now whining for pity. He felt no pity for any of them. Just as no one had felt pity for him, when he had had his life taken away from him. So, this was their problem, all things considered. Everyone is responsible for their own actions.

At that exact moment, the engineer's son understood that he would never get his old life back. So he might as well just go ahead and fabricate a completely different life for himself.

"Get dressed!" he snapped out.

He made the accountant give him his cell phone and called a taxi, loaded the girl and the tranny into the cab, gave each of them a twenty euro banknote, and urged them each, in their own self-interest, to forget everything.

Then he pocketed his pistol, smiled at the accountant, and invited him to take him and Manfredi to his bank. Where he would withdraw all the cash he possessed.

The expedition lasted no more than a half hour. The accountant managed to scrape together fifteen thousand euros. Sebastiano gave him a week to pay down the rest.

Finally, he let him go.

Sebastiano's icy calm had made quite an impression on Manfredi. If he'd possessed a fraction of his father's anima-lesque intelligence, he would have understood that the young man had long since slipped out of control. That it would have been much wiser to just let him go his way. But that's not what he did. He took credit for his friend's new ferocity. It had been his charisma as a capo that had transformed Sebastiano. He praised him and told him he was a "born tough guy." He suggested they split the coke and, when Sebastiano proudly rejected the offer, told him that he reminded him of someone, a guy who mattered in Rome, perhaps the most important of them all. That person was Samurai. Manfredi introduced Sebastiano to him the day after their caper, taking advantage of a quick visit by Samurai to La Paranza.

"This guy's cold-blooded, Samurai. You'll like him."

Samurai studied the young man with interest. What he read in his eyes convinced him. He took him aside, ignoring Manfredi.

"Tell me about yourself, kid."

Sebastiano trusted him instantly. He mirrored himself in the eyes of that cold man, seeing there the same indifference that he'd decided to don as a sort of second skin. He concealed nothing from him. In the end, Samurai told him that they'd see each other again soon. Sebastiano went back to his job at the auto dealership.

Not long after that, he sold a Porsche Boxster for cash to a tremendous slut dressed up as a sophisticated lady, accompanied by a cultured faggot.

## XXXV

A lice, this is Michelangelo de Candia, my friend the prosecuting magistrate who I told you about. Michelangelo, this is Alice . . . "

"The girl from the texts. She's even better than how you described her, Marco."

Marco shot him daggers with an angry glare and hastened to reassure Alice. They'd never talked about her, and he wasn't the kind of guy to boast openly about his passions.

Alice planted a kiss on his cheek.

"Oh, I know, I know. For that matter," she added, maliciously, "you never told me that your friend was so cute."

Marco couldn't come up with a snappy retort. De Candia broke in and, pointing with almost childish pride to the Renault 4 with a Lecce license plate, opened the passenger-side door.

"What do you say, eh? Isn't it marvelous? Be my guests, get in."

Alice let herself sink into the fabric upholstery of the aluminum-framed seat which reminded her of a lounge chair and, looking at the gear shift next to the steering wheel and the tiny dashboard that made it look so much like a toy car, put an expression on her face that was a mix of the amused and the appalled.

"What kind of car is this?"

"The legendary Renault 4. It was made in 1989. It belonged to my father. It's the only tangible thing I've held onto in my life. What's the old saying? There are only two things you can never change: your parents and the team you root for. Well, I'll say that the Renault 4 is the third item on that list, if you've ever been lucky enough to own one. Upkeep isn't cheap, but . . . "

Marco had tucked himself into the back seat.

"This was the Red Brigades' favorite car," he commented.

Alice couldn't resist. The target was too juicy.

"Do you mind if we change centuries?"

De Candia burst out laughing.

"Well, listen to her."

Marco shook his head.

Alice looked at Michelangelo. That faint Salento singsong pleased her ear. The prosecuting magistrate was definitely a handsome young man.

They drove past Viale Marco Polo and turned into Via Cristoforo Colombo. Alice and Michelangelo kept on exchanging witty banter. They'd hit it off instantly. Why had it been so hard for him, then? He shut down in a grouchy silence. He had the clear sensation that a not particularly subtle game of seduction had started up between the two of them, and the idea of feeling even a hint of jealousy made him feel both ridiculous and childish.

Cut it out, Marco.

When they drew even with the Marconi obelisk, de Candia slowed down almost to a halt.

"We have been invited here today by Lieutenant Colonel Malatesta Marco," the prosecuting magistrate declaimed, "to learn 'the truth about Rome.' *Badaboom*. Here, as far as I'm concerned, is where Rome ends. These are my Columns of Hercules, Marco: *hic sunt leones*."

Marco looked at Alice, who turned serious.

"Michelangelo, this is no joking matter," he said. "Starting tomorrow, the real city is going to start right from these streets."

"Why?"

"I've studied the maps of the Anacletis and I've gathered a little data. There's a construction project, a major piece of real estate speculation, the biggest one in history. Prestigious architects are already working on it. Millions of cubic yards of cement will cover the twenty miles from here to the sea. The client ordering this work is a company called New City. The managing director is Michele Lo Surdo, an old acquaintance of ours. The underworld's business accountant. The same guy who scooped up the state concessions all up and down Ostia Ponente after a providential little hand set fire to the bathing establishments that were already there."

"A construction project, you say?"

"Between Rome and Ardea, affordable housing. But it's a little more elegant to call it social housing. In Ostia, a new port. But there, too, it's fancier to call it Waterfront."

"That seems like something big . . . "

"It is."

"Then why haven't I heard anything about it?"

"It's secret, for the moment. The gang war has put a halt to everything."

"And if it's secret, how come you know so much about it?"

With the help of Diego, the Rebel Dragon that Alice liked so much, they had broken into the "cloud," the virtual safe of the architectural studio of Mailand & Partners. Everything they knew was the result of a series of crimes. The kind of thing you couldn't explain to a prosecuting magistrate.

"Let's just say that I have my methods. Go around this way, please . . . " Marco pointed de Candia to stay on the right and continue along Via Cristoforo Colombo in the direction of Ostia. "Before you reach Casal Palocco, follow the signs for Axa. There's a place where we can grab a drink."

"So who's actually behind New City?" Michelangelo asked.

"A cartel. It's made up of the Anacletis, the Adami-Sale clan of Ostia, and I think Rocco Perri, who is the local representative of the Calabrian 'ndrangheta, and then Ciro Viglione, who represents the Neapolitans. Ah, I forgot about the Holy Mother Church."

"Really!" exclaimed de Candia, in astonishment.

"New City, so they can build lots of cardboard houses. Every so many miles, they'll build a bell tower. Got it?"

"Interesting . . . " de Candia pondered. "And you, Alice, you're not saying anything. Maybe you gave him a hand with all this?"

"Me? No, I didn't do anything . . . these are names I'm hearing for the very first time."

"*Ma famme 'u piacere!*" the prosecuting magistrate said in dialect. "Oh, do me a favor!"

Alice wasn't much of a liar, Marco realized with a hint of relief. And Michelangelo was a friend.

They stopped outside what looked like a pub. A low wooden structure, an incongruous mountain chalet in the midst of a stand of tall maritime pines.

"Frodo," announced the neon sign outside.

"I didn't know that Tolkien lived on the Roman seacoast," de Candia commented, inviting Marco to lead them in.

"It's a curious Fascist community that lives around here," Marco started telling the story. "A mixture of veterans of the mid-twentieth century, imaginary Fascists stuffed with fantasy culture, and soccer stadium animals. An ideal substrate for the microbes to grow on, if you can just imagine the foundations on which the new Rome is going to stand."

With a nod of understanding, the colonel greeted a guy in his early fifties with tattooed forearms who had to be the proprietor. The man introduced himself as Dario. The club was deserted. They sat down at a corner table. Dario served them a tray with three pints of Menabrea beer and a platter of jamón serrano.

Marco went on.

"I arrested Dario a short while before leaving the country. He was a sort of revolutionary past his sell-by date. He's convinced that by arresting him I saved his life. Let's just say that, since then, we've formed a relationship of mutual respect. He's not a chatterbox, but usually the few things he does say are quite sound. He was the one who explained to me, when I came back to Rome, that the old Fascist comrades had put on jackets and ties and now they were pretending they were executives. He told me: 'Marco, they're all in pinstripes now. But right-wing bandits is what they were and what they still are. Deep down, Rome's never changed. A black sun with the usual satellites orbiting around it.'"

Alice couldn't resist.

"Then it's true what people say. That you Carabinieri get along with the Fascists."

De Candia delicately put his hand on her forearm.

"Forgive me, Alice. But if I were you, I'd try to be a little less cutting."

"Why? Because he's a Carabiniere and you're a prosecuting magistrate? Am I guilty of insubordination?"

"Of course not. It's just that I used to be like you. Then I understood at a certain point that if you think you know too much you know nothing. And you lose almost everything. It's not enough to just read the way things work in some book."

Alice went back to needling Michelangelo.

"And when did you have this revelation?"

"In Milan, the day I found myself face to face with a merchant banker. I had the report open on the desk. And I was convinced that he was just going to confess."

"And instead?"

"And instead he told me something that I've never forgotten. 'You, Dottor de Candia, think that I know the meaning of what I do, and so you question me about it. You're convinced that a banker is something other than what he is. I know nothing about what I sell, de Candia. I don't know what the hell a derivative is, I don't even understand interest rate swaps, much less collars. That's stuff that some kid who's good at math can do. The work I do involves people. All I'm trying to do is respond to their greed or desperation.' In other words, what he told me was, 'I don't know.'"

Alice dropped her gaze. Through the pub's windows, Marco pointed out to de Candia the patch of light that could be seen in the distance.

"Down there is Infernetto. It was an illegally built *borgata*—something between a quarter and a village. Like every other wall built in this part of town. First they amnestied everything. Then they sold them a dream. Rome just like Atlantic City. Casinos, ski slopes in the pine groves. Chairlifts. Malls every half mile. An orgy of merchandizing to make it look like something it's not."

"And especially useful in terms of laundering dirty money," Alice added.

"A perfect cop commentary. Coppish, and yet, correct," de Candia smiled, nodding.

They left the Axa quarter, heading for the sea. It was almost two in the morning by now. A couple of shivering streetcleaners were loitering outside the porchetta foodtruck parked on one of the sides of the Ostia roundabout. Marco asked Michelangelo to pull over by the wharf of the marina. A few miserable sailboats could hardly fill the spectral void of wastefully empty slips. The skeleton in reinforced concrete of a tall, unfinished building loomed over them like a mournful ruin. They got out of the Renault 4 and started strolling. Marco lit a Camel.

"Ostia had no need of this port. At least, not a port this size. Fiumicino is fifteen minutes away. But the important thing was to start to pour cement. Because a port can become a casino on the beach, because the reasons places are used for can change. *Waterfront.* It sounds good, right?"

They got back in the car. Driving back up Via Cristoforo Colombo toward Rome, the Renault 4 turned into a nameless coplanar expanse of asphalt. An alleyway sunk in grim darkness, at the end of which something glittered, a surreal apparition that looked like the entrance to a circus. They stopped about a hundred yards short of the light source.

"That's La Caverna. Officially, a discotheque. In actual fact, a monument to the peace that the Anacletis had established with the Adami-Sales, and which now seems to have vanished in a puff of smoke," Marco explained.

"And what does the peace have to do with a discotheque?" asked Michelangelo.

"Denis Sale had married an Anacleti woman. And together they ran this dive. Cocaine, hookers, slot machines. A marriage of interests that was designed to baptize a new equilibrium, shall we say, throughout the city. No more gang wars over clubs or restaurants. Instead, a salubrious new form of cooperation, where there would be room for the Calabrians and the Neapolitans, too. From the Café de Paris on Via Veneto all the way down to this shithole. Then Denis was left a widower and another tarantella began, evidently."

"It all sounds very persuasive," said de Candia.

"Open up a case file," Marco urged him, "on acts connected with a construction project. I'll draw up an official report. I can attach everything you need: not just the Anacleti maps, but architectural plans, sketches, feasibility studies, opinions of the superintendency, there's even a draft regional law that concerns . . . wait a second . . . ah, 'supplementary provisions in the domain of worship,' in practical terms, authorization to build a healthy array of bed-and-breakfasts that will be run by priests. I'll just say that I stumbled on it thanks to a confidential source."

De Candia interrupted him with a jerk of the head.

"You think that the gang war between Ostia and Cinecittà is a result of this, don't you?"

"I'm sure of it. Some existing equilibrium must have been knocked silly. I don't know why, and I intend to find out. But I do know that someone's working to restore order and put things back the way they were. Usually, when there's a lot of money at stake, the various groups bring in *regulators*. They need someone to keep the street in line, and they generally need a political sponsor, too."

"And you already know who they are, don't you?"

"As far as the political side goes, I'm in the dark. I don't know anything about that side of things, I'm happy to admit it. But for the street, there's only one man capable of putting things back on track." Marco fiddled with his iPhone, then showed de Candia the picture that he'd sneakily snapped of Samurai before confronting him at the gas station on Corso di Francia. "Samurai."

"Does he have slanted eyes?" de Candia inquired in a blasé tone of voice. "It's hard to say from these pictures." Alice burst out laughing. She adored de Candia's lightness and irony. The conversation turned frivolous. Alice said that she'd suddenly come down with a yen for something sweet. She knew a place, the best in town. The prosecuting magistrate stopped being a serious professional and begged her to take them there. Right away. Marco stuffed his cell phone in his pocket and tagged along after them, huffing in annoyance.

By the time they got to San Basilio day was dawning. Via Luigi Gigliotti was deserted, even though the crumbling, sprawling tenement blocks of the occupied apartment houses—squats for as long as anyone could remember and lord only knew who squatted there—seemed to be quivering with some form of vigilant life. Which manifested itself with sudden apparitions of shadows on the interiors of the court-yards and the lobbies. Young men bundled up in dark heavy jackets, with wool watch caps pulled down over their heads.

"Where the hell are we?" asked de Candia, disoriented.

"Half way around the beltway to the northwest," Alice replied.

"Good. Now I know less than I did before."

"We're at Rome's Supermarket," said Marco.

"Supermarket? What's that supposed to mean?"

"This is the biggest drug-dealing marketplace in the city, my friend. A supermarket for uppers and downers at discount prices. Let's just say that this is the Anacleti outlet store," Marco continued.

"Wait, Alice, weren't you hankering after some pastries?" de Candia broke in.

"That's right," she said. "That's why we're here. Because right here, aside from the cocaine, the hashish, and the heroin, there's also a little hole in the wall that sells the best *cornetti* pastries in the city."

She pointed to an anodized aluminum door that opened out onto the sidewalk on Via Recanati.

Enveloped in a dizzying scent of yeast, they stepped carefully down a steep staircase, which led into the underground heart of a tiny pastry shop with a close-packed bakery. Working in front of two large aluminum baking ovens, two young Maghrebis were greasing giant baking pans while a corpulent man in his early sixties kept an eye on them with an apparently distracted demeanor. Alice threw her arms around him, as if she were hugging her father.

"This is Mario. Mario, meet Marco and Michelangelo."

"Mhm, they look a lot like cops to me . . . no offense, eh! Alice, don't tell me that you're dating pigs these days," smiled the pastry chef.

Marco blushed. Michelangelo decided to play along.

"Let's just say that Alice used the night to test us out. You never want to buy a pig in a poke."

"And how come you're around these parts?"

"Just taking a ride. Michelangelo doesn't know Rome very well."

"It's true," de Candia said, throwing his arms wide.

"This isn't Rome. This isn't anything anymore."

Mario told his three visitors about the latest murders in the quarter. A fifteen-year-old punk who'd bled to death after a brawl. A couple of pushers. A guy from Torraccia—the new section of the San Basilio neighborhood, outside the beltway—who had just said a couple of words too many at a self-service gas station.

"The place is full of rabid stray dogs," said Mario, shaking his head as he filled a cardboard takeout tray with pastries and doughnuts: *cornetti*, *bombe*, and *ciambelle*. "They're coked out of their minds. Dawn to dusk. And they think they're the bosses around here. But they don't count for shit. They sell drugs for Anacleti and think they're God almighty. Too bad, because they're just a bunch of penniless assholes. But I told you before. This isn't Rome anymore. Even the birds have gone wrong. The other day, out front, a seagull ate a cat alive."

They went back out into the street with the 7:30 morning sun peeping out overhead.

Michelangelo turned thoughtful.

"If you ask me, you're right on the money, Marco. But what evidence do I have to proceed? A project, as long as it's just on paper, is a phantom project. Bring me evidence, solid, concrete proof. Then we'll act. But not till then."

Alice yawned. Her eyes were stinging from lack of sleep, but she'd learned a great many things during that strange night. And a number of her certainties, which until an instant before she had considered as solid as granite, were now beginning to give way. She was forced to admit that the state, the structures of power, the system, the caste, or whatever you wanted to call the entities to which those two belonged, couldn't actually be considered merely an obtuse and compact mass against which nothing was legitimate but a wall of resolute NO's. In a word, she began to feel that she actually trusted Marco and Michelangelo.

"You know," she said, "we ought to put this stuff online. All hell would break out, and someone would make a break out into the open. Let's toss a rock in the pond, and see what fish come up to the surface."

"An unorthodox, dangerous, and thoroughly illegal idea," de Candia said brusquely.

The idea was rejected out of hand.

## XXXVI

This time Number Eight had pulled the fuck-up of his life. Uncle Nino hadn't slept a wink. Back and forth he paced in his cell. Back and forth. In the morning, he summoned counselor Parisi for a meeting in prison. And to conceal his agitation, he raised his voice and spoke confidently. He told him that Cesare was untouchable, that no one must lay a finger on him. He admitted that, of course, what Cesare had done was indefensible, and that he'd fucked up not once, but three times. That his wild behavior was threatening to ruin everything they'd worked for. That in any other situation, for such idiotic behavior, there could no punishment other than death.

"But he's my nephew, counselor, blood of my blood and flesh of my flesh. He's like a son to me. We need to resolve this thing among ourselves."

"Rocco Anacleti is out of his head, Uncle Nino."

"I believe you, and he has his reasons . . . I saw him, you know, he came through here. He was in pretty bad shape. But do something for me. Go pay a call on Denis, he's a smart boy. He needs to give a couple of hundred thousand euros to the families of those two unfortunates. Then let the Anacletis know that if they're willing to overlook this thing we're willing to increase their percentage by twenty-five percent."

"If we want to be able to bring it to an end, we need to talk to the others, too," Parisi observed, pragmatically.

"Then you inform them. Talk to Rocco, talk to Ciro, talk to

Samurai, talk to Jesus Christ and the Virgin Mary, but do it fast. And tell Cesaretto that he needs to pay, and not to show his face around town for a while."

"All right, Uncle Nino. Certainly, what you're asking me to do doesn't exactly fall into the realm of the legal profession . . . "

Uncle Nino flew into a rage. Ah, now he was suddenly remembering his professional ethics, this legendary human nostril, this inveterate whoremonger, now he was suddenly reluctant, after all these years that he'd showered him with gold and white powder.

"I was just trying to say that this isn't going to be a walk in the park, Uncle Nino," Parisi hastened to explain.

Uncle Nino could tell what was coming next: as always the bloodsucker in a black lawyer's robe was going to ask for cash. It was just a matter of money. That's where they always wound up, these men without honor who were happy to hide their shameless filth behind this dirty pair of underwear they called the law.

"All right. Tomorrow I'll wire you money on the account you know about."

"Grateful as always, Uncle Nino."

That same evening, Parisi went to the Off-Shore. Denis and Robertino told him that Number Eight had taken a few days off. A fool, but certainly not a suicidal fool, Parisi thought to himself, and asked Denis to take him to the house at Campo di Carne, in the feudal holdings of a Calabrian family federated with the Perris, where Number Eight had gone to hide out with Morgana.

The lawyer explained the situation while Morgana, bare-breasted, smoked crack through a bottle covered with a lilac rag. When he realized that the lawyer was asking him for two hundred large, as a gesture of good will, Number Eight, his eyes bugging out of their sockets, burst into a hearty guffaw.

"You want me to pay them? But those two pieces of shit

ought to indemnify me, if anything; they were trying to kill me, goddamn them to hell. You know the legal term for what I did, counselor? Legitimate self-defense, is what it's called."

Parisi pointed out that it was an order from Uncle Nino and the young man instantly drew in his horns. He assured Counselor Parisi that he'd take care of it in the next twenty-four hours.

Encouraged by that initial success, Parisi summoned to his office the remaining Anacletis not yet in handcuffs. After listening to his proposition, the gypsies expressed a certain willingness to consider terms. Thirty percent, though, specified Silvio, one of the countless nephews in that vast clan, a young man you could talk to. Thirty percent, though, would be preferable. And in any case, before making any commitments, they'd have to check with Rocco.

"Just a few more days of patience and I'll have him out of there," Parisi reassured them.

The Anacletis retreated in good order, muttering their incomprehensible gypsy litanies.

The message for Ciro Viglione and Rocco Perri was entrusted to Dottor Temistocle Malgradi. The Neapolitan and the Calabrian met at Villa Marianna. They were both thoroughly sick and tired of that senseless mess, and they said they were ready to sign on for any solution that would really restore peace: in part because Uncle Nino, having shown himself willing to shoulder his nephew's debt, had proven that he was an intelligent man.

Since the bureaucratic procedures involved in springing Rocco out of jail were taking longer than expected—the case was in the hands of this de Candia, a Red toga, you know what I'm talking about—Silvio Anacleti went to the Hotel Rome, as the prison was called, and over the course of a tempestuous interview, managed to persuade Rocco to come around to the agreement.

At the end of a week, that new pact had been underwritten.

But all that optimism was unjustified.

There was someone who still hadn't expressed his opinion.

Samurai.

In response to Parisi's repeated solicitations, he had put up an incomprehensible silence. And over the last two days, just as the deal seemed to be coming to fruition to universal satisfaction, he had stopped answering his Skype calls.

The lawyer wondered whether he ought to inform the others of this development. He decided not to because he was already afraid he had ventured too far, and because he imagined that Samurai, in his notoriously far-sighted prudence, was not about to array himself against all the others.

No one had yet understood just what kind of man Samurai really was.

Finally sure of himself, certain that the storm had died down, Number Eight took up residence at the Off-Shore and, to celebrate his victorious return, organized a memorable private party. So memorable that around four in the morning, with a gusting north wind, he walked out into the street all alone to try and wear off the rivers of alcohol and the fumes of the drugs. He'd barely taken a few steps, and had just lit up an ordinary tobacco cigarette, when he saw a white Audi Q7 pull up next to him. The smoked-glass passenger-side window rolled down and a familiar voice called his name.

"Cesare!"

Max was leaning toward him, with a friendly smile stamped on his usually gloomy face. Instinctively, his hand went for the pistol that he kept stuffed down the belt of his trousers, the muzzle propped against his buttock.

"What the fuck do you want? It's all over, isn't it?"

Max got out and walked over with his hands in the air. Number Eight searched him. He was unarmed.

"Samurai wants to see you."

"But couldn't he get up off his ass and come to the party? I invited the two of you, you know."

"You know what he's like. He doesn't like a lot of noise."

"All right, but I'm pretty stoned right now. Tell him to swing by tomorrow."

"Whatever you think best," Max sighed, as he headed back to his SUV, "I'll just tell him you're not interested in the deal."

"What deal? What the fuck are you talking about? Hold on!"

"A big deal, Cesare. A metric ton of cocaine."

"Now you tell me. And just why would Samurai have suddenly remembered I even exist?"

"Because the load is coming in by ship and this is the landing point, which if I'm not mistaken, is territory that belongs to you."

Number Eight puffed up like a peacock. That's right! At last things were coming back to normal. What a good idea it had been to whack those two pieces of shit. Now everyone knew who Number Eight was, and who they were going to have to deal with. Even Samurai had decided he had to take him into consideration. If he wanted to import his shit, Samurai knew that he would have to deal with him. Samurai was asking for his help. Uncle Nino would burst with happiness when he heard.

"All right. And just where is Samurai?"

"I'll take you to him."

Along the way, he amused himself by provoking Samurai's loyal shield bearer.

"So tell me something, Max, is this story about Pigna the truth? The one where Samurai is supposed to have cut off his head with his big old sword?"

"That's the way I've heard it went."

"Thanks. I've heard the same thing. But neither one of us was actually there, were we? And from what I've heard the moniker of Samurai was given to him by Dandi when they first met in prison, and your boss was nothing more than a punk kid."

"Samurai isn't my boss, Number Eight. Men don't have bosses."

"Oh, really? But still you follow him around like a little lapdog."

"Samurai is my maestro. But you wouldn't understand."

"Oh hey, philosopher, do me a favor. Forget about it."

Samurai was waiting for them on the Capocotta beach, in the dunes. It was cold, terribly cold, but Samurai, in his inevitable black suit, hands in his pockets, face bare, seemed indifferent to the weather, the cutting wind, the roar of the surf and the rising tide, which carved, foaming, into the sandy shore scattered with soaked wood, bleached planks, the shells of dead crustaceans, and wet plastic bags.

Perhaps, for an instant, the thought that he might have walked into a blind alley flickered in Number Eight's drug-blurred mind. If he'd pulled out the gat in that moment, he might still have been able to emerge alive. But why go to all that trouble, after all: if they wanted to get him, they could always do it at the exit of the Off-Shore, they could wait in ambush near his apartment house on Piazza Gasparri, certainly. For that matter, though, wasn't there an agreement? Who the fuck was this Samurai to think he could go up against everyone? To behave like a coward, at a moment like this, meant losing face.

And so Cesare Adami strode brashly up to the figure that stood motionless among the dunes.

"Well, Samura', what about this metric ton of shit?"

Samurai spoke to Max, ignoring what he'd said.

"Max, if you'd excuse us for a moment . . . Cesare and I need to talk."

Max was baffled. Samurai had told him that he was well aware of the agreement, but that he wanted to talk it over man to man with Number Eight.

Samurai had asked Max to drop him off on the beach three, maybe four hours ago. He'd stayed there all that time, waiting. Max had no idea what he intended to do. Samurai rarely offered explanations, and the few times he did, it was impossible to take his words literally: you had to interpret them. And now why was he walking away? Maybe he was putting him to some kind of test. Maybe he wanted him to stay. Was he asking him to disobey?

"I'm going to stay right over here."

"That's your choice," Samurai commented, tersely.

Number Eight had had enough of that minuet. What were the two of them, fiancés? I'm willing to bet that Samurai . . . and in fact no one had ever seen him with a proper, regular piece of pussy . . . the image of the icy Nazi copulating with the young philosopher brought a burst of laughter to his lips.

"Hey Samurai, it's getting sort of late, if you don't mind . . . " he wheezed at last, once he'd managed to recover a minimum of composure.

Samurai pulled his hands out of his pockets, locked arms with him, and set off toward the water's edge.

"You see, Cesare, there are three components that make a man. A man worthy of being called a man, I mean to say. And these are heart, guts, and brains."

"Oh, sure, sure, I get that, but what about this shipload of cocaine?"

"The Arabs, when a son is born to them, call him 'my walking guts.' I could explain the meaning of the metaphor to you, but I doubt you'd understand it . . . in fact, I'm sure you wouldn't understand it."

"Samura' . . . "

"Hold on, just hold on a second. The heart, well you can

imagine for yourself what the meaning of that is. Daring, courage, generosity. All positive qualities, but which alone don't make a man, any more than guts do. Because of all the qualities that a man must possess, the most important is brains."

"Samurai, excuse me . . . "

Samurai stopped and stared him in the eyes. That reptilian gaze sent shivers down Number Eight's spine, it was a magnet that he couldn't resist.

"Unfortunately," Samurai resumed, this time with a hint of sadness in his voice, "you're devoid of all these qualities. You have no guts, because you can shoot but then you immediately run away and hide for fear that the mischief you've done is going to be discovered and punished. You have no heart, because you can shoot, yes, but from behind, and you'll never have the courage to look your victim in the eyes. And above all, you have no brains, because you shoot at random, you shoot before thinking through the consequences. And that's a bad thing, Cesare, a very bad thing."

Number Eight understood that things were going sideways, fast, and he tried to get his hand onto his weapon. He found the muzzle of the Mannlicher pointing right between his eyes. Samurai pulled the .357 magnum revolver out of Number Eight's belt and pocketed it.

"Samurai, I'm protected by Uncle Nino. If you touch me, Uncle Nino is going to have your heart on a plate. You and that other youngster you take with you everywhere you go."

"Get down on your knees."

"Hey Samurai, come on, cut it out. I'll just forget about you, and you can forget about me."

"On your knees, I said!"

Number Eight slipped on the wet sand and fell.

"I'll give you half of my end, Samurai. Seventy-five percent. I'll give you everything, everything, I tell you!"

"Do you see how limited you are?" Samurai sighed. "Even

at a moment like this. On the threshold of the supreme reckoning . . . all you think about is money."

"What the fuck, Samurai!"

Cesare Adami started crying. Samurai shook his head. All of that suffering, all of it, basically, useless, since what had to be done had already been decided, only irritated him. But there was still something he needed to say. To make sure the lesson was exemplary.

"I've known so many others just like you . . . One of them was your father, you know, a guy who stuck his dick places it wasn't meant to go, who thought it was fun to torture women, the one who later gave the guards blowjobs . . . We executed him. It was what needed to be done. Back then," Samurai concluded in a whisper, "we still believed that there was something resembling justice. Our kind of justice."

"Samuraaa' . . . "

A gust of wind carried off the echo of the shot.

A few yards away, Max had watched the whole scene. From his location, he'd been unable to hear what was said, but the essence of it was very clear.

That wasn't a punishment.

That was death.

Samurai had given him the freedom to choose. Like a good father.

And he had been the one who'd decided to stay.

He'd had all the necessary elements to make his decision.

And he'd decided.

He had never killed, up until that moment.

By staying at Samurai's side, he'd done the right thing.

When Number Eight fell onto the sand, Max stirred from his trance.

Rapid convulsions were shaking Cesare Adami's body.

It's horrible, thought Max. He stepped a short distance away to vomit.

Samurai walked over to him and put a hand on his shoulder.

"It's the shadow line, Max. There's no coming back from here. Help me to break down the weapons. Then we'll throw them in the sea. Their task is complete. Yours has just begun."

# XXXVII

A rms crossed, legs braced wide in the sand of Capocotta, Marco Malatesta watched as the attendants of the mortuary service of AMA, the municipal garbage collection agency, lifted Adami's corpse and eased it into the zinc casket which would be taken to the Institute of Legal Medicine. He'd been killed by a single bullet. Fired right between the eyes. But the projectile that had devastated his cranium, as had become clear immediately, since there was no exit wound, was still in the victim's body.

The prosecuting magistrates Setola and de Candia both rushed to the scene of the crime, each with his own little investigative squad following in his wake. A surreal scene. It made you want to roll on the ground laughing, only this was about a gang war like nothing Rome had seen in years. And a gang war it was, even the ineffective Setola had been forced to acknowledge the fact. In fact, given the brash confidence with which he jawed on about it, you'd think he had been the most tenacious proponent of a theory that, in fact, until just a few hours ago, he regularly ridiculed.

Beneath the sardonic gazes of Marco and Michelangelo, Setola devoted himself to his favorite pastime: issuing contradictory and largely nonsensical orders in all directions in a commanding voice. But there was little to laugh about. The slaughter seemed endless.

Marco had just lit his umpteenth cigarette when he received a phone call. Rapisarda wanted to see him. Immediately. He exchanged a nod of farewell with de Candia and headed off.

The Pisacane barracks stood at the far end of Viale di Tor di Quinto, a venerable old boulevard of the meretricious profession, where generations of adolescent males had fantasized about the streetwalkers, lit up garishly by rustic little bonfires known as *focaracci*. The last time Marco had seen the barracks was on television. In that period, he was on a mission. Together with a priest, a Coptic Christian from Egypt, he was trying to rescue from an atrocious fate fifty Eritrean refugees who were rotting in shipping containers buried in the scorching Libyan desert. He was battling against the local bandits, larger powers that were worried chiefly about not upsetting delicate balances of power, and his own government. From a news report on Al Jazeera that he'd managed to pick up on a TV set, in a ramshackle hut where he rested, exhausted after a long day of fruitless efforts, he had experienced his final and definitive humiliation as a Carabiniere and as an Italian. On a stage set up at the center of the barrack's equestrian track, in a singularly obscene chromatic symphony, with the Italian tricolor embracing the banner of the Libyan Jamahiriya, Muammar Gaddafi, dressed in a white kaftan, had harangued for forty minutes the Italian prime minister Silvio Berlusconi, eight hundred select high muckety-mucks of the earthier Italian governing class, and the Carabinieri of the fourth mounted regiment. They were drawn up in dress uniform for an equestrian exhibition in honor of that bloodthirsty dictator and the second anniversary of the Italy-Libya Friendship Treaty. That towelhead Gaddafi had decided to explain that his Italian friends would guarantee him five billion euros a year to prevent Europe from becoming black Africa. Those were the exact words he had used. Black Africa. Unless you want me to inundate the Mediterranean Sea with the desperate unwashed of the world's great South, pull out your wallets. Forget about liberating Eritrean refugees. The international world order wanted them dead, those poor wretches. They were to be sacrificed on the altar of prosperity. The best way to get them out of the first world's hair was if they were dead. Of course, in the grandstands where the vested authorities sat, there was a constant, collective nodding of heads. And the complacent nodding heads upon which the television cameras had lingered the longest belonged not only to Italy's cabinet ministers, arms dealers, and bankers, but also that of General Rapisarda, His Excellency the General of the Carabinieri Corps and Commandant of the Custoza Division. The host and master of the house for that obscene carnival sideshow. The man who, as the guard at the front gate reminded him, was now impatiently waiting to see him.

After an hour spent in the waiting room, he was ushered into the *sancta sanctorum*. Rapisarda, bent over a desk cluttered with silver baskets overflowing with Perugina candies and Venchi torroncino nougats, pretended he had been caught unawares in the midst of drafting who knows what sensitive set of notes. The Colonel's stentorian "At your orders, sir" became a sharp salute to the general's combover. Without bothering to look up from the sheet of paper upon which he continued scribbling indecipherable chickenscratch, Rapisarda invited him to take a seat. At least two minutes of silence ensued, which Marco took great care not to interrupt. Until, at last, Rapisarda took the initiative.

"We meet again, Colonel."

"It's an honor, General."

"You look like you're in shape, Colonel."

"As do you, General."

"You're too kind, Colonel. Do you have any idea of the reason you were asked here?"

"Frankly no, I don't, General, sir."

Rapisarda's voice grew in intensity, the intonation becoming harsher. The skirmish was ending, the full-fledged duel was beginning.

"What the hell is going on in Rome, Colonel?"

"A war, General, sir. And I'm afraid that this time we won't able to pretend nothing is happening."

Rapisarda was left speechless. That was a provocation. An open provocation. The very threshold of insult and defiance. What had gotten into his head?

Rapisarda's desktop landline blinked. The general lunged at the phone.

"I'm not taking calls from anyone! Ah, I understand . . . well, put him through . . . My dear, dear Dottore . . . "

Marco listened to the conversation in spite of himself. And he did his best to keep from laughing. The "dear, dear Dottore" was a powerful producer from the television network. He was inviting Rapisarda to appear on a talk show about the escalation of criminal activity in Rome. The general immediately put himself at the man's full disposal. The two men came to an agreement about how to position in the TV studio the scale topographic model that would serve for the reconstruction of the execution of Number Eight, and discussed exactly how to shape the summary of the case: but please, Rapisarda implored him, no more about this Pasolini.

Rapisarda went back to focusing on his irritating underling.

"You're just testing my patience, Malatesta. You and that prosecuting magistrate, a Communist judge, obviously."

"No disrespect intended, but . . . "

"Don't you dare interrupt me! I have to provide answers. I owe that to the country. Do you know that with the death last night in Capocotta we're at five murders? Five murders! Did you read what the newspapers wrote after the Idroscalo? A 'Pasolini-style' execution. What the fuck! Shut up, don't speak! Gang war! You're talking about a gang war. All right. Let's admit it. Four bandits firing at random at four other bandits.

Let's catch them and put an end to it. That's what the public is demanding that we do, by all that's holy!"

"The situation is more complicated than that," Marco put in drily, "and the scenario is decidedly much more complex."

"Again? What are you doing now, Colonel, trying to tell me that we're about to stumble upon some nice fat Masonic Lodge? Say, the P5, or the P6? The latter-day Magliana Gang?"

Rapisarda started laughing to himself, while Malatesta stared at the tuft of hair that was clogging the general's right ear and the array of colorful medals that studded the chest of his uniform.

As quickly as it had begun, the general's laughter stopped short.

"Have a good day, Colonel. And give my regards to de Roche."

Malatesta snapped to attention.

"Ah, one last thing, Colonel. A detail, perhaps. I've heard that you're in contact with certain circles that are . . . how to put it . . . subversive? Antagonistic? I want to believe that it's vicious gossip and nothing more. But don't make me think otherwise. Good day, Colonel. And forgive me if I haven't even offered you an espresso, but I already had two while waiting for you."

Malatesta shut the door behind him. He thought back to the face of Gheddafi, upon whom NATO was about to rain down an inferno of explosives and flame. He thought back to the expression on the face of the squad leader as he presented arms to the dictator.

To hell with him.

He hurried over to Alice's place, and she was surprised to see him in such a foul mood. She, in contrast, was beaming with joy. A famous rock singer had asked her to get his rather antiquated website back into shape. A job that paid, and paid pretty well, too! And most important of all, an ethically compatible job: the rock star was well known for his commitment to animal rights, environmentalism, civil rights, and so on.

"On the other hand, I can offer you a job that pays absolutely nothing and that's extremely risky, Alice."

"That sounds interesting. What's it about?"

"Waterfront, social housing. We're putting it all online. The project, the feasibility study by the architects, everything. We're going to toss a rock in the pond, like you suggested."

"I'll need a few days."

"Take all the time you want. And . . . welcome to the dirtiest game of all."

# XXXVIII

Sitting in a metallic gray Toyota Avensis, parked on the little piazza in front of the church of St. Mary Queen of Peace, Colonel Malatesta pointed out to Lieutenant Gaudino, who was behind the wheel, that the funeral procession was arriving. He radioed the unit's plainclothes men, whom he'd arranged along the sides of the piazza and inside the church, and ordered them to snap digital pictures.

Drawn by four bay Haflinger stallions abreast, horses that had been shipped down from the Tyrol, the hearse looked like Cinderella's carriage. But it was actually the hearse that would be carrying Cesare Adami, AKA Number Eight, on his last journey on this earth. The animals, decked out with with black ostrich-plume browbands, were caparisoned in brass harnesses; there was a chain leading back to the carriage that jangled as it shook and swayed, producing a sound that could be mistaken for the chiming of bells. Set on an immense cushion of red and white roses, the mahogany coffin occupied the entire length of the black-lacquered carriage, and was draped with a large black covering with a white number 8 at the center, the number of the last pool ball to go into the pocket.

Perched on the coachman's seat, holding the reins, sat a lean gentleman in a threadbare black suit with a top hat on his head. He wore the apathetic expression of an undertaker who normally travels to cemeteries in metallic Mercedes hearses, but who's been asked to provide a custom service. But no one was about to say no to the Adamis. Uncle Nino had decreed that Cesaretto was going to be escorted out of this world with all the honors due to a capo, which is what he had been, for better or worse. He wanted to make sure that his funeral would never be forgotten in Ostia.

The sunshine made the morning warm. The sea was calm and exuded a brackish odor.

The carriage had started out from Piazza Gasparri. It had turned onto the waterfront promenade and taken almost forty minutes to reach the church of Regina Pacis. Traffic had been halted by the vigorous enforcement of platoons of the municipal police, and the crowd that had gathered as the hearse went by and spontaneously traipsed along behind the coffin. Anxious to attend, but most important, to be noticed attending. There were a great many young toughs: none of the families who lived in the apartment blocks of Ponente would have missed this. The shops had all lowered their security blinds.

Lieutenant Gaudino was captivated.

"I'd only ever seen funerals like this one in Forcella and in the Spanish Quarter. The Camorra set the style. But if I told you that I was surprised, Colonel, I'd be telling a lie. There's a substantial part of Ostia, nowadays, that has no choice. They're either here or they're here. Cesare Adami was a violent thug who never had his uncle's charisma. Obedience to him was obedience to fear. But still, he was the boss."

"And now?

"And now the succession will begin. I'd say that Nino Adami's choice is unlikely to be anyone other than Denis Sale. The godson, and from what little we're able to pick up here and there, he has a great deal more gray matter than the guy they're burying today. Apparently he's even more vicious than the other guy was. He's already in the church. I saw him go in earlier, with a young girl who was supposed to have been Cesare Adami's woman. Her name is Morgana. At a glance, I'd say she's a junkie . . . "

"We're going to tap all their phones, Lieutenant. I'll get you the court orders as soon as possible."

"If only it would do any good . . . These people are about as talkative as the blackspot seabreams of Castellabbate . . . Hey, look who's here!"

In the piazza out front of Regina Pacis—a vast empty space now that everyone had packed into the church itself—a van for the transport of correctional police detainees pulled up just a few steps away from the horse-drawn hearse that stood waiting. Meanwhile, the Haflinger horses in harness emptied their bladders onto the asphalt.

The rear doors of the midnight blue Fiat Ducato van with the dark tinted glass windows were flung open to let an old man in a camelhair coat climb out. He was visibly tested by the ordeal.

Antonio Adami. Antonino. Uncle Nino.

He had submitted a request to the magistrate in charge of leaves and provisional liberty and had been approved for a special permit to bid farewell to his only nephew. And for something extra. Though he was keeping that to himself.

As soon as he stepped out of the van, the old man held his wrists out to the two correctional officers who freed him from the shackles and then escorted him, flanking him on either side. He took a few steps toward the carriage. He kneeled and crossed his forehead, then remained with his head bowed for several minutes. Then, rising to his feet with slow and studied theatricality, he gestured to the undertaker perched on the coachman's seat. And, immediately, four young men dressed in jeans and leather jackets broke away from the colonnade of the church. They hoisted the coffin onto their shoulders, taking great care not to wrinkle the black drapery hanging over it, and then proceeded to carry it down the vast nave of the church of Regina Pacis.

From the choir loft rose the powerful notes of the pipe

organ, and in one of the pews closest to the altar, Denis Sale wrapped his arm around Morgana's shoulders and pressed her close to him. Her eyes were dry, her skin was alabaster white, practically traslucent, and the faint application of eyebrow pencil gave her a glacial stare. The girl leaned over to his ear and carefully enunciated every word, to make sure nothing was lost in the whisper in which she uttered those words.

"That bastard Samurai is going to die."

Denis nodded and added: "I need to find out if he was alone."

"Uncle Nino is here," whispered Morgana.

Free of his escort, old Adami took a seat in the front row, the first pew from the altar. Between Robertino, who was sobbing like a little boy, and Moira, the bartender from Piazza Gasparri, squeezed into a black satin dress and torn between the emotion of her final farewell to Cesaretto and the unexpected sight of the only man she'd ever loved in her twisted, broken life. Uncle Nino leaned over and kissed her hand, brushing the wilted bow that marked her neckline, then proceeded to kiss Robertino on both cheeks, whispering into his ear the real reason he was there.

"We will avenge him."

At the altar, Don Fernando, the parish priest of Regina Pacis, was displaying courage.

"What does the Book of Sirach tell us? 'Resentment and anger, these are foul things too, and a sinner is a master at them both. Whoever exacts vengeance will experience the vengeance of the Lord, who keeps strict account of sin. Pardon your neighbor any wrongs done to you, and when you pray, your sins will be forgiven. If one nurses anger against another, can he then demand compassion from the Lord? Showing no pity for someone like oneself, can one then plead for one's own sins? Mere creature of flesh, yet cherishing resentment!—who will forgive one for sinning?'"

From the back of the church, where he stood leaning against a holy water font, Malatesta listened to the homily, doing his best to guess at familiar faces in the tangle of heads bowed in the congregation. The parish priest's voice had risen to an imploring pitch. Though he would lay odds that the plea was a pointless one, if he'd been a betting man. Still, it added to the spectacle.

"Remember the last things, and stop hate, corruption and death, and be faithful to the commandments. Remember the commandments, and do not bear your fellow ill-will, remember the covenant of the Most High, and ignore the offence. Let us pray."

Denis continued turning his head slowly, quickly reckoning up those who were there and those who weren't. Because that too would be a piece of unappealable evidence in Samurai's death sentence. Until he felt a hand touch his shoulder. It was Rocco Perri.

The Calabrians were men of few words. Perri had been making money with Number Eight for years with the cocaine and the slot machines. If he was there, what he was about to hear could not and must not be called into doubt.

"I bring you the greetings of Don Ciro. He wasn't feeling well. It was too cold out to leave the clinic. And there are too many plainclothes cockroaches swarming around here anyway."

Denis nodded.

Perri leaned in closer and whispered in his ear.

"Listen to me, because I've lived to a certain age. The Anacletis had nothing to do with this. Rocco was behind bars. The order didn't come from him. He was the last one who wanted this. Thanks to Uncle Nino's generosity, we'd come to an understanding. Everyone was in agreement. Me, Viglione, Uncle Nino, and of course Rocco Anacleti. Even Cesare had seen the wisdom. In exchange for Paja and Fieno, the gypsies were getting a fat wad of cash. Twenty-five percent of a new shipment."

Denis took a deep breath.

"What about that little asshole Max?"

"He doesn't have the balls. And why would he want to kill Cesare? Anyway, seeing that Uncle Nino is here, you can just ask him."

"So Samurai did it on his own?"

Perri said nothing. He gave a light tap of complicit understanding on Denis's shoulder and then headed up one of the side aisles. The one Malatesta was watching. The two men exchanged a glance. That face was familiar to the colonel. But he couldn't put a name to it. He followed him from a safe distance, and when he saw him getting into a black BMW waiting for him on the piazza outside, he snapped a few quick pictures with his iPhone.

Don Fernando swung the incense-burning thurible over the coffin, blessing the corpse and the black drape that covered it.

"Oh, Lord, who hast made us participants in the mystery of Christ crucified and reborn for our salvation, let our brother, Cesare, liberated from the chains of death, become one with the community of saints in the eternal Easter. For Christ our lord. Amen."

The rich sound of the pipe organ filled the church once again. For the first time, Uncle Nino stood up from the pew where he'd been sitting throughout the ceremony. He turned to the two corrections officers who were right behind him and who were urging him to head for the exit and reboard the van that would take him back to the Rome Hotel. He gestured toward Denis and Morgana.

"Could you give me just a minute? I'd like to embrace those two young people. They're the brother and sister that Cesare never had."

He took a few steps and clutched Denis and Morgana to his chest.

"Goddamned Samurai!" Denis said softly.

"Shhh, shhh. You're a intelligent young man, my son. Shhh. Shhh. Not now, not now," whispered Uncle Nino as if he were comforting a child. Then he uttered the words that Denis had been waiting for all his life. "Now it's your turn."

Uncle Nino broke free of Denis and Morgana's embrace, buttoned up his camelhair overcoat, and returned himself to the custody of his escort with great docility. The organ had fallen silent and the crowd, still thronging the church, waited for the coffin to be carried out. To one side of the altar, Spartaco Liberati emerged. His eyes were puffy and reddened, and in one hand he carried the scarves of the A. S. Roma and the F. S. Barcelona soccer teams, knotted together. He laid the scarves on the coffin and gestured to a sacristan who was standing next to the organ console. The first few notes of "Honor Him" from *Gladiator* filled the air and the church burst into a loud wave of applause. Liberati went over to Denis and Morgana, his right hand extended.

"I've lost a brother. Cesare was a brother to me."

Denis glared at him with contempt. Who did that piece of shit think he was? Did he think Denis didn't know he was on Samurai's payroll? Denis's hands, resting in his lap, remained where they were. His gaze continued to chill Liberati's blood, until he had forced him to undergo one last humiliation.

"Hey, Denis. I've worked it out with the boys. On Sunday we're going to unfurl a streamer in the stadium curve. 'Hail, Cesare,' is what we've written. Great big, like that."

"Fuck off. Just go fuck yourself."

Morgana's voice lashed Liberati like a whip, finally forcing him to seek shelter in the crowd that was now leaving the church. But it surprised Denis, too. Together, in silence, they reached the church courtyard, and there they watched as the coffin was transferred from the horse-drawn carriage to a Mercedes hearse bound for the Verano cemetery, where Cesare would lie next to his father and mother.

From opposite sides of the church, two Olympus digital cameras in the hands of ROS officers clicked furiously. But the funeral-goers didn't care. They had other things on their minds. Revenge and that bestial sensation of sudden fragility that comes from a brush with mortality were both pushing them toward Death's house, where they could try and remind themselves they were alive. Flesh and blood.

# XXXIX

Behind the wheel of the Porsche Boxster, Sabrina felt like what she'd always dreamed of being: a fine lady. And even Fabio, the leftist Fabio, the complicated Fabio, let's say it, that royal-pain-in-the-ass Fabio, made no mystery of the fact that he admired the compact lines, the cool bracing lash of the wind that tossed his hair, the frankly impressed gazes he got from everyone as the sportscar went sailing royally past.

Because there's no two fucking ways about it: everyone likes nice things. Even Communists do. Especially Communists do. Because to hear them talk, it's all revolution and fight against the machine, but deep down, they only really ever have one thing in mind: sex, oysters, and champagne.

Sabrina and Fabio had become inseparable. Eugenio Brown was never at home, always out and about, attending film festivals and dull business meetings, always in search of an idea that, as he had explained to her, prompting more than one extended yawn, "can bring together culture and show business, entertainment and reflection."

"In other words, Euge', you're looking for something that'll make you money without getting your conscience dirty."

Eugenio Brown appreciated her frankness. Sabrina was his window into a world that, before meeting her, he had even recounted in dozens of movies and TV dramas, but without ever really understanding in depth. Deep down, Eugenio hoped that he'd get the right idea, the one he'd been chasing after for too many years now, from that very world of which Sabrina was the unwitting spokesperson.

And the idea—half in jest and half out of boredom—came to her.

In her freshly bestowed gift, the Porsche Boxster, Sabrina had decided to go ransack a few designer shops in the center of Rome. Fabio was the perfect company for that kind of expedition. Like all faggots, he brought to the table considerable expertise in terms of high style as well as a great willingness to listen and discuss. Much better than any straight man or girlfriend. Because men lose interest, and women are annoying.

But that morning Fabio was distracted. He watched as she tried on one outfit after another with a look of boredom, he nodded automatically, and shook his head also as directed, in other words, he clearly couldn't give less of a damn. And in the intervals, he furiously jotted down notes in an old black notebook. Sabrina purchased a Vuitton bag and a pair of Louboutin shoes (Eugenio adored the red soles of Louboutin shoes), and dragged the screenwriter back to the car. The day's mood had suddenly turned grim. Sabrina hated being ignored.

"Do you mind if I ask what the hell you're writing?"

"I thought of a story."

"Let me hear."

"Are you really interested?"

"Yes."

"It starts with the War in the Balkans . . . "

"With the what?"

"Jesus, Sabrina, the War in the Balkans. Sarajevo . . . the seige . . . ethnic rape . . . Srebrenica . . . "

"Okay, okay, I get it, a war between Romanians, Gypsies, and all like that. But then what happens?"

"Then what happens," Fabio went on, "is that a young Red

Cross volunteer is about to be raped by two militiamen, when she is rescued by a handsome Serbian soldier . . . "

"It doesn't work."

"What?"

"The war, the rape, the Red Cross volunteer. What the fuck, Fabio, who on earth is going to go out to the movies to watch such a thing? These days, too . . . People want to laugh, Fabio, trust me!"

"Then you tell me a story, since you know so much about it!"

Sabrina burst out laughing and consoled him with a pat on the cheek.

"Don't get all worked up. I told you what I thought, didn't I? These are tough times, people want stories that are . . . "

"Nice and light?"

"That's right, nice light stories. Like that one you told me once, about that statue . . . "

"*Pygmalion.*"

"There you go, that's the one. Only maybe set in the present day. I don't know . . . Hey Fabio, has it ever occured to you that you could tell the story of me and Eugenio?"

"Sincerely, no, it hasn't," he replied, cuttingly, "I don't really think it's all that interesting, sweetheart."

"Well, I do. A girl off the streets who's seen plenty of nasty things in her time meets a producer and falls in love. He takes her in off the streets and they live happily ever after."

"Already seen it. It's called *Pretty Woman.*"

"And that one didn't make much money?"

"That was a long time ago."

"Certain things *always* work, Fa'."

When it became clear that Eugenio Brown was of the same opinion, Fabio's feelings were crushed. He reluctantly jotted down the pitch that he'd been commissioned to develop, one of the most atrocious pieces of shit he'd ever concocted. Eugenio had it translated into English and sent an email to a contact of his at the Fun Company. The reply was quick in coming. "Prime." Which, from the Americans, meant: first rate.

Not even three days after their first conversation, Fabio shows up at Sabrina's place with a digital tape recorder and asks her to tell him the story of her life, from the very beginning, leaving out nothing.

And so it was that Sabrina entered the world of the movies by the front door.

Fabio's digital tape recorder never did get used.

"That piece of shit is worthless!" she told him, giving Fabio a glare of contempt as he prepared a mojito in the belief that it would help her to remember. They had to do this another way. Her way.

"You know what let's do, Fabbie'? I'll take Eugenio on a nice guided whore-tour. You see what I mean? Forget about this bullshit tape recorder. Don't take it the wrong way. But just Eugenio, though."

When night fell, Sabrina got dolled up in what she still had left over from her previous life. Things that she'd had a hard time finding in her new wardrobe, the wardrobe of a great lady. She'd had no difficulty slipping into the hot pink microskirt, and her tits, free of any bra, still made quite a spectacular show under the skimpy black silk H&M tanktop, a thoughtful gift from an Italian stockbroker with a house and a family in London. One of her last customers, a guy who never failed to get her aroused, someone she'd always chosen to say nothing about to Eugenio. Standing in front of the mirror, smoothing her ass as she twisted and craned her neck, brushing her fingertips over her thighs, clad snugly in fishnet stockings, she decided she was quite pleased with what she saw. The monogamy and smooth sailing of conjugal life, as it were, had never really captured her imagination. Deeply amused, she'd watched as Eugenio chose a tweed jacket and a pair of heavy boiled wool trousers that rode low on his hips, along with a white shirt and a wool tartan tie.

"Sweetheart, we're not going to one of your parties. And after all, you look like my grandfather."

He had nodded with a gesture of pained reluctance, convinced as he was that this nocturnal scouting expedition that Sabrina had imposed upon him, and upon which they were about to set off, might well turn into an intolerable ordeal.

"Sabrina, are you sure we need to do this? Wouldn't it have been better to just stick with the tape recorder? We could have just stayed here, in the comfort of our home, you and I. To tell the story of your life, you don't actually have to relive it."

"Oh no . . . this again? I already told Fabio: are you or aren't you interested in making this movie? What's the matter, don't you know that certain things have to be seen? Haven't you ever gone out with a whore, you?"

"Oh please, I beg you, you know that I don't . . . "

"Sure, sure. That's what you all say."

The outfit had turned her back into a hooker in the blink of an eye. And Sabrina had decided not to sacrifice so much as drop of that defiant erotic brashness that had made her what she was and that had brought her as far as she had come. One more night. Just one more night.

Sabrina wrapped her foxtail around her neck, switched on the ignition of the Porsche Boxster, and while Eugenio, in the passenger seat, was still fiddling with his seatbelt, she rocked it into first gear and jammed down the accelerator, running two red lights on Via Conte Verde, heading in the direction of Porta Maggiore. When they pulled onto the Rome-L'Aquila highway, Eugenio started looking around with a vaguely bewildered expression on his face.

"Sorry to ask, because I don't want to spoil the surprise, but this road takes us to Abruzzo."

"Euge', it's clear that all you chic lefties have overlooked a big piece of Rome."

"We're radical chic, if anything. Radical chic, Sabrina."

"Oh, sure, whatever. Radicals, Communists. As you like it. You still don't know a fucking thing. Does Ponte di Nona mean anything to you?"

"Tor di Nona is the other way, my love, toward Piazza Navona."

"You might have gone to Tor di Nona. Ponte di Nona is what I'm talking about. Collatina, Palmiro Togliatti . . . Anything ring a bell for you, Euge'?"

He stared at her with a blank expression. Sabrina burst out in an impertinent laugh.

"I'm taking you to Patagonia."

"What's that?"

"A chow-down."

"Oh, a restaurant."

"Oh, let's not exaggerate. It's a place where you eat until you blow a gasket. And where I used to go when I first started working."

"You never told me you worked as a waitress."

"What are you talking about, waitress, Euge'? At Patagonia, you can eat a whole ox for thirty euros. All meat, only meat. You know what I mean? And do you know what happens to boys when they eat too much meat?"

Eugenio ran a hand over his forehead.

"There you go. Now you understand. The boys can't hold it in. Fifty euros, five minutes, and you're done."

The parking lot at Patagonia was a large dirt area bounded by Via di Grotta di Gregna and Via Collatina Vecchia. Another piece of Rome that they'd started but never bothered to finish. If it hadn't been for the greasy smoke from the grills and the neon sign with a stylized image of the great South American mountain, the three industrial sheds that the sign was announcing could easily have been taken for anonymous warehouses.

Sabrina locked up the Porsche, smoothed her dress over her hips, and locked arms with Eugenio.

"Beef, chicken, or pork?"

"Do I have to decide in the parking lot? Can't we get a table and sit down, first?"

"If you want beef, you go into the restaurant on the left. Chicken in the middle, and pork on the right."

"Ah."

"I'd go for pork, Euge'."

"You think?"

"I had the best luck with the guys from the pork side."

"I somehow don't have any trouble believing it."

"Hey, no, Euge'. Don't be like that, now. This is work. We're working on a movie. You're the one who told me you wanted to know."

The guy who greeted them at the monumental refrigerator counter where orders were taken was wearing a butcher's apron spattered with dried blood. His name was Enzo and he was in his early forties. He'd been born in Argentina but he grew up in Tor Bella Monaca. He had a trim physique, two muscular forearms, perfectly waxed and hairless, which he plunged into mountains of sausages, spare ribs, chops, and rump roasts. He then sliced everything into portions with a big old cleaver straight out of a horror flick according to the clients' appetite, then, after weighing it, he sent the meat to the flaming grills behind him. He immediately recognized Sabrina, and displayed exactly the kind of knowing familiarity that Eugenio had been dreading.

"Well, would you look at who's here . . . Hey, beautiful, it's been a lifetime."

"Ciao, Enzo, you're just as handsome as ever."

"Outside, but especially inside, Sabri'."

"I remember, Enzo, I remember."

"Have you decided to bring your handsome men back here again?"

Sabrina smiled, waving Eugenio over. Enzo reeked of testosterone and sausage. And he didn't even give Eugenio time to introduce himself.

"If this is your first time, you can't even imagine."

Brown nodded.

"Yes, Sabrina told me that the food here is just exquisite. You do pork here, right?"

"No, what did you think I was talking about? Sabrina, I mean. If this is your first time tonight, she'll send you right out of this world."

Eugenio delicately took Sabrina's hand and led her to one of the tables set with a packing paper tablecloth. And as he watched her he understood that she was having as much fun as a little girl.

"Listen, my love, I overestimated my powers of endurance. I don't think I'm going to be able to handle this."

Her smile faded into a sudden pout.

"But we haven't even started the evening."

"You can tell me what you used to do and where you used to do it back home."

"Oh, sure, with the tape recorder . . . Go on, get out of here."

Brown knew that the boundary between capricious and downright furious was very thin.

"Then help me, Sabrina."

"It's very simple, Euge'. Wipe off that look of someone visiting the zoo."

"Menagerie, Sabrina."

"Have you ever heard of a whore in a menagerie?"

"You're right, sorry."

"My love, when you get right down to it, men are men.

When I was in this line of work, that's the way I thought about it. What difference is there whether you screw someone who's got a platinum dick or a copper one? You worked out a price in advance. After all, it's not like you're supposed to fall in love with him. Because if you fall in love, the way I did, then you quit the business. If your prince finally arrives . . . "

Sabrina let the consideration drop with a simper. And she ran the tip of her shoe up the inside of Brown's thigh.

"Is that how it worked with your customers?"

"More or less."

During the hour they sat at their table at Patagonia, Sabrina introduced him to a round half dozen of them. A masculine sampling of variegated humanity, as Brown mentally noted. Dario, a bus driver for ATAC, Rome's public transit system. Sergio, a male nurse at the general hospital. Fernando, a bank teller at the main agency of a major bank from Northern Italy. Tiziano, a soccer player in Lega Pro, the Italian professional football league. Davide, a graduate student in Anthropology, and Silvio, a taxi driver, who also made a point of introducing his wife, a lovely young woman who hugged and kissed Sabrina like a sister. All those men shared a vitality and cheerfulness that he had perhaps never possessed. And the joy with which they greeted that woman who was now his companion, but who had given the same pleasure to them, made him think deeply about the shell he'd worn and carried with him all his life. Those horny men were brash but sincere. They had frequented whores and made no bones about it. They weren't ashamed of themselves or of Sabrina. Who was staring at him again.

"Nice, aren't they?"

"Do you miss them?"

"What a pain in the ass you are, Euge'."

"Look, it's not an issue of jealousy."

"I know exactly what the problem is."

"You do?"

"It's the reason why, at a certain point, I couldn't stand being an escort anymore. You see, Euge', when you're just a young girl and you walk the streets, you wind up with people like you. And when you start going out on dates and talking bullshit at parties, like the one at your place, then you wind up wanting to throw up all the time. Because men turn into assholes. They fuck you, but they're ashamed of themselves, the rats, Euge'."

Suddenly Brown had a splitting migraine.

"Do we have to stay here all night long?"

"No. I'm taking you to the Pashà Caffè."

Eugenio couldn't believe his eyes. What he was looking at was a hot pink rectangle along Via Tiburtina, in the Settecamini area. It boasted a crude Middle Eastern design and a large luminous sign in Arabic. Something midway between a Saudi Arabian nightclub of the third millennium and a neomelodic hallucination.

"Is that a joke, Sabrina?"

"Euge', go look on the internet. Do you know what category the Pashà Caffè is under?"

"No."

"Category 'pick-up club.' And also under 'luxury.' Did you think I was taking you to some dark spot along the boulevards? That's strictly for losers."

The space was immense. At least twenty thousand square feet, Eugenio decided as he entered the place, making a rough estimate. A slot machine room, a karaoke stage, a nightclub space and a large bar, with Asian-style chromatic light shows. Purple, red, blue, green, and yellow, in all possible shades of the rainbow. From pastel to electric. Capable of highlighting lithe young women's bodies and the dilated pupils of chronically horny older men.

Brown was standing there, frozen to the spot, as he scrutinized that mass of humanity endlessly rubbing bodies together, shrouded in a mist of cheap perfume and throbbing with a desire that you'd have to describe as chemical more than hormonal.

"My love, at least this scrap of scarf that you call a tie, please take it off . . . "

Sabrina's perfidious observation finally convinced him to step away from the terracotta floor tile in front of the bar where, in a sort of trance, he seemed to have put down roots. He went over to a little settee where two women he guessed to be Ukrainian were picking at a sampling of feijoada. It was unclear to him why, in a place that seemed to have been decorated with a sultan's caravanserai in mind, they should be serving Brazilian cuisine. But he preferred not to ask, clearly flattered by the insistent glances one of the two women kept turning in his direction.

Sabrina watched Eugenio with a smile of amusement playing over her lips, remaining at a safe distance, until a guy in his early thirties whispered into her ear a question about her price for a quickie in the parking lot. At that point she gestured toward Brown, and while the guy threw his arms wide in helplessness, she went over to him.

"Euge', you can't possibly think that you picked up these two with your charm."

"Why not?"

"*Perché so' du' zoccole.*" Because they're a couple of whores, she said in dialect.

But the way she leaned on the Z and the two C's was so emphatic that the two women on the settee seemed to be flattered, rather than offended.

"We didn't know that the customer belonged to you," said the one who looked younger, and was clearly proud of a pair of tits that defied the known laws of gravity.

Sabrina took Eugenio by the hand and led him toward the bar, where he tried to order a malt whiskey. Sabrina changed the order to a can of Red Bull.

Brown turned the can over and over in his hands as if it were some mysterious object.

"What is it?"

"It'll give you a boost."

"Please, Sabrina. I'm begging you."

And that was when she turned serious. Truly serious.

"Are you sure about the movie? Look, you can't pull it off if you don't understand how it works."

"I already know how you pick up a prostitute. There was no need for you to subject me to this torture. I wanted to understand what it was like for you, in that other life."

"And you still haven't figured it out?"

"I don't think so."

"And that's why you have to get it hard. If not, you won't understand. If you want to understand what's in the mind of a working girl, you have to start with what's in the trousers of a man, my dear film producer."

By the time they got home it was practically dawn. Without uttering a word. The time needed for Eugenio Brown to gag down the last drop of Red Bull. As they rode the elevator up to the penthouse, Eugenio tried stringing together a few mumbled sentences that could break the stony silence. But Sabrina wouldn't let him get a word out, sliding a little pill under his tongue. He put up no resistance.

Eugenio fell asleep when the sun was already high in the sky. After one last glance at Sabrina's naked body beside him, and his own erection which still gave no sign of subsiding.

*Prime*, he thought, finally closing his eyes. That's how the film would turn out, too, to use the word the Americans seemed to like: *prime*. It was the absolute best, goddamn it!

# XL

Out of respect for Ciro Viglione, who was now under perpetual house arrest, and because the possibility of wiretaps was now so clearly elevated—a certainty, according to Parisi—the meeting was held in the office of Temistocle Malgradi, at Villa Marianna.

In a half-empty medical clinic, with long hallways lit by the asymmetrical glow of security lights, Samurai arrived on time, at nine on the dot, escorted by Max.

Rocco Perri, who was the master of the house, blocked the philosopher's way.

"He wasn't invited, Samurai."

"He's with me."

"As you think best. But Ciro's not going to like it. He's already on the warpath, I'm warning you."

"What about you?"

The Calabrian didn't answer, entrenching himself behind a smile of false courtesy. Then he proceeded to carry out a thorough body search.

Once he'd established that everything was in order, Rocco accompanied them to Malgradi's office, where Silvio Anacleti and Ciro Viglione were waiting for them. Viglione was in the boss's chair, seated behind the chief physician's desk.

As soon as he set foot in the room, Samurai, bothered by the odor of the Tuscan cigars that the Camorrista practically chain-smoked, went over the window and threw it open, without bothering to say even a word of greeting.

Ciro gave him a look of astonishment. Who the hell did he think he was, this fucking Samurai? Didn't he realize that he might very easily be leaving that meeting feet-first? What the hell, had he finally gone completely and irrevocably insane?

He'd prepared a nice speech, Ciro had. A tough, decisive speech, the kind of speech a real boss might deliver, forget about Julius Caesar or even Il Duce, God rest his soul.

What the hell, Samurai! I ask you, no wait, I *order* you to put an end to the war, or let's call it what it is, the agitation, as you like to say, and instead of doing what you're told, you throw gasoline on the fire? Who on earth ordered you to kill Number Eight? And just when we'd come to an understanding . . . Now the result of this brilliant idea was right there, for all of them to see. They had the Carabinieri breathing down their necks, that bastard the colonel, and now even the judge had woken up, that son of a bitch Di Candyass who sure as could be, they had Parisi's word on it, had already planted microphones and bugs and phone taps on them all. And they'd found the papers, the papers, by the blood of Christ! And how long do you think it's going to take them to put two and two together and come up with four, eh? Excellent work, Samura'! Uncle Nino is clamoring for vendetta. We didn't even invite Denis, who's now *'o Masto*, the commander in chief, because we don't want any bloodshed in here, but you'd better watch your back, because that guy is a rabid dog . . . but most important of all, the whole deal could be about to fall through. The Great Project! So now, Samurai, either you give us a reasonable explanation, or there's no point whining about it. It's your ass that's on the line!

But Samurai's brash attitude had caught him off guard.

All right, Samura', you want to play rough? Then here, let me fix you good. Ciro Viglione puffed a cloud of cigar smoke in his face, then summarized his point of view.

"Samura', you fucked up good this time!"

"I'd have to agree," said Perri, who even when he was issuing a death sentence, never abandoned the aplomb of a silk master.

Samurai had prepared a speech of his own. He'd planned to start with the Aryan concept of caste and conclude with a less facile version of Menenius Agrippa's fable about the Belly and the Members of the human body. He intended to explain that any great project requires leaders and executors. That each one should be assigned the job that belongs to him in the overall plan. That the individual makes sense inasmuch as a part of the whole, a whole that is harmonically ordered in accordance with the hierarchical principle. And so Cesare Adami, AKA Number Eight, whose loss they were all now hypocritically lamenting, absolutely had to be rubbed out. Not out of some stupid whim or a misguided sense of justice (let the Anacletis believe this if they chose), but because he was the infected part that threatened to contaminate the whole. And that was why the sacrifice of Number Eight had become necessary.

But the quality of his interlocutors was discouraging. Ciro and Perri wouldn't have understood, and if anything they would probably have been even more irritated by his words. The only one capable of rising to his height of understanding was Max, but he hadn't come there to convince Max. As for Silvio Anacleti, his decision had already been made at the very instant that the late and lamented Mannlicher had put an end to the life of Number Eight.

Then Samurai, like Ciro Viglione, provided a summary of his thoughts.

"Cesare Adami didn't know how to keep his promises. By killing Spadino, he shattered the harmony of our group. And by killing Paja and Fieno, he broke a pact that every one of us had agreed to, he before anyone else. You may say: but we had agreed on a compensation fee. Even the Anacletis had resigned themselves to it. And I say to you: Cesare considered all this to be a personal success. And success is like a drug. That wouldn't have been the end of it. He'd have gone on killing, he'd have demanded more and more. He was sowing discord, he was fanning the flames of hatred. He was the sick part that, if allowed to grow, would have multiplied disproportionately, devouring everything else. With his death, the whole loses nothing but an insignificant part of itself. Surgery. And the Great Project is back up and running. Do you understand me now, gentlemen?"

"Fuck that shit!" roared Ciro Viglione. "I've told you before, Samura': you talk nice, but you talk too much."

"That's your opinion, Ciro."

"We're all in agreement here, Samura'."

"I'm not," said Silvio Anacleti. "Samurai did the right thing. My family's with him."

Ciro Viglione couldn't believe his ears. He got to his feet and started inveighing against the gypsy. Now what was this new development? The Anacletis themselves had signed the pact in question, the very same pact that Samurai had violated. Therefore, the individual action of that *chillu strunz'* —that asshole—ought to ring as an insult to them in particular. That was what the rules stated. Or had the rules all simply fallen by the wayside?

Young Anacleti replied. In that bloody chapter, the only ones who had paid any price at all, until the murder of Number Eight, had been them, the Anacletis. Spadino, Paja, Fieno—they were all their property. And they'd been slaughtered like dogs by Number Eight. Who had now paid for what he'd done. Samurai had restored things to their rightful balance. Now, in fact, they could proceed to a new agreement. Now, and not a minute earlier.

Viglione and Perri exchanged a glance. The move by the Anacletis had certainly caught them off guard. An alliance had been established between the gypsies and Samurai that threatened to alter the equilibrium among the various forces at play.

The first one to understand the situation and its implications was the Calabrian.

"All right, Samurai. Now the Anacletis are happy. But how are we going to take care of the guys from Ostia, Denis, and that other guy, *comu cazzo si chiama* . . . Robertino . . . ?" He broke into his native Calabrian as he concentrated.

"Number Eight's death will serve as an object lesson to them as well. If they fail to adapt, they'll meet the same fate. From this point on, Max is in charge of the street. He will be my mouth, my eyes, my hand . . . and my heart, my brain, and my guts."

"What about Uncle Nino?"

"Uncle Nino," Samurai whispered in an icy voice, "is in prison. And I'm right here. I've been entrusted with the task of bringing the Great Project to fruition. And let me assure you, that's what I intend to do."

"And we're with him," Silvio Anacleti added.

Rocco Perri, staring at Ciro Viglione, nodded his head. The Camorrista understood that the Calabrian had allowed himself to persuaded. He's let himself be fucked, is what he actually thought. But with the Pugliese Santa Corona Unita going over to the side of Samurai, the Japanese, the risk of isolation was becoming critical. Ciro could have sought an understanding with Uncle Nino.

But that would just mean more war.

And war led to investigations.

And investigations scare the politicos.

And the big deal was in the hands of the politicos.

And the politicos were in the hands of Samurai.

And to make a long story short, Samurai had won.

"All right then," he huffed, trying to conceal the scorching feeling of humiliation inside him. "All right . . . as for Uncle

Nino, we'll have the lawyer talk to him. But we're going to have to give him something to keep him quiet."

Samurai laid down his ace in the hole.

"A boat is arriving now from Greece with a shipment of cocaine. Max is taking care of this transport. A metric ton. I will transfer my entire share to Uncle Nino, as reparations. I believe that this is in his interest. The way things stand now, I don't believe business is going well for him."

At last, he gave Max the floor, and the young man set forth the details of the operation. He explained that Shalva, a Georgian middleman who enjoyed their absolute trust, would insure the shipment, and that the Pugliesi who controlled the shipping lanes from Greece were also involved in the deal. He specified the initial investment and the percentages that would be due to each of them.

Rocco and Viglione got out their calculators and started running some numbers. From their expressions, glowing with greed, Samurai understood that they'd grasped the overall profitability of the deal. A minute ago they'd been ready to strangle him with their own hands, and now they were hanging from his lips.

Disgusted, Samurai gestured to Max and left the stage.

# XLI

I t was definitely a chilly evening, a late autumn evening, but still a magnificent one. And from the glassed-in terrace of the grand hotel on the Esquiline Hill, the bundle of railroad tracks running out of the mouth of the Termini station looked like nothing so much as a dragon's tongue. Or perhaps a devil's tongue. The noises from the multiethnic souk down below on Via Giolitti reached the terrace muffled, as did the car horns facing off in the grid of streets leading to Piazza Vittorio. On the polished hardwood floor in the restaurant area, a dozen or so hostesses moved back and forth with studied composure between the Philippe Starck chairs and tables. In their flat shoes and their black pantsuits, they appeared absolutely modest and chaste. That was certainly in keeping with the etiquette of the private event organized by the publishing house Il Braciere and announced at the entrance to the roof garden by a sign on a colossal tripod.

MONS. MARIANO TEMPESTA
*ETHICS FOR A NEW MILLENNIUM*

AN EVENING WITH THE AUTHOR

In a winter Tasmanian wool cassock, the bishop was killing time by picking up puff pastry canapés with his gnarly fingers; there were trays and trays of them on the long counter lining one of the sides of the terrace. Francesco, his young secretary, dressed in a midnight-blue Armani suit that highlighted his slender gracefulness, joined him, carrying a couple of flutes of Bellavista Riserva.

Widely known in the clubs of St. John Lateran as Satanella, it was Francesco's job to choose which of the young men submitted to Monsignor Tempesta's benevolence should be employed. There were jobs at RAI TV, or in the major state-controlled companies: Finmeccanica, ENI, ENEL. There were rumors of auditions at unforgettable evenings in a love nest just a stone's throw from Piazza Navona, an apartment that was owned by a Vatican confraternity—frequented not only by the monsignor, but also by Benedetto Umiltà. There was even talk of a sort of blood oath that bonded together for the rest of their lives that budding ruling class, now gathered there on the hotel terrace.

Pericle Malgradi arrived a little late. And clutching under his arm a copy of the book, which to judge from the pages, had never been opened. He hastened to greet the monsignor with a rapidly rehearsed kiss of the prelate's hand, and followed it up with a piece of information whispered into his ear.

"Your Excellency, today I instructed my secretariat to purchase five thousand copies of your magnificent book, which we will give as thoughtful gifts to the leading constituents of my district. And, of course, we'll send the bill to the Chamber of Deputies . . . Ha, ha, ha!"

Tempesta expressed his pleasure and then turned his inquisitive gaze to the guy in the horrible shiny suit, out-of-season at best, who stood a few steps behind the Honorable. Spartaco Liberati had his mouth full, having chomped down on not one, not two, but three octopus canapes the minute he set foot on the roof garden. With a wink, Malgradi gestured for Liberati to step forward.

"Your Excellency, allow me to introduce you to Dottor Liberati, the voice of our city. You know, he was recently given an award on the Capitoline Hill."

"Delighted to meet you, my son."

Extending his clammy hand, Spartaco sketched out a bow.

"Radio FM 922 will carry the presentation live, and then we'll rerun it for a week. Mornings and evenings at nine o'clock."

Pushing Liberati away with a gentle shove, Malgradi clarified.

"Of course, Your Excellency, we also have the three state RAI network news shows, both national and regional. I saw to it personally."

"Of course," Tempesta smiled.

Benedetto Umiltà, too, seemed to be in excellent fettle, even a bit garrulous. To find himself at the center . . . well, perhaps not actually at the center . . . let's just say, "close to the center" of the Rome that counts was, for him—every time it happened—the source of fresh excitement.

General Mario Rapisarda was the last one to reach the roof garden. Pretending he'd only just managed to escape from a hellishly demanding afternoon, he apologized to Tempesta, asking him to sign the copy of the book that he too had brought along with him, which was, of course, as yet uncracked.

"At a single sitting, Your Excellency. I read it all at a single sitting. You are unyielding in terms of your principles and modern in your style, if I may venture to say."

While Tempesta, flattered, signed his copy of the book, the commandant of the Custoza division realized that at that soiree, with the exception of the hostesses, not a single woman could be found, even if you'd set out in search of one with a lantern. All of them were men, most of them under forty. And at a guess they were all young professionals. He decided that he had to agree with the guy behind him, who was whispering into his cell phone.

"Let me call you back, I'll call you back. I'm out at a party with a bunch of faggots and priests. Oh, sure, all right. Ciao, ciao . . . "

Saverio Tesi, the publisher, managed to quiet the audience, and provided a brief introduction to the luminous figure Monsignor Mariano Tempesta, mentioning his "precocious theological studies" and his "marked human qualities." Then, he confessed how proud his publishing house was.

"Let me say it. A publication of this sort has no intrinsic commercial value. It is a moral testimonial. And as such, it ought to be sufficient. But the hundred thousand copies of our first print run, I believe, prove how deeply we believe in this book, the proceeds from which, I'd like to remind you all, will be donated to Villa Marianna, a first-rate health facility in this city that, thanks to this donation, will be able to inaugurate a ward for the treatment of drug addiction."

Malgradi clapped his hands hysterically till they were sore, thinking of that sharp operator, his brother Temistocle, and the excellent line of coke that he'd snorted in the hotel bathroom the minute he'd gotten past the reception desk. By now he was sailing along on daily regimen of a good solid two grams. His last meeting with Samurai certainly hadn't helped matters at all. He'd been ready to piss his pants. What was it Samurai had said to him? "Promises are smoke, Malgradi. Just remember that everyone is replaceable. A good player always plays on more than one table."

Of course. That's why he was here. Lots of tables, dear Samurai. And that's to say nothing of the bishop's table.

Sitting with his legs crossed and holding the microphone between thumb and forefinger—which gave his pinky a coquettish freedom—Tempesta lifted the mic almost to his lips. A shaft of side spotlight illuminated him.

"Good evening, and thank you. Thank you for your demonstration of faith and friendship. Ethics is a word that has perhaps gone out of fashion. But it is a powerful word. As is millennium. The one we leave behind us, the one that awaits us and that will, one day, usher us into the Kingdom of Heaven, joined once again to Our Lord in the joys of the soul."

"Oh, sure, and maybe the joys of the flesh, too."

Although it was whispered in his ear, Malgradi's wisecrack made Benedetto Umiltà sit up a little more uncomfortably. The Honorable was clearly revving a little high. A little too high. Tempesta went on.

"As a guest of the Benedictine friars, I worked on this text in the solitude of the Hermitage of Camaldoli, taking spiritual comfort from the silence of dawn and early evenings."

"Oh, sure, and from a nice stick of black licorice belonging to that seminarian from Togo."

Umiltà blushed beet red and anxiously stared at Malgradi's wrecked-looking face.

"I beg you, Your Honor. I implore you."

By now, Tempesta's voice had the mellow, buttery texture of a DJ in the middle of the night.

"Ethics. Ethics. You might well wonder how that word applies to a century that is ushered in with the stigmata of atheism. And I can answer that question: read my aphorisms. Make of them the milestone of a new catechesis that stands in defiance of the onslaught of resurgent paganism. You see, my dear friends, not long ago a courteous journalist asked me what thoughts a man of the cloth might have on such topics as the civil union of gay people, adoptions on the part of homosexual couples, artificial insemination, surrogate mothers. Well, I answered him that there is no dialogue—that there *can be* no dialogue—with those who are trying to legitimize what is contrary to nature. The family of God is a man and a woman, and their offspring. It is in the family that we find the glory of God. The family is the cornerstone of the state. The union of two such people is a bellwether of the Apocalypse. And you all

know very well who it is who works in darkness to divide . . .
The Devil!"

Satanella started applauding frantically. And Malgradi
immediately joined in. He was now on his feet. For one of his
improvised stemwinders.

"Thank you, Your Excellency. Thank you! We shall not
allow perversion to destroy the family of God. We live in faith.
We are its guardians."

"Amen," mumbled Liberati. Who hadn't understood a
blessed thing that the bishop had said, but who felt an urgent
need to figure out whether Samurai had sent him there on a
glorified puff job or if there was something else bubbling in the
pot.

Tempesta, once the sermon was done, walked over to
Satanella and asked him to get the business cards of a couple
of young men he'd noticed in the audience. He'd been struck
by Malgradi's excitement, and didn't consider it to be a particularly good sign. He decided to confide in Benedetto Umiltà
concerning his irritation, as soon as he managed to drag him
away from Tesi, the guy from Il Braciere publishing house,
who was admiring his shoes, "which must be handmade"—
*surely you're not serious, Your Excellency, only three thousand
euros?*

"Benedetto, what's wrong with Malgradi?"

"I couldn't say, Your Excellency. He's looking tense, don't
you think?"

"He needs to take some time off, if you ask me."

"The government stands or falls in part on his vote, Your
Excellency."

"This government is dead and you know it as well as I do.
How much longer can it hold together? A month? Two
months? And after all, I have the impression that not a single
one of the things we discussed has actually come to pass, or am
I mistaken?"

"You're not wrong."

"And nothing seems to be moving forward, as far as I can tell."

"Malgradi continues to insist that the resolution is ready. There's just a technical delay."

"Hmph! Pericle Malgradi talks and talks and talks. But I've been thinking about his brother, Temistocle. He definitely seems to be operating on another level. And we need a new sheepdog to herd our flock. Don't you see them? Look, look how tame they are as they graze. They're little lambs. They're just waiting for someone to show them the way."

"You, Your Excellency, see further than the rest of us."

"It's no accident that the Church is two thousand years old, my dear Benedetto."

Pericle Malgradi continued moving back and forth in an agitated manner, pacing the roof garden like a pinball in play. He'd overdone it with the coke. He was run through with continual tremors, incapable of keeping his arms and legs under control. Once again, he tried to anchor himself to Rapisarda, who had made his way to the buffet and was stocking up on raw goat-milk caprino cheeses from the Oltrepò Pavese. He absolutely had to tell him. Right. Because then there was that other problem that needed to be taken care of.

"General, I'm afraid I'm going to have to bother you again with that matter we discussed on the Capitoline Hill, do you remember? That man of yours from the anticrime unit."

"Of course, I remember. I remember very clearly. I've looked into the matter, but let me tell you again, deep down Colonel Malatesta is a good officer. Perhaps just a little undisciplined. Sui generis, we might say. Idiosyncratic."

"Allow me to insist. This isn't a matter of discipline, we're talking about highly placed subversives within the corps. Now, now, Mario, let's take this seriously."

Rapisarda couldn't have agreed with Malgradi more.

Malatesta was a pain in the ass. And yet there was something shameless and, more importantly, reckless and panicky about the way the Honorable was pestering him. And then, there was that foam in the corner of his mouth. A little self-control, for pete's sake. Times weren't easy, after all. If it all collapsed around him, the last thing he wanted to do was let people run up debts that they very well might prove unable to repay. So, caution was the byword. Malgradi wanted Malatesta? Well, he could have him if it turned out to be necessary. But before trading the carpet, he had to see the camel. And could he still see the camel?

The general shook off Malgradi with the excuse of a phone call.

Malgradi stood stock still, in shock.

What the hell, was the general avoiding him? What is he, afraid of being bugged? Do I have a wire on me now?

He started touching himself all over, scratching as if infested by a wave of fleas.

Calm down.

He realized that Spartaco Liberati was giving him a baffled look.

"Listen up, asshole. I asked you to get busy on that asshole Malatesta and I still haven't heard a thing. Zero is the score so far. You've just jerked off a little, nothing more. Don't force me to talk to Samurai. Don't force me, you won't like how it turns out."

"But he's the one who sent me."

"You see? So get moving. Now. There's no more time to waste."

Liberati withdrew in as orderly a fashion as he could muster, renouncing the opportunity for his usual request for cash: Malgradi was unmistakably beside himself.

The Honorable's cell phone vibrated. Malgradi read: "Good job, better and better! Just keep it up!" It came from a foreign phone card. That was Samurai's hack-proof system. The tone was ambiguous: it could either be one of sincere approval, or it could be a veiled threat. Malgradi looked up and found himself face to face with Michele Lo Surdo. The accountant had a worried expression.

"We're fucked, Your Honor."

"What are you talking about?"

"It's all been posted on a blog."

"What do you mean by 'all'?"

"All of it. The project, the feasibility study, New City, the beachfront concessions in Ostia. There's even a photograph of Samurai. I don't know if you understand what I'm talking about. All of it. Except for you. Strange, don't you think?"

Malgradi took refuge in an idotic smile. A burst of narcotics surged up his verterbae, clamping his temples in an intolerable vise. The Honorable pirouetted around and then crashed to the floor.

A minor, insignificant collapse due to the stresses of a life spent in the service of his country, as the newspapers would report the next day.

# XLII

Being a disgusting mess was a fine art. And Spartaco Liberati excelled at that art. Samurai had decided that it would be Liberati's job to fight back the effect of that post that had sprung up like a mushroom on the web. And that when he went after it, there was no point in taking half measures. A nice fat avalanche of mud, during the peak listening time on Radio FM 922.

Hey guys, I'm just poisoned this morning. Poisoned sick. And for once, the problems that A. S. Roma are having don't have a thing to do with it. Listen to what I found online: "I know. I know that Rome belongs to them. Adami, Sale, Anacleti, Perri, Viglione. Do these names mean anything to you? I know. I know that New City is their Trojan horse, and that it's going to suffocate us in a vise of reinforced concrete, all the way from EUR to the sea. I know. I know that these characters aren't some good-natured trenchermen, but murderers inspired by another murderer, Samurai . . . "

So you might say to me: what of it? What the hell do you care about this garbage? I care, I care, believe me. And you ought to care about it too, my dear listeners. Because here we're talking about Rome, our own Rome. And the city's future.

But I say to you: can people just slander the families of respectable people without so much as showing their faces? Can they shamelessly libel Rome? No. No, they can't. "I know, I know, I know . . ." But what the fuck do you know? Who the fuck are you? Pasolini? And after all, excuse me for saying it, but this whole thing with Pasolini—Pasolini this, Pasolini that . . . if he was still alive, by now he'd be a hundred! What, didn't anything else even happen in the meantime? And we're still talking about Pasolini!? Go on and get the hell out of here.

New City, they say. Okay, so? What's wrong with New City? As far as I can tell, they're a solid company with plenty of cash, cold hard cash, guys! And they say: tons and tons of cement are about to flow into Rome. A great project! I personally hope this project actually goes through! What, are you going to turn up your noses if we finally get some jobs around here? What, the bricklayers and construction workers who've been scraping by on account of this damned recession, where are we supposed to send them to eat, your house? They can fill their mouths with growth and development, but they ought to rinse their mouths out and take off their hats when they talk about Samurai. They say he's a killer? Miserable cowards. Now just because someone's had some problems when they were a kid, are they supposed to be a monster for the rest of their lives? Believe you me: Samurai is better than Keynes! And sure, okay, I know that you don't all recognize that name, but now let me explain.

John Keynes, that's actually how you pronounce it, was an English economist, and during the Great Depression he used to say: put the people to work. And what could be better in terms of putting the people to work than a nice big project involving lots of cement? What's that you say? No, sorry, it's Ottavio, from the control room: ah, do I know who spreads these lies? Okay, let me tell you who it is. I talked to a friend of mine who's in the postal police. He says that the website is anonymous, that it actually comes from Hungary. Oh, sure, Hungary! This is stuff from around here. And I know . . . now it's time to use that phrase . . . I know that what's behind it is the dainty hand of an old friend of ours. Do you remember that Alice Savelli who'd already trained her sights on the good guys from Cinecittà? Well, I say that she's behind it! And you can have her! A young woman from a well-to-do family, with plenty of money, who acts all alternative and progressive . . . Now, of course, alternative is just a manner of speech in this case . . . because everyone knows that she's dating a Carabiniere, a guy who returned to Rome the other day but already thinks he's the big boss in charge . . . and maybe he's the one who gives her the tips she publishes . . . Alice, listen, you can use all the gates and bars and protection in this world, and maybe they'll never even catch you, because you know how to work the internet, you or whoever's doing it for you . . . but you can be certain that the street knows things and understands them. So you know what? Savelli, can you hear me? Or rather, can you hear this chorus, growing louder? It's the voice of Rome. Rome is spitting you out! And now, let's kick back. Randy Crawford and her *One Hello*, a negress, but with a fabulous voice."

Michelangelo de Candia fiddled around with the control panel of the Renault 4 car stereo and, as he lowered the volume, turned to Marco Malatesta, sitting beside him, with a wink.

"Not bad, this Crawford. A little dated, but then our friend Spartaco is no spring chicken. Though I'd say we've heard enough. Am I wrong?"

Marco was on his iPhone. He was telling Alice about Liberati's attack.

"Don't go home. Swing by Ponte Salario as soon as you can, no wait, better, I'll come pick you up. I can get you to a safe place . . . What do you mean, 'you already have a safe place?' Alice, listen to me . . . What the hell! She hung up on me . . . "

"Impulsive and tough. There you go, two more adjectives to string along with the trite and obvious one, 'beautiful,'" Michelangelo pointed out.

"Take me to my place, please. I need to find her."

"That sounds like a confession," de Candia commented drily. "And in any case, it's a little late to change your mind. You should have thought of it before. They already knew about you. They put two and two together. Anyway, I doubt they're going to do anything violent."

"I need to find her," Marco said again, stubbornly.

The prosecuting magistrate pulled over.

"We already talked about this, unless I'm mistaken. And we'd also come to a conclusion, if I'm remembering rightly. That spreading the news was a very bad idea. Tell me, Marco, what is it that Alice and you have achieved, eh? I'll bet the hubcaps on my Renault 4 that before the afternoon is over, the website is going to be shut down. The state shouldn't waste time chasing after anonymous posts. What's more, now all they know is that we know. And above all, they know that we've decided to play dirty, which is to say, not by the rules. Which means that this is the beginning of a very different game. Of course, one without rules. And so, why are you surprised?"

Marco tried to stammer out a justification of some kind.

"I don't like having to wait, unable to move. You should have figured that out by now. There are things that, at a certain point, just need to be done. Period. After all, Rapisarda went too far, and I just saw red."

"So the roster of impulsive fools numbers two. Now don't you start pretending to be a white knight on a rearing stallion. What you did was stupid."

"All right. What we did was stupid. Now can I consider myself to have been scolded sufficiently and go try to find Alice?"

"Luckily," Michelangelo continued, ignoring him, "someone else decided to take this terrible idea and run with it."

Malatesta furrowed his brow and gave him an inquisitive look. A sly grin appeared on De Candia's face.

"Aside from anonymously posting your *I Know*, have you and Alice at least taken a look at the reactions online? I'm not a fan of the social networks, but there's one thing I think I've figured out. That it makes sense to throw a rock in the pond only if then you're going to bother to see what effect it has, right?"

"Did someone else post something on the blog?"

"Yes. Last night."

"Then why didn't I see it?"

"Maybe because you went to bed too early," de Candia smiled.

"Maybe," Marco smiled back. "What's written in this new post?"

"They posted old court transcripts concerning Samurai. The trials for armed robbery and armed gang activities in the Eighties. Criminal conspiracy with Dandi and Freddo. An attempted murder in 1985, and something a little more recent. In 1993. The robbery of the vault of the bank inside the hall of justice."

"What are you trying to tell me?"

"Do you know how many convictions upheld on appeal Samurai has had for his turbulent past as an armed revolutionary?"

"Nothing serious, if I'm remembering correctly what I read in our archives. Aside from the five year sentence he got when he was just a kid."

"Good memory. But what I told you was that our friend posted the court transcripts of the *investigations* involving Samurai, not his prior convictions. And there's a piece of real news in those court transcripts."

"What, exactly?"

"Do you know the name of the prosecuting magistrate who spoke for the prosecution in all the trials that Samurai faced?"

"Don't tell me."

"Ah, but I will tell you, like it or not. Dottor Manlio Setola."

"I would have bet on it!"

"And let's add another detail: he made a mistake or two in those investigations."

"Are you telling me that he gave Samurai a hand? That there was collusion?"

"Take 1993. The robbery in the vaults at the hall of justice. Do you remember what happened? Maybe not, you were probably just a kid then, am I right? Maybe you weren't even a member of the force yet."

Marco's mind was shot through by a lancing lightning bolt of memory of that night at Il Bagatto. Samurai's breath, as he was deciding to show him clemency. The scar on his temple started to pulse. There were too many things about him that de Candia didn't know.

"That's right, I was just a kid. And a kind of out of control kid, too."

"Well, for that robbery, Lothar, Mandrake, and Botola, three veterans of the old gang, were sent to meet their maker, and two twisted Carabinieri went to prison."

"Let me guess. Setola was the prosecuting magistrate who conducted the investigation."

"You're perceptive, I see. But there's a detail, and a decisive one. Mandrake and Lothar wound up roasted and dead in the armored car they used for the robbery, while our friend Botola shut his eyes once and for all with a bullet hole in the middle of his forehead.

"What about it?"

"The pistol that killed Botola is a very rare weapon. A Mannlicher. And it's a weapon with a past. It was fired the first time in 1985, in a murder for which Samurai was a suspect. Young Setola investigated and only a miracle could save our friend Samurai from life without parole."

"Let me take another guess. The miracle really happened."

"That's right. The Mannlicher, back in 1985, disappeared mysteriously from the high-security evidence room and Samurai, at the request of the prosecuting magistrate Setola, was acquitted during the preliminary investigatory phase. For eight years, that pistol remained a phantom. Then, suddenly, it reappears at center stage in the robbery at the hall of justice, where it's used to blast open Botola's skull. All Setola would have had to do was add one and one. The Mannlicher is practically Samurai's signature. Which would mean that Samurai was a member of the crew behind the knockover at the hall of justice. But once again, this time . . . "

"Setola fails to notice . . . He doesn't make the conection."

"Exactly. The only thing that the investigation even moved were a few rags here and there. The lead involving the pistol is not only not followed up, but from what we read in the transcripts published on the blog, it was considered by the district attorney's office, and here I quote from memory, 'to be of no investigative interest or probative value.' At the end of the day, then, three bandits in the boneyard, two Carabinieri punished in exemplary fashion, Samurai loose on the street, and with him, his Mannlicher."

"Samurai has had Setola by the balls for the past twenty years . . . "

"Yeah. And probably not just Setola. A considerable number of the safe deposit boxes plundered in the '93 robbery belonged to men in the security services, lawyers, and magistrates."

"Sweet Jesus Christ."

"That's it, I'd say."

"We need to get word out about the level of protection this murderer enjoys."

"Get word out to who? These court transcripts are on the blog, I told you."

"In the form they're in, only you can understand those transcripts."

"Wrong, my dear Marco. Samurai understands them and Dottor Setola understands them."

"Then let's go have a chat with Setola."

"I don't think this is exactly the day for it, you know. Doesn't one fuckup seem sufficient to you for today? This stuff can prove useful. But right now isn't the time to use it."

"You're right, Michelangelo. In part because at this point,

Setola is going to be shitting his pants at the thought that someone might figure out what you just figured out."

De Candia nodded.

Marco felt the scar stop pulsating. He stared at de Candia, who stared back. They said everything that needed to be said, without speaking a word. The prosecuting magistrate opened the door of the Renault 4.

"Now you go find her, I'm going to take a walk. Inside this tin can of a car the air has become unbreathable."

# XLIII

Farideh had her back turned to Max, shielding herself from the wind. She was staring ecstatically at the labyrinth of gleaming white plaster of Hora and the only strip of asphalt on the island of Folegandros. The road vanished inland a few miles to the northwest, toward the 1,300-foot elevation of Agios Eleftherios, in the direction of the village of Ano Meria, the only other inhabited settlement. She turned to look at Max. Then she smiled at him. He stroked her hair. He hadn't told her about Samurai. After all, what risk could there possibly be? The girl knew nothing about him. And that's the way he wanted it to stay. She trusted him. She had given herself to him, unconditionally. Nothing about that trip could possibly arouse her suspicions.

"They hired me to bring a boat back from Greece to Fiumicino. It's good pay. And I want you to come with me, because I don't want to be alone anymore, or with just Kant to keep me company."

In the early afternoon, Shalva joined the couple in the hotel, a simple structure on a cliff high above the sea. Max introduced him as Misha, a rich Russian businessman.

"You know, Farideh, this gentleman produces more steel than all of Italy put together, can you believe it?"

"You're too kind, Max. Steel, at this point, is a thing of the past. And I'm really starting to feel like a man of the past."

Farideh looked the Georgian in the eyes.

"You strike me as quite young, sir, and in any case, there's a great beauty in the antiquity of things. I say it as the Persian that I am."

"Ah, I thought there was something. Something I couldn't quite pin down. You're an Aryan, then. That's where such remarkable beauty comes from. I'll have to tell our mutual friend, right, Max?"

The reference to Samurai hit Max in the gut like a solid punch.

"Don't you agree, Max? Do you think our friend won't understand how lucky you are? I think he will. And if he doesn't, I can assure you that I'll make sure he sees the light."

"Which friend is this?" asked Farideh.

"Just one of Misha's cousins, my love," Max improvised. "A cousin I transported a boat for last summer, and who was worried about the fact that I was still single."

Farideh blushed. They drank a coffee, then another, then a bottle of ouzo appeared. Shalva liked Max. Even more, he liked that magnificent amber woman who was with him. And so he prolonged that olfactory and visual pleasure until he was thoroughly sated and decided that the time had come to say farewell and impart the instructions which were, after all, the reason he was sitting at that table.

With a nod, Shalva took Max aside and handed him a waterproof bag and a bunch of keys.

"You know the *Runa* very well. It's down at the Karavostasis wharf. In case we don't see each other tomorrow morning, have a safe trip. And when you get to Fiumicino, let me know. Ah, and give my regards to Samurai. Tell him that I'm grateful for what he did with regard to the caregivers. Tell him that it's taken care of."

Max registered the information.

Shalva appreciated the young man's discretion. There was no need to get into details. Thanks to the tip that Samurai had procured for him, he'd managed to unmask the traitor. The traffic in caregivers had been momentarily broken off, but the informant had got what was coming to him. According to Georgian protocol: with his heart split open by the ritual blade, and his eyes carved out with two mussel shells kindly provided by Shalva's partners from Bari.

The two young men came back to the table.

Farideh stood up, kissing Shalva on both cheeks.

"I hope to see you again, Misha: it's been a pleasure."

"On my boat, on my boat, all of us together next summer, my Star of the East. Max will work and we'll lie in the sun. And maybe by then things will be less formal between us, given you don't think I look all that old. Oh, Max, don't get jealous now. Ha, ha, ha . . . "

Toward evening, after making love, Farideh turned her cell phone back on. She'd left it switched off ever since she'd set foot on Folegandros. She wasn't expecting any urgent calls, and she didn't have the money to pay for roaming. She just turned it on for a few minutes to check her texts. And just as she was about to push the off button, the thing started vibrating. She looked at the display.

Alice.

"Hello, Alice, ciao."

Farideh spoke in a whisper, to keep from waking Max up, but all the same she was unable to conceal from her girlfriend how happily and sweetly she had emerged from her sleep. She told her all about Greece, the trip on the *Runa*, the tenderness she felt for Max, the passion.

Alice's words made her blood run cold.

"Watch out for that young man. He might not be who you think he is."

Farideh turned off her phone and plunged back into that dull sense of sadness and melancholy she thought she'd been cured of. The sadness that had gripped ever since the day that, as a little girl, she'd clung to her father, looking at her mother's dead body, until the day she met Max.

The truth was that she was mad at Alice. Why had she called her, why had she said that? What was wrong with the happiness she was feeling? Is it true then that women don't know how to be friends in full?

She decided to ward off those bad thoughts and curled up in bed. She pressed her lips against Max's.

## XLIV

Alice ended the conversation wondering whether it had been a good idea to call Farideh. She'd put off that decision for a long time. She finally called because she'd decided she could trust Marco completely. What reason would he have had to lie to her about Max? If Max really was Nicce, then putting Farideh on guard against him was the act of a friend.

Her phone vibrated. It was him. For the tenth time.

"I'm fine, don't worry. Give me an hour and I'll be at your place. Of course, I'm fine, I told you, everything's fine, stop fretting."

For the whole day, she and Diego, from the young man's apartment, had monitored the website with a growing sense of excitement. Some anonymous hacker had posted judicial documents that concerned Samurai. They didn't understand a word of it. It was certainly a signal intended for someone in particular. But who? Anyway, she had done her part. As expected, the website had gone dark after a few hours, but the more than five hundred messages received, variously of horror and solidarity, meant that the rock they'd tossed had made waves in the stagnant waters of the capital. The news had been carried by the online editions of the major news publications. A city councilman, a member of the opposition, had announced a parliamentary inquiry. The regional news hour had interviewed General Rapisarda and the prosecuting magistrate Setola. Setola had been dismissive, alluding confusedly to unproven insinuations. Rapisarda had been more decisive; it was clearly the work of a diabolical provocateur, he'd said. Another confirmation that they'd hit a bullseye. The whole time Diego had buzzed around her, trying to narrow the distance between their bodies. She had rejected him. They'd had an affair, that much was certainly true. But that was water under the bridge by now. As long as Marco was around, the road was closed. One thing she didn't need was emotional confusion and mess in this period of her life. And after all, Marco's eagerness to protect her was flattering. Alice hesitated to use the word love. Too soon, and there were too many contradictions, still. And at night, when they finally got dressed, she had made up her mind to have a serious talk with him: he didn't need to feel guilty, that was out of place. It was clear that once they put it all up on the web, they'd trace it back to her. She'd been a target to start with, ever since she'd first challenged the Anacleti clan. Virtual firewalls might stop investigating magistrates, but they wouldn't stop people like Samurai. Retaliation could be expected. And she wasn't a delicate girl he needed to protect, she was a fighter. If you want things to change, you have to be ready to pay the price.

As she was climbing the steps of the small seventeenth-century family palazzo on Via del Corallo, she decided that Grandma Sandra's feelings would be hurt. Usually she stayed the night at her house, accompanying her gently into the troubled sleep of the elderly by reading her a few pages of her beloved D'Annunzio. That night she wouldn't be able to do anything more than to tuck her in. Too much adrenaline, too many emotions, too much desire.

She used her own keys to open the door, she peeked into the perennially shadowy front hall, and to her great surprise she was greeted by the sound of a burst of raucous laughter mixed with the background of a low, pleasant, courteous male voice.

Her grandma had visitors? But who, other than Alice herself, would spare a thought for her?"

"Grandma? It's me, Alice. Is there someone there with you?"

"Come in, come in, dear, we were waiting for you . . . "

She practically ran down the long hallway that led to the drawing room, lit by the Empire-style lamp.

Grandma Sandra was sitting in her beloved red velvet armchair, beneath a large seventeenth-century portrait of Lucrezia Borgia, the legendary poisoner. And sitting across from her, intently sipping a cup of tea, was Samurai.

Alice came to a halt at the doorway and, instinctively, clutched the bag containing her personal computer to her chest.

"Alice, come say hello to your friend. He's such an exquisite person."

"You're too kind, Donna Alessandra," said Samurai. He got to his feet, with an elegant bow.

"Grandma, let me get you into bed."

"Alice! I can do it myself."

"I'll help you, I said."

Samurai helped the elderly woman to her feet. She rested her weight on his arm. Samurai turned her over to Alice. For an instant their gazes brushed. Samurai's eyes were gelid, expressionless. They frightened her.

"He's such an exquisite person," Grandma Sandra said again, when they were in her bedroom. "You've finally started making the right kind of friends."

"Grandma, I'm so sorry, but I'm in a little bit of a hurry."

"Yes, yes, of course, dear. Go on, you go on, and when you leave, remember to lock the door behind you. Alice . . . "

"Yes, Grandma?"

"Don't you think your friend looks like Major Hermann?"

Alice sighed. During the German occupation of Rome, in

1944, the little palazzo on Via del Corallo had been requisi-
tioned by the Wehrmacht. Grandma Sandra's father was fighting on the American side, and the rest of the family was held
hostage by the Germans. Major Hermann had personally
vouched that they would be safe. Grandma Sandra treasured
that memory with a veneration that verged on hero-worship.
Major Hermann was her standard by which all masculine
charm and allure was gauged. Alice suspected that between the
distinguished, swastika-wearing officer and the young heiress
of the house of Savelli there might have been something more
than mutual respect.

"Major Hermann has been dead for fifty years," she said
brusquely.

"When you set yourself to it, you can be quite a grouch,"
the old woman replied, indignantly.

Samurai was sitting contemplating the portrait of Lucrezia
Borgia.

"Your grandmother told me that at night Lucrezia breaks
free of the canvas and comes to life. She told me that, in her
opinion, Lucrezia was defamed. She was no murderer. In any
case, I made the tea with my own two hands . . . For that matter, libel is a powerful weapon, and that's something you
should know all about, right, Alice?"

"What do you want with me?"

"I want you to sit down and get comfortable and give me
five minutes of your precious time. I won't ask anything more."

"Should I trust you?"

"You're free to leave. You could have done it the minute
you walked in the room."

"And leave you here with Grandma Sandra? I'd never have
done that."

"I understand. But do you really think that someone like
me would really try to hurt a little old lady? You underestimate

me, no doubt about it. If I had wanted to do such a thing, I'd have had all the time, in the last two hours I just spent here. And I have to say, two extremely agreeable hours. Donna Alessandra is a true lady, let me say it. In bygone times, people like her would have captured the hearts of warriors far nobler than I."

"So you consider yourself a warrior, is that it?"

Samurai poured himself some tea and offered her some. Alice declined. But, at last, she sat down on a Thonet chair, a few steps away from him.

"In this question of yours I recognize the Alice who made my old friend Marco go head over heels."

"Marco is no friend of yours!" she reacted.

"He was once. And certain things matter. They are subtle bonds that are established between people of real worth, bonds that condition them for the rest of their lives. Even beyond their own intentions . . . but we can talk more about that later. Do you know why you didn't run screaming, why you didn't call 911, why you didn't try to attack me, Alice? No? Then let me explain. It's because you are a person with a certain amount of curiosity. You want to know. You want to build up your store of knowledge. And in this eagerness, you let yourself be led by the hand by the wrong people, and you leapt to mistaken conclusions. And this, for a banner-bearer of the generation of exactitude like yourself, is unforgivable. No, don't interrupt me. The five minutes isn't up yet, be fair. You and Marco fool yourselves into thinking that you can stop history. But the Great Project is history, and it's going to move forward, whether or not the two of you want it to."

"Is that a threat?" she smiled, sarcastically.

"It's a statement of fact. That's all." Samurai adjusted the creases in his black trousers. "Does the word Bagatto mean anything to you?"

"It's a tarot card. The Magician, or the Mountebank."

"Of course. The active principle, the spirit that starts the Great Game. But try going online and searching for 'Il Bagatto social center.' You can ask Marco to explain the rest to you. In fact, since we have this opportunity, do me one last favor. Call him on your phone. And let me speak to him."

Alice obeyed, cowed by him. She dialed the number and, when he answered, handed the phone over to Samurai.

"Ciao, Marco. I just wanted to compliment you. Your new girlfriend is really something special."

Then he handed the iPhone back to her and took his leave, mocking and perfectly corteous.

Half an hour later, Marco was on Via del Corallo.

"You can put away the arsenal, he's left. And don't make any noise: Grandma Sandra is a light sleeper," Alice said.

When he tried to embrace her, she pushed him away.

"You're right. I'm an idiot. I fed you to the wolves. I'll never be able to forgive myself. Now let me get you away from here."

"Marco, what's Il Bagatto?"

Marco let himself flop down into an armchair. He took his head in his hands. And he told her everything. Everything he had kept from her till now. His father, a railroad employee, a longtime Communist. His blind faith in the Party hierarchy, from the secretary and comrade in chief, all the way down to the lowliest bureaucrat who claimed the right to shout orders at the mild-mannered multitude of the Party faithful. Marco had hated all that. His hatred had thrust him into Samurai's arms. He had believed in that man. And then he'd come dangerously close to killing him. And Samurai, for his part, had spared his life. He spoke of his mother's kindness, of his father's consternation upon learning that Marco had passed the admission exam and would be attending the police academy: what was worse, a son who was a Fascist or one who was a Carabiniere? In the end, they had made peace. But he had vanished from his life leaving too many things unsaid, too many hugs refused, too many tears choked back.

"Now you know it all."

"Now it's too late. You should have made up your mind before this."

"I would have. It was just that . . . all right, I have no excuse. Forgive me."

"For a while, we'd better not see each other, Marco."

# XLV

From EUR they had set out, thought Samurai as he stared at Il Fungo, and it was to EUR that they were returning. And in the middle lay an entire lifetime.

They'd been punk kids taught to revere the act, nourished on its mystique; they'd been brought up on the cult of the race, raised to hate the present. They dreamed of a heroic past, they yearned for superman's triumph, and in the meantime they gathered in the shade of Il Fungo to plan their next action.

They had dictated law at EUR. What better hunting ground than that quarter of Rome made up of sharp-edged geometries and spatial layouts that rejected all curves, reminiscent of the Fascist utopia that shipwrecked on the shoals of betrayal? They had fooled themselves, the others, the reds, the powerful ones, their longtime enemies, that they had herded them onto some sort of Indian reservation. They had proved with blood that for people like them there was no such thing as a reservation. They had set out from EUR to conquer the city. And now they were returning to EUR.

For a new departure? For the final surrender?

Samurai was in the grip of conflicting emotions. If he reasoned about it coldly, he could only conclude that the situation was falling apart. Defeat was in the air. The governing coalition was heading for a crackup. They were just waiting for the official death certificate at this point. The whole thing with the blog only complicated matters. They had taken emergency measures, but the damage was done. Getting the measure approved was going to be a race against time. The horses were panting, winded. Or maybe it was more a case of the trainers and jockeys having overdone it with the drugs, and now the animals were on their last legs, their internal organs ravaged by the chemical abuse. Malgradi was losing ground. In the circles that mattered, there was already talk of succession. The success of the initiative was, at this point, in the hands of the gods. Samurai had tried to bring the forces out on the street back under some kind of control. He wasn't yet ready to admit defeat, but it was just a matter of time now.

From EUR they had set out and now they were back in EUR.

Samurai remembered the afternoons of frantic consultations, the exchange of weapons, the thrill of putting on ski masks, the contact with the stock of the semiautomatic. With the money from their first armed robbery, they had gone out for dinner in the fancy restaurant on the fourteenth floor. The mythical Il Fungo. At this point, he was the only survivor of that band of heartless madmen. Now that he could go to Il Fungo whenever he felt like it, and be sure of getting a king's reception, of being revered like a pasha, it still didn't give him the hot excitement of those years. Years that he would never be able to get back.

Samurai was sad. And he wondered whether any of it had been worthwhile.

It was a bright, sunny morning. Two young hookers were taking turns baring their breasts, for the benefit of the groundskeepers.

Enough self-pity. There were other projects to get underway. There were other paths to explore. There was a whole life out there to pin down and possess. Enough is enough.

He headed back to his Smart Car, with the proud stride of a man without shadows, or who has decided, for once, not to have any.

Marco Malatesta was waiting for him, leaning on the car.

"I ought to shoot you right between the eyes."

Samurai plunged his hands into the pockets of his Tom Ford leather jacket.

"The girl took it pretty hard, didn't she? Well, that's your fault. You need to tell women the truth. Maybe not always, and not all at once. But the important things, Marco. At least the important things."

"You crossed a line, Samurai. This is something that concerns you and me. You should have left her out of this."

"You're the one who dragged her into it, not me. Anyway, I'm in agreement with you. War isn't something the ladies should be involved in. Indeed, this morning you didn't find Alice's pretty little head on your desk, in Ponte Salario, did you?"

"Fuck yourself, Samurai. You're not going to manage to win this one. Not this time. Your Great Project is going to be stillborn."

Samurai smiled. He just loved laying all his cards on the table. He loved taking on an adversary worthy of respect. It was like going back to the old days. When things were clearer, black and white, and the street and the halls of power were still the place where men clashed and fought.

"The Great Project! Do you have any idea what this is going to mean for our Rome? Thousands of jobs, homes for the poor, a new level of prosperity."

"Why don't you let Spartaco Liberati spout that kind of bullshit? You've set up a feeding trough for every filthy pig in Rome, including the priests."

"Cement is the soul of Rome, Colonel. And the priests, as you know, care deeply about all questions concerning the soul."

"There's a war, Samurai. And when there's war, there's no project. And you're not going to be able to put a halt to this war."

"War? What are you talking about? All I see is peace."

"Look more carefully, Samurai. Weren't you the one who always knew everything?"

"Once I was, maybe. Back when we were both on the same side."

"I've never been on your side. We're in two different armies, the two of us."

The two of us. Us against them, the way it used to be. In spite of himself, Samurai felt a certain admiration for men like Malatesta. *Rarae aves*, very rare birds in the dirty sky far above the common servants of the state.

"But that's where you're wrong," Samurai went on, patiently. "In the old days, the street dreamed of becoming just like you. We dreamed of normality, power, prosperity and comfort. And why not, of creating a better world."

"Bullshit. You're telling yourself a story that never happened."

"But now," Samurai resumed, in the same tone of voice, "you're the ones who do everything you can to be like us. And you do an excellent job of it."

Marco didn't reply. He'd thought the same thing when he'd questioned Number Eight, after he'd survived the ambush laid for him by Paja and Fieno. He'd wondered whether "Us" and "Them" still made any sense. Whether the priests, Rapisarda, and Setola belonged to the same state as, say, de Candia. If they were the halls of power. And what about him? Where did Colonel Marco Malatesta really fit in? On which side?

Marco stepped aside and let Samurai walk past. But this time it was the bandit who remained where he was.

"You shouldn't have it in for me. You and I belong to the same breed. The breed of men of order. We're trying to keep the ship of state on a level keel, with its prow turned into the wind, in the midst of this Babylon that Rome has turned into."

"Bullshit, bullshit, bullshit! The fish rots from the head," Marco retorted.

Samurai threw his arms wide.

"Once again, with these Cartesian categories. The fish, the head . . . The world has changed, and I'm the first to say it's a pity, but it's changed. Have you ever read Zygmunt Bauman, by the way?"

And now it was Marco's turn to burst out laughing. As if Keynes wasn't enough. Now he's throwing in Zygmunt Bauman, too!

"Say hi to Max for me," he said, turning to leave with a sarcastic grin, "I haven't seen him around in a while."

Samurai stiffened. Marco understood that the ties between Samurai and the "philosopher" still remained to be explored, and when he got back to the office, he issued an order for an investigation into Farideh's young boyfriend.

He called Alice over and over. Voicemail. She wasn't answering his calls. Marco felt himself burning deep down when he got a call on his work line. Thierry was unmistakably worried.

"Did you send someone to the demonstration?"

"What demonstration are you talking about, sorry?"

"Where the hell are you? The apocalypse is being unleashed out there! Turn on the television, if you don't believe me."

Footage of clashes in Rome. Billowing clouds of smoke. An armored car under siege by demonstrators on Piazza San Giovanni.

He grabbed his helmet and handgun and raced toward his Bonneville.

He hadn't talked about this with Alice. But if there was this big of a mess going on, she was certainly involved somehow.

## XLVI

Under a magnificent bright sun, on an afternoon baking in the warmth of Indian summer, the little two-sided hot-air balloon with the morphing faces of the prime minister and the minister of the economy that transformed into vampires hung in midair over a dense carpet of humanity, bright and colorful, from which a chorus of voices rose into the air, echoing with chanted slogans. Alice had knotted her black North Face jacket around her waist, cursing that burden of Gore-Tex which, ultralight though it might be, still remained an inconvenience, and which she had stupidly brought along with her on that cloudless day. And so she was clad in the orange T-shirt that Diego had given her. "Get Mad as Hell!" it said on the T-shirt of the Rebel Dragons. It might not be particularly poetic, that was true. But it was very clear.

Alice stared ecstatically at the spectacle she was now part of, continuously snapping photos with her iPhone. During the night she'd had something similar to one of her old panic attacks. Eyes wide open, she had asked herself whether she shouldn't give Marco another chance. She didn't know what to do. She hadn't felt that way for a long, long time. And the first decision no longer seemed like the right one to her. She had arrived at the demonstration tired and stressed out, almost without conviction. But what was happening around her verged on the incredible. The physical pleasure of community and action erased all doubts.

She couldn't remember ever having seen anything like it.

They'd done it. The event had gone viral. How many people could there be? Two hundred thousand? Three hundred thousand? Diego's eyes were gleaming. He handed her a Ceres cigarette and showed her on his smartphone the latest update on *La Repubblica*'s live feed.

"More, there's more of us than that. Police headquarters is talking about five hundred thousand. You understand, Alice? If they say half a million, then there must be twice as many of us. They're not going to forget this October 15 anytime soon."

It was almost three o'clock by now. She had trooped in behind a streamer—"Women, and That's Enough"—that for more than an hour now had been struggling to get moving. And Piazza Esedra—why not, they continued to call it by its old name, not Piazza della Repubblica—couldn't contain any more people. They still hadn't gotten started when they heard that the truck of the "United Against the Recession" contingent, marching with FIOM, the metalworkers' union, which was at the head of the procession, had almost reached the end of Via Cavour, close to Largo Corrado Ricci. She could barely make out the van of "San Precario," St. Part-Time, with the steelworkers of Pomigliano, which was also stuck on Piazza dei Cinquecento. Her gaze came to rest on another streamer, "United for Global Change," which officially declared war on the international regime of banks and bankers. She thought about Marco for a second: she wondered how he might have mocked that outsized target.

"Oh, there's no way to even move here!" Diego objected irritatedly.

She too drew from their forced immobility not only an unbridled excitement, but also a sense of vulnerability. She knew that an overextended period of stasis never promises anything good. It wears you out. It poisons the blood.

For that matter, up till now she hadn't seen a single uniformed officer. And that didn't necessarily constitute a piece of good news. It seemed that riot police and Carabinieri had vanished into thin air. What the hell had become of them? She had seen them at work during the peaceful general rehearsal of the night before, on Via Nazionale, in front of the Palazzo delle Esposizioni, where the Rebel Dragons had set up their Quechua tents for a night of Occupy Rome. Twelve hours before, police headquarters had shut off all points of access to the historical center in the direction of Piazza Venezia and Via dei Fori Imperiali. Barricades formed by armored police wagons and units in riot gear like some immense legion of heavy armored cavalry sealed off every aperture—from avenue to alleyway—between the Monti quarter, the Tritone Tunnel, and Via Barberini. Which is to say, the three symbolic gates leading in to the Forbidden City. To the Rome of the Palaces of Power. The Chamber of Deputies, the Senate, Palazzo Chigi, Palazzo Grazioli, the prime minister's extremely private residence.

Sure, of course. Let them fuck themselves over completely by making the city inaccessible not only to the Indignados and to Occupy, but to everyone. A city that in its spectral silence would thus become unmistakable proof of the very things that they were shouting in the street. That the emperor really had no clothes, and that he was marshalling his troops to protect the palaces that had by now become nothing more than simulacra of an empty power. Empty and illegitimate, too, because held only by a few, and devoid of any true representative input. The city, the real city, the *other* city, would become theirs.

All the same, there was a problem. There most certainly was. Alice found herself face to face with it when "Women, and That's Enough," the group she had joined finally managed to move the first few yards in the direction of Piazza dei Cinquecento.

Alice recognized the Neri. The Black-bloc anarchists.

They were marching at a brisk gait, arriving from the direction of the Termini train station. The lead-gray hue of their sweatshirts, the heft of their combat boots, the backpacks and, especially, those damned helmets, fastened to their waists by carabiners, said everything about them that needed to be said, much more clearly than any watchword. Alice recognized the Piedmontese accent from the left-wing social centers of greater Turin, the Venetians of the No Dal Molin movement, and the unmistakable Salento dialect of the Neri from Lecce and Brindisi. All of them soon drowned out by the heavy, emphatic accent of those Romans from Ponte Marconi. The ones who went everywhere with their dogs and with whom she'd had a set-to the year before, on December 14, at Piazza del Popolo, when they'd called her a "little hipster" in the midst of a hail of molotov cocktails and torn-up cobblestones.

The Neri sliced into the procession like a hot knife into butter. Even worse, as if it belonged to them. Without encountering the slightest resistance and, above all, without having to push through any filter. The uniformed cops were elsewhere. Guarding the flanks of the procession were now only a few scattered platoons of city constables. And the local flatfeet, safe in the comfort of their squad cars, took great care not to ask that rising black tide arriving from the Termini station what the hell they thought they were doing marching around with helmets. It was easy to say that the procession took care of its own safety. Everyone knew that was bullshit. Even she knew it. Everyone knew that that afternoon no one was protecting anyone else. And no one was responsible for anyone other than themselves. They knew it. And the police knew it.

Alice thought that their progress down Via Cavour should have broken up and diluted the poisonous slime that had first insinuated itself and by now had taken firm possession of the center of the procession. But it turned out she was wrong. The Neri marched along, preceded by three cordons in the vanguard, behind which men and women continued to congregate in orderly files, as if in accordance with some long-planned synchronized set of movements. Also, the two tattered banners with the A of anarchy, which had been fluttering on Piazza dei Cinquecento and had clearly been meant as nothing more than a gathering point, like the umbrellas waved in the air by tour guides at the Colosseum, had since been rolled up and tucked away in backpacks. Another very bad sign.

The joy of Piazza Esedra had been swept away by a contagious wave of anxiety. The police and Carabinieri helicopters that were following from high above that river of humanity and sending aerial footage back to the monitors in the interservice control center at police headquarters and, at the same time, live onto Sky TV, were now hovering lower in a threatening way. The *chop-chop-chop* of the rotors formed a sinister background noise, which clumped together the voices and the music of that multitude which still believed in a cloudless afternoon.

Alice found Diego next to her, panting.

"I don't like this, Alice, this is not good. The head of the procession has almost reached St. John Lateran, but the police are assembling at Largo Corrado Ricci. I'm afraid they want to break the procession in two."

"But why?"

Diego indicated the Neri with a nod of his head. After that, it was only a matter of seconds.

Suburra, the ancient quarter of brothels described by Petronius Arbiter, was at their feet. Via dei Serpenti on the right, Via del Colosseo and the sacred hill of Fagutal Jupiter on the left. And nearby, the very same mezzanine apartment that a cabinet minister discovered had been purchased for him without his knowledge, now as celebrated as many an immortal pasquinade, if not more.

Suburra, the eternal image of an irredeemable city. Home to a violent and desperate plebeian mob that centuries ago had become a bourgeoisie, now the city's geographic center. Because it was and still remained its beating heart.

Suburra, the origin of a millennial contagion, an irreversible genetic mutation.

That was the place. How could they have failed to think of it before now.

"Hey, you pieces of shit!"

Like the whistling through the air that announces the coming blow, the shout of the Neri preceded the tremendous crash of a street sign ripped out of the ground and now used to shatter the plate glass windows of a temp agency. Now the ski-masked demonstrators had put on their helmets and pulled their hoodies over them, and they were moving like Bolshoi ballerinas. In a nihilistic dance of fire, stones, and steel ball bearings.

Alice and her "Women, and That's Enough" reeled in horror. Enveloped in the greasy smoke of burning car tires and fuel, at least three parked cars were in flames, while through the front door of a supermarket the spoils of a sudden proletarian expropriation had begun to rain out onto the asphalt. Boxes of corn flakes, cans of tuna, bottles of water and pop-top cans of Neri Chinotto, cans of Scottish smoked salmon. On the opposite side of the street, squeezed into the cramped space of a locked street door, Alice started to scream at the top of her lungs.

"Fascists! Fa-a-ascists! You're a bunch of Fascists!"

A man in a ski mask stared at her for a few seconds. And for a brief moment he lowered the slingshot he was about to use to fire gleaming steel ball bearing into the sign outside a bank.

"Go fuck yourself, bitch!"

Now Alice was weeping. She knew the magnetic force of street violence, its capacity to overwhelm the meaning, the smell, the music, and the words of those who had peacefully occupied that street. She had curled up on the asphalt, with her head bowed over her legs, and she could no longer bring herself to behold the spectacle of destruction, though she couldn't keep herself from hearing the deafening sound of it. She tried to get out of the damned doorway, closed tight behind her, and realized that she was alone now. Diego had vanished. The women of "Women, and That's Enough" had disappeared with him. A middle-aged man with a CGIL union handkerchief around his neck was dripping blood from his scalp. He'd tried to get between the Neri and an ATM, until a steel bar cracked his head open.

Where on earth were the cops?

What were they doing?

Why the fuck were they just standing by and watching?

She tried to find reassurance in someone's gaze. In a gesture of reaction. But there was nothing. The Neri were being left free to act as they pleased. She spoke to the guy who had appeared ten steps away or so. He had a bandanna tied over his nose that covered mouth and chin, a light-colored cotton jacket with the hood pulled up. And he kept pointing his Olympus digital videocamera toward the middle of the scene with slowed, careful movements. Movements that seemed impervious to the adrenaline of those moments. He was no doubt a journalist.

"Film, go on and film everything! Everything! People need to know that the police are just standing by and watching. Fascists!"

Until *he* spotted her.

Marshal Carmine Terenzi unbuttoned his camelhair overcoat and crushed out his cigarette beneath a Timberland hiking boot above which rode the cuffed hems of his pipestem jeans. He raised the visor of his helmet, pointing his nightstick straight at Alice, who stood about fifty yards away, and spoke quietly to the private who had stepped away from the unit of the Calabria battalion, which Terenzi happened to be commanding that day.

"There she is. Come on!"

The Neri had dispersed, vanishing as if by some spell, and Alice never even had the time to figure out just who that pack of wolves lunging toward her even were. Neri like the rest of them. But these Neri had the Italian tricolor banner on their chest. And a yellow flame on their helmets.

The first blow from the nightstick caught her on the cheek, flooding her mouth with the rusty taste of blood. Alice staggered, but managed to stay on her feet. Stunned, she slipped into the on-guard position that she'd practiced a thousand times at the gym. She dodged the first cop in riot gear who came at her by leaning to the left, and with her right fist she unleashed a straight that knocked him flat on his ass. Someone shouted something behind her. Alice whipped around and let fly with another punch, blindly this time. She hit something soft, and she heard a moan. She'd put another one out of commission. Good. She assumed the on-guard position again. The second blow from the nightstick caught her off guard, between her neck and shoulders. She fell to the ground. One, two, maybe five combat boots finished the job. Curled up in a fetal position, she felt her back, legs, and ankles explode. Then she felt the stabbing, electric pain of someone hauling her away by the hair. A leather glove protruding from the sleeve of a camel-hair coat was dragging her toward an armored car whose doors had just been thrown open with a noise that was a foreshadowing of prison.

Alice found herself tossed roughly onto the filthy metal deck of the paddy wagon, paralyzed by the pain and the fear. One of the soldiers was looking at her and making comments. She recognized his voice.

"Nice work, our little slut, eh? Savelli, Alice, your fun is over. You enjoyed destroying everything you could lay your hands on with your little boyfriends, eh? So you liked Occupy? Well, now you can occupy my throbbing dick!"

Terenzi. It was that piece of shit, Terenzi.

Overcoming the pain that was locking her neck in place, Alice did her best to turn and look out the Fiat Ducato's doors, before that miserable wretch of a marshal had a chance to close them. But she wasn't fast enough.

Her black North Face jacket dropped onto her face. It felt weirdly heavy, far heavier than normal. She turned out the pockets. Steel ball bearings rained onto the floor.

Even the night seemed unwilling to carry off that shitty day. Malatesta had chased after ski-masked demonstrators until nine o'clock, on Via Merulana, where one last charge had scattered them before they had a chance to set fire to the Tamoil gas station with their Molotov cocktails. Which would have delivered the street and the neighborhood into quite different epic literary territory than that of the book by Carlo Emilio Gadda. And when he'd finally rolled through the vehicle entrance of Ponte Salario, he decided that, if there was a God, that day He had laid his merciful hand on Piazza San Giovanni. No one on Via Emanuele Filiberto had been swept away by the deranged water cannons of the mobile squad. Nor had the flames that devoured a Carabinieri armored car claimed the life of a single private. And surely none of this could be attributed to the good will of the rivals in the field.

But as far as he was concerned, that was the only piece of good news. Alice's phone continued to remain mute, indifferent to his calls.

Marco was worried. He asked Captain Bruni for a definitive list of those arrested.

Her name was the first on the list.

Savelli, Alice, born in Rome on November 7, 1983. Arrested redhanded in criminal activity by members of the Calabria battalion on Via Cavour at 16:00. Crimes with which she is charged: rampaging and looting, resisting and insulting an officer of the law. Outcome of the searches of her person: positive. Currently held at the house of detention of Rebibbia. On the authority of the judicial police: DIGOS (General Investigations and Special Operations Division), Rome.

Alba cleared her throat with a sharp cough.

"Scorpio."

"Eh? What are you talking about?"

"Alice Savelli was born under Scorpio. Just like I was."

"Alba?"

"Yes, Colonel."

"Go fuck yourself! Would you please just go fuck yourself!"

Malatesta slammed his fist down onto the table with a terrifyingly loud crash, and then delivered a crushing kick to the plastic document shredder. His hands were shaking with rage, and he crumbled two Camels between his fingers before finally managing to get the third one lit.

Alba was horrified, to say nothing of her humiliation.

"I'm going to say it to you straight from the heart, Marco. That little bitch made a fool of you."

Malatesta glared at her with hatred.

"What the fuck do you know about it, eh? What the fuck are you even talking about?"

Music. What he needed was music. He fumbled with his computer and launched the web radio. Which turned into the first station on the list of pre-sets.

Radio FM 922.

There was no music.

Christ, Spartaco Liberati at midnight? What the fuck did he have to with the incidents of that afternoon?

A bloodbath. That's what happened, dear friends. A rout, a Caporetto, like in World War One. What am I saying, a Waterloo.

Today we can say that the police force handed our city over to the Communist fury of the Black-bloc.

Alba tried to talk over the radio.

"Why on earth are you torturing yourself with this troglodyte?"

Marco hushed her.

Burnt cars, supermarkets stormed and looted. And the police, the Carabinieri? They just stood by and watched, dear listeners. They waited for them to arrive at St. John Lateran. And only there, in front of the sacred precinct of a Catholic basilica, did they remember that in the world there are the police and then there are the thieves. They even broke a cross. You might ask: why? Yeah, why? The reason why, dear friends, will now be explained to you, and you alone, by your friend Spartaco Liberati. A very, *very* well informed little birdie tells me that one of the masterminds behind this afternoon of devastation is a well known extremist. Her name is Alice Savelli. We've talked about her before, do you remember? The one who has fun slandering good people on the internet . . . The one with the blog, the one who doesn't want to let anyone build new homes in Rome, because there are already plenty. Well well, you might say. But I'm the one saying well well well. Because Alice Savelli, according to what that same little birdie tells me, is the girlfriend of an important Carabiniere who was there at the piazza today. You get what I'm talking about?

Marco turned off his PC.

"The little birdie. The little birdie. That piece of shit." He lowered his head to his chest, holding it tight with both hands. He closed his eyes and tried to breathe, sensing a pang in the pit of his stomach.

"Michelangelo. I have to call him."

Alba made one more effort to get the man to listen to reason.

"Just think it over for a second, Marco. If you call de Candia now, you'll have lost all control over this thing. It's hard enough as it is. Listen to me for once . . . "

Marco had already grabbed his landline phone and dialed the prosecuting magistrate's home number. He hadn't been asleep. Or if he had, he was a real pro at concealing the fact.

"Michelangelo . . . "

"Marco, but . . . do you have any idea what . . . "

"Alice has been arrested."

"Give me fifteen minutes and I'll call you back."

Michelangelo de Candia presented himself in person at Ponte Salario with very bad news.

The file concerning the clashes at St. John Lateran just happened to be, surprise surprise, in the hands of the prosecuting magistrate Setola. Who was known, among other things, for having kept a Moroccan butcher in preventive custody for a full year on suspicion of being the head of the Italian network of Al-Qaeda. All of which was done thanks, so to speak, to the erroneous translation done by a brigadier who, when it came to the Arabic language, knew about as much as Setola himself: which is to say, practically nothing at all.

"Our ineffable friend theorizes a link between Alice and the Greek anarchists. There is evidence of phone calls to Greece. The phone number in question, which hasn't yet been identified, answers with a voice mail message in Greek and English. Setola also says that the girl, at the time of her arrest, managed to knock two officers to the ground with her fists. You never told me that she had such a spectacular left hook."

"Do you think this is the time for that sort of thing?"

"Ah, plus, her jacket was absolutely full of steel ball bearings. The arrest report looks solid. Ten eyewitness depositions. The whole squad that detained her during the rampage on Via Cavour."

Marco shook his head. This was the end. The end. And he was the biggest idiot ever to have worn the uniform.

Michelangelo de Candia took a moment, then coughed lightly and tilted his head in Bruni's direction: she'd heard every word.

"Do you believe it, Captain?"

"Me? If there's a signed report, the solemn word of my colleagues."

"As far as I'm concerned, it's all utter crap. In other words, they've framed her."

"How can you say such a thing?" the captain retorted indignantly.

"First of all," de Candia argued, "this all comes from Setola, and that alone is more than enough as far as I'm concerned. Second, not even one minute after her arrest, the news is on everybody's lips, and *snap*, the attack on Marco Malatesta is underway. No, it's not at all clear."

Bruni couldn't believe her ears. In the orderly world in which she'd been raised by her father, a Carabinieri general, the border between good and evil, was an unquestionable ethical fact. There was indisputable evidence against this Savelli. And now these two men, the colonel and the prosecuting magistrate, two institutional figures who by rights ought to have been on the side of the government and the powers that be, were doing their best to get this terrorist out of her current fix. As if Red judges weren't enough: now there were even Red Carabinieri. She had always defended Marco, but enough is enough. She was about to interrupt, when Marco shook himself out of his catatonic state and recovered his powers of speech.

"I'd like to believe you, but—"

"Let's check the story out."

"How? Setola's never going to let this one go."

"Tomorrow morning at eight o'clock, show up at Rebibbia prison. Go and talk with her."

"Setola is never going to authorize it, Michelangelo."

"You're right. But I'd say the time has come to play the wild card that you know about . . . 1993 . . . "

Marco's face lit up. That genius, that great genius de Candia.

Alba was increasingly disconcerted. Wild card? 1993? That you know about? What on earth was going on? What had those two lunatics gotten up to? Something big, to judge from the way that Marco had suddenly come back to life. What was it about this girl Alice Savelli, that the minute a man laid eyes on her he started drooling in her direction. A perverse cocktail of resentment and jealousy was churning inside her. That was what was scalding her, even more than her offended sense of duty. But she'd never admit that was the case. Not in front of Marco.

# XLVII

At eight on the dot, Marco Malatesta showed up at the front gate of Rebibbia prison.

He waited for the great metal doors to swing slowly open, driven by electric motors, then he covered the distance between the internal parking area and the registry office of the women's wing, where the most senior female correctional officer, Silvana, took him to see Alice.

He knew Silvana well. A big strong woman in her early fifties who long ago had worked as a social worker among the junkies of the Laurentino 38 and Corviale housing projects. The laboratory neighborhoods of all those years ago. Where, according to urban planners, the proletarians would have a chance to live better lives. Would. Caracoling down the hallway that led to the interview rooms, Silvana stopped for a moment and lowered her voice.

"That poor child . . . "

"What are you saying, Silvana?"

"They beat her black and blue, Marco."

"Well, considering what she did."

"I don't know about that, you know?"

"What are you trying to say?"

"You know, don't you, that I have a good sharp clinical eye. Especially with young girls and the new arrivals."

"I certainly do."

"What can I say? When they brought her here last night, she was furious as a rattled viper."

"They always have it in for whoever arrested them."

"I know that. But it's not like she was pissed off only at you Carabinieri. She kept telling me: Those Fascist Black-bloc bastards. You understand? She called them Fascists. Now you tell me how she could possibly have been mixed up with them? I mean to say: either she really is an actress, but an Academy Award level one, or she has nothing to do with this."

"And that's exactly my problem, Silvana."

Alice was sitting at the table in the interview room, her face turned, offering Marco a glimpse of the profile battered by the furious nightsticks. A deep purple bruise disfigured the left side of her face. From her hairline—the hair was greasy and was held together in a hastily assembled bun by a hot-pink plastic hairclip—to her chin, which was marked by a sloppily sutured cut, stitched together by black surgical staples.

She didn't seem surprised to see him. She stared at him with a blank look, betraying no emotion whatsoever.

Silvana left them alone. Marco stifled the urge to clutch her to his chest.

"How do you feel, Alice?"

"Are you blind?"

"Listen to me, and listen good, you're in no situation to be acting flippant or arrogant. You get me? There are things I kept from you, I'll admit that. But you . . . so far everything you've told me has been a pile of bullshit."

"What was I supposed to tell you? Do I have to justify myself with His Excellency the Colonel, just because I happened to be present at a demonstration with another half million people? Do I have to beg forgiveness because I didn't come into the barracks with hat in hand, begging permission to go?"

"You need to tell me why you decked two Carabinieri."

"It was self-defense."

"They found twenty steel ball bearings in your pockets."

"You can ask your colleague Terenzi all about that."

"What does Terenzi have to do with it?"

"He's the one who arrested me. And he's the one who beat me up and left me looking like this. And he's the one who planted the steel ball bearings in my pocket. Do I have to explain to you how the Carabinieri work? After all, you ought to know in some detail. Remember the cocaine at the Arcobaleno movie house."

"Very nice. Just go on talking bullshit. Terenzi isn't the one who arrested you."

"Oh, he's not? Then who did arrest me?"

"A junior lieutenant from the Calabria battalion."

"That's a lie."

"Of course. And you're the one who decides what's true and what's a lie, right? There's a written report and at least ten witnesses."

"They're all lying."

"As far as I'm concerned, you're the one who's lying."

"Then I don't have anything else to say to you."

"Good for you. Because right now all they have against you is a violation of Article 419 for rampaging and looting. A sentence of eight to fifteen years. No big deal for someone who's just twenty-eight. You've got your whole life ahead of you, don't you? But if instead of that you get a nice fat charge of subversive conspiracy, since you had the brilliant idea of making friends with an assortment of Greek anarchists, then we can add a substantial stack of years behind bars to that pile. Say, another five to ten. With continuation and repetition of a criminal act, the generic mitigating circumstances applicable under the law, and the fact that you have no priors, you'll walk out of here a middle-aged lady. Excuse me, I should have said a middle-aged ex convict."

"What the fuck are you talking about? What Greek anarchists?"

"That's right. Who made a phone call to Greece from your phone number, two days before the demonstration? Do you think it was me, maybe? Do you have another Grandma Sandra somewhere around Corfú and Thessaloniki? Or maybe you were planning to make reservations for a nice seaside vacation around Christmas?"

Alice dropped her head, shaking it. She formulated a contemptuous smile.

"You're just a poor miserable fucking Carabiniere. You'd send your mother to prison without a shred of evidence. You and your colleagues are all the same, and even worse than people realize. It strikes me that Samurai was right: certain bonds are never broken."

"Fuck you, Alice."

"No, fuck *you*. Have any of your investigative geniuses even bothered to call that Greek phone number, which isn't Greek at all, but Italian?"

"It's turned off. It goes straight to voicemail, in Greek, Signorina. That phone is in Greece. Even if the SIM card is Italian."

"It's Farideh's number, oh my God, you're such an idiot."

"Farideh? And just what would Farideh be doing in Greece?"

"I found out myself that she was there, by calling her. And she's not alone. She's with that bandit, Max."

"What were they doing there?"

"Farideh told me that they were there to bring a boat back to Italy."

"And I suppose she also told you the name of the boat."

"*Runa*, if I'm remembering it right."

"Where were they in Greece?"

"Some island. She didn't tell me the name. And here's another thing: I called her because I trusted you, Marco. I wanted to warn her about Max. I believed in you. And that other guy, your handsome friend, the prosecuting magistrate."

"The fact that they even allowed me to have this interview with you is thanks to him, Alice."

"Oh, really? Well thank him so much on my behalf. Could he be so kind as to put me under house arrest?" she shot back, vitriolically.

"Did Farideh tell you where they'd be landing this boat?"

"Fiumicino."

"And do you also know when they were setting sail?"

"You've busted my balls quite sufficiently with all your questions."

Malatesta raised his voice.

"When were they leaving?"

"How would I know?! They were just leaving."

Malatesta turned his back on her and called Silvana in from the corridor to take Alice back to her cell. As she left the interview room, she intentionally slammed into his shoulder.

"So what are you going to do now, eh? Are you going to try to destroy Farideh's life too, you damned animal?"

"What I do is no longer any concern of yours, Savelli."

He stopped in a dive bar on Piazza Conca d'Oro. It wasn't even noon yet, but as far as he was concerned, it might as well have been midnight. After reviewing the dusty shelves behind the bar, he pointed to a bottle of Johnnie Walker. It had been with that red-labeled bottle that as a boy he'd exorcised his first burning disappointment in love.

"A shot?"

"The whole bottle, thanks."

He got back into his car, grabbing the neck of the big bottle in his right hand, like the most pathetic stumblebum alcoholic, while with his left hand he extracted his cell phone from the inside jacket of his flea-bitten, tattered jacket. He'd turned it off on his way into Rebibbia and on his way out he'd decided not to switch it back on.

Let it remain mute.

He felt a fever raging inside him. His eyes were burning. If de Candia had questioned him, he wouldn't have known what to say to him. He was blinded, damn it. What had he learned from Alice? Nothing. Absolutely nothing. That informal conversation that he'd bet his last few cards on had been a complete washout. Maybe Alice was just continuing to lie to him because, like all liars, she adjusted her "truths" only when her bluffs and serial omissions were no longer defensible. Or maybe what Silvana's nose told her was right, the same thing that his head, in a remote corner of his hypothalamus, continued to tell him. That girl had been pushed into that situation. The Neri and their nihilist violence had nothing to do with her. And after all, that story about the phone call to Farideh made a certain amount of sense. Could it be that that too was simply a charade calculated and planned out in advance? How could she have known that someone was going to ask her point-blank about that phone call?

His temples were bursting. He opened the door of his apartment and decided not even to turn on the light. He slipped a CD by Eric Dolphy into the stereo.

"Tenderly."

A sax solo that could rip your heart out of your chest.

Perfect notes for the agony wracking his soul.

He turned up the volume, just a few decibels below the threshold that made the thin glass in the panes of the kitchen windows shake. He pulled a dozen tiny ice cubes out of the freezer, filled one of those colorful Coca-Cola glasses that you can earn with loyalty points at the supermarket with the blessed liquor. He threw first his jacket, then his shirt and white T-shirt, all of which smelled terrible, into a corner. He

rummaged through his dresser until he found and put on an
A. S. Roma T-shirt with the number 10 of Francesco Totti.
The captain.

Sitting, legs spread wide, on a kitchen chair, he started
drinking, hoping that that swill would help him shut his eyes.
And that *Tenderly* would take care of the rest.

Maybe he fell asleep. Or maybe he just remained in a
cataleptic trance for some unquantifiable period of time.

He was awakened by the harsh, insistent sound of the
buzzer from downstairs.

He dragged himself over to the intercom. His speech was
slurred and his tongue was scratching against his palate.

"Who is it?"

Alba's voice was fuzzed over by the electric contact that
he'd never bothered to have fixed.

"It's me, Alba."

"We can talk tomorrow."

"Wait, Colonel. Let me come up."

"You really had better not."

"It's important."

"As far as I'm concerned, nothing is important any more.
At least not until tomorrow morning."

"It's about Alice Savelli."

"I already know everything. More than everything. Lots
more."

"It's a video."

He pushed hard on the button that opened the door downstairs, and heard the lock make a loud *clack*.

Malatesta left the front door of his apartment ajar and
decided to wait for Alba in the kitchen. He was having trouble
staying on his feet.

"Can I come in?"

"Anyone home?"

There were two voices. A woman's, and that was fine. But

the man? Who the fuck had Bruni brought along with her? He whipped around.

Brandolin. The young Carabiniere Brandolin. And what the hell had happened to him?"

The young man walked into the kitchen, and as he approached Malatesta he apologized for not being able to salute him with convincing military smartness. His arm was in a sling, one eye was swollen and half-shut, and he had the posture of someone with a broom rammed up their ass.

"I hope you'll forgive me, Colonel, but I have a couple of broken ribs and I have to be careful how I move my torso . . . "

"What happened to you? Did you slip and fall in the shower?"

"Yesterday, at St. John Lateran. The riot squad kind of outdid themselves."

"Were you in plainclothes?"

"No, I was off duty."

"And what were you doing there? Don't tell me that you've become a Rebel Dragon, too. Because I can handle the world turned upside down, but this would just be too much. Brandolin in Occupy."

"I was filming. And that's why they beat the shit out of me, Commander. The riot squad wanted to take away my video-camera."

"And just what were you filming? Why were you there filming in the first place?"

Alba broke in.

"As I was telling you over the intercom, Colonel, the video. Brandolin filmed all the incidents in the street, and in particular the arrest of Alice Savelli on Via Cavour and events leading up to it."

Marco lurched up out of his chair. His head was suddenly clear. Shrouded in his Totti T-shirt, he poured a glass of whiskey for Brandolin. Who shook his head no and went on talking.

"I don't know if what I did was right, but the night before the demonstration, in the barracks, I heard Marshal Terenzi working out details on the phone with Anacleti. He was reassuring him. They were talking about Savelli. The marshal was saying: 'I'll take care of that whore,' please excuse me, 'myself tomorrow. I'm going to give her the full treatment. And then they'll throw away the key. And when I'm done, you immediately inform you know who that the woman who's been arrested is the girlfriend of that piece of shit,' please excuse me again, 'Malatesta.' I really do apologize, but those were the exact words he said."

"Please, go on."

"So yesterday I decided to go to the piazza and keep an eye on everything that Marshal Terenzi did. And I saw how they framed that poor girl. She never did a thing wrong. She was standing off to one side shouting 'Fascists' at the guys who were wrecking everything. The marshal and some of his colleagues massacred her in cold blood. Then I saw Terenzi bend down to pick up a bunch of steel ball bearings and slip them into a black jacket."

Marco swallowed.

"Are you certain about what you're saying? I mean, first of all, are you certain that the person Terenzi was talking to on the phone was Anacleti?"

"Absolutely certain. He called him by name. 'Rocco,' he kept saying."

"And were you really able to videotape everything you saw?"

Brandolin set the videocamera down on the formica kitchen table. And he started running the video.

Malatesta insisted on watching it three more times. It was all true. All absolutely true. It took him a little while before he could reorganize his thoughts.

"Listen, Brandolin . . . "

"I know, Colonel, I'm sorry. I should have come sooner, but they only released me from the hospital at 3 A.M. last night. And this morning, when I tried to get in touch with you at the office, the capain told me that no one knew how to get in touch with you."

Now Alba was smiling. And he was smiling, too. For the first time in two days. He slipped off the Totti T-shirt, and stood there bare-chested. Then he started rummaging through his drawers in search of a clean shirt. He turned to look at the captain, noticing that her cheeks were blushing slightly. A blush that he recognized.

"Alba, listen. The sailboat is called *Runa* . . . "

"Sailboat? What sailboat, Colonel?"

"Forget about that. Just tell me this: do we have anyone in the coast guard? I mean to say, anyone in the national operations room, here in Rome?"

"I have a friend. Let's say a young man I haven't known all that long, who might . . . "

"How close a friend is he?"

"We've gone out . . . we've been going out for a while now."

"That's not what I'm talking about, Alba. What I mean to say is: can you ask him a favor? And I mean a big favor. Because there's no more time for official requests and pieces of paper. I need the position of a sailboat called *Runa*, which sailed from some Greek island, name unknown, four or five days ago, on a course for the port of Fiumicino. We need to use every method known. GPS location, any possible reports from our harbor offices, maritime registries. I want to know where the boat is now. And when it's going to dock here, you got that?"

"Got it."

"How smart is this friend of yours?"

"He's smart and he's fast, Marco."

"Fast?"

"I'd say yes, he's fast. He's not the kind of guy who wastes a lot of time chatting. At least, he didn't with me."

Malatesta felt a stab of jealousy, mixed with a tingling that he recognized as excitement. Which made him feel alive. Finally alive, by God. He looked at his watch. It was three in the afternoon.

"Then call him up, Alba. Call him right now."

He turned his cell phone back on, and it started vibrating insanely with all the missed calls. There was a text message, too.

General Thierry de Roche. But he didn't have the nerve to look. He closed his eyes while he brought his thumb down on the envelope icon.

"I heard about Savelli. What's going on?"

Marco stared at Brandolin.

"Can I ask you one last favor, kid?"

"At your orders, Colonel, sir."

"This video, two copies. One for General de Roche and one for the prosecuting magistrate de Candia. Take it to both of them, in person."

# XLVIII

**M**arco pulled the wool watch cap down over his ears, plunged his hands into the deep pockets of the heavy navy peacoat, and stared out at the mouth of the channel, the ancient Port of Trajan that cut Fiumicino in two, with its wharves practically deserted in the early darkness of a November evening. Perhaps it was fate that everything should happen right in that place, he thought to himself. He turned and walked slowly toward a white Fiat Ducato van parked at the end of the northern wharf, just beyond the breakwaters lit up by the faint glow of the interior lighting of the Bastianelli restaurant. Behind those broad plate-glass windows overlooking the sea, epic pages had been written in the black history of Rome. Now Russian oligarchs and arab sheiks ate there. For that matter, as he traveled the world, it had become clear to him that this is what we Italians had become: dressmakers, tailors, and cooks.

He pressed to his lips the tiny microphone concealed in the lapel of his peacoat and checked one last time with Lieutenant Gaudino that the device was ready. Twenty or so men, both ROS personnel and local cops, along with two police dog teams formed a semicircle around the ground that gave access to the channel. Their running lights off, three "sharks"— Carabinieri police speedboats—sketched out a large semicircle a mile across in the waters around the old port.

"Northwest to Northeast, do you read me?"

"I read you loud and clear, Northwest."

"I'm proceeding on foot along the wharf toward the white Fiat Ducato parked at twelve o'clock."

"Received, Northwest. Active coverage. We only see one man in the vicinity of the vehicle."

Alba's boyfriend in the coast guard had done an excellent job. Smart boy, that kid. He'd worked hard and it showed. For that matter, Malatesta had no difficulty understanding his motivation, when he thought about Alba's ass. In just a couple of hours he'd managed to identity the Greek port from which the *Runa* had set sail, and after that, the rest had been relatively straightforward. The GPS signal had allowed him to reconstruct the course of the boat that had sailed from Folegandros five days earlier. Since it had entered Italian territorial waters, the *Runa* was being tracked by a scout plane. The fish was swimming obediently into the net. And at that point, they only had to draw the mouth shut tight. Another half hour, and the *Runa* would have finished her last voyage.

In spite of the hooded down coat pulled over his head, Malatesta instantly recognized the corpulent gentleman who was leaning against the hood of the Fiat Ducato, looking out at the mouth of the channel, his back turned to him. He called out his name when he was just stone's throw away.

"Tito Maggio, why what a nice surprise!"

The fat man whipped around and a surge of adrenaline lit up his cheeks, which were purple with the cold.

"Colonel! *Mamma mia*, what a coincidence. And what are you doing out here tonight?"

Malatesta pulled out his pack of Camels and offered him one.

"I'm just like the little kids, Tito. Every so often I like to come back to ride the amusement park rides. You remember this place, don't you?"

"Of course I do, Colonel. They even shot *Romanzo Criminale* here. I just love that flick, Colonel. I've seen it three times."

"Still, it strikes me you didn't understand much of it. All friends of Libano here, eh?"

"No, what are you saying?"

"Certainly, that's what I'm saying. So tell me, now, what are you doing here?"

"I'm here for work, Colonel."

"Oh, really?"

"I have to buy fish. I'm just waiting for the trawlers to come in. You know it, I only sell live seafood."

"Of course you do."

The cigarette that Tito was clutching between his fingers was shaking like a blade of straw in a windstorm.

"Are you cold, Tito?"

"No, why?"

"You're shivering."

"Oh, really?"

"You'd better be careful. You're not as young as you once were."

"You have a point, Colonel. But work is work."

"That's the truth, you think I don't know? In fact, you know what I'm going to do? I'm going to stay here and keep you company."

"Wait, you're going to wait here too, Colonel?

"Sure, I'll wait for the fishing boats to come in, here, with you."

"You shouldn't go to all that trouble. I can—"

"Who's going to any trouble? I just suddenly got an urge for seafood, maybe a few fresh tattlers. The way you make them. I think I'll buy a nice crate of them for myself. What do you call them at the restaurant? Totani dell'Imperatore, no? The emperor's tattlers. Delicious. What's the recipe. Let's see: chickpeas, bean, boiled potatoes and then, wait, it's coming to me . . . "

"Rosemary."

"That's right, rosemary."

"But maybe—"

"Maybe?"

"No, Colonel, I'm starting to think that this isn't the right night for it."

"For tattlers?"

"No, it's just that . . . It seems to me that . . . It's gotten late. I'm starting to think I might go home. In fact, yes, I'm going home now."

Maggio started to pull open the door of the Fiat Ducato. Malatesta grabbed his arm, clamping down so hard it hurt.

"Where are you going, Tito? You just don't have the patience it takes. These fishing boats will come in eventually, won't they? Didn't you say yourself they would be coming in? And after all, where do you need to be? It's Monday."

"Sure it is."

"And restaurants are closed on Mondays, Tito. Your place is closed on Mondays."

"Is that right? Is today really Monday?"

"Yes, it is."

"Now, you tell me—"

"Just think what an asshole you are, Tito. You come down here to buy fresh fish on the day your place is closed."

The fat man started whining. Then sobbing. Then he burst into the open, melodramatic wailing that Malatesta knew by heart.

"Colonel, I'm up to my neck in shit. I'm running on fumes."

"Honestly, that's pretty old news."

"The Three Little Pigs have stripped the flesh off me. What was I supposed to do? I had no alternative, the state I'm in, Colonel! They're going to take my restaurant away from me."

"That's just terrible. The news comes as quite a shock."

"They just told me to wait for this sailboat . . . "

"Ah, so you're waiting for a sailboat, not a trawler, not a

fishing boat. And who told you to come down here with the van? What are you supposed to load?"

"No, I meant to say something else."

"There, you see, I was right after all. You're really just a poor asshole, Tito."

"And now what's going to happen?"

"What's going to happen? You're going to rest up for a while."

"In prison?"

"What do you think? In fact, you know what let's do? Let's just smoke another nice cigarette and we'll wait for it together, this boat. After all, it seems to me, we're already here."

The silhouette of the *Runa*, by now, could be clearly made out in the roadstead just off the mouth of the channel. The sails were furled, the running and anchor lights were on, and the water at its bow was just slightly ruffled by its three knots of headway. On deck, you could just make out two silhouettes. One was standing, working one of the two stern rudders, the other was crouching just to the port of the boom, which was bound to the cockpit by a taut bundle of shrouds.

Malatesta smiled. Uttered under his breath, the words merged with the nebulized gust of water vapor that he exhaled, a gauge of the dampness and chill of the night that surrounded them.

"Dear Max and Farideh, welcome home."

"What did you say, Colonel?"

"Tito, don't tell me you don't even know the friends you've been waiting for."

"To tell the truth, Colonel . . . "

Malatesta raised his pea coat lapel to his mouth.

"Now, Northeast. Now."

The beams of two powerful spotlights lit up *Runa* as bright as broad daylight, with a cold, blinding glare. For a moment, the man at the helm seemed to be frozen in a flash of sudden frenzy, as he attempted a fruitless about-ship, revving the engines and turning the wheel. Three police speedboats appeared abaft of the two-masted sailboat, turning on their flashing blue lights. An amplified voice ordered the skipper to ride in slowly to the wharf.

In just seconds the wharf was alive with Carabinieri, while Malatesta asked Maggio to get busy hauling on the hawsers that had been tossed from the cockpit of the *Runa* toward a large rusty bollard.

"Come on, Maggio! You're not going to make us do all the work, are you? We seafarers like to help each other out."

Max had switched off the motors and, standing in the cockpit, clutched Farideh to him as if she were a castaway. Preceded by a couple of uniformed Carabinieri, and by Alba Bruni, all of them with their firearms leveled, Malatesta presented himself with his badge held high.

"We all know each other, unless I'm mistaken. And let's not forget that we ran into each recently at the restaurant of a mutual friend, didn't we, Tito?" he said, turning to Maggio, who was standing on the wharf, extending his pudgy wrists to be handcuffed.

Farideh's voice was throbbing with tears.

"Max, what does this mean? What's happening?"

But there came no answer. Malatesta tried to prompt her.

"I'd like to know what's happening myself, Farideh. Maybe, if Max doesn't know how to explain it all, you can help out."

The girl shook her head. In her eyes, the colonel could read the anguish of someone looking out over the abyss.

"Come on, Max, since when have you developed a taste for autumn cruises?"

"I have nothing to say."

"Well that's a bad idea on your part."

With a wave of his hand, Malatesta ordered the drug-sniffing dogs aboard the *Runa*.

"How long do you think it's going to take them to find the cargo?"

Farideh grabbed Max and shook him.

"What cargo? My love, what cargo is he talking about?"

"Come on, Max, didn't you hear her? Do it for love. Provided the two of you aren't staging an impressive masquerade, and I still wouldn't rule that out, why don't you tell Farideh what kind of cargo I'm talking about. Come on, speak up. I'm sure that you're a sincere kind of guy. And I'm sure that you also told her all about the night last summer when you brutalized her father in Romanina. Didn't you?"

Farideh fell with a scream, huddling at the bottom of the cockpit in a fetal position. Every muscle in her body stiffened, her legs kicking frantically as if she were having an epileptic fit. Max watched her for a long time as she was helped gently into the back seat of a patrol car, with a blanket wrapped around her shoulders. Then he turned to lock eyes with the colonel.

"You're a bastard, Malatesta."

"You think? I only see one bastard aboard this boat. And he's standing right in front of me. Let me ask you one last time, you fucking dickhead. Where is the shit?"

Belowdecks, the drug-sniffing dogs were going wild, and they'd started scratching at an exact place on the sailboat's internal bulkheads.

"Find it yourself."

The voice of one of the ROS men called out to Malatesta.

"We've got it, Colonel. Take a look."

The soldier pointed to the gauges of the potable water tank, indicating that the thousand-liter tank was full to the brim. Malatesta went back to the cockpit. Max had been handcuffed, his hands behind his back.

"You made that poor girl go without water. Three days

aboard this ocean liner and you never drank so much as a drop of water. You didn't even let her take a shower, what the fuck. Nice going, Max. You're done for."

They marched him off, pushing his head down with a hand to the back of his neck, while the ROS cameraman was capturing footage of the arrest that general headquarters would hand out in time for the midnight newscasts. The specialists were working with axes and oxyacetylene torches on the water tanks in the *Runa*. On the wharf, there was no one left in handcuffs but Maggio.

"Colonel, what should we do, take him away, too?"

"No, he'll wait with me. Won't you, Tito? An hour more or an hour less doesn't make any difference. After all, the Rome Hotel never closes. Let's see what you were supposed to pick up. You must be curious too, no?"

Marco stayed on the wharf in the old port until one in the morning. Until the last brick of cocaine had been extracted from the false bottoms built into the *Runa*'s water tanks and loaded into the Carabinieri's Land Rover Defenders. Until even the car taking away the handcuffed Maggio had vanished down the road to Rebibbia prison. That pain in the ass had never stopped whining and whimpering for a second.

"Colonel, oh my God, Colonel, don't ruin me. No one ever told me a thing. If you do this it'll kill me, Colonel . . . "

As he climbed into his car, Malatesta switched on the radio to cleanse his brain of that repulsive litany. The lead stories on the late-night radio news broadcast all had to with the sensational drug-smuggling bust. And once he'd heard enough, Malatesta turned down the volume and put his smartphone on speaker. There was just one last thing to get out of the way. Maybe the most important thing of all.

"Hello, Roberto? This is Marco. I hope I didn't wake you up. Do you have a minute to talk to me?"

Roberto Zanni was the head of DIGOS (General

Investigations and Special Operations Division). They'd known each other for years. They were the same age, and they'd grown up in two rival operations, so they'd eventually learned to respect each other. In time, they'd even become friends. Though that was not for general consumption. Most important of all, it didn't hurt their friendship that Roberto was as diseased a fan of A. S. Roma as Marco was.

"Ciao, Marco. As for being awake, I'm wide awake, and I certainly have the minute in question, but if you're calling me up to bust my balls about the championship, let's make it some other day, okay?"

"Don't worry, Roberto, I wanted to talk to you about—"

"About the *brilliant move* you just pulled at Fiumicino? What are you doing, calling to get congratulations?"

"Roberto, what do you say I hang up right now, call you back, and we can start over, would that work?"

"Sorry, Marco, I always assume you're a little less of an asshole than you actually are."

"Listen up, I have a video that would interest you. Something you guys are working on."

"What in particular?"

"The incidents at St. John Lateran."

"Well?"

"What would you say about a Carabinieri marshal who beats an innocent person black and blue, draws up a false arrest report, and defames that person with false evidence?"

"What is this, a practical joke?"

"Never been more serious in my life."

"How come this time you decided not to wash your dirty laundry at home?"

"It wasn't something 'we' decided. It was something 'I' decided."

"I understand. We never talked, and I found the film online."

"And you think I'm the asshole."

"Go fuck yourself, Marco."

"One more thing. Your marshal is the one in the camelhair overcoat. His name is Terenzi. Terenzi, Carmine: he's on staff at the Cinecittà station. And the girl is called Savelli. Savelli, Alice. And she's in Rebibbia prison."

"Do you want to come over and take my place? Maybe you could write the report yourself. You know I'm not a stickler about these things."

"I love you, my friend. Give me an hour and the flash drive with the video will be on your desk. That way tomorrow morning you can get to work bright and early."

# XLIX

Two hours of sleep that were more like a duel to the death between his adrenaline and his sense of guilt. A completely shitty condition for Marco Malatesta: to be unable to enjoy his well-deserved triumph, to feel no joy at the thought of Rapisarda's long face, to feel like pounding his head against the wall at the idea that he had ever doubted Alice. The thought of her, innocent, sitting in a jail cell and the thought of his own blindness wouldn't let him alone. His brilliant move had suddenly catapulted him into the dizzying, stellar heights of the untouchables. Rapisarda had been muzzled. Thierry was delighted. Michelangelo de Candia was excited and ironic, though he remained too much of a gentleman for a sarcastic and richly deserved "what did I tell you?" Untouchable, certainly. He had the clear sensation that he was going to remain untouchable for a long, long time, because that confiscation, more than just a commendable exploit, was a full-fledged turning point. A *result*, to use the terminology of the bureaucrats who infested the Carabineri corps, just as they did every other vital nerve center of the Italian state. But most important of all, the first crack in the wall of a system that had long seemed completely invulnerable.

And yet, unless he was misremembering his readings in the mystical period, a time when he moved along cheerfully from *Howl* to *Zen and the Art of Motorcycle Maintenance*, "untouchable" is an ambiguous term: it describes not only those who are too high above the masses to be besmirched by suspicion and slander, but also those who are too low to be considered worthy of the slightest interest.

Untouchable means to be alone. Deplorably alone.

And the idea that solitude amounts to the splendor of eagles, the clear-eyed, indecipherable gaze of the wise man, well, that was just more of the Fascist nonsense that he would gladly leave to Samurai and his comrades.

He'd disappointed her, no question. No, even worse. He'd betrayed her.

Had he lost her, too?

Alice would be released from jail that afternoon. Enough time to allow his friend Zanni to make his own brilliant move, and to let Setola swallow the bitter pill of her release.

He wanted to be there, and he was going to make sure that he was. Perhaps all was not lost. And, in any case, dodging out the side door at the moment of truth would be the act of a coward.

In the meantime, only a solid dose of hard work would be enough to stave off the demons of anxiety. And so, equipped with an authorization issued by de Candia, at exactly eight thirty that morning he was standing at the front gate of Rebibbia prison. Impeccably shaved, hair neatly combed, and with the mask of martial composure he usually wore when he had something to hide, he had Max summoned to the private interview room.

The young man must not have been having a much better time of it than he, at least to judge from his pallor, the dark circles under his eyes, his unkempt hair, and the first whiffs of the smell of confinement that wafted off his muscular body. Max had never been behind bars before. He'd get used to it quickly enough, the colonel decided. He was looking at a nice, long vacation. Unless he had other plans.

"*Buongiorno*, Nicce. How does a superman enjoy himself at the New Rome Hotel? Did you sleep well?"

The other man's icy glare made it clear that, for the moment, there was no point in talking about other plans. Max was putting on his hard-guy persona. But you could never say for sure. He'd seen plenty of hard guys cave in. Professional armed robbers. Heartless murderers. Among the younger Mafiosi and Camorristi, after all, there had been a period when it was all the rage to turn state's witness. To such an extent that the government had turned to stalling maneuvers, Marco thought back sarcastically, hastening to churn out a series of rules and regulations that made it increasingly difficult for bad guys to turn to conversion. So much the better, though. If Max really was a tough guy, it would become clear in the fullness of time. In the meantime, he could still put forward a proposition or two.

"Don't waste my time, kid. Tell me what I want to know, and I'll keep Farideh out of this mess."

"She has nothing to do with any of this," the "philosopher" replied in a rush.

"Convince me," Marco replied, "that's why I'm here."

"I give you my word."

"I wouldn't know what to do with it."

"So what is it you want, exactly?"

"We could start with your friend, for example. Samurai."

Max seemed to take a few minutes to think it over. Marco sensed an opening. He dug into his pocket for the pack of Camels and offered him one. Max grabbed the ciggie and rolled it around in his fingers. The colonel clicked his lighter into flame. Max crushed the cigarette into crumbs and blew the shreds of tobacco at him.

"You're a piece of shit, pig. You're much worse than I am."

"I'll take that as a compliment."

He put the pack down on the table, got to his feet with studied leisure, tossed his head to summon the marshal who stood outside the interview room, keeping an eye on them, and had him open the armor-plated door.

Max continued to sit there, motionless, doing nothing but eyeing him with contempt.

"Think it over. The offer is still good."

This was followed by hours of cigarettes, pointless walks, and rides on his motorcycle. Marco switched off his cell phone. But it was his brain that refused to be quieted.

Was he playing dirty with Farideh? Was there a real possibility that she really had known nothing about the boatload of cocaine? To hell with that, the girl had eyes in her head. There was a metric ton of shit aboard the *Runa*. But what if she was nothing more than a naïve young girl who'd fallen in love with the wrong man? Well, it was his duty to squeeze every last drop out of that story. He couldn't let himself get swept away by sentimentalism. Still, perhaps, he might be making a mistake with Farideh. Just like he'd been wrong about Alice.

And there it was: his thoughts turned back to her. His obsession. The hours ticked by with exasperating slowness. He turned back on his cell phone. Congratulatory text messages and emails, one from the Minister of the Interior in person, the Northern League representative with the red-framed eyeglasses who believed in a "free Padania" and who now governed all Italians in uniform. Five unanswered phone calls from general headquarters. Maybe that was Thierry. Or else, who could say, it might be Rapisarda. Two saccharine text messages from Alba. One teasing text from Zanni, dismissing him as a misguided S.S. Lazio fan. Any other time he'd have called him back, and they would have wound up exchanging opinions over a couple of cold beers. He turned off the phone again. On impulse, he stopped and bought two dozen red, red roses from a Sinhalese flower vendor on Via Tiburtina.

He still had a half hour to wait. He parked the Bonneville within sight of the gate of the Rebibbia Women's Wing and unwrapped his third pack of the day.

A young man with a ponytail pulled up in a fancy little city car. Diego from the Rebel Dragons. They shot each other hostile glares, then settled down to wait at a safe distance.

Twenty minutes. Out of the gate emerged a procession of official cars. He thought he glimpsed the silhouette of the assistant district attorney Setola. He turned away, and immediately regretted that instinctive move. What, was he ashamed? Of Alice? Diego was keeping an eye on him. He started to head in his direction, then changed his mind.

The little metal door, sloppily painted a military gray, swung open and a vivid beam of sunlight illuminated Alice.

Marco broke into a run in her direction, shouting her name and waving the roses.

The girl look around, saw him and, ignoring him, started walking toward Diego.

She was limping. And she had one hand pressed to her back. Terenzi, you bastard, I'm going to rip your balls clean off.

With a final burst of speed, he caught up to her while she was still just a few steps short of Diego.

"Alice! Stop, Alice, I just want to apologize!"

Diego stepped forward.

"What the fuck do you want now? Haven't you already caused enough trouble?"

Marco took a step back. Alice laid a hand on the young man's arm.

"Could you just give us a second, please?"

Diego shook his head, by no means convinced. Alice smiled at him. He nodded and walked a short distance away.

Now they stood facing each other. Marco, with all the stupidity that a man in love can muster, handed her the flowers, hinted at a bow, and flashed a smile that he meant to be taken as humble.

"Forgive me, Alice. I'm an idiot."

She scrutinized the roses, heaved a sigh, and delivered a straight-armed slap to his face. The flowers flew away. Diego rushed over. Alice waved him off, with her arm held high.

"Let me take care of this asshole."

Marco rubbed his face, the smile never fading a bit.

"I deserved that. Forgive me."

"You deserve far worse, you piece-of-shit Carabiniere."

"Now don't overdo it, Alice."

"You're the one who's overdone it. You need to release Farideh, and right away!"

"I can't do that. And even if I could, I wouldn't. A metric ton of shit, Alice, a metric ton. Shit that was going to the Anacleti clan, shit that was going to Samurai, shit that was going to the people you claim you're fighting. Farideh needs to convince me that she really knew nothing about that. Can you seriously not understand that?"

He was taking the wrong tone and he knew it, but there was nothing he could do about it. That was his life, for Christ's sake!

"You're the one who doesn't understand. She has nothing to do with any of this, and you know it. You never even gave her a chance. And you used me, you fucker! You treated me like a . . . what's the phrase you guys use? A stool pigeon?"

Alice had a point. He had used her. He could come up with only one argument in his favor: he'd also saved her from an unjust accusation. Still, he hadn't believed in her. So all things considered, silence was his best tactic.

"Give me a cigarette," she ordered him, without warning.

Marco hastened to comply. Alice took a long drag.

"Does it even occur to you what life's like in there? Do you think about that when you arrest someone? Do you have any idea of what a horrible place prison is, Marco?"

Hearing her say his name filled him with hope. He reached out to touch her, but she recoiled, indignantly, before his fingers could so much as graze her.

"Don't you touch me, don't you dare!"

"You're right, I'm sorry."

"And stop saying you're sorry!"

"Yes, I'm sorry!"

Alice flicked away what remained of the cigarette. For a moment her eyes shone with a gleam of irony, the prelude to a liberatory laugh, or at least so Marco fooled himself into believing.

Alice sighed. Her tone grew gentler. But it was a firm gentleness, unappealable.

"You're not a bad person, Marco. But you do have one problem. A big problem. You don't know which side you're on. Whether you're with the people doing the beating up or the ones getting beaten. You can't seem to make up your mind. So you're sort of on one side and sort of on the other. Which means you're not really on any side at all."

"Alice . . . "

"Don't follow me. And don't try to find me. Ciao, Marco."

She went back to Ponytail. He wrapped his arm around her waist, and she leaned on his shoulder.

Marco watched her get into the city car, backlit by the sun which seemed to be mocking him, and realized that once and for all he had lost something priceless.

Marco, the Untouchable.

L

Number Eight had gone off to meet his maker a good twenty days ago or so. And getting to Il Tatami wasn't that complicated. Denis took aside a couple of punk kids from Ponente, two ferocious stadium hounds who still had zits on their chins but had already graduated to switchblades in their pockets. He'd gotten word that they were going around boasting that they'd been ushered "into an important network" in Rome. Some sort of quasi-Nazi confraternity that met on a weekly basis at a Japanese fitness club well beyond the Giustiniana zone. Where some guy in his early fifties they called the Maestro trained them like young chimps, along with other dickheads, no smarter than them. For that matter, unlocking their silence concerning this precious secret cost him no more than a couple of grams of coke. A price perfectly in line with the price of disloyalty at age sixteen.

Bingo. They'd nailed Samurai.

"We absolutely have to go slaughter that pig."

Morgana was out of control. Hatred, in women, at times can be more obsessive and enduring than in men. And she was swollen with it. By now she reeked of vengeance. But now Denis was a boss. In fact, he was *the* boss. And if there was one lesson he'd learned from Number Eight, it was the pointlessness of ferocity without method.

Samurai alive—at least for a while—was an opportunity. And it certainly didn't take a genius to understand that. Uncle Nino was in prison, and he was going to rot in there. The

Anacleti clan were tangled up with the cops who were breathing down their necks, and they couldn't so much as take a step. The ROS had snapped up Max with a metric ton of cocaine, and he was going to gather cobwebs behind bars for a good long while. The market was demanding new masters and new rules. Meaning, then, that an understanding had to be found. And with a pistol pressed against his temple, even Samurai would become an obedient little lapdog. They just had to go step on his tail in his lair.

Morgana raised no objections.

Denis knew perfectly well that she wasn't happy with the arrangement. But he considered the silence with which she agreed to his terms a sign of submission that was worth every bit as much as a blood oath, if not more.

"When the day comes, I'll give him to you."

Flat on his back on the bench in Il Tatami's Finnish sauna, Samurai didn't see them coming. And when the door of the wooden cabin swung shut behind them, he felt suddenly defenseless. The way he'd felt only once before in his life. The time that Marco Malatesta could have put an end to the whole story. A woman's finger pressed against his sternum, exerting a menacing pressure. A man's firm grip held his arms motionless.

Morgana's voice was a whisper.

"Are we intruding?"

The question dropped into the void. But Samurai's silence left them both indifferent. The pressure against his sternum increased slightly, causing a stab of pain to his ribcage. Denis leaned down and spoke into his ear.

"A man with manners answers when someone asks him a question, Samurai."

They'd described him very well, this Denis. Ferocious, sarcastic, shameless in his way. No resemblance to the crude troglodyte he'd replaced. While Morgana was a discovery.

That stiff forefinger was an icepick, and she could have finished him off in an instant by shattering his sternum.

"I'm not in the mood for small talk. And I wasn't expecting visitors," Samurai said to Denis, doing his best to conceal the sense of physical and psychological constriction that was crushing him to the sauna bench.

"We thought we'd just make it a surprise."

"I hate surprises."

"Then maybe you should have been more careful."

"There's only one thing worse than impulsive visits. And that's threats you don't mean to back up."

"Who says that's what this is? How we back it up depends entirely on you."

"What is it you want?"

"Morgana is dying to cut you to bits. I wouldn't mind either. All things considered, we could wrap things up right here. And now."

"Then go ahead."

"You're accustomed to working with Number Eight. But I'm not Cesare. I'm here to offer you a deal."

"What do you want?"

"Everything."

"I need to take a shower."

"First, I need to hear a yes."

"You've got it."

Shalva was running a little late. And as he walked into Il Tatami's locker room, he noticed that Samurai was huddled in conversation with some guy over by the showers, someone he'd never seen before.

What struck him about that man was his excessive physical proximity to Samurai. Strange that Samurai should allow that. And so he was tempted to get a little closer, but then Samurai and the stranger shook hands firmly.

The stranger, clearly quite pleased, walked off into the locker room without saying goodbye. Shalva memorized his facial features.

He looked around for his terrycloth towel but couldn't find it, and so he decided for once that he'd do without it. At that time of the afternoon, the sauna was always deserted.

But not that afternoon.

Morgana was seated in the lotus position. Sweat pearled her flesh, giving a glow to her body. Shalva nodded hello to her, the way you do with women you don't know. She responded by freeing her forehead and her eyes from her bangs, which were drenched. A sign of focused attention. Shalva leveled his eyes into the young woman's gaze, and then proceeded to explore every square inch of her flesh. Firm, well proportioned breasts, a flat belly that widened into generous hips. Full, fleshy lips. It was a ravenous form of play, and he did nothing to conceal it. She seemed to lend her complicity. That man, with his entirely hairless body and his lily white flesh, had the beauty of a classical statue. Even though he was a man in his prime, he had perfectly defined muscles. His pectoral muscles opened out into broad shoulders, his abdominals highlighted a perfect washboard, and his back, sculpted by powerful dorsals, merged high and smooth into his buttocks. Like a black man's, without wrinkles or creases. Morgana felt an intense wave of excitement that she saw clearly mirrored in the man who stood looking at her. She stood up from the bench, slowly scrubbed the palm of her hand across her breasts and belly, then left the sauna, shutting in the unknown man behind her.

Samurai joined Luca in the driveway that led up to the Japanese house. He had just left those rabid dogs Denis and Morgana with a commitment that, as far as he was concerned, had as much value as a gob of spit in a pond. Those two were demanding a place in the sun, but like all their peers in that gutless generation, they lacked the balls to take it to the limit. Their inclination to seek a compromise with the older players like him simply condemned them to utter irrelevance. They said that they wanted to take what was theirs by right. But they didn't want it badly enough to tear it out of the hands of those who had stolen it from them and had no intention of giving it back. He'd been twenty himself, just like them. But he'd sworn defiance to the world at large. He had killed. He hadn't asked permission. He hadn't loaded his pistol with blanks. Forcing the old generation to make way for the new was no longer just an option. It was necessary for the survival of the species. The wonder and fury of a new virginity was what they needed. The surging whiff of testosterone that filled the room he was walking into was what they needed.

"The boys are here," said Luca, pointing to a small crowd of skinheads. "There's a new one today."

Samurai looked where Luca was pointing and identified Laurenti, the engineer's son. He exchanged a nod of the head with him.

"Do you know him, Samurai?"

"His name is Sebastiano. He's a right guy. I have plans for him. Am I wrong, or are there more kids than there were last time?"

"You're not wrong."

"So finally a few of them are willing to listen."

"They're all here for you."

"We need to be careful and to avoid making mistakes."

"Why would we?"

"Because it's happened before. And this is no longer a time for mediocrity. There is no redemption in the sewer we're swimming in, Luca. We need to work to create a new era. The one we live in reeks of carrion. We must reeducate ourselves for pure ego. The tension toward the act. I'm sick and tired of the superfluous. And the trite bric-a-brac that it engenders. This anti-Semitic racism out of some operetta, this glamorous Fascist fetishism and these cinematic street thugs turn my stomach. The difference between an Aryan and a kike is a matter of the spirit. Not the facial features. We must work within the conflict that exists between the yearning for redemption and the lure of dull matter. The recession is offering us immense spaces in which to maneuver. Social hatred will soon wash over the Europe of bankers. And we need to be ready when that happens. As far as the near future is concerned, re-read your Evola."

"I've already started to. And in any case, I don't know if you've had a chance to take a look at that draft document."

"*Dawn*. Yes, the title seems pretty good to me."

Shalva interrupted them. He'd stayed in the shower longer than usual to extinguish, or perhaps prolong, the desire that had exploded in the sauna. He gave Samurai a hug, and Samurai told Luca to give them a minute to talk alone. The confiscation of the load of cocaine in Fiumicino was not a matter for public discussion.

"Was it an accident, or did someone tip them off, Samurai?"

"I'd call it an accident, Shalva."

"Should I be worried about that Max?"

"Don't worry. I know him. He won't say a thing. He's got head and heart. But also guts."

"What about the Iranian girl who was with him? Farideh, I think her name was. Max introduced her to me on Folegandros. I have to admit, a very nice choice, but still . . . "

"The girl wasn't expected."

"Exactly. You say it was an accident, but I'm wondering whether the girl wasn't something other than what she seems."

"If I know Max, she wasn't in on a thing, and still isn't."

"You're right, my friend. Still, Max ought to have told you."

Samurai smiled.

"That's true. But I trust him. And in any case, the beautiful Persian girl is going to keep her mouth shut too. She has no alternative. If she talks, she gets sent up for international narcotics trafficking. If she plays dumb, she might get off entirely and be set free even before the trial. We can keep an eye on her, but she doesn't strike me as a problem."

"By the way, who were those two in the locker room?"

"Two annoying little flies from Ostia. His name is Denis. She's Morgana. Just think. Just think, the cross and the Celtic sorceress."

"Problems?"

"Delusions, I'd say. Foolish delusions. Which we'll take care of once and for all when we've finally implemented the Great Project and we can clear the air of the last few insects. And maybe I'll ask you to crush those two."

"With pleasure, my friend."

# LI

In the end, Pericle Malgradi made it through by the skin of his teeth.

The knot that he had to untangle, the boulder that threatened to thwart the Great Project, was the sudden and unexpected splintering of his group. The city council members he had been counting on to pass the bill had risen in open revolt. The underboss, the politico that had started all the trouble, was a greedy old member of the Fascist nomenklatura of years gone by who had earned himself the nickname, both for his gelatinous appearance and for his total lack of scruples, of Jabba, as in Jabba the Hutt, the criminal batrachian from *Star Wars*. The old Fascist, who controlled a faction within the council, had let the dynamic of what he saw as "political momentum" get to him. Once he saw the granite mass of the center-right majority coalition begin to crumble, the race to "reposition" had begun. And Jabba had moved with lightning speed. He'd established a clear distance from the existing regime in its death throes. And in doing so, he had brought with him what had once been the Malgradi gang. Which meant that now the Great Project was starting to look like excess weight, and would have to be heaved overboard.

Malgradi confronted Jabba in no uncertain terms.

"What the hell, don't you know who's involved in this deal?"

"The fact is that the Great Project is going to split public opinion. Already all this mess with the blog has provoked an array of reactions. There's going to be an endless stream of controversy. We're going to be overwhelmed by a tidal wave of appeals—"

"But it's all strictly legal, you know that, don't you?"

"Of course, no doubt. But times have changed. The future is uncertain. We're too weak to pull it off alone. I'm not saying that nothing's going to come of it, just not right now, Pericle, not right now."

Oh, sure, all strictly legal! Oh, sure, not right now! Go explain all that to Samurai, to Ciro Viglione, to the Calabrians . . . and to the Monsignor.

"So, help me understand, if there was a broad consensus, then it might be feasible in any case."

"Of course, but where are you going to find it these days, this broad consensus?"

"Leave that to me, you just need to keep cool and promise me that when the time comes, you won't pull out at the last minute. You and all the others."

All the others who had been eating from his feed bag for years, God damn them to hell, the ones who were bound to take to their heels at the first sign of trouble.

Jabba promised. Jabba was a refined politician. A promise, as we know, is the future, but in politics the future and the past don't even exist. In politics the only thing that exists is the present.

Jabba underestimated Malgradi. When it came to matters of political promises, the Honorable considered himself to be unbeatable. Now he was looking for consensus, this jumped-up Fascist who until just a short while ago was serving as a pall-bearer for his bomb-throwing comrades. Consensus. I'll create consensus for you, you little asshole.

And in the end, you'll no longer be able to tell me no.

Malgradi forced himself to show some pride. From one day to the next, he gave up cocaine and sluts, because there are times when you need to be clear-minded above all, and he launched his campaign of acquisitions.

Because when friendly fire is about to do you in, that's the time to extend a hand of friendship to the enemy.

He identified three minority-party councilmen, two old hacks nearing the end of their careers, without any hopes of reelection, and a lusty young political climber who, in his furious, elbowing progress had so alienated his party that it had just kicked him sideways into city government. Another politico with no future, excellent fertile soil in which to sow seeds.

He started working them.

He explained what the Great Project was.

"We've heard all about it," they replied, at first, "and we don't like the rivers of cement."

"Then I'll help you learn to like them."

A couple of dinners at La Paranza and free servicing from several of the most noteworthy members of his fleet of whores softened up their initial attempts at resistance. A few crisp high-denomination banknotes unleashed a sudden interest in the "social benefits" of the operation. The commitment to enlightened and profitable business practices put down in black and white in front of a notary won them over to the cause.

On progressive blogs and local magazines think pieces began to sprout that attacked Jabba. Already a target of Communist propaganda for the deeds of his misguided youth, the old Fascist became the subject of increasingly violent attacks for his opposition to that Project which, even though it had been flagged by certain agent provocateurs as Evil Incarnate, would actually produce thousands of good jobs. Obviously, in the most rigorous respect for the environment and the letter of the law.

The campaign spread over local radio stations and websites,

emerging eventually in the news pages of *Il Messaggero*, and from there ricocheted onto the leading national networks. And when an article appeared on the front page of the most respected publication of the progressive bourgeoisie under the byline of a respected economist, who indicated in no uncertain terms that social housing was "the intelligent Keynesian response to the economic crisis," Jabba finally lost it and openly confronted Malgradi, employing every bit of his traditional Fascist plain talking.

"What the hell kind of ideas have you got into your head, you fucking asshole?"

"You wanted consensus? Now you have it!"

"What are you talking about? You're fucking crazy. But believe me, I'm crazier than you."

"No, at the very least you're handicapped. I figure that with all the holy water you sprinkle over yourself to show off to your little friends, the priests, you've wound up waterlogging your brain."

"Malgradi, you're done for."

"Listen up and listen good, asshole. Tomorrow three opposition councilmen are going to present an item to be tabled, a request to immediately schedule debate and subsequent vote on the Great Project. That was what you wanted, isn't it? Bipartisan consensus. What are you going to do? Or rather, what are you and your people going to do? Are you in, or do I have to destroy your reputations once and for all?"

Jabba turned pale. Malgradi paused for a moment to savor his rival's debacle, then he laid out the scenario.

"At least half of the councilmembers on the left are going to fall into line immediately. The others will follow soon enough. There will be negotiations. We'll slip in a few variants, a couple of benches, half a dozen plane trees, a nursery school for the kids, the kind of thing that these dickheads love so much. You'll deliver a nice hot speech about the importance of producing jobs at a time of economic crisis, and the trade unions will be good as gold—"

"But there's still going to be a few people against it," Jabba ventured, just to avoid surrendering at the first assault.

"Of course there will. There's always someone who'll bust your balls. But it'll just be the usual losers. We'll send the riot police around, a few swings of the billy club, and *raus*, we'll send them all home. Have I made myself clear, comrade?"

Jabba capitulated. One after the other, the renegades, in a somber, hopeful procession, came and paid homage to Malgradi, who bestowed upon them, with magnanimous equanimity, handshakes, sage advice, and kicks in the ass.

The matter was brought up for debate. And the vote was set for November 14.

Malgradi celebrated the end of Ramadan at La Chiocciola with three girlfriends. He had required them to wear wigs, each a different color: red, white, and green. So that it would be perfectly clear that this was the holiday commemorating an Italy that never surrenders, a healthy nation that refuses to cry over its sorrows, an Italy that couldn't care less about the spread. In a burst of generosity, he handed a hundred euros to the Albanian porter. But when that loser came out with his tired old litany, asking when he'd get his citizenship, Malgradi told him to go to hell.

Kerion Kemani took it without blinking and decided, at that exact instant, that Malgradi was going to pay for that.

When counselor Parisi gave him the news, Samurai, usually so calm and composed, couldn't conceal a surge of genuine surprise. He had clearly underestimated the Honorable Malgradi. The gears were starting to mesh again, things were starting to move. Still, he couldn't seem to shake that vague sense of impending doom that had been pestering him for days. Could he really have been so spectacularly off-base? No.

Not a chance. Things were still bound to end badly. Samurai had too much confidence in his nature as a superman not to prepare a backup plan.

And so he gave Parisi precise instructions that left the lawyer flabbergasted. Samurai had become an bona fide pessimist.

"But why should it all go so horribly wrong, excuse me?"

"I don't recall having hired you to ask questions."

"As you wish. Ah, I'd almost forgotten. Tonight there's going to be a little party at a restaurant that belongs to a friend of Temistocle's. We'll all be there, the Anacleti clan, the Honorable, Ciro, Perri. And of course, a few girls."

"You know that I detest group sex."

"But you're supposed to be the guest of honor, Samurai, after all it's all your doing that—"

"Time to stop wagging your tongue, Counselor."

Samurai shuttered his apartment and went to stay with Shalva, in Trevignano.

Marco Malatesta and Michelangelo de Candia learned of the upcoming city council vote with a blend of rage and help-lessness. They were both too pragmatic to labor under any illusions. The Great Project was going to be approved, and they had no way of stopping it. The investigation had run aground with the confiscation of *Runa*. Max, Farideh, Tito Maggio, who had all invoked St. Denial during the questioning, avail-ing themselves of their right to remain silent, were the ideal guilty parties in a major cocaine-trafficking ring.

But the matter went no further.

Public opinion had been been skillfully manipulated, or perhaps it was distracted by other matters. There was no evi-dence linking the Great Project with the murders.

If de Candia dared to open criminal proceedings, even if it were under a John Doe heading, establishing grounds for indictments, he would be roundly reviled as an enemy of the people. A wingnut. What possible reason could the district attorney's office have to go after people who were working to provide bread and jobs to a city that had been so badly hit by the recession? It was hardly a criminal offense to build housing and port facilities. Who would believe him if he tried to explain that what this was going to lead to would be corruption, not expansion, slavery, not good jobs? In fact, he'd look like lunatic raving on a street corner. Now they even knew the name of the operation's political sponsor: Malgradi, whom Alice had described as an inveterate whoremonger. But the Italians were notoriously inclined to go easy on everyone involved in the sex trade. Unless he could link the project to the corpses of Ostia and Cinecittà, the prosecution was a losing bet.

A few dead bodies remained, but they could well have been results of hoodlums murdering each other, a gang war that had started and ended for no good reason and deals involving any number of incorrigible pieces of shit.

In an office where the air was thick with cigarette smoke, at last the horrible word echoed like the clap of doom: failure. Michelangelo tried to lighten the atmosphere with one of those pat phrases that diehards love to say to themselves:

"Hope springs eternal. We still have a whole week until the the vote. Let's try to make good use of what little time remains to us."

Marco played along. He promised, he swore that he'd redouble his efforts. He'd go back to prison to see Max, once again offering to negotiate Farideh's release. He'd send his men out to follow all the suspects. He'd dip into special funds to pay old informants and recruit new ones, he'd . . .

Michelangelo, without warning, asked him about Alice.

Marco's eyes frosted over.

Michelangelo started fooling around with a CD by his beloved Petrucciani.

"I have a confession, Colonel. I like that girl. I liked her the minute I met her. And I'll admit that I thought about trying to start something up with her. I wouldn't be able to put my conscience to rest if I didn't tell you. I even thought about . . . getting in touch with her, in other words, giving her a call, inviting her to come listen to my music."

Michelangelo.

"I know, it's despicable. But each of us has our weaknesses. I apologize. In any case, I didn't do it."

Marco went back to Ponte Salario. De Candia had reopened the wound. A sense of defeat had taken hold of him. Alice, Alice, Alice, Alice. She had dissolved in the slow drizzle of the chilly Rome November.

As he was leafing through the reports for the umpteenth time, searching for the damned link that continued to escape him, Marco decided that November 14 was not merely the deadline for the Great Project, it was also his own deadline.

He could give up the investigation and keep Alice.

He could lose Alice and wipe the entire gang of shits off the face of the earth.

It wasn't the same thing, and it amounted to human sacrifice. He'd grown resigned to it, in the fullness of time.

But he could only tolerate one loss at a time, not all of them together.

Losing everything, and all at one fell swoop, was just intolerable.

It meant losing Rome.

All right. He'd leave Rome.

Rome doesn't change. Rome can't be redeemed. Remo Remotti had been right. So Rome could go fuck itself.

Alba walked in without knocking. It had become a habit. The more remote he became, the harder she worked to break through the blockade, without results.

Alba watched him as he sank ever lower and she couldn't resign herself to it.

If she could only lay her hands on that damned dark-haired *zecca*. How could she have managed to suck his soul out of him like that?

But she had no intention of giving up on him.

"I have Spadino's cell phone," she said, dumping a boxful of phone records onto his desk.

"That's not possible," he retorted, wearily. "We don't even know what SIM card he was using and the phone itself was destroyed in the fire.

"I tracked back to it by looking at the calls to and from Max's phone. It's all in there," she shot back in a defiant tone, pointing at the documents.

Marco sighed. Spreadsheets weren't his strong suit. The phone providers gave out information with an eyedropper, each time it was as if someone had asked if they could screw their sisters. The data arrived broken out and scrambled. It was up to them to find their way through the maze of SIM cards, IMEI codes, fictitious account holders, incoming and outgoing calls, cell towers engaged. Alba had a genuine talent for that kind of painstaking work.

"It'll be faster if you just tell me, Alba."

The captain sat down.

"Spadino used a SIM card taken out in the name of a non-existent customer. A Romanian."

"How can you be so sure?"

"Can you imagine a nonexistent Romanian repeatedly calling Spadino's mother and sister? I can't."

"Go on."

"There are phone calls to Max and other members of the crew, Paja and Fieno, for example. Nothing connected with Number Eight, but that's not the point. Let's go to the night of June 12. There are incoming and outgoing calls to the phone number of a prostitute, who plied her trade under the name of Lara. I checked it out. This Lara's cell phone turns out to be disconnected, out of service. And you know when it went dead? Two days after the death of Spadino on June 20. Anyway, I went ahead and chased down this Lara's list of contacts. Lots of incoming and outgoing calls on the cell phone number of another prostitute, a certain Vicky Krulaitis. Excellent. This Vicky was found after the August holidays in the Marcigliana nature reserve. Eaten by dogs. From what was left of her, we were able to determine that she'd been dead for a couple of months. Her last phone contacts: the night of June 12. And that's not all. Lara had a website, which had been taken down. www.larasecrets.com. It was two of them, working as a team, her and a girlfriend . . . "

"Vicky."

"Exactly. On June 12, this Vicky stopped communicating. Two months later, she was dead. Her best friend vanished two days after Spadino's murder. She shut down her site, got rid of her cell phone. She's involved. And Spadino's involved, too. For two reasons. First: he and Lara reached out to each other on the twelfth. Second: a few days later, Spadino was dead, too."

"Right. The two events seem to be connected. Spadino's death triggers the war. But do gang wars break out over a dead whore? And how did she die anyway?"

"That's something we'll find out," Alba smiled, adding, after a well-timed pause: "And now let's see if we can't dream a little. It's June 14. Vicky has been missing for two days and it's reasonable to think that she's already dead. It's nine in the morning. Spadino calls the switchboard at the chamber of deputies. Now, Colonel, unless your dark-haired *zecca* has boiled what's left of your brain away, then I say to you: whores, Spadino, that is, a lackey of the Anacletis, and the chamber of deputies . . . who comes to mind? The first one to guess wins, eh, those are the rules . . . Now, a-one, and a-two, and . . . "

"Malgradi!" they both shouted, in unison.

Alba fell back against her seat back, eyes glowing with pride.

From that point on, it was a race against the clock. Alba added a detail to her presentation that would eventually prove fundamental. All of the phone calls made on the night of June 12 went through the same cell tower in the historical center of town. Lara, Vicky, and Spadino, then, had to have spent that night within a perimeter that ranged, roughly speaking, from Piazza Venezia to Ponte Sant'Angelo. Marco remembered another detail: Alice had told him that Malgradi had a habit of taking his escorts to the hotel La Chiocciola.

"And how would you happen to know that?" Alba asked.

"Forget about it," he replied, feeling a stab of pain in his heart as he remembered that asshole with the ponytail. And after all, who even knows if the two of them had ever really been in the Anna Magnani suite at the hotel.

They decided that that was as good a place to start as any. They went there around midnight, disguised as a couple up to no good. The night porter, an Albanian with a lean and hungry look about him, along with a strong smell of broccoli, shut the issue of the *Corriere dello Sport* that he was reading and didn't even give them a chance to speak.

"Are you police or Carabinieri?"

Marco and Alba exchanged a guilty glance like a couple of kids caught with their hands in the cookie jar.

"Carabinieri," said Marco.

"What rank?"

Alba was on the verge of taking offense. Marco placated her with a kick.

"High ranking. You can trust us."

"I'm listening."

Alba showed him the pictures that the RIS cyber technicians had extracted in record time from the reconstruction of the altered website. They were the two women who called themselves Lara and Vicky.

The Albanian looked, looked again, and smiled.

"I really love Italy," he sighed, "but Italy doesn't love me. My sister and I have been waiting five years to get citizenship."

Alba erupted in anger. Just who the hell did this Albanian think he was? This wasn't a bargaining session, this was an official inquiry, part of a police investigation. Did he know something? Then he'd better tell them about it, with no more beating about the bush. Or they would subject him to the most unpleasant of experiences. Did he understand that they could expel him from the country whenever they chose, with a sharp kick in the ass? What the fuck, he was dealing with the Italian state now.

The Albanian took the upbraiding she dealt out without losing his composure, then shook his head.

"I've never seen either of these women, I'm sorry."

Marco shot Alba a furious glare and gestured for her to step aside. He pulled out his police ID and laid it down in front of the night porter.

"Here's what we'll do. Right now, you go make a photocopy of my ID. Then I'll write on it that I personally promise to get you and your sister Italian citizenship, as quickly as possible. I take back the sheet of paper. If your information proves useful to me, I'll give it back to you."

"Marco!" Alba cried.

"Otherwise," Malatesta concluded, still speaking to the man, "this very night I'll take you to Regina Coeli prison on charges of pimping and profiting from prostitution, and your sister will wind up in the refugee center of Tor Cervara, with all the other illegals scheduled to be expelled from the country in the next forty-eight hours."

Without another word, the Albanian took the colonel's

official ID card, asked for fifty cents—"Xeroxes cost money here, like everything else"—and vanished into the back office.

"You're out of your mind!" Alba hissed.

Marco kissed her on the cheek.

She shoved him away from her, infuriated.

"I'm no one's third wheel."

The Albanian returned, gave Marco back his original and a Xerox of his document, and asked to see the photos again.

"This is Lara, but she's out of the business by now. Says she's living with a film producer. This other girl, poor thing, said her name was Vicky. They worked as a pair. Two professionals, no offense, Signora. She died here. The night of June 12."

"And how do you know that?"

"I saw her. If you ask me, she overdid it with the drugs. What is it you say here in Italy? Overdose. They were girlfriends with that politician, the one you see on television. Malgradi, I think his name is. That evening they were together in the Anna Magnani suite."

"Let's go upstairs," said Marco.

The porter coughed.

"Sorry. Right now, there are guests. But there's something else to see."

Kerion Kemani took them to his sister's apartment and handed them the pillowcase and the cell phone with the photos that he had taken that night, when Spadino and Lara had taken away Vicky's corpse.

Marco and Alba went to Michelangelo de Candia's apartment in the middle of the night. They asked for immediate warrants for the arrest of the woman and Malgradi.

The prosecuting magistrate gave a frosty reply.

"First find her, then we can talk about it. As for Malgradi, not a chance."

"But he was the john. The Lithuanian prostitute died in his hands."

"Prove it. He could always say that they were having a good time together when he was called away for an urgent matter, and that when he left the girl was still alive.

"We have the pillowcase! Her DNA must be on it."

"What's the chain of custody on the pillowcase? It was kept with the dirty laundry of an Albanian who's probably an accomplice to the Honorable's high jinks. And to whom you recklessly made promises of assistance in securing Italian citizenship. With that kind of a situation, any two-bit lawyer could make mincemeat of us. I'm not saying that you didn't do a good job, I'm just saying it's not enough. You need to find this Lara. She's the key to the puzzle."

"Still," Alba suggested, "we could get the word out. Ruin Malgradi's reputation."

Michelangelo burst out laughing.

"Then this is a bad habit with you all. Do they teach you this stuff at the police academy?"

Marco locked arms with Alba, who didn't understand, and got the hell out before a diplomatic incident could degenerate into a declaration of war.

He had to find Lara, then. Her legal name was Sabrina Proietti, and she had a long record of hooking it. The day of the vote was approaching, after which all this effort would become pointless.

They alerted their informants, they roped in the sex-crimes prevention squad, they even considered broadcasting an appeal to the public at large, a solution that they quickly discarded because, once their interest became part of the public record, the first one to hear about it would certainly be Malgradi. And Malgradi meant Samurai, Anacleti, and all the giddy rest of them. For poor Sabrina, better known by her

stage name Lara, that leak of information would be tanta-
mount to a death sentence.

Once again it was Alba who solved the situation. It happened the morning of November 11, three days before the vote
to approve the proposal.

For years, Alba had been a passionate reader of gossip magazines. She enjoyed reading about the love affairs of screen
kings and starlets, and especially loved hearing the losers from
reality TV pompously announce their various schemes. Seeing
the extent of other people's vanity in this mirror, in a certain
sense, made her feel like she was a better person. It was in the
pages of the Italian gossip rag *Chi*, the bible of the sector, that
she saw Sabrina's face beaming out at her defiantly. Her arms
were wrapped around a well-dressed man in his early fifties
with salt-and-pepper hair, a well-known producer, as she
announced that soon the story of her life was going to be made
into a film, a major international production with a stellar cast:
Charlize Theron, Uma Thurman, Michael Fassbender, and
Viggo Mortensen. That's right, Italy was landing in Hollywood
via the adventures of our own Roman-born Pretty Woman.

It was with immense pleasure that she brought the maga-
zine to Marco.

"While you titillate yourself with radio programs for Zulus,
there are others who drink directly from the spring of genuine
popular culture, my dear colonel."

The final act played out in Eugenio Brown's penthouse
apartment. It was noon, it was raining, and the most famous
couple of the moment were still in bed when Marco and Alba
rang the doorbell.

Eugenio Brown put on an understated cashmere sweater
with subtle shades of green. Sabrina, in a pink dress, was lovely
even without makeup, and she didn't bat an eye when the
colonel called her Lara.

"My girlfriend's story is in all the newspapers," Eugenio broke in, coming to her defense, "and we have nothing to hide."

"No, she certainly doesn't," Marco said softly, finding himself suddenly well-disposed toward the producer, "but there might be certain details best discussed with the lady. In private."

"No," Eugenio objected. "Sabrina and I have no secrets from each other."

Marco agreed. Poor fool. He'd recognized the stigmata of a man in love. What he was about to do pained him, but there was no other solution. He turned and spoke theatrically to Sabrina.

"Spadino is dead, Lara. They murdered him like a dog. And you're in danger too. The same way we found you, those guys are going to find you too. And they're not just going to question you. So, you really have no choice: You have to trust us."

The ladylike mask crumbled. Sabrina stared at Eugenio Brown as if she wished she could incinerate him on the spot. She snapped open two vials of an echinacea-and-ginseng tonic that she purchased by the twelve-pack at the local organic herbalist, and poured them into a glass of water, because that brand of tonic formed part of the foundations of a genuine lady. She chugged it down at a single gulp.

"I told you that this whole idea of the publicity launch was a stupid idea! But you never want to listen to reason. The true story of Sabrina Proietti, the whore. You've ruined me for good, asshole!"

Eugenio gave her a stunned glance.

"But, my love, I . . . "

Sabrina ignored him. She crossed her legs, let the crestfallen producer hand her a cigarette. Then, clamping it between her lips, she snapped off the filter, which she spat out into the ashtray in the center of the table. She turned to the colonel, truly a handsome piece of beefcake, no doubt about it, with a lethal smile.

"And what do I get out of this whole thing?"

"It depends on how much you have to lose," Marco specified.

"Let's just say that when the girl died, I was there too. And that maybe I helped out in procuring pious burial for her mortal remains . . . "

"Sabrina . . . " Eugenio Brown moaned in despair.

"Shut up, you. You opened Pandora's box, and now it's too late to put the cork back in. Well, Colonel?"

"Well . . . let's just say that certain information not essential to our reconstruction of events wouldn't necessarily need to become part of the public record."

"That's good by me," Sabrina concluded. "You want to know about that swine Malgradi, no? Then let me tell you exactly how things went."

# LII

The Subaru Outback pushed slowly down Via del Corso, its flashing blue dome lights lighting up the Saturday afternoon crowds, which were much larger than usual. The lights slapped patches of blue onto faces overwhelmed by incredulity and happiness. On foot, riding mopeds, on bikes, from Piazza Venezia to Piazza del Popolo, men, women, and families were all flowing in a giddy disorder toward Piazza Montecitorio. Obstructing sidewalks and special preferential lanes.

Marco shot a glance at the thermometer on the dashboard—sixty degrees—and slapped his hand down on the driver's leg.

"Andrea, what day is it today?"

"Saturday, Colonel."

"I know that. What about the date. What's today's date?"

"November 12. Do you want to know the name of the saint today, too, Commander?"

"What?"

"This car has everything, right here on the GPS. Here it is. Today is St. Christian's Day."

"Then people say that there's no such thing as divine providence."

"I don't get it."

"Never mind, never mind."

He tuned in to the frequency of the operations center.

"All right then, to all cars and personnel . . . Situation on

Piazza del Quirinale rapidly evolving. At the moment, we report two to three thousand persons, number climbing. Large crowds gathering on Piazza Colonna, traffic blocked solid on Via del Corso. We recommend to all personnel currently on duty in the area to not REPEAT NOT prevent free access and departure between Quirinale, Montecitorio, Dataria, Via IV Novembre, and Piazza Venezia. Report in with any critical situations that may develop."

Now the Subaru was stuck in traffic in the middle of Via del Corso. Malatesta reached out and grabbed the driver's arm.

"Forget about the siren. It's not the time or the place."

"Of course not, now that that guy's leaving, it seems like just yesterday that he first took power. What was it he said? 'Italy is the country that I love.' But it wasn't yesterday, it's been twenty years, eh, Colonel?"

"It seems more like forty."

"And now who's going to be in charge, Colonel?"

"A technocrat."

"Anyway, it doesn't seem to me as if anything's going to change for us. We're still just going to have to chase after thieves. Right-wing, left-wing, eh, Colonel? All the different ones we've seen."

"Andrea, it's a good thing you vote every five years."

"Colonel, between you and me . . . I stopped voting a good long time ago."

"That's just as well."

Malatesta went back to staring through the side window at the crowd surrounding the car. Some middle-aged guy was carrying a boombox on his shoulder—*fuck, where did he find that piece of antique junk?*—which was emitting the amplified melody of Handel's "Hallelujah Chorus."

Maybe tonight wasn't the right time to light the fuse, he thought. Or maybe it was. St. Christian's Day, the night that marks the end of his twenty-year rule. Of course, the kabbalah was sure to have something to say about it.

He thought back to the story that Sabrina had told him in the penthouse apartment over Piazza Vittorio.

"Now let me tell you how it went."

Of course, then this was the last twist.

He looked at the time. It was seven o'clock. He opened the door of the Subaru and got out.

"I'm going to walk. It'll get me there quicker. Wait for me at Largo dei Lombardi."

Marco noticed that the neon signs out front of the "Back On Your Feet, Rome" foundation had been prudently turned off. But from the shapes that he could just make out behind the windows that were illuminated from within, he realized that his trip over here had not been made in vain. Without slackening his pace, he went past the bodyguards at the front door, waving his Carabinieri badge and ID under their noses; he also took care not to say so much as a word in response to the repeated questions from the young woman who barred his way at the reception desk and then tottered after him on her five-inch heels as far as the lounge.

"Excuse me, sir? Sir, can I help you? Who are you looking for?"

Mauro Lotorchio introduced himself, with an enthusiastically unctuous handshake.

"With whom do I have the pleasure?"

"ROS, Carabinieri. Anticrime Section. Lieutenant Colonel Marco Malatesta."

"There must be some mistake. We didn't call for anyone. Maybe the bad guys you're looking for are right out here in the street. Ha, ha, ha!"

The laughter of that piece of dried cod in a double-breasted suit who reeked of French cologne ought to have been met with an open-handed slap. But deep down, he knew he could do better. He could crush his pride. His and his master's pride.

"Listen, my dear Lotorchio. Nobody called for me at all. Let's just say that this is a surprise visit. And let's also just say you tell the Honorable Malgradi I want to see him."

"I'd be very happy to do that for you, Colonel. But right now the Honorable is involved in an exceedingly sensitive political meeting. You surely understand, these aren't easy hours for our country. We each have responsibilities and we are obliged to make decisions . . . "

"Let me guess. Irrevocable decisions, is that the phrase? I must have read it somewhere already."

These bagmen were trained to be more flexible than modelling clay, but the guy had registered the lunge and had changed his expression. On the lips of the idiot, the smile straight out of a toothpaste ad had vanished, giving way to a visible tremor of rage. Now, Malatesta. Now.

"All right, then, my friend. Given, as you well know, ROS doesn't take action for apartment burglaries, if you're not going to announce me, I'll take down your name and I'll interrupt the Honorable's meeting myself. That way all three of us can take a trip down to the barracks."

Malgradi rushed into the waiting room outside the large conference room.

Christ, now what the fuck did that Malatesta want? He'd known it all along, damn it. He knew that he should have gotten that asshole out of his hair long ago. What the fuck was Rapisarda up to? Hadn't he settled Malatesta's hash with the whole story of that Red Brigades terrorist they'd caught at St. John Lateran?

The Honorable shook Malatesta's hand and waved away Lotorchio with the kind of gesture you'd use to dismiss a butler. He put on a stony face.

"I'm entirely at your disposal, Colonel. If you'd only called ahead, I'd have arranged to meet you in a more fitting place, at a more fitting time."

"I hope you'll forgive me, Your Honor, but you know how things go with homicides. You never know what thread you'll grab next. Day, night, investigations don't go according to the clock or even the calendar."

"Homicide? Frankly, I don't understand."

Malgradi had taken on the color of the immaculate shirt that he was wearing, upon which a gold tie clip gleamed, with a miniature tricolor banner, a memento of the 150th anniversary of Italy's unification.

"Homicide. You understand perfectly, Your Honor. For me, what's important is to understand whether you've ever heard the name of a certain Spadino. Or if you prefer, Marco Summa, which was his name until last summer, when they roasted him to a turn in a pine grove. All we found of him was his teeth."

"How horrible."

"Maybe he asked for it. Or maybe someone else had it in for him because he'd gotten too big for his britches. Or maybe he got smart with someone he shouldn't have gotten smart with. Or maybe he saw something he wasn't supposed to see."

"Excuse me?"

"I was just thinking aloud. But tell me, answer my question. Does that name mean anything to you?"

"Absolutely not."

"Think it over carefully. Spadino."

"Nothing."

"Then maybe I'll have better luck with a certain Vicky. She's a Lithuanian citizen. Excuse me, she was."

"No, I don't know any Polish women."

"We were luckier with her. The dogs had only eaten half her head. And when we found her, the worms working on her decomposition hadn't entirely digested her."

Malgradi was seized by an uncontainable urge to vomit.

"Listen, Colonel, I wouldn't want to seem discourteous to you in any way, but I honestly don't see what help I can be. And so, if you'd be so kind as to excuse me, I need to get back to my meeting. Naturally, I am completely at your disposal if you happen to think of any other circumstances concerning which you believe I can be of some assistance."

Malatesta smiled. The Honorable had taken the hook. And now he tried to lessen the tension on the line, letting a little play into the conversation. The man could have just burst into a black rage. He could have shouted that he was a member of the parliament of the Italian Republic. Kick him rudely out of the foundation and demand—he certainly would have been well within his rights—that Malatesta observe the traditional formalities required for an interview with a person of interest or even a suspect.

He hadn't done any of that. Malgradi hadn't done it, because he couldn't. He was up to his neck in shit. Guilty as sin. And now Malatesta knew it. And so the countdown had begun.

St. Christian. St. Christian.

"Thanks, Your Honor. We'll see you again very soon. You've been much more helpful than you could ever imagine."


The villa in the Parco della Caffarella was immersed in a shade and silence that seemed unnatural given the fact that it was not even two miles as the crow flies from the plaza of the republic where everything was taking place. On the 43-inch high-definition screen of the Sony television set in the oval living room with its large bow windows, a room that constituted the architectural heart of that 22,000-square foot villa—"An exact replica of the office of the President of the United States," the master of the house boasted coquettishly—the footage from Sky TV's coverage on Piazza del Quirinale arrived live and larger than life. Even stripped of the voices of the correspondents. Voices, chants, mutterings, and then, loud and clear . . . A shout from the square that turned into a roar, transforming the whistles into a throbbing stadium cheer.

"Buffoon! Buffoon! Buffoon! Buffoon!"

It was 8:57 P.M.

"Mafioso! Mafioso! Mafioso! Mafioso!"

The procession of motorcycle cops and the midnight-blue Audi A8—bombarded by flashbulbs that illuminated, behind the bulletproof glass, the face of the Italian prime minister in the last act of his show—streamed into the Quirinal Palace.

Benedetto Umiltà gestured to the Filipino butler, dressed in a jacket encrusted with gold braid. The guests were all sprawled out on cream-colored sofas arranged in stadium seating around the big screen TV. The houseboy served champagne flutes of spritz and handed around crab canapés on a large silver tray.

"Isidro, delicately, if you don't mind."

Monsignor Tempesta lifted the aperitif to his lips without taking his eyes off the immense television set. Samurai asked if he might have a cup of white tea.

"Sri Lanka or Zhejiang? They're both biodynamic teas, sir," the Filipino asked, as he bowed stiffly from the waist.

"Whichever is stronger. And no sugar."

Umiltà tried to break the tense silence that kept them chained to the images of the prime minister's farewell.

"You'll see, you're about to drink something absolutely out of the ordinary. A friend of mine sends these teas to me, a general manager at the Ministry of Agriculture. Do you remember him, Your Excellency? He's the one whose situation we looked into a year or so ago, he purchased that magnificent building in Borgo Pio from the Confraternita Dei."

"Dottor Pavetta? No, wait, perhaps I'm mixing him up with the one who made mozzarellas."

"Yes, Your Excellency, Pavetta is the one involved in fish farming in Maratea. The one who arranged for the EU financing and who helped out on the construction job on the Salerno-Reggio highway. And, yes, we're going to be eating his buffalo mozzarellas today. Earlier, I was referring to Dottor Giansi."

"That's right. Giansi. Galeazzo, right? With a brother at SACE insurance and a daughter at the Palazzo della Farnesina, the Ministry of Foreign Affairs."

"You have a mind like a steel trap."

Samurai interrupted them.

"Speaking of ministries. Does this evening change anything?"

Tempesta smiled. And with him, Umiltà.

"Nothing. A thunderclap in Palazzo Chigi becomes a faint breeze in the ministries. That's what makes the Italian Republic such a stable institution. And after all, we've had reassurances, haven't we?"

Tempesta put his hands together as if in a gesture of prayer, brushing the tip of his nose.

"We've had extensive assurances that the transition is going to be painless. And after all, and here it is the churchman in me that's speaking, from the height, if I may, of the thousands of years of wisdom of the institution that I so imperfectly represent . . . the storm will move on, and we'll only have to reckon with the eternal and immutable conundrum of human nature. And in particular, with the very peculiar nature of our own people."

Amen, thought Samurai with a twinge of envy. It was the same identical moral approach found in Mafiosi and members of the 'ndrangheta: *càlati, juncu, ca passa la china.* Bow down, reed, and the flood will pass. The tea arrived. Samurai took two exquisitely scented sips from a cup of Chinese porcelain.

"Just as well. If the ministries aren't teetering, then I think we can be reasonably confident about the solidity of the city government. Our bill is scheduled to go up for a vote in the city council on Monday. Another forty-eight hours and we can finally get started. In the end, unbelievable but true, Malgradi actually did what he was supposed to."

From Piazza del Quirinale, once again, the voice of the Sky TV correspondent could be heard.

> We've just been informed that Prime Minister Silvio Berlusconi has formally submitted his resignation and has left the Quirinal Palace by a secondary exit. Beginning tomorrow morning, the Italian president and head of state will start a round of consultations and by Monday ought to appoint a leader, and announce the formation of a new government . . .

Umiltà grabbed the remote control and held it up, so his guests could see it.

"What if we put on some music instead?"

The sound issuing from the eight lollipop-stem Bang & Olufsen speakers enveloped the three men in a cradle of powerful sonic waves.

"Magnificent. Mozart, Symphony No. 25 in G minor. First movement. Allegro con brio. Even though from you, Umiltà, I might have expected Beethoven's Fifth, or the *Eroica*," said Samurai with a sarcastic grin.

"You think of me as such a banal person."

"I prefer to have people surprise me. I so detest being disappointed."

They hadn't noticed the reappearance of the Filipino. Isidro announced the arrival of Pericle Malgradi. The Honorable had the overwrought expression of a shipwreck survivor. Benedetto Umiltà walked to meet him with a studied demeanor.

"My dear Honorable Malgradi, please come in. In your absence we ventured to comfort our stomachs with a few canapés. Crab, actually. Would you care to partake?"

"If I'm not being indelicate, I'd like to use the restroom. I don't feel at all well."

"I can imagine. The tension of an evening like this can play some nasty tricks on your stomach."

Isidro accompanied the guest to one of the three bathrooms on the ground floor. Seven hundred fifty square feet lined with Pompeii red wallpaper, the sinks and toilets all made of black Carrara marble.

"What the fuck is this place, a crypt?"

He reemerged from the toilet as empty as a piece of bamboo. But if possible, more wrecked than before. Returning to the oval living room, Malgradi lunged at Samurai with electric intensity.

"It's all over. That damned Carabiniere, it's all over."

Samurai resumed his reptilian gaze. Benedetto Umiltà consigned Mozart to the pause button.

"What are you talking about? What the devil are you talking about?"

"The ROS . . . They know everything. Two hours ago, Malatesta came to the foundation. They know everything, I tell you! We're all in danger, Samurai, all of us, even you."

Samurai indulged in a faint giggle that left Malgradi blank with terror. He raised his voice.

"And just what kind of danger would I be in, in your opinion? Come, come, tell me, Malgradi. What do I risk? A little cocaine? Between the two of us, I'm not the one who snorts coke. The whores? You're the one who fucks whores. And always has. The Lithuanian girl? Who was with her the night that she died? And who called Spadino? Not me. And who asked Number Eight to remove him? Certainly not me. Could it have been you?"

"I could . . . tell about certain things . . . " Malgradi let slip.

"How many children do you have, Malgradi?" Samurai resumed, in a surprisingly gentle voice. "Two girls, I think, am

I right? Very pretty, from what I've heard. It would be a shame if anything happened to them. They have their whole lives ahead of them . . . "

"Gentlemen, please!" Monsignor Tempesta pleaded melodiously. Samurai put his hands together and fell silent. The bishop approached Malgradi. The Honorable was sprawled out on the sofa, his hands pressed against his tear-streaked face, as if awaiting extreme unction. "Honorable, I believe that what you need is some rest."

Malgradi let his hands fall from his face and shot like a weasel in the bishop's direction.

"Rest? On Monday the council is going to be voting on the Great Project: it's my political masterpiece. Our masterpiece."

"Honorable, there's nothing in this whole story that can be called ours. And there never was. You of all people would know that. Two days in politics can be a geological era. The government has fallen and, what's more, I don't know how much longer your little secret with the Carabinieri can last in this city, drafty and leaky as it is. Believe me, you can stop thinking about the debate and the vote. Rather, I'd like you to imagine a place."

"A place?"

"You badly need the benefit of silence. It's a great boon, a balm, like solitude. You need to find yourself, frankly. I was in need of the same thing. Since you read it, you no doubt remember where my *Ethics for a New Millennium* was written?"

Samurai asked Isidro to pour him another cup of white tea.

"Superb."

"The tea or His Excellency's words?" asked Benedetto Umiltà.

"I'd say both. And now, if you don't mind, I'm afraid I have to leave you."

Samurai got to his feet and Isidro held out his black Prada overcoat. Malgradi was on the sofa, beached like a whale. He seemed to be fast asleep. His shirt was unbuttoned to the belly, one of his legs, dangling from the sofa, displayed a cotton lisle sock that had slipped down to his ankle, and his eyes were half shut. A whitish film encrusted the corners of his mouth. His labored breathing emitted a sort of bronchial rattle. Samurai looked at him with the same indifference he showed as he stepped around homeless men sleeping on cardboard boxes at the Termini train station. He held out his hand to Tempesta, and then to Benedetto Umiltà. Isidro accompanied him to the villa's internal parking area, holding open the driver's side door of his black Smart Car.

Samurai bade him farewell with a pat on the back.

"Now, when you go back in, make sure you air out the living room. It smells of death."

Samurai took less than an hour to reach Trevignano. It was time to start the clean-up campaign.

Shalva was wide awake and watching TV. Live coverage of the prime minister's farewell was continuing nonstop. Now they were broadcasting old footage from the archives. 1994. The videocamera with the lens covered with a nylon stocking was filming that man throwing his hat in the ring, back when he still had hair.

The Georgian had a broad, amused grin on his face, and with circular movements of his wrist he was oxygenating a glass of Bas-Armagnac.

"Lookie lookie. And I always thought that a swine like you was only interested in watching porn. Do you find the spectacle exhilarating, Shalva?"

"My friend, the politics in this country is more entertaining than Russian and Georgian politics put together."

"Let's just say that it's never boring."

"Whores, corruption, betrayal. Better than porn. It's life, Samurai. Your politics is a mirror held up to life."

"And to think that instead I wanted to see to a nice funeral."

"Life is given, and life is taken away. Tell me what I have to do."

"Do you remember the two insects you saw at Il Tatami?"

Shalva thought back to Morgana with a rush of lust.

"Unforgettable."

"They need to be whacked. The two of them, and a third one, in Ostia. His name is Robertino. I'll just point you to them. I'll rely on you to finish the job. And . . . Shalva?"

"Tell me, brother."

"This is just the beginning. It's time for a breath of fresh air, in Rome."

## LIII

They really were members of a generation that was as naïve as it was unholy. Ready to believe that a handshake with a "graybeard" in a locker room was a guarantee of who knew what kind of commitment.

On Sunday morning, the Skype call that Samurai made to Denis lasted only a few dozen seconds. It was sufficiently concise to leave no room for questions. But not so hasty as to seem fake.

"Denis, I need to see you all. We need to get to work. Right away. Tomorrow, we're getting the green light in the city council for the Great Project."

"Why 'see us all'? Aren't I enough?"

"Unless I'm misremembering, the last time we spoke you weren't alone. Or has your company changed?"

"It hasn't changed."

"Exactly. Since I'm not interested in changing the formation of my team in the middle of an operation, we'll just keep going the same way we began. And let me say something more. I want Robertino to be there, not just the girl."

"Whether he's there or not doesn't make any difference. The less he has on his mind, the fewer faces he sees, the better. And after all, you know how little he fucking understands about zoning plans."

"Everyone I have an agreement with, I need to look them right in the eyes. Robertino is a problem of yours, not mine. And until you've solved that problem, he's a member of the team, as far as I'm concerned."

"Whatever makes you happy. He'll be there. Where?"

"I'll come to you. At the Off-Shore."

"When?"

"Tonight, around eight."

"Understood."

The preparation was the fun part. Better than the actual execution. Always. It allowed him to savor the details, allowing the adrenaline to build up. Shalva had learned this in Serbia from Zoran, a sniper who, after the war was over, organized bear-hunting parties for narcos and Russian oligarchs. And the M-93 Crna Strela Black Arrow 50-calibre precision carbine whose burnished barrel and anatomically shaped stock he was now caressing had been a gift from Zoran. Shalva had saved Zoran's hide one fine spring day, helping him escape the death-grip of a professional killer from St. Petersburg whose wife Zoran had fucked. And the only form of gratitude that Zoran had shown himself capable of had been the ceremonious and emotional delivery of that fantastic instrument of death, manufactured by the Zastava Arms Company, based in Kragujevac, Serbia.

"Bears?" Zoran had said. "I've killed more than a hundred of them with this. At a distance of five hundred meters, there's no difference between a man and a bear."

After painstakingly checking the bolt and the optics of the infrared laser sights, Shalva slid two clips holding five rounds each into the capacious pockets of his khaki trousers, and slipped under his belt, behind his back, two Noz tactical knives, the kind once used by the army of the former Yugoslavia. It was quite cold for mid-November, and he rummaged through the closet for a black wool-knit watch cap with the word Grand written on the rolled cuff—the name of the Tribeca hotel in New York where he'd first taken a black fashion model to bed. A wonderful memory. An object strictly for important occasions. And this was one of them.

He checked the time and climbed into his car. It wouldn't take long to drive from Trevignano to the Coccia di Morto shoreline.

The Off-Shore was deserted. It had been shut down ever since Number Eight's death. The searches done by the Carabinieri, and the investigation conducted by the attorney general's office, had both militated in favor of a lengthy period of renovation. And after all, Denis wanted to scrub that place of its patina of South American bordello.

"I want something new. Something minimalist," he had said to Morgana. And in response he had been given a laconic reply.

"Sure. As long as it doesn't look like one of those faggoty places."

For this reason too, as they killed time while waiting for Samurai, Denis kept going into and out of the VIP lounge along with Morgana, putting on the air of an architect ruminating over surprising insights.

"This seashell-shaped bed has got to go."

"Sure, but it works perfectly."

"And the dancer cubes in the bar . . . get rid of them. We can't turn this into a Nineties discotheque."

They seemed like a couple of newlyweds at Ikea, and Morgana couldn't really say whether that reassured her or just drove her into a blind fury. She had never fully belonged to Number Eight. And she certainly had no intention of becoming the property of Denis Sale. She was his woman, not his good little wife, whom he'd first get pregnant and then get to manage a "basic" place, as he put it, where maybe she'd be in charge of looking after some other, younger slut.

Robertino generally kept to himself. He took walks up and down the beach. Watching the two of them fuck meant twisting the knife over and over again in the sore left by Cesare's death. His own Cesare. He should have told Cesare when he was still alive that that slut Morgana was fucking Denis. Denis, his brother, sure. Who claimed he was going to take his revenge, just as he'd sworn on the day of the funeral. And why not. There he was. Good and docile, waiting for Samurai to show up. But not to whack Samurai. Not at all. To do business with him, bastard that he was, by name and by birth. This damn *uoterfront*. The day he'd first heard about it was the day Cesare's death warrant was signed.

Robertino was furious. And he was too deeply immersed in his rage to be fully aware of the sounds around him. So he missed the car that pulled into the parking lot of the Off-Shore.

Shalva switched off the engine of the Audi and rolled down the window. From where he was, he enjoyed an excellent line of sight. The first silhouette that he could make out in the darkness, barely illuminated by the interior lights of the bar at the Off-Shore, was that of the little man who was pacing anxiously in circles out on the dunes, several hundred yards from the club. He must be the third guy that Samurai told him about. Robertino. He sat there watching him for a few minutes, until he was sure that Denis and Morgana were nowhere around.

He opened the trunk. He slipped on his soft chamois leather gloves. He picked up the M-93, and checked the clip and sights one last time. He screwed on the silencer barrel. He crouched down at the front of his car. He leaned into a perfect firing position. Then he pressed his eye against the telescopic sight.

Head, chest. Head, chest.

At a distance of five hundred meters, there's no difference between a man and a bear.

*Crack.*

The .50 caliber projectile knocked Robertino back thirty feet or so, carving open a hole at the height of this sternum that was big enough to fit your arm into.

Shalva stood up and, walking at an exceedingly slow pace, headed for the dunes. The blood and bits of flesh and bone of his target were scattered over a radius of several yards. The expression on Robertino's face was a beaming smile. His eyes were wide open. The Georgian reached behind his back and extracted one of the two Noz knifes from his belt. He castrated the corpse with two rapid slashes of the blade and pushed the bloody trophy into the dead Robertino's mouth. Then he turned and headed toward the lights of the Off-Shore.

Denis had opened the door to the storeroom where they kept the alcoholic beverages, the room from which the arsenal had been spirited away in a timely fashion the day that Cesare died. He turned on the light and invited Morgana to come in. But she remained motionless.

"Hey, don't just stand there. Come on, give me a hand. What's wrong?"

"I heard something."

"It must have been the wind."

"No. It's not the wind."

"Then maybe it's that asshole Robertino."

"Why, do you know where he is?"

"How would I? He left to take a walk on the beach."

"I know that. But half an hour ago."

"Don't you worry about him, no one's going to kidnap him."

"Buonasera."

Shalva's voice froze them in place.

The barrel of the M-93 kept both of them covered, moving imperceptibly from the forehead of one to the other.

Denis stared at the Georgian.

"And who the fuck would you be?"

Shalva smiled.

"We know each other. We share a passion for saunas. And I'm here to give you Samurai's best regards."

Denis Sale's brain spattered a crate of Corona Light beer. The bullet from the .38 handgun had centered his temple with great precision.

Shalva turned to look at Morgana, who was clutching the pistol in her right hand and continued to extend her out-stretched arm in the direction of the corpse.

They stared at each other.

Shalva pointed the M-93 toward Denis's corpse. And he fired again, blowing his cranium wide open.

Then he set the carbine down on the floor, never taking his eyes off the girl.

Morgana did the same with the .38. Then she took the Georgian by the hand, leading him to the large seashell-shaped bed in the VIP lounge.

It was the first time she'd ever experienced such pleasure with a man. And once she was done trembling from her last orgasm, she found the strength to speak.

"What's your name?"

"Shalva. My name is Shalva."

"I'm Morgana."

It hadn't been especially hard for Shalva to convince Samurai that leaving the girl alive hadn't been a mistake and that she wouldn't turn into a threat. The two men both spoke the same essential language.

"I vouch for her, brother. My guarantee. She solved the problem. She's going to be useful for us," said the Georgian.

"Just remember that she's still and always will be a woman."

And so it fell to Parisi to roll up his sleeves and get to work. The job wasn't finished. Samurai's phone call woke him out of his sleep in his villa in Grottaferrata as he slept next to his good little wife, who knew nothing about any of it.

"Counselor, I pay you to answer on the first ring. Not the tenth."

"I hope you'll forgive me, but . . . "

"Tomorrow morning at eight o'clock I need you to go see Max in Rebibbia prison. Not a minute later. Tell him that not a fly is buzzing at the Off-Shore. And that Denis and Robertino, God rest their souls, have shambled off, the same way that bears shamble off. Heavy caliber. Slavic-made weapons."

"Is there anything else I need to explain to him?"

"That young man isn't like you. There's no need to waste a lot of words on him."

## LIV

On that sunny Monday morning, looking out the window of Jabba's office, the Roman Forum was heartbreakingly beautiful, though that did nothing to reduce the sheer physical agitation of that cleaned-up Fascist comrade now facing his most challenging test. The television news screen and all the online news sites were leading with the news flash that already dominated the front pages of the newspapers:

PEDDLING NARCOTICS AND CONCEALMENT OF A CORPSE.
INVESTIGATION OF THE PARLIAMENTARIAN MALGRADI.

The three Judases on the opposition side in the city council didn't even need to be announced. Jabba harangued them like three guilty schoolboys.

"It's clear to you that with what has happened, our plans have had to change, right? That bill no longer exists. It won't be debated, today or ever. I'm not signing my name to something put forward by a whoremonger and half a murderer."

The youngest of the three assumed a solemn expression. It's one thing to be compliant, but it wasn't a good idea to overdo it with that stinker.

"The agenda is set by the caucus leaders. And I believe that they've already modified it. Unless I'm mistaken, we're going to vote on Malagrotta today. And so the problem is solved. Rather, I'd assume that we can reconsider the social housing project, at some future date . . . 'Never' is a word that we just don't use in politics. And for that matter the last thing we want to do today is wade into a counterproductive polemic concerning Malgradi's friends in the city council, on the Campidoglio."

The ex-Fascist comrade dissolved into a hyena's smile.

"You took the words right out of my mouth, councilman. In fact, what I had in mind was a nice fat bipartisan motion in which the majority and the opposition declare their mutual agreement in postponing the vote on the project to some more suitable jucture, because of their awareness of the limitations constraining the new executive coalition in terms of the spending review. Eh? What do you think? Rome sets an example for all of Italy. A new season begins. And that way nobody gets hurt."

And with that, he thought to himself, goodnight, Malgradi. Goodnight and good luck.

The phone call from the RIS laboratories came into Ponte Salario around ten in the morning, amidst the blizzard of documents and examinations and analyses that had surged in the wake of the bloodbath at the Off-Shore. After much time had passed, they'd identified the weapon that had killed Number Eight. Marco Malatesta immediately forgot about Robertino and Denis's ravaged corpses and paid gave his full attention to the young captain on the other end of the phone line.

"Well, Colonel, the bullet fragment that was extracted from the cranium of Cesare Adami belongs to a batch of Borghi cartridges. We're talking about antiques. It's a type of ammunition that was manufactured in Argentina in 1947. We've turned our archives inside out and examined all the possible compatibilities. And—"

"And?"

"And we came to the conclusion that the pistol that fired that bullet cannot be anything other than a Mannlicher."

"An Austrian pistol made in 1901."

"If I may venture to say so, my compliments, Colonel. Do you know that pistol?"

"Let's drop that line of pursuit. Just go on."

"Well, the only thing that seems really interesting is the fact that this pistol . . . "

" . . . had already been fired in 1985 and 1993."

"Goodness gracious. Then it seems to me that we haven't discovered anything at all and that what I'm telling you is . . . "

"You've done an excellent job, Captain. You have no idea how excellent."

Malatesta ended the conversation with the same haste that he next used in dialing de Candia's number.

"The Mannlicher killed Number Eight, Michelangelo, do you understand that? Now we've got him in our grip. Samurai is fucked."

De Candia didn't warm up all that much, and that fairly chilly reaction aroused a sense of apprehension in Malatesta.

"You don't sound fully convinced, Michelangelo."

"What should I be convinced about? The examinations carried out by RIS or the fact that we have our friend by the balls?"

"Excuse me, Michelangelo, but Mannlicher equals Samurai. We've said this a thousand times."

"Certainly, but the pistol, where is it?"

"We don't have it."

"Exactly. And so?"

"But we do have someone who can tell us where to find it. Max. He has no choice. He's in a world of shit."

De Candia remained silent for several seconds.

"Go talk to him. And get going immediately. You'll find the authorization for your investigative interview waiting for you by the time you get there."

\*

It wasn't eleven o'clock yet, and when he got to the registry office at Rebibbia, Silvana welcomed Malatesta with a hug.

"You're not going to see my girls today, are you?"

"No, I'm heading for the men's wing."

"I know. They let me know from the district attorney's office. One more thing, I never had a chance to tell you, but you can't imagine how happy I am about that young girl caught up in the mess at St. John Lateran. What was her name again . . . Ah, that's right, Alice. I told you so. My nose is infallible . . . "

Silvana noticed that Malatesta's expression had suddenly changed. So she dropped the subject. "Are you going to see the guy involved in the coke bust at Fiumicino?"

"That's right: Max."

"There's a lot of traffic through here today."

"What do you mean?"

"This morning, first thing, his lawyer came in to talk to him. That Parisi. The kind of guy that, normally, unless it's at least noon, doesn't know his own name. But instead, this time, it wasn't eight o'clock yet."

Damn it to hell. Damn it to fucking hell. Malatesta would gladly have shot himself. Eight in the morning. Fucking eight in the morning. Samurai had screwed him. But how could he have known about the Mannlicher?"

Max was beaming. The asshole.

"Here I am, Colonel. I can guess what you want to talk to me about."

"And I can guess that you know exactly what it is. Maybe someone even woke you up to give you the news."

"TV, Colonel. All-news networks are a great invention. *Slaughter on the Waterfront* . . . "

"Well?"

"So I have no reason to remain silent now."

"Seriously?"

"Last night's slaughter at the Off-Shore is the vendetta of the Slavs for the cargo lost at Fiumicino."

"So you're a dead man walking too?"

"Maybe. Or maybe not. That depends on what Dojcilo has in mind."

"And just who would that be?"

"A Bosnian Serb. He's the guy who arranged for me to take the cargo from Folegandros. He must have concluded that the people in Ostia sold him out to you guys. And he settled matters in his own manner. And as far as that goes . . . "

"As far as that goes, we found Serbian-made cartridge shells and Robertino had his own balls stuffed in his mouth."

"That's something you know."

"Maybe I'm not the only one who knows it. Is that all?"

"No."

"Don't tell me that you want to tell me about the rest."

"I have nothing else to lose. So I might as well get it off my chest. Cesare Adami was my doing. I killed him."

"And you expect me to believe you?"

"Number Eight had gone too far. Paja and Fieno were my boys."

"You held them in utter contempt."

"You were misinformed, Colonel."

"Then why don't you inform me correctly. Why did Number Eight kill Spadino?"

"Why don't you ask him?"

"What are you, trying to be funny?"

"No. It's just that I see no reason why you shouldn't get an answer to your question."

"Because Spadino was one of your men, too."

"That's right, *was*. Before he died, I was told that he'd gone into business for himself."

"What a nice fairytale of death you're telling me."

"That's the way it all went."

Max was false as Judas. He was heaping blame on himself but he was lying, and by now Malatesta had proof. But unless Max agreed to swear under oath that Samurai was to blame, there was no way for Malatesta to drag him into that case. He'd remain unindicted, yet again. And Marco also understood that Samurai hadn't needed to know anything about the Mannlicher, because he'd already foreseen that sooner or later they'd work their way back to it. And that meant that everything—starting from the murder of Number Eight, to Max's confession, including the bloodbath at the Off-Shore—everything was part of a plan. RIS had taken a long time to track down that bullet, but even if they'd been quicker off the mark, there was always a Max waiting patiently to be sent on ahead into the slaughterhouse.

"All right, Max. Now you listen to me, and listen good. Let's just pretend that that's the way it went. And let's pretend that I believe the heap of lies you just told me. But let's also just say that in exchange for a great deal of good will on my part, you tell me one single thing. Which can remain between you and me."

"If I can, Colonel, why would I keep the truth from you . . . "

"Tell me what you did with the pistol you used to kill Number Eight. Or, if you prefer, seeing that you're so crazy about the truth, tell me where Samurai put it before convincing you to take the rap for a murder you never committed."

Max burst out laughing.

"If I'm not mistaken, I threw it away."

"You're just a miserable asshole, Max."

"And anyway, Colonel, since when has getting your hands on a gat ever been a problem in Rome?"

"A 1901 Mannlicher. A collector's piece, a rare weapon. Samurai's weapon . . . "

Max held the colonel's gaze without dropping his sarcastic attitude.

"You can get gats like buying toys. With all the accessories that go with them. What does it matter if a toy is an antique or brand new?"

"I understand. I imagine you'll be happy to put all this down in black and white in a deposition, am I right?"

"You know where to find me. I don't have anything planned in the next few days."

"You're never getting out of here alive, you know that, right?"

"The problem isn't me. I got what I deserved. The problem is Farideh. I want to be deposed so I can tell the truth about her too. She didn't know anything about the cargo. I told her that I was a skipper and I dragged her with me to Greece. I told her that I'd been hired to bring a sailboat back to Fiumicino. On Folegandros, she had dinner with me and Dojcilo, who introduced himself as a Russian steel oligarch who owned the boat. Ask him about it. I know that so far, he's been unwilling to talk, but you'll see, he'll be willing to confirm what I'm telling you. She deserves to be kept out of this."

Malatesta grabbed Max by his lapels, lifting him straight up out of his chair at the interview table. His forehead was just inches from the young man's face. The scar on his temple pulsated frantically. He was searching for a squirm of discomfort in those eyes. But Max remained composed, indifferent. Even if now he stank of fear.

Marco dropped him, hurling him into the chair. He turned his back on him and knocked on the armored door to signal that the investigatory interview was over.

"One last thing, Colonel. I shattered Farideh's father's hand. I want to get that down on the record too. That girl needs to know the truth."

The colonel turned and looked at him one last time. To Max, the colonel suddenly seemed tired and disheartened.

"I understand you, Max, I understand you. Your maestro has done an excellent job. But you and he are both laboring under great illusions. The street isn't what it used to be. And to tell the truth, you're basically fucked."

For an instant, it seemed that he had breached some shell. Max turned grim. There shot between them a sort of bolt of comprehension, subterranean and unstated. As if between two enemies who discover that they speak the same language. But it was only for an instant. Max took refuge once again in the martyr's melancholy grin.

So long, Max, thought the colonel with a hint of regret. You made your choice. Too bad. You're better than so many others. But you made your choice, so go fuck yourself, you little piece of shit.

Marco shut the armor-plated door behind him.

Game over. All the dominoes were in place now.

He rummaged through his pockets for the Camels. He saw himself again at Il Fungo, face to face with Samurai.

The Great Project had been aborted. Malgradi had hit a brick wall. Other champions of similar breeding were getting ready to take his place.

## EPILOGUE
### *Tomorrow is another day*


*Pisacane Barracks.*

On December 20, in the presence of Thierry de Roche and a half dozen high-ranking officers in full regalia, in the windswept courtyard of the Pisacane Barracks, General Rapisarda presented Marco Malatesta with the Carabinieri Corps' solemn certificate of encomium "in recognition of his achievements: the recovery of a vast quantity of narcotics with an elevated level of purity, and exceptional investigative skill shown in the resolution of numerous homicidical crimes."

As Rapisarda was shaking his hand, his face glowing with pride like an illustration on the Carabinieri's official calendar, Marco, grim-faced and impassive, muttered:

"Homicidal, General, sir, homicidal crimes. The adjective homicidical doesn't exist in the Italian language."

"Ah, yes, of course, of course . . . very good!" Rapisarda responded, even though he hadn't really even understood. "And I wanted to take advantage of this opportunity to add to the official praise my own personal congratulations, in the hopes that certain misunderstandings that have divided us in the past might now be put definitively behind us."

Marco said nothing, grabbed the parchment certificate, bowed mockingly and half-heartedly in the direction of the "Carabiniere on Horseback," and started to turn away. Asshole. Opportunist. A month ago you were ready and willing to kick me headfirst into hell. I ought to have just let you do it. At least, then, maybe, I'd have felt at home.

Rapisarda, this time speaking confidentially, put a hand on his arm.

"Terenzi, that miserable individual . . . I've taken him under my direct supervision. At the Custoza station. I put him in the stables, where he can clean up horse manure all day. The decision was made to avoid an embarrassing trial. No one at DIGOS raised any objections, and we came to a reasonable understanding with Dottor Setola in the district attorney's office, too. These days, when law enforcement is in the midst of a delicate operation to improve its public image, we might just as well do our best to avoid excessive ruckus . . . I certainly hope that you're in agreement . . . "

"If that's everything, General, sir . . . "

"Perhaps it might have been advisable for you to have a few words with your friend, Dottoressa Savelli. A less . . . aggressive attitude on her part might have been a good idea."

"Considering the state of my relations with Dottoressa Savelli, I'm afraid that anything I might have attempted would only have been counterproductive, at the very least."

Rapisarda was clearly hurt. For an instant he stared at him, with flash of the old, completely sincere hatred. But he regained his composure almost instantly, mollusk that he was.

"I understand, I understand. We'll solve that problem in some other way. Well, the corps is proud to be able to count an investigator of your caliber in its ranks. Ah, one last thing. About that young Carabiniere, the one from up north, his name slips my mind . . . "

"Brandolin."

"That's it, very good, Brandolin. Your request has been accepted, Malatesta. He'll come to work with you at the ROS. Are you happy about that, Colonel?"

Marco nodded, just to put an end to the misery, and left to join Thierry, who had witnessed the pantomime with a sardonic little smile that required no commentary.

Protected by his superior officer, he dodged and evaded smiles both envious and sincere, slaps on the back that were both malicious and affectionate, handshakes both hypocritical and heartfelt. He finally found a little peace in a drag on his Camel cigarette and in the comfort being offered by his friend the general.

"Don't take it the wrong way, that's not worthy of you."

"At your orders, General, sir."

"Just think," Thierry resumed, overlooking the other man's sarcastic tone, "you missed a lovely homily from our friend Spartaco Liberati. You've suddenly shot up into his top ten. You should have heard him, this morning. Colonel Malatesta . . . the hero who sweeps the streets clean."

"Let me guess: cleaning the streets of gypsies and every other kind of *zammammero* . . . "

"Now you're going to ruin the fun of the surprise. I recorded the whole thing for you."

Marco, with a smirk, shook his hand.

"Emanuele, I'm sick and tired of all this."

"I've heard that before."

"And I can imagine what you're going to say to me. But this time you won't be able to talk me out of it."

The general gave him a slap on the back. Marco had his reasons for what he was saying. But they were the reasons of a wounded animal, irrational reasons. No matter what the argument he employed, right then and there, it would do no good. For that matter, the Carabinieri as a corps, and the government itself, could ill afford to lose an officer like him. This state, crumbling to pieces as it is, a state that needs to be glued together in defiance of its innate tendency to fracture, needed to be kept united against its all-powerful *cupio dissolui*, its "desire to dissolve."

"Did you get here on that?" Thierry asked, pointing at the Triumph Bonneville.

500 · C. BONINI & G. DE CATALDO

"It's one of the few things left I can rely on."

"I've dreamed of taking a spin on it for what seems like for-ever, Marco."

Without another word, Malatesta handed him a helmet.

"I'll drive," the general said brusquely, "and that's an order."

From his office window, General Rapisarda had followed the skit with increasing disgust. Sure as death those two were talking about him. And what they were saying wasn't hard to guess. After all, that Steve McQueen-style motorcycle. An offi-cer riding a Triumph was already an anomaly, but everyone knows that Malatesta is an anarchist. Let's even admit that this round had certainly gone Malatesta's way, but it was just one round and the match was long. Still, two senior officers riding a motorcycle was something close to a lethal insult. The over-all degeneration of standards had contaminated the corps by now, the last bulwark of order and decency in a larger context of intolerable degradation.

His assistant knocked on the door and then extended an elegant envelope.

The general acknowledged with a shiver of pleasure the invitation from Temistocle Malgradi.


*Trevignano sul Lago and the Villa Marianna Clinic.*

The lake was starting to get on her nerves. The little biting flies were killing her. You want to put Trevignano up against Ostia? But in the end Morgana had gotten used to it. Shalva's silences were priceless. That man never wasted a syllable. He talked the way he fucked. Spare and essential. And the coke to get fucked up on was available in plentiful abundance in the villa, which by the way, upon her arrival, had suddenly been populated by a pair of extremely helpful and solicitous middle-aged Georgian women who had been sent up from Bari. She was waited upon and held in the highest regard. Breakfast in bed, lunches and dinners served at a table with a tablecloth seven days a week whenever she felt hungry, clean linen every morning. A princess, she had become. And so, to shake up that perfect of idyllic boredom she'd wound up in the middle of, Morgana had decided to give heroin a try. She smoked it. She only ever smoked it. None of that filth from the last century, tying off with surgical tubing and shooting up.

She'd started out with no more than a gram a day. And the thing seemed to amuse Shalva a great deal too, the sight of her wandering around the house with aluminum foil and glass pipes. Unlike cocaine, heroin gave her a sense of profound, definitive peace, something she'd never before experienced in her life. Getting fucked up had turned into an inner exploration, an armistice with a painful past, a sedative against the call of the street that, nonetheless, assailed her from time to time. Like that afternoon, when it swept over her without warning.

She had driven down to Bracciano in the black Toyota Aygo to do some shooting in a nearby quarry—Shalva was insistent that she needed to keep her skills honed. "I've never seen a woman shoot the way you do," he kept saying—and at the stoplight two kids pulled up next to her on an SH motorbike. Age sixteen or seventeen. The one on back had stared at her and, after lifting his hand to his mouth, had started pushing his cheek out with his tongue.

Blowjob queen. They were calling her a blowjob queen. Just for the fun of humiliating her.

She could have just laughed it off. When she was a kid, she often used to do the same thing in Ostia. With Marzia, her best friend, whose life had ended at age sixteen when she'd slammed into a maritime pine on Via Cristoforo Colombo. They would single out men driving alone. Especially men over sixty. And they snickered at the idea of the effect that their prank must have on guys who maybe even couldn't get it up anymore.

Sure, she could have just laughed off what those two little assholes had done at the stoplight. But she didn't.

She followed the kids outside of the town of Bracciano, and when they hit the first hairpin curves heading up to Via Cassia, she screeched ahead of them, cutting them off. She made them take off their trousers and underpants and kneel in the weeds. Then she forced each of them to suck on the cold barrel of the .38 as she clutched it in her fist, until they were docile and good as little lambs.

She went back to the villa, pursued by ghosts. Cesare, Denis, Robertino, the Moroccan from Cinecittà. They were calling to her. They were laughing, but then their heads exploded. Like balloons.

She rummaged around in the big mahogany credenza in the living room where the heroin was bagged in a one-ounce cellophane wrapper, and decided that she wouldn't bother with the little scale this time. No need to weigh it. She lifted the pipe to her mouth and started filling her lungs.

"Keep your eyes open! Keep your fucking eyes open!"

Sprawled on the front seat in the Audi, she could hear Shalva shouting. With his left hand, the Georgian was miraculously keeping the car on the road despite the insane speeds at which he was driving, while with his right hand he shook her, making her chin wobble over her cashmere sweater, which had been reduced to a sponge soaked in vomit, bile, and mucus. They were expecting them at Villa Marianna.

Temistocle Malgradi gestured dramatically to two ogres wearing scrubs, the scrubs being the only thing that identified them as nurses. And he devoted to that overdose the attention you'd expect from a veterinarian asked to look after a dog with indigestion. He was in a hell of a hurry.

"You're going to have to forgive me, eh. But I have other things to do. Today's the big day. The big day."

With the eyes of a wolf, Shalva followed Professor Malgradi as he climbed into his Audi Q7.

If she died, Malgradi was a dead man.

Morgana was tossed onto a gurney that they trundled straight into intensive care.

Shalva was holding her hand.

"You're going to be all right. You're going to be all right."

Summoning up all the strength that remained to her, she looked at him, her eyes open wide.

"Don't save me," she said.

The doors into intensive care swallowed up the gurney with Morgana on it, and Shalva was left alone in the corridor. Paralyzed by the words he was listening to.

"I love you. I love you."

Words that he was speaking.


*Hall of Justice and Bar Necci.*

The day after receiving his certificate of solemn praise, Marco, accompanied by Alba Bruni, attended the first hearing of the summary court procedure for the incidents at St. John Lateran. When the prosecuting magistrate Setola called for acquittal in this preliminary session, in accordance with Article 129 of the Penal Code, for Alice Savelli, "a victim of mistaken identity," a spontaneous burst of applause erupted in the courtroom of the third judicial division, which was packed with demonstrators of varying degrees of innocence. The chief justice threatened to clear the courtroom. Quiet resumed. The defense attorney seconded the prosecuting magistrate's request. Alice got to her feet and asked if she could make a statement.

"In my case, Mr. Chief Justice, to call it a case of mistaken identity is a euphemism at best. As Dottor Setola knows perfectly well, I've lodged a criminal complaint against Marshal Terenzi for defamation and battery."

A new burst of applause and reckless cheers. The chief justice lost his patience and threatened once again to clear the courtroom. Once again, silence fell. Setola took the floor. He explained that Alice's complaint against Terenzi was a part of the record and that further investigation was currently underway. Alice started once again to launch an objection. Her lawyer grimly yanked her back into her chair, apologized to the court, and indicated that, as far as he was concerned, the matter was closed. The chief justice exchanged a glance with his fellow judges, then he read the document that had clearly been prepared in advance.

"In the name of the Italian people, and in view of Article 129 of the Code of Penal Procedures, Savelli, Alice is fully absolved and acquitted of the charges."

When the third round of applause erupted, not even the judge could muster an objection, and Alice walked out of the trial and the courtroom on a wave of frantic joyful cheering. Next to her were Diego Ponytail, Farideh—who had been released a few days earlier as a result of Max's deposition—and old man Abbas, who had finally left the wheelchair behind and was now hobbling along on crutches.

Marco waited for the ruckus to subside and then, outside in the hallway, he stopped right in front of her. Instinctively, Ponytail put his arm around her with a tenderness that made the lieutenant colonel's heart bleed.

"I'm just here to say hello," Marco justified himself, "and to tell you that I'll come to the trial to testify against Terenzi."

"Do you think there's going to be a trial, Colonel?" Ponytail challenged him.

"Diego, please . . . " whispered Alice.

Ponytail nodded, and backed off.

Marco and Alice stood there gazing at each other for a moment. They didn't know where to begin. They didn't know if there was anything left to say to each, or if it had all already been said.

It was she who broke the silence.

"I was hard on you, I'm sorry for that."

"Are you happy?" he asked her.

Her face lit up in a friendly smile.

"That's not really the point, Marco. It never could have worked between us. I . . . I'm one thing, and you're another."

Marco handed her the unsightly little package he had brought from home.

"This is for you, Alice."

"What this is? Some kind of liquidation bonus?" she joked, without sharp edges. But when the unwrapped it and recognized the Burmese Buddha head that she'd liked so much the first time that she'd visited his apartment, a sweet and sincere smile finally lit up her face.

Marco turned around and put an end to his self-pity. Her cry of *"Ti voglio bene!"* reached him when he was already several yards away.

*Ti voglio bene.* Italian for "I love you," though not exactly "I love you."

Marco was reminded of that verse from a poem by the ancient Latin poet Catullus: *plus amo minus bene velle . . .* the more I love you the less I wish you well. The heartbreaking wisdom of the young and disappointed lover. His high school teachers would declaim it according to poetic meter . . . *plusamò | minús | benevélle . . . plusamò | minús | benevélle . . .* euphonious, cute, amusing, no? What better epitaph for a love affair throttled in the cradle by ideology? Or by the stubbornness of the hunter of human scalps? Or by the uniform? Or by the state? Or by all those things together? And, most important of all, had any of it been worth it?

He kept the question to himself, since after all, there was no answer.

But that mocking refrain, *plusamòminúsbenevélle*, continued to obsess him, until Alba, the sweet, sharp-edged Alba, who was staring at him with those big eyes of hers that blended strength and submissiveness, pointed out a small knot of gentlemen in grey tweed who were festively heading for the exit.

"Viglione, the Camorrista. The appeals court just acquitted him."

"He'll sue for wrongful arrest, no doubt," Marco commented drily.

Sitting at a table in the Bar Necci, Farideh was writing to Max.

"My love, they say horrible things about you, but I don't believe them. I believe in you. And I'm going to get you out of that prison. I want you beside me, for good. Because I can't live without you . . . "

*Millennium Pride.*

The New Beginning was 400 feet above ground level. In a bright December sunset. In the magnificent and luxuriant towering winter garden on the twenty-eighth floor of the tallest granite skyscraper in the country. The Millennium Pride. A vertiginous deluxe erection in the midst of the green space of EUR. A breathtaking view of the sea off Ostia, the circuit of the Castelli Romani, the ancient city of the amphitheaters and the Suburra. Six hundred "housing units" destined to the Best of the Best.

Them.

It had been his idea to christen the new electoral platform in that location—*New Beginning, what an evocative name*, chirped a couple of matrons smelling of mothballs as they hurried into the event—a platform that would be welcomed into the Third Republic of Italy by the main entrance as it "helped Rome to get back on its feet."

Temistocle Malgradi.

The Candidate.

The leader of a new reform movement, "part of the moderate center, but still progressive. Catholic, but secular. Free-market conservative, but libertarian."

The Professor.

The new champion of a Civil Society.

The guardian of the new Open Home, as the party might be called. Ideological orphans and tactical political maneuverers straight out of *The Leopard*. Intellectuals and politicos putting on the feedbag.

"My Home will be your Home!" That was the slogan that Temistocle had arranged to print on the invitation in heavy, recycled stock, and it had been sent out to three hundred of the best names—and surnames—in Rome. Managers, powermongers in state-owned industry, major bureaucrats, film producers, actors, university professors, lawyers, notaries, chief physicians, senior officers such as Rapisarda, big names from television journalism and print media, high prelates. A vast swamp of overcoats, garish synthetic fur coats, and down jackets that now, like a black swarm of ants, were being devoured in shifts by the construction hoist that was shuttling up and down between the base and the summit of the tower still under construction.

Temistocle Malgradi was beaming. Behind the shelter of a hibiscus plant, he couldn't stop thanking Mariano Tempesta and Benedetto Umiltà with a hand on his heart. They looked back at him with all the satisfaction of a buyer gazing at the new SUV ready to drive out of the dealership.

The *damnatio memoriae* of that human shipwreck of a brother of his, Pericle, had been their masterpiece. They had basically buried him alive in the monastery of Camaldoli, in expectation of a trial that might be a long time coming. And in the meanwhile, everyone could be allowed to forget. Amen.

The Candidate tapped gently on the gooseneck microphone. He cleared his throat with a short, studied cough. He breathed in the cool scent of the mentholatum spray he'd just used to clear his stuffy nostrils, which were reacting to the line of coke he'd snorted just half an hour ago. As he was snorting coke on the twenty-eighth floor, he'd contemplated Il Fungo, fourteen floors further down. Poor old Il Fungo. Its days were over. As was only right, when the Present takes the place of a Past long since buried. And when the Future is a new, luminous adventure.

"Ladies, gentlemen, all my dear friends. First of all, thank you. Thank you! Thank you! I speak to you as a man of science and therefore with words of truth. Above all, as a man who is deeply moved because I have been given the chance to participate in this magnificent adventure, upon which we are setting off today, an adventure that I am honored and proud to call Politics. With a capital P. The same Politics that made my father great and proved my brother's undoing. You may wonder, just as the people closest to me have wondered in recent days, with what spirit, with what strength, after everything that has happened to Pericle, my family can have decided to return to the public stage. Well, it was exactly what happened that gave us no choice. It was a duty we owed to ourselves, to you, and to the country. There is only one way to make up for wrongdoing: you must expiate it in your service to the community. And politics is service, as I have learned, and as you may too, in the pages that have accompanied me in my solitary reflections over the past few days, pages from *Ethics for a New Millennium* by Monsignor Mariano Tempesta, the shepherd of souls who is here with us today, and to whom I can claim the distinct honor of enjoying a close friendship. This is the trustworthy raft of faith and hope upon which my brother, so sadly shipwrecked, has finally taken refuge."

Malgradi's culminating blather caught Eugenio Brown in the hint of a yawn. Sitting next to him in the small audience surrounded on all sides by luxuriant greenhouse vegetation, Sabrina, swathed in a breathtaking black tube dress, was fuming.

"Hey Euge', leaving aside the fact that with all these vines and dwarf trees I feel like I'm at the zoo, excuse me, the menagerie, I still want to tell you that these Malgradis are a family of fucking whoremongers, no matter what they say."

"Please, my love. Please. Language, my love, language . . . "

"How could it ever have occurred to you to get us sucked into this herd of dickheads?"

"My love, you can't always delegate things in life. We too need to do something for the good of the country."

"I get that. But with the Malgradi family, of all people, after everything that's happened?"

"You know, just because they're brothers doesn't mean they're the same people. I've heard a lot of good things about this Temistocle. A progressive Catholic."

"Oh, sure."

Temistocle finished up in a crescendo that he had tried out over and over again in the past few days, with his latest sweetheart, an attractive dental hygienist, as his audience.

"The old style of politics has failed us, my dear friends. Its failure, ladies and gentleman, marks the end of the twentieth century. I say it in the most definitive and irreversible terms available. Enough! We cannot continue to look toward the future if our eyes are perpetually turned toward the past. And this is something that I say to our friends on both the right and the left, who have both committed so many errors in these recent troubled years of our life together as a nation. There is a rising tide of indignation, rancor, and antagonism all around us. In part, we are all responsible for it. We cannot allow it to sweep us away. Let us, rather, look toward the coalition of the finest neo-conservative and pro-labor tradition. Enough with the old oppositions. Our path will be neither easy nor short, and that is why we must begin today, because the Future will not wait, because it is eager to become the Present. The Future begins today. It begins right here."

There was a wave of applause that brought the house down.

Brown turned to Sabrina.

"What did I tell you? This guy is cut from a very different cloth. And anyway. It's with them that we can start over, after everything that's happened and that's happened to you, my love. Do you have any idea of the symbolic power of our presence here? Do you know what it means? That your past is now a closed book. Over. Erased. A New Beginning, my love. Also, I have a surprise for you."

Sabrina's pout dissolved into a smile. She knew the preamble well enough to recognize what was coming. She leaned her ear over to Eugenio's mouth like a cat.

"It seems to me that you like this place."

"Aside from this jungle, I like it a lot. I saw that they have a movie theater. And a gym. And a swimming pool."

Brown smiled.

"I talked to the builder when we first got here. You see him? That good-looking man in the front row."

"Yes, indeed. Not bad at all. And he's probably dripping money. Well?"

"I bought you a little something here in the tower. A thousand square feet or so. That way, whenever you're bored on Piazza Vittorio, you can always use this place as your office and your refuge. I figured that with the movie and the various series, you ought to have a space all your own."

Temistocle Malgradi had finished up and now he was greeting folks in an orgy of handshakes and cheek-kissing.

Sabrina brushed her fingertips over the nape of Brown's neck. She kissed him sweetly on the forehead.

"I love you, Euge'. You're my life."

*La Paranza Restaurant and Samurai's Villa.*

Tito Maggio was beaming.

Out of jail, awaiting trial, with good odds of beating the rap thanks to Max's confession, reassured by Samurai concerning the age-old matter of his debts to the Three Little Pigs, on the very day he reopened La Paranza—*damn him to hell, this fucking Carabiniere*, he had really hit him hard—he had seen himself honored by visits from Perri, from Rocco and Silvio Anacleti and, naturally, from Ciro Viglione, guest of honor inasmuch as he was fresh from his acquittal—*the triumph of justice, no small deal!*

Moreover, the fact that it was Viglione the party was being thrown for, was in and of itself another piece of good news: while the Anacleti clan and the Calabrians were notoriously stingy, the Camorrista loved an opportunity for lavish display. He unfailingly demanded, as he put it in Neapolitan dialect, "*chillu ca costa 'e cchiú*"—whatever cost the most. He paid in cash and he left extremely generous tips. For that matter, even if he had wanted to pay with a credit card that would be out of the question for at least another little while, as a result of frozen bank accounts, court orders, and preventive confiscations, and other legal quibbles. An understated little card, left almost carelessly on the white linen tablecloths, informed the diners that "due to temporary difficulties with our lines, it is impossible for us to accept credit or debit cards." But luckily, at least to judge from that first evening, things were starting to stir again. Yes. The clientele couldn't care less about Tito Maggio's legal problems. Was the seafood good? Were the wines up to snuff? Well then, fuck judges and cops, you only live once, right? The only sour note was Samurai's absence. Tito would have expected to see him enter, tailing after the usual crew, or maybe even a step or two ahead of them. Instead, nothing, not even the shadow of Samurai. An absence that astonished and embittered Ciro Viglione, too.

"That fucking asshole Samurai could have gotten up off his ass just this once, no? What do you all think about it?"

"I did that," Rocco Perri admitted, "or I guess I should say, I didn't do it. That is, I didn't invite him to the party."

"Why not?"

"Because it's better if we have a talk amongst ourselves first."

Ciro Viglione looked at the Calabrian, still unctuous and smiling, and saw that the Anacletis were nodding their heads. The map of the alliances was being redrawn, then. This wasn't going to be a very good time for Samurai.

"Do I catch a whiff of *ora pro nobis*?" the Camorrista inquired, sinking his teeth into a scarlet gamba prawn that had only left the land of the living moments ago.

"It's premature," Perri explained, "but no doubt about it, he's been kicking up a fuss lately."

"And we've all lost money on account of it. Every last one of us," Silvio Anacleti pointed out.

"And Uncle Nino's been busting my balls!" Viglione finished up, clearly in tune with the rest of them.

The other men at the table all nodded in agreement.

"He wants revenge," said Perri. "But I told him to keep calm. The time will come. Right now, we need to rebuild our crews, figure out whether there's any life left in the Great Project, or whether we should just draw an X over it . . . "

"Samurai says that it's only a matter of time," Silvio Anacleti ventured.

"And you believe him?" Viglione queried.

What followed was a profusion of arms thrown wide and deep sighs of indecision. They knew and they didn't know. They believed and they didn't believe. And most of all, Ciro Viglione, they were still afraid of him. In other words, the Camorrista decided, Samurai still carries some weight, but he's like someone out on parole. The next time he fucks up, he's a dead man. But why waste time? The truth is that Samurai has broken our balls. Why not just get four or five young bravos, send them over to take care of him, and then after explaining the rules of life to them, promote them on the field of battle for their act of bravery, and start over again with them. The way they used to do in Naples, back in the good old days.

"If it was up to me, you could do it tonight," Viglione summarized.

"Let's wait for the politics to work itself out, Ciro, trust me on this."

"I'm sick and fucking tired of politics!"

"And that's why politics has changed, right, Ciro? You do remember the old blood oath we swore, don't you? 'The big fish became small, and the small fish became sharks . . . '"

Ciro reined in the more impetuous spirits. Rocco Perri had fallen back on the ancient Mafia oath of allegiance. It was a way of reinforcing the message and making it clear that the matter had been examined and resolved in all possible venues. Samurai was being given an extension. There was nothing more to be said.

Snapping his fingers, he summoned the waiter's attention.

"Bring another bottle of Krug, boy. This one is warm."

Sebastiano, the engineer's son, and Manfredi, the shylock's son, showed up on Manfredi's motor scooter a little past one.

Manfredi stood watch, as they'd agreed. This was a job for

the young man; he had shown some real ability and would soon make a name for himself.

Sebastiano shot a glance at the restaurant's plate glass windows. The lights had been turned down, and the waiters were preparing the tables for the next day's business. Another twenty minutes, half an hour, tops, he said to himself. He exchanged a glance of understanding with Manfredi, and to vent his anxiety he went for a walk through the empty streets of the center of town. Christmas was coming, and the season's festoons and decorations hit him with the painful intensity of nostalgia for the way things were and would never be again. Just a year ago, he'd been a happy young man. He'd held the world in his hands and he hadn't even realized it. Now he was just a guy with nothing left to lose. But, at the same time, he was coming to a fork in the road. He was impatient. He went back to La Paranza and stood out front. Manfredi was hiding somewhere nearby. The waiters were going home, straggling out a few at a time. The last one to leave was the chef. Finally, the last light blinked off. The engineer's son pulled the nylon stocking over his head, gave the barrel of his revolver a spin, gripped the handgun firmly, took a deep breath, and was ready and waiting when Tito Maggio's corpulent silhouette appeared in the front door.

"Shut up, don't move, get back inside," he ordered the man, aiming the revolver at him.

"What the fuck—"

"Get back inside, I said."

Tito Maggio obeyed.

"Shut the door and turn on the lights. On the dimmer. That's right. Now go to the cash register and get the cash."

"I have it right here," said Tito, pointing to the pouch clipped to his belt.

"Give it to me."

Tito Maggio was hardly a lionhearted soul. He thought to

himself, what the hell, let him keep the money, that poor idiot, and he can go fuck himself. But then it occurred to him that, given his situation, there was always the risk that the Three Little Pigs might refuse to believe there had been any robbery at all. They were capable of saying that he'd made up the whole thing just to squirrel away the cash. Rumors might make their way to Samurai. Samurai might believe them. If he lost Samurai's protection, it would all be over. He'd be done for. And so he screwed up the courage that he lacked.

"Hold on, listen to me for a minute, kid . . . I don't know if you're clear on who I am . . . I'm Tito Maggio. Here in Rome I'm friends with everyone. And most important of all, I'm friends with Samurai . . . you know who Samurai is, don't you?"

"Give me that fucking pouch. I'm starting to lose my patience."

Who the hell was this asshole? Where had he come from? Did he or didn't he know that Samurai held Rome in the palm of his hand? That whoever takes him on was just so much dead flesh?

"Look, let's just say you made a bad mistake, kid. Now you just turn around and head out of here the same way you came in. Look, if you want I'm happy to spot you a hundred euros, hell, two hundred . . . Let's just say I invited you to dinner, eh? A nice free meal at La Paranza, oh, that's not the kind of thing just anyone can afford."

By now, Sebastiano was possessed by a unnatural cool. He thought back to the instructions he'd been given by Manfredi, that poor idiot; he thought back to his easy-going and occasionally mocking tone of voice.

"Tito Maggio has a bad habit. He doesn't pay his debts. So we're going to have to teach him a lesson. Nothing serious, we don't want to put him out of business, heavens no. You go in, you make him hand over the day's take, then you tell him: look, Tito, you have to pay your debts, that way he'll understand where this is coming from and that he needs to stop playing the asshole. Then you head on back home and I'll tell the notary to record the document that, in the meantime, we'll have drawn up."

"And what if he tries something? What should I do, should I shoot him?"

"Try something? Tito? He's just going to wet his pants."

Well, Tito Maggio was trying something. And that made things simpler.

Tito Maggio was like Manfredi, like Sor Scipione, like the buzzards that had cleaned the flesh off his bones, like his father's executioners. Samurai was the only one who was any different. He was cut from another cloth, Samurai was. He had instilled the meaning of revolt in Sebastiano, Samurai had. He had transformed hatred into pure energy. All right. All right.

Sebastiano fired. Once, twice, three times. Tito Maggio dropped to the floor without a shout, with a stunned expression in his eyes. *Wait, did you really just do that, kid? Now, you tell me, what a way to end the . . . "*

The engineer's son took the stocking off his head, reached down and grabbed the pouch. It was fat with cash.

Alarmed at the sound of gunshots, Manfredi rushed into the restaurant.

"What the fuck did you do? Have you lost your mind? Give me that fucking pistol, Sebastia'!"

Sebastiano swung around and aimed the gun at him, amused at Manfredi's dismay, and then shot him. Twice. Once in the crotch. That's for Chicca. And once in the head. And that's for the life you stole from me.

When the message, sent via Skype, reached Samurai he was naked, on the terrace of his villa, dancing the solitary t'ai chi of the strong, of the indestructible ones.

"All done, Maestro."

Sebastiano was impassive. Samurai nodded.

"Good work. Now get out of circulation for a while. You know where to go. I'll take care of the rest of it."

When Samurai got to La Paranza in his SUV, the place was crawling with cops who refused to let him get any closer. He locked eyes with Marco Malatesta. With a nod, the lieutenant colonel ordered his men to let the bandit enter.

Inside the restaurant, poor Sor Scipione was caressing his son's corpse, in a grotesque parody of Michelangelo's *Pietà*. Samurai shot him a sorrowful glance of formal acknowledgment. They were "deluded," those wretches. They wanted to "lay him down." They'd never understand a thing.

Then he bent over the fat restaurateur's corpse and put his hands together in the Hindu greeting.

"Namaste, Tito!"

Inside the lieutenant colonel a rage that was as savage as it was healthy began to build up. No, no, no diplomatic leave, no "I'm dropping everything and quitting this job," nothing of the kind. In war, turning on your heels is known as desertion. And this, fucking hell if it's not a war.

"There's one thing you were right about, Samurai. Rome no longer has a master. Not even you know how to keep these dogs on a leash. I'll start over from them. And I'll nail you."

Samurai cocked an eyebrow. Too bad. Marco still didn't understand. The rules of the game had changed.

"La Paranza was no longer the place it used to be. Lately, you couldn't get a decent meal here. Poor Tito, he was getting old. We'll see you again soon, Marco."


*Out on the street, shortly thereafter.*

While RIS strung fluorescent tape around the perimeter of La Paranza's front door, Marco took one last glance at Scipione, kneeling in the puddle of his son's blood, and at Tito Maggio's corpse, which the rigidity of death was now turning even more grotesque in the stupefied grimace of his final farewell.

Bruni and Brandolin had arrived as well, and he had nothing more to say to them than a few gruffly muttered routine instructions and an appointment to meet the next day in the offices at Ponte Salario. Then he trudged off in the direction of Via del Gonfalone, where he had parked his Bonneville.

Rome was deserted. The night was chilly and the air was redolent with wood smoke, the wood they still burned in the fireplaces of the "important" palazzi of the historical center. How long had it been since he'd lit a fire in the fireplace, he wondered. When was the last time he'd allowed himself an evening of peace and quiet, letting his thoughts stop tormenting him for a change?

He crouched over the starter of the Bonneville and waited until it grumbled into life and the two chrome-plated exhaust pipes began to spit out white puffs.

The noise disturbed a seagull that was digging its beak into the carcass of a pigeon. The seagull seemed to glare at him, a long, angry look. Then it flew up into the air, squawking out its anger.

With slow, ritualistic gestures, Marco pushed his hands into the gloves, tugging them tight, fastened the chin strap of his jet helmet with the Union Jack emblazoned on the back, lowered the Plexiglas visor, and raised the pashmina scarf over his nose; that scarf reminded him of the other life, from which he had decided to return to settle this account.

The *clack* of first gear echoed in the silence of the alley behind the family courts building, though it was not loud enough to drown out the sound of an engine starting, the engine of a vehicle that, in the shadows, he did not immediately recognize as an SUV, an SUV that followed him with its lights out until it emerged onto Lungotevere dei Tebaldi.

As he was riding upstream along the river, passing one bridge after another and the blinking traffic lights that separated him from the Lungotevere Flaminio, he started keeping an eye in the ovals of his rearview mirrors on a pair of headlights that had had been following him at a constant rate of speed.

When he reached Ponte Duca d'Aosta, Marco felt sure that the car that was following him was still with him. He could have just pulled over, made a single call on his cell phone, and put an end right then and there to that undisguised tail, that threatening dance. But he didn't. He turned his eyes to the far bank of the Tiber, to the Olimpico Stadium immersed in the darkness, and thought back to the words Samurai had uttered on the day their eyes had met again after many years.

"Forget about the motorcycle. You're too old for that now, Marco. And Rome is a dangerous city."

He rapidly downshifted into fourth and then third gears, twisting the throttle and heading straight for the stretch of the Lungotevere Thaon di Revel that led to the on-ramp to Corso di Francia. He shouted as if trying to drown out that other piercing scream. The scream of the horsepower throbbing under his saddle.

"I know that it's you. I know that it's you. Come and get me. Come and get me!" he shouted, rising to a standing position on the footpegs.

The SUV shortened the distance between them in a matter of seconds, and at the beginning of Corso di Francia the distance between the bumper of the huge roaring beast and the fairing of the Bonneville narrowed to a few yards. Marco stared at the straightaway ahead of him. He remembered the nights they'd spent as kids pulling wheelies on that kilometer of asphalt, defying the cement and marble of the parapets of the viaduct that loomed above the river.

The SUV swerved into the left lane and pulled up parallel

to him. The needle on the Bonneville's tachometer shot up into the red zone, while the massive wheels of the SUV came dangerously close to touching the front tire of his motorcycle.

Marco revved the engine, rearing up on his rear wheel to avoid impact. The SUV swerved to the right. The noise of the impact that followed was like the last sound of a wasted life.

Malatesta staggered to his feet. Blood was filling his mouth and drenching the pashmina scarf. His left leg was burning with a stabbing pain. He decided not to look down. He hurled his helmet into the distance and, looking up, saw that the SUV had finished its run and had come to a stop just fifty feet or so from where the Triumph Bonneville had been pulverized as it slammed into the asphalt. The SUV had wrapped itself around a traffic light. From the half-open driver's side door, a man was trying to extricate himself from the interior.

Malatesta grabbed a piece of wreckage from the ground. It must have once been the motorcycle's clutch handle. The impact with the asphalt had turned it into a sharpened icepick.

When he reached the SUV he saw him.

Samurai, of course.

He started pounding the chunk of razor-sharp steel clutched in his right fist against the car door, and then against the driver's side window, which finally exploded into shards.

Face-forward on the airbag, the driver seemed unconscious. Samurai's face was a mask of blood. Malatesta grabbed him with a vast surge of hatred and dragged him out of the car. His legs must be broken, because he collapsed like a sack. Supine on the asphalt, Samurai stared up at him without a whimper, eyes wide open. Marco spat on his face, freeing his mouth of clots of mucus and blood. Then, with just his right leg, the only one he could still control in terms of force and movement, he started stamping down on his ankles and shins.

A stream of tears inundated Samurai's eye sockets.

"Do it, Marco. Do it now, or there will never be another chance."

Malatesta raised the icepick high, then suddenly felt the impact of a massive hurtling body as it sent him slamming to the ground.

Sprawled on one side, he lifted his head and met Samurai's gaze. Captain Alba Bruni was handcuffing Samurai's hands behind him. Then Marco turned toward the man who had kept him from ruining his life. Or doing justice.

"Are you all right, Colonel?"

"Never better, Brandolin."

"You missed your opportunity, Marco."

Samurai's gasping wheeze reached him, tangled up with the piercing screeches of the seagulls. They both came out of the night. Or out of who knows where.

ABOUT THE AUTHORS

Carlo Bonini is a staff writer at the Italian national daily, *La Repubblica*.

Giancarlo De Cataldo is the author of the bestselling novel, *Romanzo Criminale*, an essayist, the author of numerous TV screenplays, and a judge on the circuit court of Rome.